Samba Dreamers

Camino del Sol A Latina and Latino Literary Series

Samba Dreamers

A NOVEL

Kathleen de Azevedo

The University of Arizona Press ⟪ Tucson

The University of Arizona Press

♾ This book is printed on acid-free, archival-quality paper.

Manufactured in the United States of America

11   10   09   08   07   06   6   5   4   3   2   1

Library of Congress Cataloging-in-Publication Data

Azevedo, Kathleen de, 1955–

Samba dreamers / Kathleen de Azevedo.

p. cm. — (Camino del sol)

ISBN-13: 978-0-8165-2490-7 (pbk. : acid-free paper)

ISBN-10: 0-8165-2490-4 (pbk. : acid-free paper)

1. Brazilian Americans—Fiction. 2. Emigration and
immigration—fiction. 3. Immigrants—Fiction. 4. Brazil
—Fiction. I. Title. II. Series.

PS3601.Z483S26 2006

813'.6 — dc22

2005016871

Publication of this book is made possible in part by the proceeds
of a permanent endowment created with the assistance of a Challenge
Grant from the National Endowment for the Humanities, a federal
agency.

For Lewis

Preface

The military coup that rocked Brazil forty years ago reached its peak in 1968 with the creation of the Fifth Institutional Act, which severely curtailed the freedom of political expression. But even in the presence of torture, disappearances, and exile, many Brazilians refused to be silenced. Their response to oppression gave birth to a cultural movement known as *Tropicalismo*. The movement based its philosophy on Oswaldo de Andrade's *Cannibalist Manifesto*, which used *antropofagia*, "cannibalism," as a metaphor for how Brazil devoured and was devoured by other cultures as it formed its national identity.

During Brazil's colonization, cannibalism — or fear of cannibalism — played into the imaginations of European explorers and intellectuals. In the latter half of the twentieth century, when Brazil was once again being devoured by a military government, intrepid Brazilian artists used images from American pop, indigenous peoples, African culture and, in particular, exaggerated tropical stereotypes as a way of asserting an alternative nationalistic vision. Carmen Miranda was one such stereotype used by the movement.

Não permita Deus que eu morra
Sem que eu volte para lá;
Sem que desfrute os primores
Que não encontro por cá;
Sem qu'inda aviste as palmeiras,
Onde canta o Sabiá.
—Gonçalves Dias, "Canção do exílio," Coimbra, 1843

God let me not die
Without returning home
Without savoring the primeval beauty
That here I cannot find;
Without even beholding the palm trees,
Where sings the Sabiá.
—Gonçalves Dias, "Song of Exile," Coimbra, 1843

A large fern covered my view. Slowly I moved the greenery aside. There, I saw my first Amazon: large, her skin painted with black *genipapo* dye. The long wound on her shoulder, smeared with balsam, opened slightly as she prepared her bow. A twine belt around her waist cut into her thick flesh. A magnificent cluster of purple flowers dangled from a tree above her. She raised her bow, shot her arrow and brought down a capuchin; she scoffed at its small size and stuffed the poor fellow into a bag made of human hair.

—*Carta de Carlos Manoel Teixeira da Cunha a João Vicente Cardim da Almeida* (Letter from Carlos Manoel Teixeira da Cunha to João Vicente Cardim da Almeida), *O Ano* 1639

Senhor da Cunha, You have let your pen wander, for exploration of a new land brings a fever. To be a part of history, there must be truth to your tales.

—*A resposta de João Vicente Cardim da Almeida a Carlos Manoel Teixeira da Cunha* (Response from João Vicente Cardim da Almeida to Carlos Manoel Teixeira da Cunha), *O Ano* 1640

Chapter 1

O Ano 1975

Clouds brushed the wings of the airplane. José Francisco Verguerio Silva looked out the window and suddenly had the feeling of bursting through the glass, tumbling slowly through white heavenly wisps, and finally colliding with the ground, his long Brazilian name smashing into pieces and scattering. He got up to his feet, sobbing as he looked for all the parts of his name, but he had lost them. He filled out the landing card and gave his passport to the airline attendant. Now he was Joe. Joe Silva. It was all the name he had left.

BRAZAIR Flight 605 touched down in Los Angeles and shot down the runway. BRAZAIR had filed for bankruptcy, and Joe was on their farewell flight. He clung to the satchel containing small presents bestowed on the passengers by the melancholy but gracious crew: a child's pilot hat, a Tom Jobim cassette tape with his famous "Girl from Ipanema," and a small blue toothbrush. After years of searching his soul, Joe was finally here. The Rio movie premier of *Carmen: Você ainda está no meu coracão*, dedicated to the memory of the irrepressible Brazilian star Carmen Socorro, had kindled his desire to come to America. Then, with the violent disappearance of his beloved Sonia, his desire burst into flames.

Joe's footsteps creaked on the cold linoleum of the long, wide airport halls, the leather soles of his shoes sticky like a dry tongue. The halls echoed with human noise. He carried his duffle bag and flight satchel past directional signs that seemed vaguely familiar — "Exit," "To Customs," "Baggage Carousel," "Gates 55–79," "Things Go Better with Coke" — as if they had popped out of phrase books. But other signs were brief and cryptic, words cut and censored, other words added. One needed to know these new secret phrases to survive, and Joe didn't know them. He saw people coming toward him, pushing through the airless rooms, getting up from chairs as if suddenly in a hurry, snatching up their belongings. These people whispered to themselves and peered through dark glasses as if their eyes had been gouged. Speaking of gouged eyes! How could Joe not see it coming when Sonia marched up to his newsstand and announced a new love in her life: Ação Popular! The student political movement! She wanted to overthrow the military government, but all he wanted was to marry her. He had waited a long, long time, and now this? But she was not in the mood for love. "Where is the Truth around here?!" she shouted and hurled one of his newspapers onto the floor. "What a bunch of lies! Why do you sell such crap!" He panicked, fearing they would be caught, and pinned her against the corner to kiss her into silence. Her eyes blazed fiercely, half for her love of politics, half for her love for him. His feet dismantled the *Jornal do Brasil* Sonia had thrown on the floor. He peered down at the sly weather forecast: "Weather is black. Temperature suffocating. The air is unbreathable. The country is being swept by a strong wind. . . ."

Joe struggled to make his way through the airport, clawing through the raw and vivid memories that always blended into his present sadness, as they did now, when the memory of Sonia turned into a craving for *biscoito de polvilho*, which he knew he would never taste again. Clever *cariocas* sold these wonders in the bakeries and on the beaches of Copacabana, Ipanema, and Leblom. Dark-legged men and women trekked on the sand and shook rattles as they toted large sacks of biscoitos, selling their wares to toasty sunbathers. Those sacks, though enormous, must have weighed less than ten kilos because a crackly biscoito de polvilho, shaped like a small ring, is no more than crunchy, intricate chambers of air flavored with salt or sugar. Joe imagined these delicious bits of enchantment crumbling in his mouth, a memory that *saudade* would never let fade.

Joe continued to the front of the terminal to catch some kind of bus. His saudade for home now came furious and fast, not only for the biscoitos, but for the samba and the jangling strains of *forró* music and hot afternoons spent over a cold beer. He longed now for all the places in Brazil he had neglected. He longed for Iguaçu Falls and its multitude of rainbows, though he'd never been there. He longed for Fortaleza and its sand dunes, though he'd never been there. He longed for Teresina, the hottest place on earth; for the Amazon and the ghosts of lawless *bandeirantes* haunting the mangrove swamps; for the yellow birds and green frogs; for the Rio Negro and Rio Branco, where he'd never, ever been. He longed for Salvador, where he had gone once as a child—Salvador, with its vendors selling cheap plastic clocks and vinyl wallets and pet roosters tethered to chairs. He imagined his dark-eyed *mamãe*, with her wavy hair tied in a bun, mouthing something he couldn't pick up, her Portuguese jumbled into the clamor of flight bags and jet engines. He hungered for her black beans and *carne seca* with *farofa* and hot sauce sprinkled on top, and he sucked his lower lip.

Outside the terminal, fresh air hit his face, and he felt better. Hotel passenger vans rumbled past like a parade of army tanks. He heard the shrill metal whistles of parking attendants and saw them fling their hands at parked cars. Suitcases on wheels bumped along the cracks of the concrete. Here he was, a carioca in a strange land, a land of lazy rudeness he'd been told. But, oh, he had wanted to come to L.A., he had longed for it—even though Sonia's friends told him that American capitalistic desires were to blame for the military tanks that came rumbling from Minas Gerais to Rio and for the period of unhappiness that followed, the Anos de Chumbo — Years of Lead, as it was called, and now he wore his longing like a splash of ash on his forehead for penance, but most of all for sorrow.

But no matter. Enough of this. Joe, stunned with jet lag, had to figure out what to do next. His little bit of English disappeared and left him muttering in Portuguese. Like any Brazilian, he was thinking that of course there would be someone here to help him, give him a little advice, a little ride maybe.

Next to the curb was a passenger van with large dark windows and writing on the side, "Hollywood Celebrity Tours," spelled with small yellow spotlights set against a dark-blue background. The sliding side door was wide open. Maybe this van would take him downtown. Maybe he could get a job working at a newspaper stand like he had in Rio. The driver was probably having coffee. Joe looked around and, seeing no one watching him, decided to climb inside and just wait for what would happen. He made his way to the last seat in the back, set his duffle bag and satchel on the floor, and sat down. The heat of the van made new sweat pour over his old sweat, coating his skin like plastic. Out of the tinted windows, crowds with flickering legs and quick-midget chatter swam in sepia, like a silent movie. No one looked through the van windows from the outside, and probably no one could see him. He remembered those horrible one-way windows with terror, and he shuddered and rested his forehead on the seat in front of him. He had come to America to forget, but the memories attacked him like spears.

Joe heard footsteps stomping into the van and two men speaking Spanish, not like high-brow Argentinean, but like Spanish slooped off the tongue and mixed in with English and heh-hehs. One of the two men wore a plaid shirt with American-style pointed cowboy pockets and a large beige cowboy hat. He slid into the driver's seat, and the top of his hat knocked against the doorway. He took it off, repinched the crown with his thick thumbs, and stuck it back on his head. The driver looked at himself in the mirror, but didn't notice Joe. Nothing here was real, as if Joe were in his bed in Rio, dreaming this whole trip and getting tangled and sweaty in his bedsheet. Joe studied the man's face for clues of generosity or contempt. The man's head was thick and oval, his skin a warmish brown, and his wide nose a friendly triangle.

Another man slipped into the front seat beside the driver. This other man carried a small suitcase, with tags dangling from the handle. Obviously, he had just arrived. He tossed the small suitcase on the floor behind him and shut the door. This passenger was skinny like a peasant and wore his white shirtsleeves rolled up. His combed black hair pressed down on his head so that little curls flipped up behind his ears. The driver cracked a joke in Spanish, and they both laughed, the way close friends laugh.

The Hollywood Celebrity Tours van swung into a line of cars, airport shuttles, taxis, buses, and God knows what. Then, after a bottleneck, the van and a million other vehicles spilled onto the freeway as if nothing could stop them. Spanish tumbled from the two in front; they opened the windows, and the one not driving pulled out a pack of cigarettes, drew out two, lit them, and handed one of them over to his driver pal. Both held their cigarette between two fingers and rested their wrists on the sill, letting the smoke spin into the air. They poked and laughed at the "No Smoking" sign on the dashboard and took a puff at the same time.

So this was it, L.A., the city of fantasy. Sure, Joe had expected movie stars and Disneyland and all the treasures of this unknown land, but here the city reminded him a bit of a difficult woman: the pastel-colored houses were like boxes of scented soap. The cars formed crazy beaded necklaces that broke and whipped around freeway turns. Large billboards wanted this, wanted that, wanted a good smoke, wanted a bottle of gin, wanted a leather suitcase, wanted a baby wrapped up as a present. This city drummed its long red fingernails, making an impatient clickity-clack. Still, this city, indifferent and painful, glittered when it smiled and exposed its breast.

Just then the driver looked up at the rearview mirror and called to Joe in Spanish. The friend turned and looked at him, his arm outstretched on the back of the seat, his head wobbling with the movement of the van. Joe had to speak. He rose slowly and crept toward the front, stepping over his bags, then over the passenger's bag, taking his time to think of a good answer; as he sat on the seat behind the driver, he could only manage "Como?" The driver grinned like he understood and started speaking English, which was worse. "This isn't a city bus, compañero. Where do you want to go? Adónde vas?"

Joe looked out the large front window. "Maybe Hollywood."

"Where in Hollywood? Sunset Boulevard? MGM studios?"

Joe shrugged. The words left him. "Desculpe. I forget much."

The driver and his friend laughed. "Brasileño, eh?" They knew by the words that didn't fit in the new world. There was no mistaking his Brazilianness. Round eyes with half-moon lids that always look a little tired, black curls too lush to be hot oiled. The type of immigrants with some kind of past, those in their thirties who can only shake their heads as if to say, "What in the hell did I do to get here?" Joe shrugged languidly, luxuriously, like a Brazilian, because Brazil was a big country to carry on his broad but soft shoulders, and he flared his fingers as he spoke, as if to say, "Of course I danced naked to get my visa. We all do."

"If you spoke good English," the driver said, "you could drive a tour van and make a lot of money from tips. You understand the word *money*? *Dinero*?"

"Of course."

"Money is very popular here. The tourists come to Beverly Hills to see people with money, but they all get depressed because they'll never be rich though they work twice as hard as Vaughan Peters or Elissa Baden. Those two make millions for one little movie." Then the driver had to translate in Spanish for his friend. Joe and the friend nodded in agreement, for Joe understood the Spanish better.

The passenger offered Joe a cigarette. "Yes, please," Joe said, so thankful. The passenger struck the lighter and held the flame steady. Joe lit the cigarette and nodded thanks. The driver said, "He's Rufo, a good friend of mine," then tapped himself on the chest. "I'm Tony. And you?"

"Joe. Joe Silva." The new shortened name startled him. It didn't fit right in his mouth. Joe took a puff and held the cigarette out the window. He felt his tired eyes caving in and wondered how long it would take him to get a room somewhere and how far he would have to walk.

"Joe," Tony looked at him in the rearview mirror, "necessita trabajo?"

Joe scooted forward carefully. *Trabajo?* Work? Could he be so lucky?

"Yes," Joe said, "very much."

Tony grinned. "I'll set you up," he said, "I can set you up with work, even a place to stay, no great shakes as they say here, but—"

Joe held his forward position, afraid that maybe he didn't understand correctly; he didn't want to get eaten alive by hope.

The driver waved him back, "OK. Deal is done. Relax, amigo."

Joe settled down and flicked his cigarette ashes out the window.

"So, *you guys*," the driver took care to show off his American slang, "I'll take you on a Beverly Hills tour, for free." Then he flipped on the radio. "Tejano! Es bueno, no?" The music broke through the speakers on the dashboard, and the accordion wailed to the skies and told of the time Sonia accused Joe of being *brocha*—the humiliating time when a man's member remains innocent and soft. She accused him of sleeping with another woman. He couldn't admit how nervous he was for her, for her safety. For her life. But his manhood knew. Like a man, he stormed out of Sonia's apartment and went to the corner *botequim* to drown his sorrows. The radio moaned: "When you get home, your young woman will be wrapped in your sheets, waiting for you."

Joe caught his breath, trying to calm himself down. This is what people don't see in an immigrant: how he stumbles in two worlds, trembling, clutching a cigarette with his broken but healed fingers, and bargaining with the devil to give him peace.

Beverly Hills. The van meandered through quiet streets lined with thick, leafy trees. The fallen reddish-pink blossoms of the jacaranda trees made purple stains on the pavement. The lemon trees scattered their ripe fruit onto the plush grass. Juniper bushes had been pruned into large tear drops or made to look like shallow walls surrounding the front yards. Of course there were famous houses too; quaint houses with blue shutters; mansions that rose thick like fists, with stone lions at the front steps; and modern houses with alluring bay windows that sparkled like eyes, full of wonder and a bit frightened.

The driver gunned the motor as he drove along a narrow road going uphill. There were fewer houses now, hidden among trees. Then the driver announced, "I am going to show you my favorite house. This house is not on the tour, but I love it in spite of its faults, eh? You, amigo, especially," he nodded to Joe, "will love this one."

Just then he pulled up in front of a wide iron gate, the entrance to a large, white, Spanish-style split-level house with an adobe tile roof. Brick stairs led to a porch and then to a heavy churchlike double door. On either side of the door were two decorative arched windows, each trimmed with a row of blue tiles and a grillwork basket. On the second story was a balcony with a railing shaped by someone who knew how to work with good wood. A large sliding-glass door led from the balcony to what Joe imagined was a sexy bedroom, the size of an entire Rio apartment, just the place to have made exquisite love to Sonia from sunset to sunrise. If things had been different.

"This is the house of Carmen Socorro. Do you remember, Joe, Carmen Socorro?" the driver asked.

Joe nodded and settled back. Of course, the house had to be Carmen's, she of the Brazilian legend! Who doesn't know the story? She began as a humble hat maker and became a movie star who wore enormous hats loaded with bananas and grapes and real animals and even small villages. *Que loucura!* Joe had seen pictures of Carmen's furniture in one of his mother's old movie magazines. Carmen had leopard fur covers on the couch and a round white swimming pool. But she had died young because Hollywood didn't want her anymore, just threw her away. He remembered when Carmen's body came back to Rio, just some dried-out coconut hull. His mother went to the funeral and almost got killed in the crush of the hysterical crowd. But Carmen's fate wouldn't happen to Joe because he didn't want to be a movie star. It was the furthest thing from his mind. He wanted to be normal, everyday normal — chit-chat with Americanos and "make a few bucks," as they say.

The driver crooned, "My mother loved Carmen Socorro and Ricky Ricardo. Loved them like they were family. She even liked the Cisco Kid. Now we are not supposed to admit that we enjoyed those things. We are supposed to be ashamed, but who else sang our songs, eh? Of course, everyone knows that the movie star Vaughan Peters lives here now. He does movies where they blow up buildings. Machismo Americano, eh?"

The driver continued, his hand tracing the parts of the house, the eight carved squares of the double front doors made of incense cedar brought from the hills around these mountains, "but notice, one square there"—he pointed out the van window—"lower your eyes, the one with the design. It is a carving of a face with its eye open, mouth apart, and somehow people in Hollywood thought it was a curse, but in fact it is a design from a church somewhere in Brazil, I don't know where."

Joe strained to see the mysterious carved figure, but the large wrought-iron gate blocked his view. "Yes," the driver said, "once there was no gate here, and the driveway was open and welcoming, especially to all her Brazilian friends who drove so crazy. And see the balcony? Ah . . . Carmen used to sit there under an enormous rubber plant, and she used to rest her feet on the railing, and imagine, my friends, this sight! As we drove in, we'd see her legs stretched above our heads, showing a bit of her underwear, and she'd be surrounded by big leaves like she was a jaguar in a tree ready to attack us with those beautiful red nails of hers. How we wished!"

The driver laughed to himself and moved the van farther up the hill to where a large garden spilled over low brick walls and crowns of palm trees swayed. He pulled over to a smaller wrought-iron gate, stopped again, and continued: "She planted this garden; it goes on for nearly a mile into the hills. She brought many plants from the Amazon and put birds here, too, and so many monkeys it was like a zoo. She was homesick, of course, homesick in the worst way." He turned to everyone in the van, "we all know what that is like."

The passenger began wiping his eyes, his tears on his fingernails.

The driver leaned back in his seat and gave the passenger's arm a small squeeze. Joe strained his eyes to peer through all those trees and branches. Then the shadows swelled and rubbed together, and in the friction he caught a glimpse of a woman standing among the trees. Her frizzed-out hair mistook itself for moss. Her lips were red and buttery. She moved naked through the trees, and the sun made her skin glow like mother-of-pearl, and leaves seemed to grow on her body as if she were an abandoned tree. She turned toward Joe and stared straight into his heart. The shock brought out the flashbacks, which started always from the same place. Joe sweated and shuddered like he always did when the painful memory deep inside him — the one he wanted to forget, the one he came all the way to Terra Nova to flee — urged itself forward and pounded loudly on the door —

Sonia cradles his head in her hands. Her expression is soft, and the moon outside the apartment window is as white as bone. José leans over and carves the words "I'm sorry" with his lips and tongue on her cheek. For the argument. "Sinto muito. Me perdoe."

Suddenly there is a banging at the door. José slowly lowers his face into her hair, hiding as the military police burst into the room. One group drags Sonia out of bed, another grabs him. Handcuffs bite his wrists. He sees Sonia being dragged out, the shadows down the hall like jungle leaves. The last thing she says to him, in a shout because there is no more time, "Me perdoe!"

Forgive me.

Along the river, the mighty warrior women prepared for battle. They scratched underneath their leather breastplates and gold collars as if their heavy weaponry pinched the tiny hairs on their bodies. The small bites of pain seemed to keep them on the edge of a delicious wildness. As they drew back their bows, their shoulder muscles quivered like the flanks of their steeds. We considered these warriors fiercer than the cannibal Petiguares, so we remained hidden. These women charged on horseback into battle, throwing their heads back, and letting out a war whoop so magnificently watery that their spit formed into rain clouds.

—*Carta de Carlos Manoel Teixeira da Cunha a João Vicente Cardim da Almeida, O Ano* 1640

Chapter 2

O Ano 1977

Rosea Socorro Katz heard the heavy iron doors of the prison clang behind her like steel curtains, but she didn't look back. In her ironic imagination she almost expected a clapping throng to be waiting outside with TV cameras to witness the daughter of Brazilian bombshell Carmen Socorro being released from Frontera Institute for Women, where she had served time for destroying rare and precious Amazon artifacts. The fortress behind her burgeoned with the wild and the wounded, their hands calloused and scarred from paddling Amazon war canoes, hacking escape routes with machetes, hanging onto ledges — and occasionally jumping. Her only greeting was the clatter of an old oil drum rolling in the wind.

Outside the prison gate, the land spread out flat with its knotty soil, curled and angry weeds, and frazzled gray brush. The distant hills rested together like fat thighs. The sun scoured the sky with blue Ajax. The open space scared her; she and her large body had been cooped up in the four walls of her cell and in the prison yard, but now the earth and its forceful wind threatened to swallow her, then regurgitate her like dried bone shards. She hunched her large shoulders into a prisoner slouch, and her ill-fitting T-shirt stretched across her back like sinew. A guard motioned her toward the van, courtesy of the California Department of Corrections, that would take her to the nearest Greyhound bus stop. With a small wad of gate money in her pocket, she couldn't go far. It was all the money she had.

Soon after the van dropped her off, the bus to San Bernardino pulled up. Rosea climbed up its stairs, taking with her a bag of pathetic belongings, not much more than an extra set of underwear and a T-shirt. Her six-foot self rumbling down the aisle got passengers staring upward, most of them women huddled in the middle of brown shopping bags. They looked like a parade of sorry-looking mules. One old woman had an infant over her shoulder, a five-year-old girl by her side, and a bunch of other stuff. Rosea sat in the seat directly in back. The baby, her tiny cheeks red with a rash, peered at Rosea who smiled, something she hadn't done much lately. The little one with her cap of black hair started to whimper. Already a bad beginning.

Rosea had served time for arson, for burning down her own house. She couldn't say why she did it, except that she had to save herself from going crazy. Some people would say, "How could you? The world's most interesting house, the home of Dr. Jeremiah Millard, Anthropologist, Collector of South American Art, Friend of the Natives. Humanitarian." Her Husband. He brought the Indians radios and deodorized soap. So what! Rosea could say: "So what's a few burned up jars of rare seeds, Yanomami spears, yellow bird collars, and one live monkey?" Luckily, Jeremy's most prized possession, Birdboy, hadn't been around. Birdboy was SAFE. But who could stand him? Birdboy, his swollen belly, his high-water pants on his thin legs, the bristle of tiny feathers creeping on his hairline at the nape of his neck, his beaky heck-heck cry. If the fire had snuffed out Birdboy, she'd still be in Frontera. For good. She'd have disappeared from existence, she'd have been an artifact in a cage until she dropped dead. "Splendid," Jeremy's excellent college friends would say, "it's what we all wanted."

Rosea had burned down her husband's house because of the monkey. Right. It would have been something to have told the true story in court: I tried to kill a capuchin brat, but instead burned down the house. It was the stinky monkey in that big custom-made cage that took up half the living room. It was him or me, your honor. First, I flung matches into the cage, then flung in lighted paper towels. Boy, do monkeys go crazy with insane eeking, trying to squeeze through the bars of the cage! Hilarious. Then I thought, why not lighter fluid? So I splashed some into the cage. The capuchin huddled in the far corner and stared at the splash as if it had pissed an inordinately big puddle. Then I remember watching my fingers, snapping match after match, and tossing them toward such a dangerous little pool of piss. The matches kept missing, then finally one landed in the lighter fluid, and the cage immediately exploded in flames. The brat didn't even cry out. Then I turned on the stove and oven and ran out to watch the whole fire from across the street. The flames spread throughout the house and finally burst out the windows. By then, our neighbors had dragged out their feeble garden hoses and tried to squirt out the fire. But the flames grew, and the house exploded. I heard a big screech. I loved the flame fiercely because it was mine, your honor. If some dashing Mexicano or Brasileiro had passed in front of me, I probably would have fucked him on the spot. To celebrate.

Am I sorry your honor? Yes.

Am I *really* sorry?

(Pause)

Not in my heart.

Rosea looked out the window and squinted. A truck passed by like a dream, its front bumper shiny with heat, and the radio left behind a whiff of a love song. Rosea caught the last few notes. It sounded like something new, a song she hadn't heard before. Her throat caught, about to cry, but she groaned down the grief just as—

The grandmother on the bus started to cry, blubbering out words tangled in a barbed wire of pain. Then the baby started to cry. In fact, a lot of people on this bus were crying because the vision of hope that hovers over one's head like a white dove had flown away. We all know what that's like.

Rosea had no choice but to go to Pachito's house; she hoped he would remember his little offer that she could stay there for a couple of days. She knew Pachito from their wild days of long ago, when they got into "Mexican trouble," which meant fights mostly, fights that brought the whole excited LAPD into town. Rosea hadn't seen Pachito for a while, until she ran into him at Frontera during visiting hours. He was checking up on a cousin of his wife and found out Rosea was here, too. Pachito and Rosea sat across from each other with a glass window between them and spoke on telephones. "Ése!" Pachito said tenderly, "Hola, carnal, que pasa? Long time no see." Rosea asked, "How is your kid?" "Growing," Pachito said, "Teresa is really growing. Can't believe how things change."

"Yeah," Rosea sighed, "I can believe it."

The toughs, the *vato locos* from East L.A.! Though Rosea was the daughter of the famous movie star Carmen Socorro, she used to hang out on street corners, wear a leather jacket, and make jacking-off motions to the white wannabes driving by in their Volvos. She stole money from the donut store wino. That's how she met Pachito: by hanging out on the street. He wore vato gear, wishing it were a zoot suit, and spoke a blistering *caló* that made it hard to understand him sometimes. He frightened people with his silver tooth. But surprise of surprises, he got married somehow, and not to a homegirl, either, but a Catholic schoolgirl.

She and Pachito gazed at each other like old times. Then he took a quick glance to check for the guards, reached into his shirt pocket, and pulled out a business card with his name and home address and pressed the card against the glass so she could see. He laughed with that silver tooth. "I'm pretty ambitious now, not like I was before. Don't have my own business yet, but at least I got the cards, eh, Rosea? Please," he put his card back into his pocket and lowered his eyes, "look me up when you get out, eh? I know what it's like."

Yeah, a Brazilian hanging out with Mexicans hardly made sense. But in those days Brazilians in the United States were few and far between. Millionaires and exchange students mostly. And, of course, Carmen Socorro, Banana Lady. Rosea needed *uma chama em sua alma perdida*, the flame in her lost soul, and she looked where she thought she could find it.

❰

Rosea got off the bus at the San Bernardino station. She took out of her pocket a slip of paper with Pachito's address and asked a baggage handler for directions. The stooped old man put down a suitcase, squinted, then pointed in the direction of a subdivision way off near the foot of a scrubby mountain with a TV tower. "A bit far," he waggled his thin blond finger, "unless you got a ride."

She started walking. Ride, my ass. She'd have to find a way to get tough again even after years of snuffling out "excuse me's" and "no problemas." She'd have to listen to people say, "Jeez, we thought you were dead!" and "So why did you burn down your house? If you hadn't, you'd have had a place to stay! Couldn't you just have *divorced* the man? It would have been cheaper and made everyone happier."

Rosea stopped from time to time to catch her breath. Humiliating for a six-foot, thirty-five-year-old woman. She wasn't used to all this wide-open space. Sweat turned her armpits into smelly swamp coolers. She kept on walking and finally arrived at the house.

Pachito had made good with this simple *casita*, half covered with white aluminum siding, the other half painted beige. The little lawn was no more than shrunken dry tufts on either side of the wood stairs. Red volcanic rocks made a border around the lawn, and a small faded plastic gnome and a cleaning bucket guarded the entrance.

Rosea knocked on the door and roused a rumble and a sigh, then the door was flung open, and a teenage girl stood before her. She wore a soft, powder-blue blouse with a scoop neck, black Ben Davis pants, and black eyeliner that made her eyes look like seeds.

"You must be Teresa," Rosea said warily.

Teresa slowly nodded. "Yeah." Her warm brown neck velveted into soft breasts, and her black hair spilled down her shoulders. "Wow," said Rosea, "I didn't realize you would be so big." Teresa shrugged, "You're kinda big yourself." Then Rosea peered over the girl's shoulder into the house. She saw a bulletin board and a table piled with bills. "Is your father here?"

"He's not home," Teresa said, "he's WORKING." Rosea stood there, but didn't know how much to explain. I was your father's hang-out girl and bla-bla and so forth. Teresa must have been used to fast talkers because she let Rosea in with a swoop of her hand. "You can wait here," Teresa said, "no problem."

Teresa was watching her soaps. The ones in English were good, she reminded Rosea, but she hated Mexican *telenovelas*. She plunked back down on the couch, surrounded by empty cups and plates, and put her feet up on the coffee table. She lifted up her shagged hair from her neck, reached over to the table, grabbed a hair clip, and made a small pony tail. Her legs were thick and restless, and she crossed her feet at the ankles and swayed them back and forth. She slid down with her head back as if she were bored, but kept her eye on the screen. When the commercial came, she eyed Rosea on the couch. "How's it going?" she asked as if Rosea had just been to the mall.

Rosea thought Teresa needed a jolt. "I've been in prison."

Teresa smiled. "Whoa. You too?"

"What do you mean 'you too'? You've been in trouble?"

Teresa shook her head nonchalantly. "No. But tons of people have. Prison is a fact. Like death." Then she got up and went into the kitchen and offered Rosea some iced tea. "Yeah, if you got some," Rosea called. Teresa shuffled around in the refrigerator, then returned with two full glasses. Rosea gulped the whole thing at once. A young man came on the screen. He had a tiny mouth like Birdboy. Teresa motioned to the TV. "This guy got this girl pregnant but can't tell no one."

Rosea leaned forward. "Well, he's telling someone now."

"Yeah, but that ain't no one. That's his pregnant girlfriend." Teresa
looked sad, watching the soap.

"Go to school?" Rosea asked.

"Duh."

Rosea turned away and looked around the house. She wondered if she could stay. She had nowhere to go. She sized up the house as to who slept where. There was a stack of pillows and a folded blanket in the corner. A bad sign. That meant someone slept in the living room. It would have been better not to burn down her house, come to think of it. She should have just lived with Jeremy and his exotic treasures and his insidious adopted bird son. She didn't have to be Birdboy's stepmother. She wasn't a mother hen.

This was the first time she had been in a home since her arrest. Rosea sat back on the couch with Teresa. Her shirt clung to her sweaty skin, the small casita was so hot. She closed her eyes and drifted halfway to sleep. She could hear the girl's young strong breath, so involved with the pregnant girl on the TV. Teresa's shifting on the couch made Rosea feel like she was in bed with someone else. Someone like Pachito. Forget it. Don't even think about him in that way.

But now, dozing off in a comfortable home, Rosea remembered her mother's belongings, things she hadn't wanted burned: the *fantasia* costumes, the *balangadas* and bracelets, the tango shawl, the sweet red lipsticks, the I-love-you lace, the old curled posters, the old kissy-kissy letters from Brazil with *abraços* and *beijinhos* of love and of painful saudade, an old locket, and crusty basket hats with straw fruit chewed up by moths and nits.

The tires of a pickup truck crackled in the driveway, then the truck's door slammed, and footsteps trudged up to the house. Rosea jolted awake. The front door thumped open. Pachito stood at the entranceway, a lunchbox in his hand.

"Hey!" He seemed surprised to see her and was pleasant in a Pachito kind of way. "How've you been?"

Rosea rubbed her eyes and yawned, "Well, I'm out, aren't I?"

"Didn't go AWOL, did you?" He laughed and walked over and kissed Teresa on the cheek. "Hey, princesa, qué pasa?" Then he took his lunchbox to the kitchen. He called to Teresa in Spanish, but she answered in English. Something about food. Pachito opened the refrigerator door and called out, "Rosea, a beer?"

"Sure."

He grabbed two beers and a bag of Fritos and sat on the couch between her and Teresa. He watched the TV for a few seconds as Teresa reached over for a handful of Fritos. Then he turned to Rosea. "Hey," he said, "you don't look too bad. Didn't get the gas chamber at least."

"For god's sake, I didn't murder anyone but a monkey." Rosea squelched her tortured anger because she needed to ask Pachito if she could crash. She wasn't used to asking for things. Bellowing at the weaker girls, perhaps, or at the guards when all hell broke loose. But not polite asking. He had invited her here. Things could be worse. Tomorrow she would go to her parole officer and try to get a job, maybe, and a place to stay. But tonight she had nowhere to go. She'd ask for TONIGHT. Tonight ONLY.

Pachito took off his boots and lay back with a beer; he talked kindly to her, kinda unwound — the slow, soft, after-a-long-work-day way. He worked at a construction job, a good one that would last him a while: a new shopping mall where people would come from miles around. Then Pachito said, "Mannie should be home soon," and sank into watching the soap opera with Teresa. Rosea sipped her beer. Both father and daughter crunched Fritos in unison. Rosea hated watching TV because that was all she had done in prison. She looked at the walls of Pachito's house, at the graduation and wedding pictures, including the one with his wife, Mannie, who worked with teenage girls climbing on the cliffs of the penal system, the ones released from Juvie. Other things on the walls: an embroidered sacred heart, a bulletin board with bills and store sales. A fancier carpet lay over the dirty tan wall-to-wall carpet. The weave of the couch upholstery was like a comfortable old coat.

Pachito turned away from the TV. Rosea felt his eyes splashing on her and smiled shyly. "Yeah?" Rosea said, almost hoping Pachito was making a bit of a pass.

He always wondered, he said, how she could burn down her house.

It would be like burning down your soul, and it's so wonderful to have a home, no matter how much stuff needs fixing. True. Pachito's home wrapped around him with *cariño*, with big arms and adept fingers that pinch fat cheeks. Pachito relaxed with his beer, dropping his head back with a tired sigh and looking at the ceiling above his head, stained and cracked from an old water leak. The plaster puckered like lips poised for a loving *besito*.

Rosea felt desperate. She couldn't stay here. It's too much, if the house is a guy's soul, for god's sake. She thought of darting out, catching the next bus out of here. Pachito rose, went back to the kitchen for another beer, and called out, "Why don't you stay the night, Rosea? Teresa can go to her aunt Lupe's." Rosea held her breath as she expected Teresa to squall the way a teenager does when she's uprooted from her sprawled-out comfort, but Teresa didn't mind because Aunt Lupe's house was hers, too, and she said OK.

Rosea sighed. "Sure."

Well, no hassle. Rosea woke up the next morning in Teresa's room. She had gone to bed early so Pachito and Mannie could have the living room — their bedroom — to themselves.

Today she'd try and find some kind of job. She lay in bed and gazed around Teresa's room and how it shouted with teen love and thrashing: a holy card of a heart with a sword pierced through it, a poster of Mick Jagger, a photo of a girlfriend holding a cat, a magazine picture of a girl kissing a frog with the caption "Quién dice que las princesas tienen que besar los sapos?" On the small desk was her homework, books stacked in an angry I-don't-care mess, a slim book of love poems, and a math book with crushed papers stuffed inside.

Rosea heard the shower going as both Mannie and Pachito got ready for work. She listened to Pachito shouting over the shower and Mannie's dim shower voice, then Mannie's voice emerging from the watery clatter. They had taken a shower together. God, when will that ever be for her?

Rosea got up and slipped on her jeans. She looked at herself in the full-length mirror. She saw her image clearly for the first time in ages because the prison didn't allow glass. The top of the mirror cropped off her head; a six-foot Amazonian body was too much for this world. Her shoulders filled the mirror, and her gut was solid, like a man's. Her long hair was ratty as if she had slept in the woods of her mind, her dreams all shot up and burned. She brushed her hair and braided it so the frizz would calm down. She had dark inky eyes and a full mouth like a split-open plum. Without enough sun, her face had grown lighter, gray-yellow like a blank stare. She brought her paper bag of clothes into the living room and found coffee waiting for her. She sat down and had coffee and a slice of bread.

Pachito and Mannie came out of the bathroom, laughing and looking clean. Mannie was dressed for work wearing a slim denim skirt and a tailored beige blouse. Her short, dark hair was wet and crisp from the shower.

"Hi, Rosea!" she chirped lightheartedly. "Sleep well?" Even this early in the morning the sun was burning through the slit of the closed curtains that she flung apart. "I bet it's good to be out." Mannie had tried to talk to Rosea about prison last night, but Rosea was too tired, and she responded with Amazonian politeness, a ready answer, clean and precise as the cleft of water at the bow of a canoe. Mannie had talked about how hard freedom would be—*freedom*. She swooped up the dirty glasses on the coffee table and put them in the sink as she continued chattering, shifting back and forth in comfortable work clothes, pulling out from the kitchen cabinet a box of cornflakes and a box of Grape Nuts. She talked about picking up Teresa at Aunt Lupe's and taking her to school. Teresa had her schoolbooks here, so Mannie apologized for rushing because she had to leave a bit early. But she still kept asking, "How was it, how was the food, how were the other girls?" Her loop earrings brushed against the brown skin of her neck as she poured the coffee, then she sat down across from Rosea and asked pointedly, "I mean it, Rosea, how is it for the girls?"

Mannie counseled girls on probation. Hard to believe someone like Mannie could face the toughs. Rosea didn't feel tough anymore. She looked into her coffee, as black as night, as black as secrets, as black as

Amazon drums. She said she thought jail was bad for girls, but not like in South America, where they burn your feet or things like that. But jail is jail. Something inside flies out your mouth and takes wing, flapping away into a horizon made smoggy from the thousands puffing their cigarettes into the night, contemplating the futility of their lives.

Indeed, there are great things in this Terra Nova, but it is these women who fascinate me most. Even the wealthy landowners remain terrified of them, yet none have born witness to such sights as I. I saw a group of these women surrounding a campfire to keep warm. The fire lit their great calves the color of bronze greaves. Three salamanders leaped out of the fire like I have seen them do in sugar furnaces. One woman snatched two of these creatures and ate the delicacy promptly. These open fires produce many such salamanders, as they are wont to dwell in its flames.

—*Carta de Carlos Manoel Teixeira da Cunha a João Vicente Cardim da Almeida, O Ano 1640*

Chapter 3

O Ano 1970

By this time in Brazil Sonia had disappeared. The voices of Tropicalismo were being silenced; many went into prison or into exile. The heaviest blow of the dictatorship, the Fifth Institutional Act, now two years old, had muffled the cries of revolt. Joe, fallen and fearful after his time in prison, lived in his mother's apartment and left it only to go to work. Brazil's World Cup four-to-one victory over Italy briefly interrupted the country's deep despair and then —

—the sunlight splashed on the front windshield of the speeding Hollywood Celebrity Tours van. Tony's voice spun in the haze left by their
illegal cigarette smoke and sounded almost as if he were still giving the
tour: "You see, my Brazilian friend, the palm trees grew somewhere else
and were planted here. Brought in as children of the tropics and grew to
be Angelenos. Nothing in L.A. is native except sand and cactus. We are
in the middle of a desert, can you believe that? Pipes bring in water from
rivers north and east. It's like everything green here has been forced to
grow. . . ."

The passenger was sleeping with his head fallen back on the seat,
and his carefully greased and combed hair separated into a crack. Joe,
through his jet lag, watched as row after row of squat apartment buildings appeared and slid back into the sepia tint of the window glass. The
dull pastel and beige apartments had intriguing names: Tropicana, Linda
Mar, Buena Vista Estates. The stairwells of welded metal seemed to
dangle like broken zippers. The driver pulled to the right lane, then
finally glided up along the curb in front of the boxy, light-green Casa
Rica Apartments. Tony motioned for Joe to come along. Joe grabbed his
duffle bag and shoulder bag and stumbled out of the van.

He followed the driver through an entranceway of busted mailboxes
to a dirt courtyard, surrounded on four sides by two floors of apartments, the doors facing an open corridor. On the floor above, a pair of
wet blue jeans hung over a rusted iron rail, and plinging drops made a
small pool of mud on the ground near a broken lawn chair. The glass of
nearby windows shuddered from the vibration of blaring televisions.

The driver walked down the first-floor corridor to a door at the far
corner. He rang the bell, removed his beige cowboy hat, and peered into
the peephole. The door opened, and a man stood there, his large body
filling the doorway, and he croaked, "Eh, Tony." Joe hung behind, watching the two as they discussed his fate—in English. Tony cajoled, holding
his hat by the pinched front of the crown, and gestured, sweeping the hat
gracefully from side to side. The big man, his scowl forming a firm button between his eyes, stood in the doorway and shot glances from Tony

to Joe—then finally motioned them into the smoke-filled living room. "I'm the *ger-rente* as you people call it."

Tony rolled his eyes and followed the manager into the apartment, leaving Joe huddled by the doorway. "You can trust Joe," Tony called as he waited in the living room, "he came by plane."

A black-and-white TV blared with a children's show. Joe stared at the TV, trying to figure out all of the words because words for children are easy. There were two characters, twin puppets with little noggins and googly eyes. Jeffy and Keffy. They were talking about being lost, chattering oohhh-oooh—he-he-he-he. Bloop. Bloop. "Oh, Keffy, I'm so lost, what should I do?" "Oh, Jeffy," the other one said, "Ooooh, Jeffy. Find a policeman. Tell the policeman your address. Policemen are our friends. Always know your address, Jeffy, that way you can find your way home." "Ooooh, thanks, Keff. Thanks a bunch. A lot. A zillion times."

The manager brought Joe a key attached to a metal slab showing a room number, 212. Joe stared at the key, so tired he almost forgot what the key was for. Tony took ahold of Joe's arm. "Eh? You OK?"

Joe nodded.

"Mañana por la tarde, te llevaré a tu trabajo. You'll be ready for work tomorrow?" Tony slipped back on his beige hat. It made a soft shadow over his eyes.

"Thank you," Joe said.

The manager sat in his big armchair and went back to watching TV. Joe stared at the back of the man's large, fleshy head. Jeffy and Keffy were onto something else. "Close the door, will ya," the man called.

Tony shut the door and tapped Joe on the cheek with his whole hand, hugged him hard, and whispered in his ear. "Tienes cuidado, huh?" Then he left, and Joe was alone. He took his duffle bag up the metal stairs and passed some apartments on the second floor where he heard a woman speaking Spanish on the phone, an argument in Chinese, and a sob from someone near a front door. He found room 212, put the key into the lock, pushed the door open, and flipped on the light.

Water had wept long stains on the wall. A box-spring bed shoved to one side was his empty altar on which to lay himself down, to sacrifice himself in the name of saudade, of *confusão*. He dropped his duffle bag and his coat and looked into the closet and chest of drawers for blankets, sheets, a pillow, but didn't find any. That meant he would have to buy some, go to the store and ask. In English. *Lençóis*—sheets. *Cobertor*—blanket. *Travesseiro*—pillow. *Estou morrendo de cansaço.* I'm so tired I could die. He pulled out a sweater from his bag and rolled it up into a ball for a pillow. Then he lay down on the bed, rested his head on the sweater, and pulled a jacket over him. Thank God he had a job. So quickly. He could rest if he had no nightmares of Sonia. Please God. You give me a boost in this world, I'll give you a boost in the next. We are not talking of a *suborno*, no bribes. Just a *jeitinho* or two. If God is Brazilian, He knows perfectly well what I mean.

Sonia's body lay abandoned in the woods, near a waterfall.

Joe woke up. It was night, and he had had the dream again. The muscles down his back spasmed from the chill. He sat up, trying to erase the nightmare, yet trying to figure out where the wooded place was that so terrorized him in his dreams. Neon lights from outside fluttered across the dingy curtains, making the room flushed and feverish. Footsteps shuffled outside his window, and someone called out, "Where do I live?" The lost man broke a bottle against the side of the building and shouted again, "Where do I live?" Joe lay down and tried to close his eyes again, but he began crying—his first tears in the new land. First, his sobs jolted as he tried holding back; finally he wailed out loud. The voice of the lost man outside floated up to his window. What an idiot! *Vagabundo!* If a man doesn't know where he lives, how can he possibly find his way home?

Joe stood at the sink at Wranglers' Eye and Rib restaurant and sprayed hot water over dirty dishes. The steam made him sweat, and he licked the saltiness from his lips. The cooks called to each other in Spanish, and it was enough to make him miss Portuguese. It was an OK job, so grateful he was to his Mexican friend Tony. So thankful to be working, my goodness; he could have been that lost man wandering the streets looking for his home. He thought back to his newspaper stand in Rio, a nice one with the sturdy corrugated metal roof, and how every day he had worried that it would be blown to pieces by a bomb like so many other newsstands during that awful time. Yet his *banca de jornais* had survived bombs and had blossomed with gossip rags, *Quatro Rodas* travel guides, pamphlets of horoscope advice, newspapers, and bright lotto sheets flapping on the outside racks like flags. His friends would hang out after work to talk soccer, and with their supreme soccer player Pelé astonishing the world, they could almost believe in miracles.

He took another handful of dirty plates and with the rubber spatula scraped the cold orange meat fat into the garbage. Then he sprayed hot water over the dishes and stuffed them into the large automatic dishwasher. He looked up to the serving window and through the steam saw a waitress, a young woman with blond hair in a ponytail, bounding up to pick up an order. Her face was round and soft, her lips shaped like a bitter heart. Freckles spilled on the bridge of her nose, and she had small wrinkles in the corners of her eyes. She picked up the plate, then let go of it with a clatter. "This isn't what I asked for," she hollered above the water and the sizzling grills. "Dammit. I wanted the short ribs. This is a damn Porterhouse."

Everyone looked at one another.

"Where is that fuckin' Manuel? Jesus!" she demanded.

The others looked at each other knowingly. One clucked, "Ohhh Sherri, ohhh Sherri."

"What do you mean, 'oh Sherri'? Is it my fault you can't speak English? I bet you order these things by mistake so you get to eat the food later on. MANUEL! Where is that güero?"

Manuel appeared from the storage room. "Hey, Sherri," he said. He was light-skinned and wore his full brown hair in a net. He grinned with a wide mouth. "Hey, Sherri."

"Short ribs, Manuel."

Manuel grabbed the plate, took it to the grill, slapped the porterhouse back on it, and stuck his prongs into a side of short ribs. Sherri rapped her fingernails on the counter. Her fingernails were painted orange like the leftover meat grease. She rolled her eyes; sweat smeared the eyeliner under her eyes. Manuel brought the plate back with ribs. Sherri swooped up the plate, hissing, "Hot, hot."

"Hot, hot," one of the cooks laughed.

Hot. Hot. Sherri. Joe felt a pang of delight. Her nasty impatience . . . women's outrage—ah! Don't ask why he loved their loud mouths twisting in pain because someone else had betrayed them, their sexy waddle, their feeling of entitlement, their demands that you treat them better. He liked when women talked on the streets about their boyfriends, their mouths boxy and angry, jetting their eyes at male passersby, gesturing to them with a roll of their shoulders burdened with a purse, with a toss of their hair, a clink of their earrings. "Jerks." He liked how they said it; their lower lips looked full, their eyes squinting and dark like small cracks of a cliff. *Babacos*. Jerks.

"Speak English!" she had shouted. "Speak English!" He liked her anger. He wished she were wearing sunglasses; he wanted to undress her and see her amazingly white skin. He wondered for a moment if she was scared, if she had slashed up her torturer, if she was into torture herself with those frighteningly pink cheeks. He sprayed water on a dish directly, and it splattered on his shirt. He worked faster and imagined touching her, running his brown fingers down her arms, stopping at the small bowl at the joint of her arm. If she flinched, he would calm her with "don't move, don't move." He would force her to be still and tell his story of torture and escape, whispering in her ear, until her blue eyes filled with tears, until he could see his hopeless little face reflected in a woman's sorrow.

Manuel, the kitchen supervisor, made himself a large salad and called, "I hope you will eat something, Joe." Just before Joe spoke, Sherri came in with rueful grin, snarling, and her playful contempt pierced his heart. The grill twinkled its hot, leering smile. Joe looked at Sherri and said, "It's OK. I am not hungry."

Manuel laughed and glanced at Sherri, too. "Sherri is never hungry either. She is always on a diet."

Joe smiled broadly and flicked the dishwasher on. The water rumbled.

"Well," Sherri tucked a strand of hair behind her ear, "I hope everyone is happy because the Dictator just came in again."

Joe's face fell. Sherri touched his shoulder and pointed out the window. "Check this out. The Dictator."

Joe looked past the counter and into the dining area. He swallowed hard and had to look away for a moment, then he peered out again. The Dictator had a large belly and wore a beige military uniform with medals covering his chest and a cap with the brim pulled down to his eyebrows. The Dictator grabbed another waitress by the skirt, a skinny girl with short dark hair, but she pushed him away and headed toward the kitchen.

"We have names for weird customers," Sherri said close to his ear, but Joe only heard the hum of her words as he backed away from the kitchen window. Sherri touched his shoulder again. "Relax, kid, it's an act."

"Or maybe he is a movie star, yes?" Joe said under his breath. Joe looked out the window again. The Dictator sat at the table with his wife. She had on a flowered dress made of shiny curtain fabric. She wrapped herself in a large knit sweater and wore a straw hat that she had attempted to slouch, but the hat was old and stiff, and the brim stuck out like a broken plate. They sat opposite each other and waited in silence.

Sherri was funny when she didn't like people. The Dictator wanted this and that, pointing to her and the skinny waitress as if he were condemning them. Sherri had the little snoot of politeness. When she approached the kitchen window, she made a crazy face and stuck out her tongue. Joe smiled through the steam as if he understood Sherri to say: "Don't worry, fique tranqüila, coitado, I love you, babee, and we can fight the Dictator like partners in crime."

When the Dictator finished his meal, he rose, posed as if standing in front of a crowd of well-rehearsed cheers, looked over his people, and reached under his jacket near his pants pocket as if to pull out his wallet. His wife sank deeper into her sweater. Suddenly he took a pistol from a small belt holster and aimed it at the ceiling. The diners dived under the table, and the cooks backed away from their grill and left the meat sputtering. Sherri screamed, dumped the tray onto a table, ran back to the kitchen, and pulled Joe down under the sink. His knees hit the concrete hard, and on his hands and knees he shivered like a frightened dog. Sherri wrapped her arms around his waist, and he could hardly breathe with her grip and his fear. He looked down at her soft white hands clasping at his belly, and even that could not calm him.

A gun went off with a wham. The diners screamed, and Joe cried, "I'm going to die!" Sherri pressed her body closer as she held on tighter, digging her chin into his back. He wished he could comfort her. He wished he were more of a man. The Dictator's footsteps shuffled to the front door, followed by his wife's clicking high-heels. The bell clanged, and the door closed with a whoosh of air.

Slowly, Sherri let go, then crawled over toward the door. "Melinda," she called to the skinny waitress, "is it safe?" The people in the dining room stirred. Sherri stood up. "He never used his gun before!" She looked back at Manuel. "Call the police?"

Manuel shook his head no as he pointed to his no-green-card cooks easing out from the storage room and returning to the grill.

Sherri grabbed a broom and dustpan and went out to the dining room. Bits of dust drifted from the bullet hole in the ceiling. She began sweeping around the Dictator's table, looked up at the hole, and laughed defiantly. She beckoned the customers out from under their tables, teasing them with her broom. She chattered them back to their seats, declaring that the Dictator was no more than a frustrated actor, and "we all know what THAT is like!" She swooped over to the table, swiped the unpaid bill, and waved it like a flag. "He's cheap, too! He forgot to pay his bill! Should we call him back?" The customers laughed and drew out their wallets and gave her money, not only for the dinner, but extra for her bravery. Then she bowed heroically, swung back into the kitchen, grinning and fanning herself with the bills.

Meanwhile, Joe had managed to hoist himself up to the sink. The old ache in his shoulder joints came back, and his skin seemed to peel in pain. He leaned over the basin, rested his forearms on the edge, and stared blankly at the food-splattered porcelain. He thought he would be sick. He felt the supervisor's calm hand on his back; Manuel's Spanish words blew against his hot skin. "Es nada, amigo, the worst is over." Joe nodded, wiped his stinging eyes with his thumb, then went back to washing dishes. He let the warm water run over his hands and forced himself to remember something beautiful, like the carioca summer rain.

After the restaurant closed, Joe waited a bit for courage, then followed Sherri through the back door and out to the parking lot. He wanted to talk to her, but his English needed to be perfect. He said in his head the kinds of sentences that he could say to her. But what if she gave an answer that he wasn't able to understand? He lit a cigarette and watched her as she wandered over to her car, chugging down a large paper cup of 7-UP as if nothing had happened. She mumbled something to herself, took a few more drinks, then threw the rest out. He could see through her cotton slacks, the cheeks of her *bunda* rubbing together, muscular, mashing, gnashing, eating each other alive, then kissing each other good night, and rolling their heads together on one pillow, relieved.

Chapter 4

O Ano 1975

Just like Joe, Brazil had started out with a longer name. In 1500, when explorer Pedro Alvares Cabral, thinking he was going around the coast of Africa, instead spotted a strange and unexpected horizon in the west, Terra Desconhecido e Escondido became Terra Nova Descoberto, Finalmente! (Or, as others claim, he had a feeling that the new land was there all along. Some say it came to him in a dream.) Weeds and reeds floating in the water scraped against the hull of the caravel. Finally, Cabral and the exhausted crew headed toward land in rowboats, landed on the beach, and called the mysterious place Terra de Vera Cruz, Land of the True Cross—land with a cross to bear.

Once the country showed its true face, the name was chopped short to Brazil.

Joe went to adult school at a community center to learn English. The lesson started right from the beginning: "This is a table. This is a chair." He was sitting with some Chinese people who couldn't understand a word. Joe knew about tables and chairs and dishwashers and knives, but he wanted to know about the words of love. He wanted to say in English: "You are trembling," "Your scent reminds me of a pot of beans," "You make me cry out in my dreams." The teacher wrote some words on the board. She was young and small and wore bangs like a girl. She used the book and her notes a lot as if she weren't sure of English herself and pointed to this and that in the room, saying the names and patting herself gently on her girl-like belly. This lesson he already knew. He had taken some English in Brazil, for god's sake, and working at his newspaper stand, he had run into Americans and liked to *bate-papo* with them, or, as it is said here, "shoot the breeze." He cracked open his Portuguese-English dictionary, looked up certain words, and wrote them down. Then he started composing a letter to Sherri, tangled but true. The rest of the class struggled along with the furniture, but he was on to better things. He finished the note just as the class ended, with everyone individually saying, "Good-bye, see you later." After class he showed the letter to the young teacher, but she shook her head, bewildered. Her eyes were baby blue, and she squinted. "I'm sorry. Can't understand a word of it. What are you trying to say?"

How could he explain?

But eight months later he proved to be a star pupil. The teacher said he needed a more advanced class. Maybe at a junior college. "You have the will," she said, rapping her small fist on the desk, "you have the will, the need to learn. That's what English is all about." She gave him a little diploma of completion. "Where are you from again?" she asked.

"Brazil."

She smiled to herself, then cocked her head so that all her hair swept to the side. "That's cool," she said. "If you have a question about English, you can still come over and ask me." Joe smiled. She almost seemed like a grown woman.

And to celebrate his graduation he decided to ask Sherri out, even if his English wasn't perfect. The restaurant hadn't opened for dinner yet, and Joe wandered around the dining room for courage, examining the table tops of plastic wood and the Western lamps with red-glass covers. He tried to figure out the autographed pictures on the wall. He recognized the one Gary Cooper photo, but the rest were new: Chi Chi Rivera, Solomon and the Mambo Kings, the Cucaracha Jumpbirds, and Tex Green on his horse Flipper.

Joe came into the kitchen. Manuel lit the grill. Pots of chili and soup boiled on the stove. Sherri hovered over the pots, lifting the lids and peering through the steam at the contents, then decided on the soup. She ladled herself a bowl of minestrone. Joe grabbed a bowl and stood behind her. "Hi," he said.

"Hi," she said. With that knowing glance. "Como está usted?"

Everyone thinks he speaks Spanish. It's maddening. He should have taken Spanish classes instead of English. Shit.

"Hablas Ingles muy bien now?" she blew the steam from her bowl in his direction.

"Of course. I finish adult school. I was the best student."

"There you go!" She announced to the cooking staff. "Now he's learning English; let that be a lesson to you."

Manuel crunched a tomato between his teeth. "They speak English when you're not around."

She threw her head back and laughed. "Are they saying bad things about me?"

"I would not say bad things," Joe said and gave a broad smile that made her smile, too. Her thin blond hair, wet and smelling of shampoo, was in a bun, and she wore small gold earrings. Her full chest urged the white blouse forward, and the skin of her back puckered from her bra clasp. The tight black pants of her uniform covered her round bunda with mystery. She winked and carried her soup to the staff room. Her wink was better than food.

Joe drifted into the staff room, holding the empty bowl at his side. He had to say something more than "Hi."

Sherri looked up from her soup, the steam misting over her face. "Name is José, right? Hoe-zay?"

"Joe."

"Joe or Hoe-zay? I know *that* much Spanish,"

"My name is Joe. Joe."

Sherri stirred her soup with the spoon to cool it off. She looked up slyly. "OK. Joe-Joe." She started eating her soup. He stood there watching her. She looked at Joe again. "When did you cross the border?"

Joe raised his eyebrows. "I'm from Brazil."

"Whoa," she spoke with her mouth full. "They got a beach, yeah?"

Joe nodded slowly. He wanted her to be more reverent when it came to Brazil. If she knew how Guanabara Bay embraced the blue water and how the mountains surrounding the bay were covered with jungle and resembled the garden of a madman, she'd be more serious. Only the favelas of cast-off brick and wood — like fragile ladders climbing the faces of the hills — deformed the city with misery. Rio is like you, Sherri. You are beautiful, alluring, but angry and corrupt, and you think, "Who can love me?"

Just talk to someone who knows.

She put her spoon down, a bit annoyed at his just standing there. "You better grab some food before the place opens. You won't have a chance to eat otherwise."

"Do you have a boyfriend?" he blurted out and knew it sounded rude, but he didn't know the polite words to say this.

"Don't get any ideas," she snapped, then ate, not looking at him, and gave a sharp slurp. "I'm through with the dating racket."

Then she completely ignored him and continued eating. He backed out of the staff room into the kitchen, set his bowl on the prep table, and pulled out a small notebook and pencil he kept in his back pocket. He wrote "dating racket" to add to his increasing rush of English words.

During the evening, he drank in Sherri with his gaze; he scraped the dishes and watched her through the kitchen window, chatting with the customers, gossiping with skinny Melinda, who twitched her shoulders when she laughed. Sherri grinned with a bright, tight smile. Oh, she must hate her job. She was too polite, just too polite. Now she was pointing to the wall menu, explaining the differences in the cuts of meat. She seemed oblivious to love, but that didn't matter because Joe had been rejected many times, and here, in this new land where dictators and hate were not dangerous, love should not be as dangerous either.

After work, Joe asked Sherri if she wanted to go out on their day off, and she said fine and laughed with a twinkle that made her look like a small animal on an American cereal box. "Where would you like to go?" Joe asked, holding his breath because he was too poor to take her any-where. Her eyes did a slant motion to the side, her small gold earrings quivering. "The beach," she said. "That's a cheap date. And it's not so cold, even this time of year."

Joe grinned a smile of relief, and his excitement churned like the waves and dazzling undertow of this new land. Oh, Terra Nova! Oh, this new country with rivers of gold. Oh, the hidden life of Los Angeles. Terra Incognita. Land of lovelorn sighs — oh, this city of thighs!

❨

Women wearing sunglasses drove Joe mad with desire. They seemed mysterious and had their own language. Dark-haired women who hid behind sunglasses looked bitchy, as if their eyes were bloodshot from partying or fucking all night. Women with sunglasses walking along the beach seemed to whisper among themselves: we have tongues of silence — we pretend we want a man. We speak many languages. We are compli-cated. We want two lovers. We paint our skin with lipstick. At the beach, we want the fish to bring us gold. We like dangerous waves. We search for children, bawl them out, give them swats — Doesn't your mother know you're misbehaving? We wear straw hats to keep monkeys out of our hair. We pretend we're exotic trees. We exchange rings. We get jealous of others with diamonds. We like to make trouble. We do it daily.

All of this went on in his head as Sherri came toward him. The early-morning haze of Santa Monica made her look soft like a thick Ameri-can blanket. Her ample legs curved gracefully into her smallish feet. She wore an old sweatshirt with a faded print of a pink shell on the front.

Gold strands of hair fell from her ponytail. Joe slipped his hands into his pants pockets and watched her walking in the sand, hips swaying in her tight jeans. She carried a straw beach bag with a plastic starfish clinging to the side.

"Hi," she said, so cheery, not brash like in the restaurant. Her lips were heart shaped like American love. They ambled silently to where the water touched the sand. Cold water rushed around their ankles and pulled away. Their heels squishing in the sand sounded like kisses with wet tongues. Joe took the beach bag from her and offered to carry it, and she smiled. "Sí," she said. "Is it *sí?*"

"*Sim.*"

She chuckled and threw up her hands. "Spanish," she said, "was not one of my favorite subjects in school."

He looked into the bag and saw wrapped sandwiches nestled under a sweatshirt. They wandered for a bit without saying anything. Sherri looked toward a wave rolling out like a white sheet of lace. "Sherri," Joe finally said.

Sherri turned, those eyebrows raised again.

"I don't speak Spanish; I speak Portuguese."

"Oh," she said, "really? Why?"

Joe shrugged. "In Brazil we speak Portuguese. It's different than Spanish."

"How is it different?"

"I don't know," he said, "just a bit." What he wanted to say was that Portuguese lingers in your throat like velvet. The words float upward warmed by the humming of your thoughts, then they come through your mouth, pushed out by the desires of your heart.

"Cool," she said. "I learn something new every day. Say something in Portuguese."

He started talking to her in Portuguese, how much he wanted her, how he looked at her every day, and how lonely he was with the drunks in front of his apartment and the burning flesh of the Eye and Rib. He admitted that he couldn't make his life work right, that he had become obsessed with his newsstand business and with all the newspapers' printing lies, which he sold, betraying his heart. Then everything had collapsed when Sonia and he were dragged away by military police.

Sherri didn't understand a word, but she nodded as though she did. "Beautiful," she said. "Beautiful words." Then she reached into her bag and slipped on a pair of sunglasses, not dark flashes of seductive malice, but pink and round and innocent like two antacid tablets.

They came to a small sandbank. The water swirled up, and the foam left a creamy mustache on the surface of the sand. They sat down facing the ocean. "I used to come here a lot," she said, "but now I don't so much."

"Why?"

"First, I came with Susan, my twin sister. Then later I came here to do drugs." She smiled slyly. "You know. Drugs? Weed?" She pinched her thumb and forefingers together and sucked in. "The teachers used to tell us we'd have children with three heads if we messed with it. You know, mar-i-juana?"

"Of course I know marijuana."

Sherri laughed quietly to herself and sprinkled sand on her feet. "Well, I was big trouble in those days, believe me. Sometimes I can't believe I'm alive."

Joe had the urge to touch her aliveness. He wished he could pick her up like a seashell, hold her next to his ear, and listen to her breath.

Sherri leaned her forehead on her knees.

"Who's Susan?" Joe asked.

She got a little impatient with him. "Susan. My twin sister. Sister. You understand? She was killed. Died, OK? When she was a teenager. Got hit by a car. Pow." She demonstrated by hitting her fist into her cupped hand.

Joe nodded. "I understand, of course."

"Yeah," Sherri snorted. "She died the L.A. way." Then she turned away, "I bet I remind you of a soap opera, huh?"

"Of course not, how sad."

"Really," she said, her lids were half-closed now, "having a twin was like — well, she's half of me, of course. She was the heart twin, and I am the head twin. When she died, life became fucked — kinda like with no heart." She ran her hands up and down her calves. "Twins run in my family. I have two aunts from my mom's side that are twins and another aunt *had* twins. I think my grandparents had some twins floating around. I would love to have twins. I'd love to get married and have twins, man." She chuckled and rolled her eyes. "I hope you're not understanding all of this, Joe. I'm making an ass of myself."

I understand all of it, he thought.

"At any rate," she pulled the basket between her legs and started fishing for the sandwiches, "I'm a waitress and pretty much a dull person. The best I can hope for is a beer drinker. A Budweiser kinda guy."

After the beach, they went to Sherri's apartment. She lived upstairs in a two-story complex like his. Beige. There was a railed corridor that went along the front doors and windows and a stairway of stone slabs welded to a metal frame, the kind that reveals the long drop below, that gives the fear of falling. Sherri unlocked two locks and bumped the front door open with her hip. "Shit, this place is stuffy," she said and opened the beveled kitchen window. Joe tugged on a cord that snapped open the curtain.

"Oh great," Sherri threw up her hands, "let's do a porn movie for the public, why don't we?" Joe pulled back. For a minute he thought she was serious and didn't know quite the polite words to handle this. He looked at the living room, where her bed lay sprawled, unmade. Like him, she lived in one room.

Sherri apologized for her spare apartment because she moved a lot and threw away a lot of stuff. She said that the apartment was usually clean, but she got so damn busy. She flitted around, closed the blinds, turned on the light, got a glass of water, kicked off her shoes, and leaned on the breakfast counter that separated the kitchen from the living room. She motioned to a small bookcase with a few paperbacks, a few china clowns, and some pictures of girlfriends making rabbit ears behind their boyfriends' heads. "I got some books. At least I'm a little educated, huh, Joe? Did you go to school?"

"Of course. When I was little." He smiled uneasily. She grinned, gulped the rest of her water, then went back into the kitchen and clattered her glass down hard on the counter. He didn't really want this, if she didn't. But just as he formed in his head an apology, an excuse, Sherri began undressing. She didn't look at him as she slipped off her shirt. Her smooth white shoulders looked fallen, and the folds of her underarm and upper breast were puckered. She shoved her old, worn bra to her waist and unhooked it, then tossed it aside like a rag. She unzipped her jeans. "God, I'm fat."

Joe didn't answer and began unbuttoning his shirt.

She whirled around, the fly of her jeans open. "Am I?"

"What?" Joe stopped undoing the buttons midway.

"Fat."

"Of course not," he smiled and lowered his eyes, flinging off his shirt. He stroked his chest of black curls and hoped she wouldn't mind. In fact, her eyes lit up. "Haven't seen *that* in a while," she said, a bit of snideness from her side glance, a bit of seduction in her heart-lips pursed like a rose bud. Then they struggled out of the rest of their clothes.

Joe stood naked in front of her, but was embarrassed with a new woman. He had been ridiculed naked — the military police had made fun of his man part — and he folded his hands over his balls. Sherri gave a smirk. "I won't bite," she said, "I'm not that fancy."

Joe nodded again. "Of course," then went over to her. She expected him to do something. He unbuckled the barrette of her ponytail, and her hair unraveled blond, her white chest expanded. It was soft and curved, and he smoothed his hands down her face and over her breasts. His skin felt tight, and he eyed her hand, afraid she would touch him.

She kissed him on the lips. He drew back and kissed her. Then she put her hands on his waist. "Aren't you Latins supposed to be good in bed?"

Joe coughed, a bit embarrassed. Of course, why not? They are better than the English, he had read. He touched her shoulders, not sure what to do, then he said, "Lay down."

Sherri shrugged, "Sure," and she climbed into bed awkwardly, her legs clamping shut, then opening. He got on top of her, hung over her like a roof. She reached up and put her hands around on his back. Suddenly, the flashbacks came roaring through—

He feels the searing pain cutting through his skin, jolting his ribs and his guts. He cries out as he keeps his face pressed against the concrete floor dotted with blood—

"Are you OK?" Sherri asked, but her voice was in the distance. He could not will away these horrible memories, even with the act of love, and his desire was crushed by a scream from the other side of the wall—

The leather belt crashes against his skin—

"Are you OK?" Sherri asked again, this time more concerned.

His eyes focused on her, and she seemed to tilt her head. Her hair spilled around her as if she had fallen in a puddle. She touched him again.

"Don't—!"

"Estuprador—!"

To be called a rapist makes him vomit. As he shudders with sickness, the skin on his back cracks open like a rotten fruit—

Then, quieter, Joe said: "Don't touch."

"Whoa," she said, "no touching?"

"I'll manage."

He saw her face fall, her eyes weaving close together. She tucked her hand behind her head, and he could hear her feet sliding apart. "OK then. Whatever."

He slid his *pau* inside, hard only because he began remembering how he loved her creamy skin and her contempt. He finished in no time, as quick as an Englishman, and, without touching her, he lifted himself up and lay beside her. He felt terrible the way he had treated her, like a *puta*, but he didn't have the words to explain.

She sighed, "The water must be different here." Then she curled up her knees and lay on her side facing away from him. Joe sat up and looked down at his rumpled stomach and how it folded into a pair of thick brown lips. His nipples were the purple eyes. The hair on his pubis was the goatee. In fact, his hairy belly looked unnatural, dark and sneering. Sherri got up, slipped on her panties, and let his cum slosh around without washing herself off. Then she turned on the TV, slid back into bed, and turned her back to him. He sat up, leaned over, and grabbed his shirt from the floor. He felt around in the pocket and got out his cigarettes. "You want one?" he asked.

"No," she said languidly, "believe it or not, it's one vice I haven't picked up. You can smoke. I don't care."

Joe lit one for himself. He leaned back on the pillow, the gray smoke clouding his humiliation. He gazed at her white back and the shadow of her spine that reminded him of the middle of a butterfly. Her bikini panties barely covered her ass, and he reached with his big toe and stroked the upper part of her crack. "I'm sorry," he said.

She flinched. "Toe is cold. Don't."

He turned to watch the TV. It was that children's show with two puppets named Jeffy and Keffy again. He didn't know what sex they were because they talked like excited animals. They sang a song about love, about will you be my friend at school, can I paint your lunch box blue? The music in the background had a lot of bells and silly laughter. Jeffy and Keffy heard a horse coming up the street, and they said, "Let's toss our hats in the air." And they tossed their cowboy hats in the air to the sound of a slide whistle. All at once Joe felt it, as if he could see inside her womb; he knew something was forming. He pictured the yolk inside her smiling with its big creamy face, then splitting into two yolks. She rubbed her belly. He even heard them chattering inside Sherri's body, Jeffy and Keffy. "Ooooo-bippidy-bop-ooo—bleedeleedeedee—ooo—it tickles, Jeffy; no, you're tickling me, Keffy."

"Maybe you are pregnant," Joe said.

Sherri shrugged. "You should have worn a rubber."

He took a puff of his cigarette and looked at the burning tip. "I will support you. I will not run away. I am that much of a man."

"That's what they all say," Sherri grunted, yanking up the sheet and pulling it to her neck.

"I mean it." Joe watched the TV for a while. The two puppets were bopping each other with a small red hammer. Ooop. Aap. Ooop. Aaap. Oh, Jeffy! Oh, Keffy!

"If you have twins," he said, "I'd like to name them Jeffy and Keffy. Those names seem American to me."

"Well," Sherri's voice softened as she drifted to sleep, "you seem pretty American to me alright."

Chapter 5

O Ano 1977

Rosea watched as Pachito's old truck, chugging with a bit of vato cockiness, drove away, leaving her in the middle of open farmland. Pachito had to be at work early and could take her only this far. After a week or so, Rosea knew her presence tainted Pachito and Mannie's proud little home, her having to sleep in the living-room floor beside their bed, practically on top of them, it seemed. She listened to them whispering heavily, their bodies shifting the same way every night. She decayed everything she touched; she always reminded people what they were most afraid of, the part of the past that haunts them. She reminded people of what happens when others forget you exist.

Rosea had to walk a quarter of a mile or so to the job her parole officer had lined up for her, some damn fruit stand out in the boonies. The manager had specifically requested her, had followed her mother's career and the arson trial, and now was willing to rehab her in exchange for a few cha-cha lessons. Ain't that something! Rosea, savage offspring of Carmen Socorro, desired all of a sudden, loved by fans the world over.

She trudged down the road and looked out over the flat farmland with broccoli fields on one side and plowed brown planting rows converging at the horizon on the other. The broccoli, their leaves and small green heads, shriveled in the sun and smelled like chemicals from nearby portapotties. The telephone wire above wagged in the unsheltered breeze. Hawks alighted on fence posts, and mosquitoes buzzed in dense bouncing clouds. This desolation looked like the lonely freedom she feared most of all.

The produce stand—really a small hut—gleamed in the distance like a silver tooth. Above it a string of colored plastic flags purred in the wind. A small white car was parked to one side. As she approached, a man came out to greet her. He waved his arms in the air as if she were an airplane flying in. On closer look she saw an old thing with a fringe of gray hair around his extensive bald spot. He wore sandals, a cotton shirt, and loose pants, and his whole figure rippled like a mirage. Once he got through waving her down, he ran toward her with his hands out, stepping carefully over dirt clods. He clutched her arm and held on, taking deep breaths.

"Don't kill yourself over me," Rosea said.

"No," puff-puff, "I'm so glad you're here."

"A pleasure, I'm sure."

He wouldn't let go of her arm, but clung on, ogling at how tall she was. The skinny guy came up to just under her chin. "You must make yourself at home," he said. You must and you must. He practically led her like a horse, until finally Rosea jerked her arm away with an "I'm not crippled." He nodded and backed away, muttering to himself.

The stand was made of old lumber and patched with plywood. Shelves lined with cardboard boxes contained mostly small swarms of tumbling fleas. Rosea looked into a box of crookneck squash, all rotten except for one, yellow and fresh and shaped like a question mark, that for some reason seemed oblivious to time.

The man throttled up his voice. His mouth was dry. "As Isaiah said, those released from bondage will kiss the dirt." And with that, he got down on his knees, curled up until his backbone showed like a dorsal fin. Then he touched his lips on the ground, right next to her feet. She looked up, unable to bear the geezer. The sign above the cash register said "Beno's Fruit and Vegetable Stand."

"Are you Mr. Beno?" Rosea flicked some dust with her foot.

He got up and stared into her eyes. "My name is Melvinor," he said, then took a deep breath. "Melvinor."

"Alright," Rosea backed away, "good to know what to call you."

"I can't believe you are Carmen Socorro's daughter."

At that, Rosea grit her teeth and paced around the stand, looking at the whole rotten mess. "My name is not Carmen Socorro's Daughter. My name is Rosea Socorro Katz."

"It must be hard for you," he said, "to remember what happened to your mother, the legend, the greatest star in Hollywood. Oh, I loved your mother, I loved Carmen Socorro. So did Bing Crosby. All the fellas wanted her."

"Oh really?"

"Maybe to you I'm an old man. But I'm not blind. As Isaiah said, 'A field that is fallow is ready for a new crop.'" Then he puttered over to the cash register and continued babbling, "Oh Carmen — how her hair was dark and her lips were red and her hips so round and her skirt so tight!"

"Hey!" Rosea hollered. "I didn't come here to talk about my mother. Don't ever say another word about it. I'm only stuck with you because I have to be, got it?"

Melvinor raised his eyebrows. "I wanted you. I followed everything you did."

"That doesn't mean we have to like each other."

Melvinor nodded and shuffled over to an ice cooler of soft drinks floating in icy water. He pulled out a Coke and eagerly shoved it in her hand. She took it and nodded, then restlessly reeled away only to hit her head on the low-hanging beam of the ceiling. She howled and grabbed her frizzy black and angry hair that hung past her shoulders.

A hand rested on her scalp. Melvinor was poking around in her hair, trying to find the bump. "Leave me alone," she said and pulled away, pressing the cold Coke can against the sore spot.

Melvinor stepped back and nervously tugged at the upper button of his shirt. His hands were so old and stiff he could barely twirl the button. "Rosea. There's something I want to know."

Rosea cracked open the pop top and took a drink, not answering him.

"Rosea," he said after a long silence, "Do you sing?"

Rosea lurched crazily and hurled the Coke hard against the wall; the aluminum can exploded like a grenade. Coke rained from the ceiling and dripped onto Melvinor's head. God, she was imprisoned with adoration that didn't even belong to her. And there was nowhere else she could go.

☾

Autumn and still a hot motherfucker. Three months slaving out here seemed like Melvinor's biblical forty years and forty centuries in the desert. The day had a look of danger on its face and prayed desperately for luck. The telephone wires above crackled with dread. It was a day off kilter, a cola-for-breakfast kind of day.

Melvinor slouched and sat back down on his crate in the half-shade outside the stand. The old man wore a visor that had "Beno's" printed on it in large black letters. The sun had burned a pink cap on the exposed part of his bald head. He eyed Rosea from under the visor's rim. He was probably staring at her butt again. Bet he liked her long, strong legs, too. Old Melvinor hung out here every day, no matter how hot it was. He and his white Pinto and his large green thermos. He was probably alone before, but now he had her and her butt. He looked off into the dizzy haze, into the fields, watching the migrant workers snatch dragonflies and pinch them dead between their fingers.

Melvinor scraped a stick in the dirt. "Boy, we used to have watermelons here. Nice juicy things."

"Uh-huh." Rosea sat on a stool outside the stand, smelling the ripe rinds rotting away. Five watermelons lay split, and Melvinor just left them.

No one would come here; there was nothing to buy. Rosea lit a cigarette and used an empty Coke can for an ashtray. The haze of the fields already made her sleepy. She numbly smoothed her hand over her hair, and her mind, dormant with bitterness after all those years, began to open, and she remembered having her hair braided by her mother. She remembered how Carmen Socorro spoke in a sexy hush in order to "nurse" her throat so it would be ready to sing, and she used this voice as the hairbrush massaged Rosea's scalp and tugged deliciously through her thick black hair. As Carmen brushed and wound Rosea's hair around her hand, she told of how the Amazons blended into the trees and waited in camouflage for their enemy. Imagine, her mother said, their warm brown bodies and heavy hair blending into the fierce jungle. Imagine the enemy in their last doomed seconds, seeing a bunch of Amazons, women with hair like a horse's mane, a dark curtain of glory, the enemy feeling an instant pang of excitement, even delight, as they stared at the sharp point of the flying spear coming between their eyes. Then her mother, unable to contain herself, wept and used Rosea's locks as a handkerchief to wipe her tears. Her mother mourned for her own hair, which she had to keep bunched in a turban, bound and gagged under tons of fruit and frufru. Her wonderful Brazilian camouflage had been stripped, and now, with the costume, Carmen was as visible and vulnerable as a toucan on a tea table. Her mother eventually calmed down and continued with the braiding, working Rosea's hair into two long black vines.

Melvinor leaned against the hood of his car, drinking coffee from the tin cup of his large green thermos. He didn't say anything, but looked at Rosea glassy eyed and lifted the steaming cup to his lips. Then out of nowhere he began talking. Melvinor always began talking out of nowhere, but it was the third time this morning, another sign of dread. He stood up and started again on Isaiah, the exile, and how one had to wander in the desert for a long time before one found the way home. He made sweeping gestures. He acted bizarre, but he seemed funny. Rosea stood there grinning. "What are you talking about, old man? Who in the hell is this Isaiah?"

Melvinor calmed down and stroked the little fringe of white hair around his bald spot. "I still can't believe you're Carmen Socorro's daughter."

Rosea crushed her cigarette. "I told you not to talk about it, didn't I?"

Oh no, he wouldn't stop with that. Then he started babbling again, about how he used to go to Latin clubs and admire women with lipsticked mouths and black-lined eyes. But it was Mona, oye vey! His wife. "Imagine," he said, "a little Jewish couple free with their dancing feet; the short, noisy Mona, who wore a red dress from Bloomingdale's, who did up her black hair in two long rolls that framed her face like a Hasid woman's wig. Mona's thick square feet stuffed into red pumps could do fast footwork. We sailed into banana land with the rinka-rocka of maracas and congo bongos. Oh! Mona could not move from her gut like Latins do, but she *could* wiggle her butt like the pendulum of a too-wound-up clock. And when she laughed with that 'yek-yek' nasal flatness, the trumpeter in the band, holding the horn to his chest as he kept with the beat, gave a little smile, his thick maroon lips dented from where his mouthpiece pressed down on his kisser."

"And Carmen Socorro! Wow! What a gal!" he continued. "Her hips, her flouncy skirt, her cupped hands, her twiddling fingers! Her tutti-frutti hat became the cornucopia for starving Americans, hungering for fresh fruit and world peace. I know you don't like me to talk about her, Rosea, but Carmen reached out to us when the distant war haunted our soul. During the war, everyone in America, everyone was good because no one could be as bad as the bad people were. Perhaps, for the only time in history, our half of life was cheerful because the other half was so sad. But oh the orchids and roses, and high trills from the tongues of bangled women and men with thin spicy mustaches. And Mona, God rest her soul, bore me a daughter, Heddie, but both of them died of cancer. The funny thing is, I can only remember loving Mona and Heddie; I don't remember their faults. I would have done anything for them."

Rosea bristled. "Would you do anything for me?"

He closed his eyes for a moment, then opened them. The rims right below his eyes were red. "Yes."

Rosea backed away quickly and grabbed from the shelf a case of rotten oranges hopping with fruit flies. She took the crate out back and dumped the old fruit in a pile. She stomped back inside, got a box of black limp bananas, went back out and threw those in with the oranges. Tangy carcasses. She dumped out a crate of peaches that oozed pulp through the cuts in their skin; after that went the squash and finally those famous watermelons. The fruit lay in a black, breathing heap, pits swelling out of the sour, watery pus.

Rosea's nails became claws, her breath rapid as she charged back into the stand and snatched a spade from the corner. She went over to Melvinor, flicked her long mass of hair away from her neck, and rammed the shovel into the dirt at his feet, making a slash. "Take this," she fumed, "you're gonna bury the old fruit out back."

Melvinor took the shovel and gulped, "It rots on its own."

"It smells like shit," she gritted her teeth. "Rotten fruit smells. I feel sick when it smells."

"I don't think we want—"

"Yes," Rosea seethed, "I *want* it."

He stared at her darkly, then went over to the pile of rotten fruit while humming "Copacabana" softly to himself.

Rosea laughed bitterly. She knew she could drive men crazy. Before prison made her thick and dull, she had been attractive, so tall and daring with her black hair and made-up eyes and hips as thick as a mound of earth. Men loved her long legs and powerful calves stretched long by cha-cha shoes, fuck-me red with poisonous high heels. Rosea didn't deal with men the way her mother had, no. She wanted to make *that* perfectly clear. Her mother seduced Rosea's father, Moses Katz, a little Jewish man who came to fix the filter of her pearl-shaped swimming pool, by opening her robe like wings and luring the little man in his bikini trunks over to the Promised Land of warm naked flesh and tropical fruit. He must have clung to Carmen's Amazonian thighs like a little tree frog, and they must have rutted in amphibious ecstasy. Rosea could only imagine this because she had never seen her father; he took off after the egg was deposited. Rosea, on the other hand, would take her lovers to Malibu on the back of her motorcycle, and she'd force them to stand at the edge of the cliffs at night, looking over the ocean and into their own dark abyss while she threatened, in her wild street caló, to push them off. *"I am not like my mother,"* she'd hiss, her words like the sound of a flying whip. *"Hollywood did not eat my brain. I am ME! You cannot just kiss me without paying a price."*

Melvinor sighed patiently and repeatedly tried to jam the shovel into the ground. He pinched his lips into a line, and a dribble of sweat swizzled down his neck. Rosea glared at him, but her sticky eyelids felt heavy. Every time Melvinor whacked the shovel blade into the ground, she took a deep breath, and the whack became a slap on his face. Whack. Yeah, hack away at the dirt. Pretty damn futile, huh? It's futile . . . plants grow futilely . . . futilezation . . . tiny futile veggies could be sold as pathetic gourmet greens. Whack.

The pounding of the shovel became like rhythm, like samba, like cha-cha, and she closed her eyes and pretended to think like coconuts do, rotting and basking in the sun, getting kicked into the water, bobbing, soaking, dancing. Rosea started to breathe hard and imagined coconuts drifting past fish scales in the lower depths of the ocean. Melvinor was wheezing loudly.

"Fuck it," she said, "stop digging."

❨

Melvinor dropped the shovel and babbled of how he had to wander the earth and live out in the desert like Isaiah and eat dirt clods and scorpions, and then he got in his car and just drove away, didn't even say good-bye. As if burying the fruit had traumatized him. Rosea sat on his crate and looked out. A tractor bounced around in the distance, driving monotonously straight. She had visions of the land being plowed and uprooted, the plants sighing and yielding to the tractor blade. Nobody was interested to see if the crops would grow. If the plants aren't putting out, it's BAM, out they go. Her mind attacked the tractors—pulled the drivers down from their small tractor seats and stuffed their faces into the powdery, drought-ridden dirt. Her mind was blowing up into a thousand cherry-colored flames.

She watched the sun go down. What does one do when one has tried everything? She wondered what her mother would do. Her mother had made herself a legend and could not control her real life, not even the size of her hats. Carmen's hats weren't decorated only with bananas, but with whole bowls of fruit, coconut trees—the whole Amazon rain forest had been uprooted. Monkeys swayed from the trees and dropped off into the jungle. Carmen wore a neck brace in rehearsals because her hat was so heavy. Wearing the large hats gave her headaches, so her husband-cum-manager gave her pills for the pain. Still, she cried because her feet hurt, and she couldn't look down to see her toes. She kept taking pain pills until she became so immovable she might as well have grown roots.

Rosea had spaced out, forgetting to hitch a ride with a migrant truck. By nightfall, the wind was quiet, and Beno's plastic flags were still. The moon lit the dried-up fields. Mice skittered on the floor of the stand, and she could hear their tiny feet on the empty crates. She felt like swooping down and killing them. From the fields she heard a low rumble.

The faint roar grew and massaged the inside of Rosea's throat. She felt curious about the noise and wandered toward it. She could feel the powdery soil puff on either side of her tennis shoes. Grains of dirt stung her chapped lips. A small curious light appeared, winked at her, faded, and lowered its lid, then winked brightly again as she broke into a run.

The roar approached, and Rosea saw a light coming from a giant tractor bumping along the field. She let out a sigh, and with it all the anger in her flushed out in waves. She held her breath and plunged herself in front of the light. Rosea wanted the tractor to run her down. Suicide had that euphoric lilt to it, the rushing of headlights, the stampeding of massive steeds, the taut bending of the bows and the flying of arrows. The freedom of bobbing on the ocean! Rosea had a sudden longing to return to some forgotten river, to push against the current, and knock stray coconuts against the sides of war canoes. She searched for the one belly, that familiar brown navel belonging to the woman who could not sing, but only scream until her spit formed rain clouds. The tractor bellowed. Rosea imagined herself surrounded by silver slivers of metal, deep-sea fish with razor fins and delicately pointed snouts. A silver tail fin darted at her head. Beaky snouts goaded her shoulders, then slunk back, smiling and twisting as they gleamed, suspended and curious. She reached out.

Light flashed, the fish dived for her neck, then shimmered at her eye-balls. Her eyelashes touched the metallic fins, but they froze, then slowly swam away until all she could make out were the tiny, pointy fish eyes. Rosea heard the driver of the tractor shout. She decided not to be afraid. She stood in front of the tractor, outstretched her hands, and looked up at the night sky and its ocean of stars.

The next morning Rosea found herself lying face down in the dirt. The tractor must have missed her. The morning sun soaked into the long black hair tangled around her neck. A new morning breeze whistled in her ears. She touched her wrists and felt her warm, dry skin. Then she looked up and saw that the whole field had been plowed under. Rosea eased herself up on her knees and brushed away the dirt from her shirt and face. She looked toward the fruit and vegetable stand and noticed that the wood and corrugated tin concoction was leaning to one side. Probably been that way all along. The Pinto was there of course. Mel-vinor appeared from behind the stand, obviously looking for her. His eyes scanned the horizon, and she heard faintly, "Rosea! Rosea!" Rosea clenched her hands. She wanted to run away from him, but he would see her.

Melvinor finally spotted her and pointed. Rosea started to shiver as she saw him approach. He was so thin and old; he moved lightly on the earth as if he were wearing sandals and a long robe. He jogged a few steps, then caught his breath, held out his hands to her, and brought with him a warm gust of wind.

Rosea stumbled to her feet, but she was too shaky to run off. Melvinor reached over and snatched her shoulders. She pulled away and wandered back toward the stand.

"I had a dream about you," he said, trotting after her.

"Leave me alone."

"I had a dream that you—" he caught up with her and grabbed her arm.

Rosea pushed him away, and he stumbled backward, patting his heart.

"Don't touch me." She staggered over to the tin shade.

"Rosea, he said, "I had a dream that you swam out into the ocean and died."

She caught the doorway of the stand.

His bony hand rose and touched the top of her head, floated, touched her cheek, her lower lip. Then he passed his fingers lovingly across his mouth and cupped his hands around his own face the way he would cup hers.

She could see through his skull as if it were crystal, and she became frightened of his oldness. Her mother rose in her memory—savage, breast-plated, bristling, harsh, and blazing. Her mother's hair burst out of the fruited turban and turned into a whirlwind. Rosea threw her head back and screamed. She screamed until she sucked up the clouds and all the potential water in the sky. She sucked up the fields and the whole oceans. She watched her hand grab and pull down on the string of plastic flags that flapped in the valley gusts. As the walls of the stand started to crack, she jammed her foot hard against the wall and loosened the tin from the frame. Melvinor stood back and stared. Little threads of his white hair wisped out. She almost imagined him to be her father, even though she didn't know what her father looked like. His mouth gaped into a silent scream, and she wanted him to scream for her and her mother, scream in torturous longing.

She yanked at the flags again and pulled down the front of the roof, then moved to the side to watch. The warped wood planks buckled, and part of the tin roof caved in submissively next to her in a gentle roar. The shelves crashed into splinters. The last ceiling beam collapsed. The two halves of Beno's Fruit and Vegetable Stand split and fell open like a coconut. Rosea was amazed how beautiful the land was. The field was rippling; the wind made a sound like oars dipping into the water; and the corrugated tin glittered like sunlit jewels of the Amazon.

The Fruits: the figlike *berjaçotes*, pomegranates, guavas, tamarind, *abacaxi, cajá, araticu*, the pinecone-size *oiticoró*, the delicious *mangaba*, the red *jamacaru, pitomba*, the cherrylike *maçaranduba, guabiroba* that looks like an olive, the egg-size *oiti*, the long white *gravatá* that one eats by sucking, the *uvaias, macujé* that tastes like pears, and the *jaboticaba*.

The Women: the one with one long breast, the one who smells like oily *bacalau* stew, the one with spiders in her hair, the one with lips the shape of a war canoe, the one who washes her hair in the Rio Nhamundá, the one who lives by the Mirror of the Moon, the one with the insatiable lust, the one who gives birth to babies the color of blood, the one who was poisoned by snake venom, the one who became the star that we call Beta Centauri, the one with a hut that attracts fireflies that glint with pleasure.
—*Carta de Carlos Manoel Teixeira da Cunha a João Vicente Cardim da Almeida, O Ano 1640*

Chapter 6

O Ano 1975

Joe had finished cleaning up the kitchen and now stacked the chairs on the tables for Sherri while he waited for her to finish her shift. Sherri, instead of rushing to get her usual midnight 7-UP, lingered, almost reluctant to leave. She touched a chair here, caressed the top of a table there, and the red-beveled lamps of the dining room softened her pale flesh into pink, highlighting her lids as if he had licked away the shadows in her eyes. Joe placed the chairs upside down on tables, and she looked past him, almost looked through the walls and onto the street. He mopped the floor cautiously, watching, dreading. Today he had learned the phrase "to give someone the boot" and feared her American silence.

He went to the small closet, dumped the water from the cleaning bucket into the large sink, and put away the mop. When he returned to the dining room, her look had changed; her face rippled through the room of metal chair legs, her skin glowering, and she looked hot and irritated as she untied her apron. "I'm pregnant," she said simply, then without stopping, "Don't worry, you don't have to support me. It's no hassle for you. None for me, either, because I want to keep it."

What was she saying? Pregnant? You don't have to support me? How could she say that? He ran his fingers through his hair, mixing mop water into his curls, and took a deep breath. Her stomach still looked normal, the size of a small salad bowl. But it would grow with his child. How could he not support her? Not marry her? He pressed his fingers against his lips and gave a small secret kiss, thinking of his Sonia—how they were going to get married after she finished school and how he had lost her. Oh no, he wouldn't lose Sherri now. And what was this expression on Sherri's face? A little angry now with that glare she got when she met someone who couldn't speak English?

He went up to her and took her face in his hands. Her cheeks tightened, and she pulled away. The face of the mother of his child! "I love you," he said. "This makes me so happy."

He would be with her, holding the globe of her belly in his hands, sketching on her stomach the map of Brazil so his child would know the way back to his father's home. All of a sudden, the English that was pent up inside poured out of him, and he spoke glibly like an americano, but passionately like a carioca. I love you like the hills, like the gold arm bangles of Yemanjá, like floating lighted candles in the water. I love you like the Iguaçu Falls and the rainbows rising from the mists below. I love you like the pool of Guanabara Bay, the mirror reflecting the beautiful mountains that surround it, and the small sailboats dotting the waters with pleasure.

He drew her close, and he heard her struggle, her nose snorting against his shirt. He was afraid she would leave him if he let go, so he hung on, trying to keep his mind off the men on his doorstep with their hopelessness and harsh night coughing. He didn't want to end up that way. He was in his thirties, and at this age he wanted a home; he wanted to hear her peaceful breathing when he woke up. He knew what love was by now. This was hope in the new land, hope that he needed. He kept talking, flinging out stars of good fortune and joy. "I want children more than anything," he said, and "I'd do anything to keep you."

(

Sherri hollered and pushed in her labor. Joe dropped his head; he felt dizzy from holding his breath. He could use a little *cafezinha*. "Don't pass out," the nurse said, "we can't carry you." Joe slipped an ice chip into his mouth and one into Sherri's. The water dripped down her cheeks, and she grunted like a man lifting bricks. He mopped her sweaty brow with a washrag; finally he could be gentle to his wife, who was in too much pain to brush him away. Sherri pushed again, and finally, with one last yell, a child tumbled from between her legs in a gush of blood, already hollering as it landed in the doctor's outstretched hands. The nurses squealed with surprise, and Joe, close to tears, reached out for his child, covered in maroon-colored blood.

The doctor eyed him strangely, handed the baby to a nurse, who took it over to a table with a scale. Joe could see it was a boy. He went to his son and cried, "I want to hold it," but a nurse with a white mask across her snout blocked his path as she wiped the baby. "There is still another one," she snapped.

Yes, Joe knew. *Gêmeos!* Twins! Sherri screamed and writhed again. The doctor's and nurses' lips grinned under their white face masks. With another rush of nurses and another gush of blood came another baby. Twins! Joe slapped his forehead. "Meus filhos!" Even before the doctors told him it would be twins, he had predicted it, the creamy yolk inside her belly splitting in half! His heart burst with happiness for his two little boys! He'd hold one, and Sherri would hold the other, and that's the way life would be! He thrust out his brown hands again, but the second boy was also carried over to the table, weighed, and cleaned up. Sherri lay back, her eyes glittering. Two nurses took the babies, and each put a baby on the crook of Sherri's arms. Even with their reddish newborn skin, Joe could see they would be pale like her. They did not look Brazilian, or at least not like him at any rate, and for a jealous moment he wondered if the father was someone else—a Norwegian skier, perhaps. But when one of the boys kicked his tiny feet like a little frog swimming in the water, Joe knew they were his. He wanted to snatch one up, but was afraid he would break the little one, so he reached over and took their small bean-like toes between his thumb and forefinger and gently tweaked one toe at a time. Yes, you've come from a land far away, *meus filhos*. Welcome to the New World.

And now, my world must change, Joe said to himself as he stretched across the double bed at home and watched his identical sons sleeping. Identical, but different—Joe could tell them apart. Keffy slept on his back, his arms and legs splayed out and soft, his fists relaxed; but Jeffy curled his body as if trying to roll over to his side, his fists clutched as tight as walnuts. Your *papai* needs to find a bigger place for you and *sua mãe*. We cannot live in her small place, and your papai cannot be a dishwasher. His English and his ambition had increased his appetite for better things, just like you, my little *filhotes*, my little cubs, drinking your milk bottles with enormous appetites. *Seu pai* is going to ask for a job at Hollywood Celebrity Tours; I can explain it better when you get older. Your papai came to this new country, over warm but troubled skies, and the little combivan rescued me and put me near the breast of your mother. Though your mother teases that all I will see at my new job are badly dressed midwesterners, and though she says everyone in Hollywood is on drugs and the scum of the earth, remember that you, too, were born out of a fear and contempt that miraculously disappeared the day you were born. Now papai's skin, so hardened from his past, tickles when air from your little nose puffs against his cheek. This is the new fresh breeze blowing across Terra Nova. It is how it should be.

Joe walked up from the parking lot and found the Hollywood Celebrity Tours office, squeezed between a small clothing store and a souvenir shop. The reflections of passing pedestrians rippled on the blue-tinted window with the name spelled in gold lights— HOLLYWOOD CELEBRITY

TOURS. Joe made a wish on each light like a star, crossed himself, and lightly kissed his fingertips. He opened the glass door, and the hinges creaked as a rush of cars roared over Wilshire Boulevard. His footsteps shuffled softly on the light-green carpet. The small soft-glo lights dotting the ceiling made the shiny threads of his suit—his brown church suit from Brazil, his out-of-date immigrant suit—glitter like copper. The smiles from the movie posters that hung on the walls made him nervous, frightened him in their nonchalance, but he recognized them all: John Wayne in *Stagecoach*, Clark Gable in *It Happened One Night*, Marlene Dietrich in *Blonde Venus*, the Marx Brothers in *Coconuts*, Bing Crosby in *White Christmas*, Gary Cooper in *High Noon*, Greta Garbo in *Ninotchka*, and, of course, Carmen Socorro with her turban spilling over with red cherries, her face in comic alarm.

He wandered to the front desk. An electric typewriter hummed with a letter in progress on the roller as if someone had left suddenly. He could hear people's voices floating from the small hall in back, doors slamming under the croon of soft music playing from an antique radio on a small bookshelf. Finally, a woman stepped out from the back, laughing as she headed to her desk. She frowned when she saw him. Her black hair was styled in two side rolls that stuck out from her thin face. They looked like bat wings. She looked a bit odd, about as out of date as he, with her polka-dot dress, the skirt gathered into a big bow on the side of one hip. Her gaze slanted, matching the cat-eye glasses that dangled from a chain of small fake pearls. She was not young, and her wrinkled, thin neck looked like it had been twisted, then let go.

She jabbed with her voice, her chin jutted forward like a hatchet. "What do you want?"

For a second, his English left him because it didn't seem like America, but seemed instead like an American movie in which he must say something clever. He looked back at the poster of Carmen Socorro. Carmen's luscious smile prodded him, another Brazilian immigrant, and Brasileira to Brasileiro they toasted each other with imaginary chilled glasses of Brahma beer. Joe turned to the secretary, smiled broadly, and finally announced the name he had mastered: "My name is Joe Silva."

"Well?" she twitched. "Well, Joe, what do you want?"

Joe asked for a job, a tour van driver maybe. This made her raise her eyebrows and howl, "Oh no, no openings," and she hobbled back to her typewriter, whacked a few words, then stopped, shook her head, "Nah-ah. Nothing here, Mr. Silva."

No, Joe could not give up. He remembered Tony, his friend, king of jeitinhos, doing such a brave thing, picking him up in his van, probably against the rules. Joe thought he shouldn't mention that he had met Tony. Joe could pretend he had guided tours for years, his lie as smooth as oil, inflammable, a bit dangerous, and, yes, he could break her silence. Flash! went Joe's smile. She saw it and gave a little jolt as the buzzing typewriter carriage return slammed.

"What is your name? Have you been in the movies?" Joe asked in a carioca accent so smooth it would unravel her large hair buns in an instant.

She looked at him askance. "I'm Desiree. What do you mean?"

"Desiree, you seem — ah — " and Joe raised his eyes, searching for the words as he had seen foreigners in American movies do, "like an actress, I don't know."

Her grimace disappeared. "Oh. A bit," she smiled wanly, "a bit. Like all of us here. And you?"

Joe smiled ruefully. "I have acted, yes."

She laughed lightly as if she thought his bitterness a bit sexy, paused with her head tilted — and sprang from her chair. "Wait here," she said.

Joe tilted his head to look at a photo on a small gold frame sitting on her desk. He nudged it with his finger so he could get a better look. A picture of a cat. He glanced down the hall and could see her standing in someone's doorway. How strange, Americans with pictures of animals instead of children.

The secretary came back out. "Go inside. You can speak to Chucky Weaver, our boss."

Joe stepped into Chucky's small office. Chucky, dressed in a pin-striped gangster suit, leaned back on his chair and rested an ankle on the other knee. The man pointed to a chair facing the desk as if he were shooting a gun. "Sit down. Name's Chucky Weaver." Joe, taken aback at the man's costume, eased down on the chair a bit too carefully and marveled at Chucky Weaver's perfectly knotted necktie. He smoothed a hand over the front of his out-of-date Brazilian suit, then spotted right above Chucky's head on the wall an ominous-looking machine gun hanging from a hook by its leather strap. Joe gasped, and his throat tightened against his shirt collar; he could smell the old familiar sweat of a nervous tropical afternoon. This was the type of gun carried by policemen who leaned against doorways of old colonial churches and waited for night-fall.

"Ah," Chucky said, "the gun." The man fingered his wide lapels and peered out of his slouch-brim hat and spoke with a low-slung voice. "Jimmy Cagney used that in *Angels with Dirty Faces*"; he whisked his pointed finger over to a large poster of Jimmy Cagney holding the very same gun. Joe nodded stiffly, so impressed. Then he broke out laughing, and this rattled apart his tension. Only in America is a gun used for decoration.

So. Chucky softened with Joe's laughter and chortled, "Whatya say, pal, what brings ya' in so bright 'n' early?" Joe looked into Senhor Weaver's deep-set blue eyes staring earnestly from an overhanging cliff of blond eyebrows. "I am looking for a job here. I have heard of this place, and I would love to work here. As a driver." Joe flashed another grinning gleam.

"Yeah? Yeah?" Chucky stroked his bottom lip with the knuckle of his thumb. "Why here and not elsewhere?"

Joe spoke rapidly, imagined himself swimming in his bobbing words. "Amigo—" With the first words came the assurances of his American wife and American kids and how he had an American driver's license and that he could learn how to drive a combivan easy. Who doesn't know how to drive? He drove in Rio, but of course *here* he didn't drive the ca-rioca way; in fact, he just loved the American way of driving, less reckless, more cautious. And most of all, amigo, he loved American movies, especially these musicals with Fred Astaire and the Westerns with Gary Cooper, and, God, he couldn't remember them all, but who can remember the names of friends? But oh, amigo, he loved these movies, his whole family did, and oh how they would go to the theater so air-conditioned on a hot summer day, the wonderful coolness of movies. Of fantasy . . .

Chucky nodded seriously.

Joe was out of breath, his throat raw and dry, his sweat now soaked through his shirt. He ran out of gold nuggets to fling before this man. His *amigos* sounded heavy and stupid. Hell, he could drive a van, and he could speak. What more did they want? Joe grinned stiffly, looked back up at the machine gun, and wondered if it could automatically go off, spraying bullets everywhere.

Finally, Chucky spoke. Joe could hear the gangster's tongue unpeeling from the roof of his mouth. "Well, you might do," Chucky said. "Do you get along with people?"

"Of course."

"Been in trouble with the law?"

Joe laughed nervously.

Chucky leaned over, beamed with pleasure. "Been a gangster?"

"Oh no. Not that."

Chucky laughed as he took off his hat and combed his thinning hair with its nervy little end curls. "Well," Chucky said, "well, you are another Spanish speaker, I presume. We need one, and you look good. Pretty handsome guy, you. I'll give you a shot at the training."

Joe was about to say, "I speak Portuguese," but the whole thing struck him as so absurd that he threw his head back in a full laugh and proclaimed sure, he spoke Spanish. He knew he could fake it; he could fake anything at this point. A lie is almost the truth anyway. They say truth is your wife, the lie your mistress. You love them in different ways, but you never give up one for the other.

Weaver swiveled dreamily back and forth on his chair and began describing his clever "concept." The "concept" was that every tour guide dresses and acts a movie character—for instance, their Bogey does the tour bit in a cool mumble, off the side of his mouth. Their Mickey Rooney wears short trousers and a little beanie and does kids' stuff, gives cars the raspberry, makes the carload sing songs. "We got the Cowboy, too—Tom Mix, I think he's supposed to be. You, my friend, are a Rick Ricardo. Your uniform could be a tropical print shirt for summer, baggy linen pants, then for winter maybe a sequined babaloo coat. Can do open neck with no tie, slicked back hair. Gold chain. Act Cuban. No cigar smoking, though. Say you play bongos."

"I am not Cuban; I am Brazilian."

This revelation seemed to stun Chucky. "Well? You want to be Carmen Socorro?"

Joe's smile faded. "Of course, I can't be Carmen Socorro. I am a man."

❨

The next morning Joe came in for his tour-guide training. Desiree showed him to the staff room in the back. The room had a punch clock and a calendar, clipboards hanging on hooks, a table and some chairs, and a poster of small portraits of movie stars making an arc over the silver-glitter words *Hooray for Hollywood*. Just outside the room was the back door leading to the company garage and parking lot.

The Cowboy came in through the back door, carrying a large cup of coffee. He nodded to Joe, then turned to the clock and tipped his hat back. His bolo tie held the collar tight around his skinny neck, and his Adam's apple knobbed out like a bulging eye. He snatched his time card, made a quick jab into the punch clock, got a clipboard with what looked like a checklist, set down his coffee, and began to draw. Someone thumped open the back door. "That must be Bogey," the Cowboy mumbled, shading the drawing with his pencil. Bogey shouted to someone in the garage. Then he swooped into the room, holding a cigarette in the cleft of his fingers, and grabbed a clipboard. He wore a tan fedora and a trench coat. "Where's Mickey?" he grumbled. "That faggot." Just then Chucky bounded into the room, slapped Joe on the back, and introduced him as the Cuban Rick Ricardo. Bogey responded with a "huh!"

Chucky roared, "Hey now, Casablanca! Welcome our little Cubano! Hey, partner," Chucky called to the Cowboy, "show cha-cha man the ropes." The Cowboy took his clipboard and motioned Joe outside.

They went up to a van, the same blue van with yellow spotlights that had rescued Joe on his first day in America. There were six other vans just like it in the parking lot. The Cowboy took the clipboard and slipped into the driver's seat for the inside inspection. Joe watched from the passenger door. The Cowboy started the motor, checked the gas, and then he howled like a coyote into the microphone. "That works," he said, jumping out and handing Joe the clipboard to show what he was supposed to do. The checklist included a diagram of the van and a sketch of the Cowboy crashing through the windshield. Joe chuckled. The Cowboy smiled. "Don't do this until you really got the job."

Bogey stepped out the back door and headed for the small fleet of buses at the far end of the parking lot, but stopped short when he saw Joe. He slipped his hands into his trench-coat pocket, clamped the clipboard tight under his armpit, and ambled toward them. The Cowboy straightened his hat. "Bogey gets to drive the buses out yonder. Those are for full-city tours, or sometimes they head on south. A bus driver is about as high a horse as you can get around here."

Bogey glared at the Cowboy, then turned and scowled at Joe. "So you're the Cuban," he sneered, "and a communist? Ain't it enough to have had the hippies for a while?"

"A communist? No, don't you worry." Joe gave a hard cynical smile. "The communists are all dead now, my friend."

The Cowboy thought for a moment, then hooted and slapped himself on the thigh with his clipboard. "Oh you're good, partner, you're real good."

Bogey shrugged his shoulders and headed toward the buses.

The Cowboy told Joe to get in the van. As Joe slipped into the front seat, he wished Tony were here because there was no one he really liked. He wondered if Tony had to wear an absurd costume. Maybe Tony had refused, maybe he was that much a man. Joe leaned his elbow on the sill of the door and looked out the window. This place made him a bit afraid, but he didn't know why. He peered into the sideview mirror and saw his own Americanized eyes—now more afraid, but less innocent.

On the first day of his tour-guide job, Joe modeled his tropical shirt and new tan pants for Sherri. She lingered in bed with the two little ones on either side of her, each sucking on a bottle propped up by a pillow. She laughed and called him Babaloo Barney, Mr. Ronrico Rum, and Joe chuckled a bit, sensing an uneasy cruelty, but no matter. A man has to work. He put on his Panama hat, gave the rim a tilt forward, and kissed both his sons and Sherri, but she didn't like to linger with kisses; her love **63** was the Eye and Rib kind—quick service and OK food, she always said.

He assured himself he was perfect for the job; his English was good, his foreign accent "sexy," and he had memorized the information about each of the movie stars' houses—how much they cost and all that. Joe also knew by heart what films each star had made, how much money each star earned, a good hard-luck story of breaking into the business, and a tender story about their children.

He drove his Hollywood Celebrity Tours van to Mann's Chinese Theatre—changed from Grauman's a few years ago, which, he was informed, you may have to *tell* some people—and pulled up to the loading zone in front. The front of the Chinese theater was easy to spot, gaudy with its spiky gold dragon heads, bright red panels, red Chinese pagoda tops of ticket booths, and Coke machines. You could tell the small-time crooks by the way they laughed and looked at the women's purses and tapped their binders filled with special offers. The tourists meandered as they tried to find the hand- and footprints of their favorite celebrity lovey-dovey, as Sherri would say.

Joe stood in front of his van, and tourists placidly handed over their tickets and climbed inside. He smiled and said, "Welcome to Hollywood," and they gave a nod. All the men and women seemed to dress in the same knee-length shorts, sleeveless cotton shirts, and small straw hats or Disneyland caps, with cameras slung around their necks. One woman with her small son stepped up and warned Joe not to crack any obscene jokes during the tour. Joe laughed nervously. "No, of course not." The woman frowned and stepped in. Joe grew nervous. The management had given him the jokes, and he had memorized them; they seemed fine to him, and he had recited them for Sherri, who said they were OK but not hilarious. "Don't worry, ma'am," Joe crooned as he slid into his seat. "Don't worry."

Joe looked up at the rearview mirror full of eyes looking at him over the tops of the seats. He adjusted the "tips appreciated" placard, made a sign of the cross in his head, and sailed into the street traffic. He cracked his first joke, but no one laughed, and he looked in the rearview mirror again; the tourists stared straight ahead. He wondered what had happened, if he had said a dirty word by mistake or forgot part of it, or if his language skills didn't quite work because of his nervousness. He almost wanted to apologize, but that would seem worse. At his first point of interest, he said, "If you look to the left" — and the heads turned all at once to look out the window, as if he had pressed a button — "you will see a large cutout of the Marlboro Man." Then he spoke about how L.A. was a desert, and the water came from north and east, and everything green here had been forced to grow. One tourist said he knew all that, and the others said nothing.

When he got to Beverly Hills, he told of how much the average house cost and how the celebrities decorated their houses for Christmas. The tourists sat there as if stuffed with straw. The men held cameras on their laps, and the one child on the tour fell asleep leaning against his mother's shoulder. Good God, they were falling asleep! Joe spoke into the mike, "Are you warm enough? Too cold?" The Cowboy had said extreme temperatures made tourists uncomfortable. The tourists shook their heads no, silently.

This bus of dead people was getting Joe mad, not just nervous, but a bit angry. First, he didn't like how they dressed; their clothes made them look fat. Then he thought of how Sherri could be a little snide and didn't like him to touch his sons. He tried to figure what to do, debated, then in his distress a wave of saudade came over him, the longing for home, for warm words, for the feeling of not being a stranger. His mind wandered back to Brazil again, its tropical beauty and warm smiles and a mamãe who adored him so. Suddenly Joe felt his van turning into a long, hand-rolled dreamy Cuban cigar. He tasted yellow palm oil on his lips. Yes, he continued to take his pilgrims to the temples of Bel Air and Beverly Hills. But as the days progressed, he dared to change the usual bla-bla-bla because, as he knew from torture, a lie can be a lot more productive than the truth. He passed by the home of Jasper Wilkens, maker of movies, man of twelve wives, and of Chet Kastlebaum, who tried to design a new hanging tower of Babylon, which got destroyed in a fire, and on and on with famous people who didn't exist, but so what? Joe devised adventures for them — one who had an underwater palace in Cuba; another who dreamed of being a soccer player, but his looks were so beautiful that somewhere in Hollywood there was a church with a small altar where people could worship him. He spoke of the houses, too, not about their cost, but about how the tiles on the roof were carved from real red turtles shipped directly from Baghdad. The cameras snapped furiously, and his bus came to life; people slid forward on their seats and asked him enthusiastic questions, wanting more of the fantasy than he could possibly hold in his heart.

Gradually Joe felt his Brazilianness drift away like a green coconut bobbing out to sea. *A Weekend in Havana* was creeping over him like the celluloid iguana he was becoming, a bit frightening with its hard flat mouth and expressionless gaze. But he kept reminding himself that America was an exotic country, so he continued to tell his fabulous tales, clinging precariously to a thin branch, his skin growing tough, green, and brilliant.

I would caution you, Senhor da Cunha, to separate the truth from your dreams. Either these women are so widespread as to take over a continent, or they are the tales of Man's constant and troubling desires. Your endless delirium will lead to your death. Hunger and thirst are not longings for love, but for food and drink. Longing for the arms of a beast is not longing for flesh, but for your loved ones at home. The jungle leads men into confusion and causes them to wander. Do not tend to your heart for advice, but remember that the will to survive was well known at the start of your journey.

— *A resposta de João Vicente Cardim da Almeida a Carlos Manoel Teixeira da Cunha, O Ano* 1641

Chapter 7

O Ano 1977

Rosea left the little holy man Melvinor standing in a mess of corrugated tin and fallen wood beams that had been Beno's Fruit and Vegetable Stand. As she left, Melvinor shouted that she had "destroyed his Israel." She wanted to scream at him, "My God, man, I just got rid of your belongings. Now you really can wander the earth! Your life isn't spare enough, get sparer! You're not humble enough! Be humble like a razor blade in a safe place! Can't you see? No one changes; they just get in a bigger mess than they were in before!"

Again Rosea found herself on the bus, this time to L.A. She had burned out her charm at Pachito's house, and so he had kindly convinced Ento put up with her—for a few nights. Pachito's deal included two hundred dollars and a bus ticket.

Rosea leaned her head against the window and let her skull rattle against the vibrating glass. Freezing air blew through the vents. She hated Southern California. The rolling mountains reminded her of the dry hills near Frontera, like the ruffled backs of royal lions who hide their vicious teeth from those passing through. The pale sky always seemed laced with powdery cocaine. Once Amazons had terrorized California, and wild griffins had pecked apart the eyes of conquistadors. Still, new conquistadors kept coming, by foot or by Jag, until they found a treasure chest called Hollywood, and when they smashed open the treasure chest with their boots, they found nothing but sand.

❰

Enrique Gonzales lived in a sweet barrio house—porches with busted screens, windowsills with peeling paint, thistles growing among the short buzz-cut tufts of grass in dusty yards. The neighborhood had been good once, but misfortune had taken it by surprise. Enrique's house had a white pickup in the yard, so he was probably home. Rosea knocked on the door, and Enrique floated from the dark house, carrying his mail. He still had on a jacket as if he had just come home from work. First, he squinted, a bit gruffly, as if someone had disturbed him; then his face opened, not too surprised, but trying to be polite: "Rosea! Just got home from work, come in."

Rosea stepped inside. Again, the strained welcome, the gracious offering of something to drink. The information about what he's been doing —he has a wife and kids and an OK job. He knows what you've been doing. Silence.

And the familiar: the exhausted wife, Nita, drove into the driveway in a green Pontiac, and their kids, who had been playing with friends, jumped out of the car, burst through the front door, and raced through the house. Nita followed them, yelling at them to slow down. Then came the children's hugs for the exhausted *papi*, then the "oh-my-God-she's-tall" line when people first saw her. Enrique and Nita discussed something about a bill, something they'd talk about later. Nita was friendly, but didn't have much to say because she didn't know about Rosea being in prison. In fact, Enrique took Rosea aside and told her not to say anything about it because Nita was a Christian, and he didn't want the hassle of explaining his past.

Rosea quietly ate dinner with them. The kitchen smelled like bacon fat and penny casserole. The oldest boy plucked the slices of hotdog from the cheese noodles with his fingers, and the younger one put his toy truck on the table next to his milk. They chattered and nudged at each other and tossed looks at Rosea. Nita fired off something in Spanish at the two to make them behave. The kids pretended not to understand. Enrique spoke in careful English, a low polite voice, "Adam, use your fork," "Carlito, put away your toy." The kids eyed Rosea suspiciously, as if blaming her for their parents' sudden burst of etiquette.

Then Enrique leaned his forearms on the table and spoke seriously to Rosea. "Pachito and I have a friend who drives a tour van in Los Angeles. Or he did drive one; I'm not sure what is happening with him now. But he says there is an opening at this place. He thinks maybe there is something you could do. Kind of a crazy, movie star place or something, but why not, it's a job."

Rosea nodded. "Do I have to work with people?"

Enrique smiled and plowed his fork into the macaroni, making a big stack. "Everyone has to work with people. Even a bracero."

Rosea smiled weakly. "Of course." She continued eating, not looking at them. "When do I go?"

"Tomorrow. Tony arranged for an interview and everything. You have a dress to wear?"

Rosea looked up stunned. She couldn't say, "WHERE WOULD I GET A DRESS? DON'T YOU KNOW I'VE BEEN IN PRISON? YOU THINK I RAN A FRENCHIE BOUTIQUE OR SOMETHING?"

"No."

Enrique didn't get it. "No dress? For the interview?"

"No." Rosea looked down at her food and spread the noodles with her fork.

"Nita! Ella necessita un vestido. ¿Tienes algun vestido que ella puede usar?"

Nita looked at her compassionately, like a nun. "No problem. I have a bag of things for the church. I can fix something."

Rosea grimaced. The pasty sounds of teeth chewing noodles almost made her sick. Enrique broke the silence. "Nita, did you know her mother was Carmen Socorro?"

"Who?"

"The singer?"

"Does she sing on the radio?"

"No, Nita, the Brazilian bombshell, in the old movies. You know, Miss Tutti-Frutti—the hat with a lot of fruits."

Nita smiled and shook her head. She was a bit newer to this country and had never gone to American movies, so she didn't know too many American movie stars.

Rosea said a bit too loudly, "It's OK, really." She looked to the side and realized the two boys were staring at her again.

Nita snapped to attention, "Don't stare at her, huh? Eat."

Early the next morning an old copper-colored Chevy with a smash on one side near the front fender pulled up to the yard. The driver came into the house and strode into the kitchen, calling out to Enrique in Spanish. The two boys were sitting at the kitchen table and eating cereal. The driver removed his beige cowboy hat and stuck it on Adam's head. Carlito grabbed the man's arm, and the man bent down and gave the little boy a loud smacking kiss on the cheek.

Rosea sat at the kitchen table drinking coffee. She was stuffed in a dress that Nita had altered for her, a blue-gray swirl print of nylon-blend fabric that stank of armpits. Two wide strips of plain blue cloth had been sewn to both side seams to widen the bodice and waist for Rosea's thick curves. The loose bow and collar that had looked so typically *abuelita* had been dismantled and resewn so that the two ends of the bows joined together in a 1950s round collar. Nita had also given her a small silver crucifix to wear to make a good impression—to show that she was moral and that they could trust her. Rosea kicked around her too-tight shoes under the table. She had spent the night on the couch and hadn't been able to sleep, so now she felt raw and cranky, watching all this South of the Border Brady Bunch to-do. The bitter coffee dried out her mouth.

Enrique came into the kitchen and greeted the guest with a burst of Spanish, and they both turned to Rosea. "He's Tony," Enrique said, "he used to drive a tour van for Hollywood Celebrity Tours. He says maybe there's a job for you. I told him your mother was Carmen Socorro, and he almost went crazy."

Tony grinned, and his eyes wowed when she stood up. Another adoring fan that made her feel even more like a loser. Criminal or celebrity — there must be something in between. She would have to do well in this job because people were getting tired of her, and Enrique was the last of her sympathetic friends. Rosea followed Tony out, hobbling on her tight pumps as she carried her duffle bag. Tossing it into the back seat of his car, she said, "Gotta find a place to crash," realizing it was a pathetic hint.

"No problem," Tony waved his hand, "I know of a perfect place to stay. No 'great shakes,' as they say, but enough. Deposit is super cheap."

Yeah. Rent. Almost forgot. She had wanted to use some of the money Pachito gave her to buy some big earrings, the kind she adored. She couldn't wear pierced earrings in the pen because somebody would have yanked them and ripped her ears. Looked like the two hundred dollars already had a landlord's kiss marks. Well. As her parole officer said, you gotta pay your own room and board now. Gotta stop sponging off the good people of this world.

Tony pushed down on his cowboy hat and got into the car. Rosea slid into the seat beside him, slammed the door, and they pulled out into the road. Tony spoke animatedly of all the Carmen Socorro movies he had seen and how she just cracked him up . . . *Copacabana*, *Weekend in Havana*. "Mind you," he squinted under the brim of his hat, "I can't say Hollywood knows anything about us Latinos. I mean, it was strange, those cha-cha movies and the Cisco Kid. I mean, let's face it. Most of us can't dance and don't own a horse. But we used to see these movies because it's all we had. I mean, a hungry man doesn't turn down bread because he really wants a bologna sandwich, you know what I mean?"

Yeah. She'd have preferred bologna up the butt. Finally, they reached

the "perfect place to stay," and Tony took her down the hall, past a courtyard of dirt, a rail draped with dripping jeans, and an open door with
some kid screaming to holy hell at the far-end apartment. Tony knew the
manager, and, Jesus, what a fat man! The manager said another Brazilian had lived here, but had moved out because HE TOO managed to get
married and have kids. The fat man showed her to her room — bare, dripping with wallpaper piss, a single bed with a slunky mattress, and a motel
dresser. Ground level, too. Rosea moaned and threw her bag against the
wall. She could hear Tony outside in the courtyard calling, "Hurry up!
You have an interview!" Rosea paused, then grabbed the damn crucifix
from her neck, gave a quick yank, and hurled the holy wing-ding into the
corner, where it disappeared behind the dresser. She seethed, her body
fat pushed below her waist, her thighs melting into her nylons. Then she
left, not even locking the door because there wasn't a fuckin' thing in
that room worth stealing and going to prison for.

Tony drove her to Hollywood Celebrity Tours and pulled into the parking lot. He motioned her out of the car, but remained inside a bit longer,
then snuck out quietly, not slamming his door. He hovered near a group
of dark-blue vans and peered around, secretively. "Why don't we go in?"
Rosea asked. "Why are we playing hide-and-seek?"

Tony waved his hand rapidly, motioning her to hush. Just then the
back door of the office swung open, and a man in a tropical shirt, white
pants, and white shoes headed over to one of the vans. When Tropical
Man saw Tony, he let out a small whoop and a "My God! I can't believe it!"

The two men ran and embraced each other, and Tropical Shirt broke
into an almost desperate ramble, gesturing dramatically, wrestling in his
pocket, and pulling out his wallet. He pulled out some pictures, and Tony
made that familiar "Ahh-haa," cooing at the picture of the guy's kid.

Rosea stared at this escapee from a Bing Crosby–Bob Hope Road
Tropicana flick. Curly hair and tan skin. He looked like an exotic bird
with a florescent underbelly. She fought like hell not to burst into a tweet-
tweet; she had to suppress her smart-ass hiss because she needed this
job, even if she had to spend the day siphoning gas into her mouth.
Then Tropical Man took another look at the picture, smiled to himself,

and slipped the wallet back into his pocket. Rosea noticed dark, curved eyebrows above heavy-lidded eyes. Jesus, he would be cute if it weren't for the Dole pineapple wrapping. Tropical Man started babbling to Tony again, telling his whole life story; almost in tears, he looked away for a second, took a deep breath, and swallowed. Then Tony rubbed him on the back, and they embraced again like long-lost relatives or faggots or whatever.

Tony ambled back to Rosea. "It's lunchtime. You need to wait until the afternoon for an interview."

"Interview?" Rosea huffed. "You know the guy, right? I mean, I'm not just waltzing in here cold turkey—"

"The boss needs someone," Tony said simply. "My friend says you can take his lunchtime tour—free. You can interview later on."

Mr. Tropical grinned and motioned for Rosea to step inside the van. His smile faded as Rosea came closer. Tony, about to get in the car, remembered something and rushed over to Tropical Man and told him that she was the daughter of Carmen Socorro. Mr. Tropical's face lit up again, but his smile hardened as he held out his hand to help her into the van. Rosea brushed him aside, raised her skirt up to her thighs, climbed in, and plunked herself down on the last seat.

The driver turned. "My name is Joe, eh?"

"Rosea." He made her nervous.

He paused. "I have to go over to the Chinese Theatre to pick up the tourists." He turned on the ignition, pulled the van out of the parking lot, and headed toward Hollywood.

Joe spoke into the microphone, "Hola," and the tour group chanted back: "Oh-la." The tourists had faces like babies watching fish in a tank. Joe spoke in his little microphone about how he was from Cuba and had played with the Desi Arnaz band, how he and Desi were close like this— he raised his hand and crossed two fingers—"amigos." Then of course they all asked what Lucy was like, and he stopped for a minute as if he was thinking and said, "She's really nice, he always liked blondes." "But she's a redhead," someone said. Oh. His eyebrows lifted. "Oh, normally

she's blond. She colors her head — I mean — hair." "Oh really?" someone
else said. "*That's interesting.* I never knew that."

Rosea smirked. She knew this guy didn't know a damn about Desi or
Lucy or anything, and he was faking fast. He had an accent very much
like her mother and her mother's Brazilian friends. Rosea sat back and
looked at his dark and anxious eyes dancing in the rearview mirror. Obviously, he was supposed to pretend to be Cuban. Oh, that's the story.

His van inched up hills as he talked about the insane movie stars:
the ones found dead and mummified, the has-been damsels locked up
in asylums, the voodoo queens, the obsessive-compulsive director who
painted everything he owned in green, the starlet who painted her body
gold. The passengers flicked their fingers on the glass and began madly
clicking their cameras. Rosea rolled her eyes. Jesus.

Then he did it. He drove up a narrow, familiar road, with wild greenery
and a few luxury bungalows off to the side and headed toward the house
she knew. He pulled up, parked, and told everyone this was a special
treat and normally this wasn't on his route, but it was for someone special
with them today. "This, my friends, was the house of Carmen Socorro,
but now Vaughan Peters lives here." Rosea pressed her nose against the
window. Yes, the balcony where her mother had sat, those doors, the old
wooden pair with the one odd panel of a face that her mother had seen in
a church in Brazil! Now the place had a nasty iron gate because Vaughan
Peters lived here now, but probably — oh, the garden was there, it *should*
be there!

Rosea started to panic, and she felt her knees shaking; then her whole
body rattled as if being demolished. Sweat prickled on her upper lip, and
she felt faint. She wished he would drive away, just go. But no, he knelt
on his seat and faced the tour group, and in his lilting English, with a
beautiful accent, told everyone how this was one of the first things he had
seen in America. He said he believed the house had some magic prop-
erties because Brazilians bring magic from across the seas. He thought
once he saw a woman with a white dress wandering around in the garden. "Did you know Carmen Socorro?" one of the tourists asked dopily.
"No," the driver said wistfully, "I was just a boy at that time, before I went
to — college." One of the group said, "Aaahh, an educated one." Then the

driver said that Carmen was discovered on the beach here at Malibu, as beautiful and as white as a pearl. They found some coconut shells floating in the water nearby. "What can I say, a happy accident? She could only speak Portuguese but sang like a bird. One could say the sea gave us Carmen." Then he whispered with his eyes half-shut, "Many times we wish the sea could take us somewhere out of our misery."

The tourists looked at him strangely. Joe straightened up, got practical again. "They say Carmen had a daughter, but no one knew for sure."

Rosea hollered, "Você fala como um bobo!" (which her mother used to say in an argument). His shoulders flinched as if she'd whipped him. The passengers turned around and stared at her.

"Fuck you!" Rosea felt her mother's house on top of her, crushing her skull, and she tried to heave the enormous weight off of her.

The driver looked at her calmly. "Are you OK?"

Suddenly Rosea burst into an unusually raw cry; she hadn't cried all these years, and her sobs weren't lubricated and warm. She curled up and tried to muffle herself by stuffing her face against the vinyl seat, but her moans came out in snorts. She rocked back and forth, churning her sadness into thick anger, wanting so much to see her mother, maybe in her orchid bathing suit, oh! She wished the driver would just leave, but she heard him get out of the van, open the sliding side door, and climb in the back. The people shifted, making way for him. He shuffled some stuff around, then she heard him pouring something, and he brought her a thermos cup of water. She sat up, her face sticky and wet, and she sipped the water. She wouldn't look at the mansion. Everyone watched her quietly, as if they were expecting her to make a speech. One man with a sunburned nose who looked like W. C. Fields said, "Here, honey," and handed her a large handkerchief. Rosea waved it away, drank the rest of the water, and handed over the cup, but couldn't look at the driver's face. What of it? He reached out his golden brown hand and took the cup.

"Sorry. Get on with the tour." Rosea sighed. The driver took the cup and the thermos, got back in his seat, and drove along the garden, where he turned the van around and headed back down the familiar hill. He continued his tour and his fantastic lies, and the cameras clicked and buzzed in response. She looked in the rearview mirror at his eyes, the sadness, the rich brown. Whereas others in this town made up stories because they got paid, he made up stories to live, she was sure of it. The accent, she knew now—Brazilian, no mistake, his nasal Ns were a giveaway. He was absolutely beautiful, too, golden like a penny, but not so dark, and the way he smoothed his hands up and down the steering wheel. He caught her staring at him, and she could see in the mirror his eyes smiling and his smooth, thick eyebrows.

Then he spoke low into the microphone, and the warmness of his voice filled her heart. "Se sente melhor?"

She knew. She knew. Her love couldn't be weak, though. An Amazon can't function that way. She wanted him, wanted him at all costs. This man had skin kissed by the sun and by the drumming of the waves. The part between her legs spasmed, softened with saltwater, and she felt the mouth of the Amazon pulling him in for a downward spin.

☾

After the tour, Rosea went in for the interview, cold turkey just as she thought. Joe led her through the back door, then went ahead to the boss's office and said a few things. Then he headed back down the hall, nodding, "He's expecting you," and disappeared into a staff room next to the back entrance.

Rosea stepped into the office and saw a man in a gangster suit sitting at his desk. He took one look at her and hooted, "My God, if you don't look like your mother! But your mother was quite a bit—shorter—and she used to give that look, all sexy, foxy eyes. Yeah. But—she had long hair like you when she'd let it out. Loved her, saw all her movies."

Rosea grinned stiffly. "Good for you."

"Name's Chucky Weaver." He leaned back on his chair, clasped his two hands in back of his head, and swiveled back and forth.

"Rosea Socorro Katz."

"I know. I've been expecting you."

Rosea waited for the lechery to come out of those gangster lips of his. You know. The proposal. The "deal," as they say here.

"I can't believe you're Carmen Socorro's daughter," he said.

"I can't believe you're Jimmy Cagney's son."

Chucky burst out laughing, "Ah, ah, oh oh. You've got the humor, you've got it." Rosea clenched. Then he started on about how the employees here were close, and it was important to be honest and open in order to have a good "ambience." "Oh," Rosea quipped, "like restaurants?"

Chucky chortled. "Like restaurants."

Then he leaned forward, his arms resting on his desk, and went on about her mother again, her beautiful hips and dazzling personality. "She could be five minutes on screen, and shhiipppp, she'd steal the show just like that, rob it from the hands of Betty Grable and Alice Faye. And *they* were the hottest stars during World War II. Almost could be said if we didn't have Hitler, we wouldn't have had movies. But her spirit, something about the Latins, who knows. They taught us Americans to have fun, to appreciate good nooky. Who knows the secret?"

Yeah, Rosea knew the secrets of the Hollywood jokers who lived their lives in costumes from a failed role they didn't get, their snazzy fuck-me gold rings on their thumbs, the corners of their mouths with beads of lascivious spit. She wondered where people like Chucky came from and if they ever got homesick for who they really were. She wondered why the guy just wasn't a real gangster so that he could make more money. Chucky's eager, sickening face as he discussed the job seemed to say: Hire you if you fuck me. Hire first or fuck first? Did you get the part? Are you DEALING WITH the ambience, the togetherness? It's tough in This Business, it's tough even for parasites in The Business.

"Well?" Chucky finally said in a haze, "well, how about it, *dah-link*?"

Rosea spied the machine gun hanging on the wall. She thought of something she could do for his fantasy and grinned so wide she could feel her teeth dry out. "I dare you to take that off," she pointed to the gun.

"Oh that," he chuckled, "is unloaded. It's a *prop*."

"Well then, take it down, I want to see. Let me hold it." Rosea still had her way with stupid men.

Chucky nodded, rising from his desk with a little stretch. His eyebrows met in one solid line. He turned, scooted his chair toward the wall, climbed up carefully, and removed the machine gun off the hook. He climbed off the chair, one foot and then the other, held the gun in front of him cautiously, and presented it to her like a gold sword.

Rosea took the machine gun carefully. "You know," she said, "I never held one of these. My mother was never in gangster movies."

"Most mothers aren't," Chucky quipped as he sat on the edge of the desk.

"True." Rosea examined the black barrel, the cold sloops and loops. The tiny snoot and the metal ring at the end. The handle of the machine gun a steel flag. She imagined herself pointing the gun and pulling the trigger, shattering his face into a bloody red flat-splat. Rosea felt a rat crawling up her shoulder. "My mother was in musicals," she blurted out.

"Musicals. Wonderful stuff. Don't make them anymore."

"Nope. They don't." Just then she pulled the trigger. A hail of bullets shot out and ripped the drywall, splattering plaster like snow. Chucky shouted and slammed back into a filing cabinet. The gun stopped. The bullets had made deep, long holes. Chucky stood frozen, wheezing.

Down the hall someone jumped from an office chair, the wheels squealing like a scared child. Rosea watched as dust from the drywall swirled and started to drift. A woman rushed in, squeaking, "Chucky, you OK?" The skinny squealer wore a polka-dot 1930s-style dress, her hair in two rolls like the guy's on the Quaker Oats box.

"Yeah, Desiree. Baby. Don't call the cops." Chucky grinned stiffly.

Rosea still held the gun and couldn't believe it.

Several people crowded into the doorway of Chucky's office. The skinny woman jabbered while Chucky stood there in shock. Rosea smiled quietly to herself. "I'm sorry. You told me it was unloaded," and she placed the gun on top of his desk and hung her head the way she'd seen actors do in the movies. "I guess I don't have a job anymore."

Chucky looked at the people standing at the doorway. One man had a cowboy hat, and one was a grown man dressed as a kid. Chucky's lips went sideways in a smirk, then he started laughing, "Oh-ho-ha-ha, yeah. You got a job alright. Don't worry about that. Always nice to start off with a bang bang."

Rosea suddenly reeled and headed down the hall, her shoes and nylons so tight she thought she'd burst through the neck of her dress. She flung the back door open, ran down the steps, and flopped onto the small stone ledge under a pepper tree. She plunked her elbows on her knees and shoved her head in her hands. Threads from her underarm seam ripped. She tore off the pins she used to keep her hair up and let her black frizz fall in a furious mess. She closed her eyes and breathed slowly. She was so ungainly and awkward, and they didn't know how angry she could get.

The back door opened, and someone's soft footsteps shuffled behind her. She clenched her jaw. "It's going to be a bumpy ride, as they say." A pair of hands stroked the top of her aching head and smoothed down to the ends of her hair. She held her breath. It felt so good.

"Menina, não chora. É nada."

It was Joe and his sweet Portuguese. Rosea didn't know much of his language, but she knew those words. After her mother had the shock treatments and even her hair hurt, she would comb her daughter's hair, comforting them both and cooing, "Rosea Socorro Katz, sweet coconut, não chora. É nada."

By the time Rosea got home, her body was screaming for Joe. José. Sex. What a dismal apartment—the peeling wallpaper, the wooden doors warped into the doorjambs, the double locks that were too heavy for the fragile doors that some psycho could just kick in. She flicked on the light to her dingy hole, then went over to the window and snapped open the curtains, only to find the neighborhood kids playing right in front of her window, kicking around the overgrown weeds, lurking like thieves. Their laughter was hard and demanding. They were playing football, and one threatened to kill so-and-so if he didn't throw the ball. Rosea stood at her window, and slowly the kids turned, their bitter eyes staring at her through the weeds. They wore clothes that didn't fit. The game stopped, and the bully boy, the one making the death threats, raised the ball and hurled it against her burglar bars with all his might.

The bars wanged, and she drew the curtain closed again. She flung off her old-lady dress, her pumps and nylons, bra and panties, and stood there, a naked savage, her crazy big-bunda self. She could never bring anyone here. No pictures, no flowers even. Looked like a prison cell or a whore's bedroom. Once you've been in jail, you can't help but create your cell all over again.

She hungered for this Joe. She wanted to stuff his entire body into her mouth in an Amazonian frenzy. She wanted to stuff him up her cunt and then give birth to him. Crazy love. She slammed her body against the wall, jangling something in the apartment next door. Someone hollered and thumped back, so she threw herself on the bed. New rules, everything new, new. The only skill she had from her past was luring men, catching and hopelessly snagging them. She knew the satisfaction of seeing them gaze upward in awe from her dexterous and wicked hand. She had never learned this power, but had always possessed it. It's the way it was. Geezer Ortiz, Paul Banyard, Chulee Marx, and Jeremy Millard all fell for it. Kids in the toughest neighborhoods knew about her — East L.A., Compton — they stood back, aloof, even after they came out of prison. They wanted her, but were afraid to want.

Rosea rolled on the bed and gave a big groanlike roar. She opened her legs and combed her fingers through her curly bush. She imagined Joe's tanned hand with a swirl of black hair on his knuckles. She imagined it soft, his fingers combing and combing through, his fingers refreshing and tingling like the delicious grief in his eyes.

Creatures of the air: *Sabía* the thrush, *currasow*, the henlike *jacus, jabiru* stork, *canindé* with its small body and long tail, the *cujujuba*, which when captured closes up its anus and dies, toucans, *tamatião-açu* with its humanlike cries, *juruvas* with sea green feathers, the *quirejuabe* with beautiful blue feathers, the rheas that eat iron, and many parrots and large *araras*. But none is so strange as the half-children–half-birds that are left on the banks of the river to die. Their heads are flat on the top, their necks grizzled with short feathers that appear florescent in the sun. These strange ones cry out in high-pitched whistles, which neither birds nor humans can understand.
—*Carta de Carlos Manoel Teixeira da Cunha a João Vicente Cardim da Almeida, O Ano 1641*

Chapter 8

O Ano 1977

Birdboy climbed up the bookcase and crouched on the top shelf, wrapping his arms around his bowed legs. The tiny feathers on back of his neck, barely discernable from the black grizzled hair at this hairline, glowed in aqua green fluorescent flecks. He was fourteen with the body of a six-year-old, slightly barrel chested with delicate but shortish limbs, knotty at the joints. He curled his bony toes on the edge of the shelf and pursed his humanlike lips into the memory of a small beak. The kid gave a loud shriek for attention.

Jeremy snapped, "I'm ignoring you, Bird." Then he opened his well-

marked copy of Claude Lévi-Strauss's *Tristes Tropiques* — The Sad Tropics. And how sad they were! Jeremy passed his fingers down the pages of
wisdom that made Lévi-Strauss into a different man. The anthropologist
had traveled the rivers of the Amazon, observing tribes, contemplating
the purity of culture, pulling his canoe so deep into the rivers that his
mind couldn't find its way out. Primitive cultures in their purity cannot
sanctify those of us with restrictive clothes and tight shoes. The primitive reminds us of our own corruption. This is why anthropologists de-
tach themselves from their world. This is why Jeremy felt he was floating through the academic world, mouthing a strange language — cryptic
texts of academia's explanations of things that cannot be. In this world
of vacuous thought was the very concrete contempt for those who got
caught in their dreams like birds snagged in jungle nets of the Juarouá
tribe.

The memory of Dr. Robert Maxwell came to Jeremy with a vengeance.
Dr. Maxwell, Jeremy's mentor, was a man so obsessed with the memory
of his strange deflowerment that he had wandered back into the Amazon
wilderness never to be seen again. And before Maxwell, his colleague and
main competitor, Dr. Franklin Bisby, had also succumbed to the charms
of the jungle. Even the famous Brazilian anthropologist Darcy Ribeiro,
who had recorded the existence of hundreds of Amazonian tribes, gar-
nered himself daughters of caciques, women who, like delicious whores,
painted their toenails red for his pleasure.

Look at Jeremy Millard, professor of Amazonian artifacts and ephemera, left in bone shards and feathers by his ex-wife, Rosea Socorro Katz!
Even with his home in a heap of ruins and ashes, destroyed by her dev-
astating anger, he still longed for Rosea's thunderous body thrashing in
the sheets beside him, her leg half out of the bed in her nightmares, her
other hand plowing through his hair. Don't ask how his love for Rosea
endured, even while she, at least as far as he knew, was still in Frontera
prison. Jeremy was never the type for her: he was lean and square jawed,
a bit nervous like a monkey. His kneecaps were flat, and his long fingers
waved at the imaginary flies buzzing around in his head. His eyes blue
and staring, his hair hanging lank and covering his ears, he reminded

people of a Protestant preacher, one boiled by cannibals (so they say), naive and stupid and ignorant of the ways of the jungle. But Jeremy thought he knew the ways.

Tristes Tropiques spoke: "Get out of your library, foolish man! You need air! Plow through the outdoors, scoop away the clouds from those damn student papers exploring the 'otherness' in natives of New Guinea, and take with you that poor confused thing who is now your son!"

In the depths of the Amazon, the local *caboclos* had told Jeremy that Birdboy was the child of a bird and a woman warrior. These women lived with no man, but sometimes went on rampages and mated with anything that moved. It was a sight to see, he was told — the women howling in ecstasy, holding the birds between their legs, the vivid blue or red *arara* wings beating against their thighs. Then, when the babies were born — some with one wing, some with no wings, all usually delicate like the avian father and devoid of any maternal robustness — the women left them on the bank of the river for the crocodiles and jaguars or for some well-meaning anthropologist to rescue and figure out. But you don't tell things like this to child psychologists. You don't tell them these things, or it is YOU who goes to the funny farm. Instead, you tell them that your strange son has a compunction to fly — though he has no wings — and that you have to hold him back from leaping through a window, and they tell you that the boy is autistic, depressed, suicidal.

Jeremy tucked the book carefully into his jacket pocket and looked up at Birdboy still sitting quietly on the top shelf. He motioned for his adopted son to climb down from the bookcase. "OK, let's go for a ride. Please try not to fly down," he quipped.

Jeremy drove north of Los Angeles, through the Grapevine and down into the valley. In the rearview mirror, the city folded into a champagne-colored haze. Dust blew from empty, combed fields, and the smell of plowed-under crops wafted through the car window. Jeremy often drove out here to show Birdboy the many regional birds, to assure the child he was not alone. There were twitchy Angeleno city birds flying in spurts from tops of billboards to the tops of fence posts, and the tireless blackbirds of the Central Valley that soared among the rows of high-voltage towers and disappeared in the haze of the distant mountains. Birdboy watched intently, his hands scratching the seat like he did when he became agitated, longing for the freedom to fly.

At the side of the road, Jeremy saw a large hand-painted sign, "Beno's Fruit and Vegetable Stand," and down a dirt road a ramshackle produce stand swirled in dust and smog. A small car was parked beside the stand. Maybe they could pick up some fruit and take a little walk. Jeremy turned into the dirt road, parked near the stand, and they got out of the car. Birdboy shuffled behind him, kicking up dust. "For god's sake, Bird, pick up your feet," Jeremy snapped.

The produce stand had collapsed on itself and sections of corrugated roof had fallen on top of empty shelves. It was now nothing but overturned boxes, pieces of wood and metal, and fruitless desolation. An old man wearing white baggy pants and a white T-shirt stood stunned in front of it all. He raised his hand in greeting.

Jeremy and the old man stared at each other. The wind rattled a loose piece of the tin roof. Jeremy looked into the man's chalky blue eyes and at his white wiry hair and dry stretchy lips. The man looked like someone torn by disaster, like Dr. Maxwell after he was ravaged by the Amazons, stunned, humiliated, and strangely turned on.

"Some trouble here?" Jeremy said.

The old man slowly turned to the busted corner of the stand and pointed. "Could you fix this?"

Jeremy inspected the corner. The nails that held the crossbeams were twisted, wrangled, and one of the beams had a long, lengthwise crack. "Looks like a tornado hit," Jeremy said.

The old man didn't reply.

Birdboy hopped up and down and gave little hoots.

The old man didn't care, but shifted from one foot to another.

Jeremy shrugged his shoulders. "I'm no carpenter, I'm afraid. Just a dumb college professor."

The old man paced back and forth as if haunted. He mumbled something, tossed his hands in despair, and cried out "Why me?" to an uncaring God. The cry held pain and abandonment, the vacuousness of despair, the muted stupidity of fate.

"What happened, my friend? You look in a state."

The man told him of this girl he had hired, a surly one, a bit brutish, who tried to tear up the stand and nearly did. Her presence made the fruit rot, made him broke because she drove customers away; then she tried to get run over by a tractor. He lived out here now in his Pinto, in the remnants of his little business. Jeremy felt a surge of mercy, remembering how he had come home to find his house in ruins, his Amazon treasures burned to black sticks, his monkey mummified. This old man did not have Claude Lévi-Strauss biting his heels; he did not have pompous department chairs; he did not have obtuse grad students with their limp and sweaty papers filled with their whines and his own gruff crib marks reflecting his bitterness at their youth; he did not have weasel-like trustee committee members regretting giving him tenure and barely enduring what they called his autistic son (for so explained the strangeness of Birdboy—the thought of an Amazon copulating with a bird was too much to bear). The man was pure grief. Like a tear.

"Old man," Jeremy said, "I have a spare room. I have plenty of space actually, just me and the Bird. We can cry over the cruelty of women, what do you say?"

The old man squinted. "So you've had your share of sorrow?"

"Oh . . ." Jeremy laughed to himself, looking at his adopted son jumping up and down, yerping, his socks coated with dust. "I've had a few close calls."

The old man nodded, then was silent.

"I can't call you 'old man,' " Jeremy said.

The man held out his hand. "Melvinor. And you can call me an old man; I am pretty old."

"Dr. Jeremy Millard." He extended his hand rather formally. They shook on it. Then the two men passed by the Pinto and walked over to Jeremy's car. Birdboy shuffled behind them, his breath coming out in panting wirts and birts. Melvinor glanced at the child, said nothing, then got in. Jeremy decided against the walk and drove home, thinking of how his indulgence for strange ephemera—the everyday castoffs of any given culture—led him toward connections to strange and puzzling creatures.

Jeremy Millard had met Rosea for the first time at a party sponsored by the Brazilian consulate—or a party with a Brazilian theme, he couldn't remember which. He had published several articles about Birdboy and wanted to move swiftly and scout out some sources of possible funding so he could go back to the Amazon. He wanted to bend ears with carefully chosen words and interesting plans. He wanted funders to think he was a serious fellowship candidate, not an anthropologist obsessed like Dr. Robert Maxwell and Dr. Franklin Bisby, who had shocked the academic community by deliberately disappearing into the jungle. It would be hard for Jeremy to convince funders that he was still sane and had kept himself single for the good of the anthropology department.

The party was at a mansion in Bel Air, one of those places where the owner seems only vaguely present. A bandstand in the main room featured a group playing bongos, trumpets, and guitars. The musicians wore ruffled silk shirts with sleeves that fluttered as their hands flapped and rapped on their instruments. Jeremy couldn't get over the tight pants Latin musicians wore and wondered how they could father the number of children they did. In fact, the band seemed more Cuban than Brazilian. That Jeremy knew this difference set him apart from his colleagues. The music was Perez Pradoish, much of it a soothing could-do-a-tango-if-push-came-to-shove. The MC, a handsome man with conked hair, announced to the audience that he had worked with Desi Arnaz. He introduced the other musicians as having been members of the Banda Lua, the old Carmen Socorro band. Jeremy vaguely remembered Carmen Socorro as the movie star who wore large hats with glued-on fruit and other things, but beyond that he didn't know much.

The evening felt strange to him—him, the timid overworked soul with skin smelling like the soap of library restrooms. It felt strange because the party wasn't about scholarship at all, but about money. Nobody really wanted to hear about Birdboy or about Jeremy's trip to the Amazon, but about who got what grant and who didn't deserve it.

But ah, an awakening! Because of the boredom and the secret longing for the Amazon warriors, he began noticing women. He liked the dresses now; some hung over the women's breasts only to be swooped up and gathered at their hipbone with a jeweled pin. Others wore spaghetti-strap dresses, tight knits that sleeked over their bodies like a long sock. The smoother lines of dresses had open bowl-like necks that showed ridges of collar bones. The women with swizzle-stick bodies wore full-fashioned earrings, triangular and Aztec, quizzically exotic, and their hair was cut short and blunt like Chinese orphans or left long and blond like bridal veils.

Jeremy stood there among the hum of exquisite chatter. He was disgusted with himself and didn't see anyone who would care about his anthropological ideas. Then someone called his name. He turned, first seeing a clash of upraised martini glasses, then catching a glimpse of Julian Bemis, who had helped him fund his first trip to the Amazon. Bemis motioned Jeremy over with a cigar-shaped fat finger. Jeremy gave a cry of relief and squeezed his way through jewels and silk jerseys and groans and glasses.

Bemis was older than Jeremy and had a nonacademic job, which meant he had more money and a truer love for the exotic. Bemis's satin cummerbund went smoothly over his round belly, and he wore two large diamond rings on one of his chubby hands. Jeremy also noticed that Bemis was with an unusually tall young woman who stayed alongside him, though she seemed a bit detached. This woman towered, but not gigantically so. While the rest of the women at the party wore their hair in orderly smoothness, she pushed her long black hair to one side like the Amazons he remembered who could hurl and catch knives. The woman spotted him between people's heads, as if she were hunting him down. Her eyes were heavy lidded and dark like beetles. Then her mouth curled in a half-smile as if she were challenging him to a duel. He was so taken with this tall woman he didn't realize that he had worked his way through the crowd, and Bemis practically had to yell in his ear and jab his diamonded fist into Jeremy's upper arm. "Hey, Dr. Millard. Wake up!"

Jeremy shook Bemis's hand vigorously, then extended his hand politely to the tall woman. "A pleasure."

Bemis motioned with his finger. His thick prominent digits seemed to dominate the conversation. "A friend of mine, Rosea Socorro Katz."

Jeremy smiled. "A nice choice, Bemis."

"She's not my girlfriend," he blathered out loud.

Rosea gave a grimace. Her teeth were large; the muscles on her neck shifted in anger, but she said nothing.

They sat at a small table, and Jeremy talked about his Birdboy articles, but all the while eyeing the woman, who seemed a bit bored. He continued talking, for Bemis was interested, then he stopped suddenly, mid-sentence, as if struck down by the realization that he himself did not care a hoot for Birdboy at this moment. Something about the woman had overwhelmed him. Bemis looked at both of them and winked as if he knew. Then he introduced the woman further—he had hardly paid attention to her all this time—as Carmen Socorro's daughter, Rosea.

"Oh yes," Jeremy said, "the band was—"

"Right," Bemis said, "right. Rosea has been doing things in Hollywood, little B flicks. Jungle pictures. Her mother was from Brazil. Where the nuts come from."

Rosea rolled her eyes.

Bemis got serious. "She needs a little quiet now. And more kindness than I can give."

Jeremy looked deeper into the woman's face and saw that, yes, she did seem a bit sad. She touched him somehow, with the compulsion to kiss her madly or something. Jeremy whispered, "I need a drink," because his tongue felt dry.

"Sure," Bemis got up from the table. "I'll get them. Would champagne be OK for you folks?"

Rosea nodded at Bemis and then gave Jeremy the eye. She opened into a smile, and Jeremy almost felt as though he could fall into her mouth and slip down her throat. Bemis left for the champagne. Rosea tossed her head. "He was a friend of my mother's. One of the weird ones," she said.

Jeremy chuckled, knowing the reputation Bemis had for funding madcap adventures. One expedition was to find the Yeti in Tibet.

Rosea seemed to roll Bemis off her shoulders and send him splashing in an imaginary river somewhere. She then began talking about her mother, the movies mostly, and her eyes would shoot around, here and there. Her gaze lingered on a woman wearing an Audrey Hepburn slink dress, sizing her up and down; but just as Jeremy was getting worried that maybe this Rosea was a dead-end street, she leaned forward and rolled her lower jaw. "I hate skinny women like that. They're like insects," she said.

Rosea grinned when Bemis came back with a small tray and three filled champagne glasses. She took one, but found the skinny stem hard to maneuver in her powerful hands. In fact, she was beautiful — bronzed and a bit brash looking, as if she were struggling to control herself. Frustrated, she drank the champagne in one gulp. As she set the glass down, her face seemed to dim, so incredibly sad. Jeremy held the glass to his lips, watching her, then he slowly took a sip of champagne. She smiled cynically and settled back.

Something about her didn't seem quite right. The dress she wore seemed too tight; it pressed on her breasts, and the silk and lace didn't suit her. The two side seams from her underarm to waist were split where the armhole was, as if she had tried to alter the dress but never finished. Her velvet belt had a second large button missing so that the end of it dangled. Jeremy talked again to Bemis, but cautiously, worried about upsetting Rosea. She started looking around the room, searching for a way out, then she seemed to give up, resting her elbow on the table and leaning her forehead on the back of her hand. Jeremy stood up, "Please, let's step outside." She got up quickly, almost overturning the table.

Bemis took a bit of Jeremy's sleeve. "Take care of her now, I'll get back to you."

Jeremy followed Rosea to the veranda, and for a moment it seemed like in the movies. There was even a moon. She leaned on the railing, and he gazed at her broad back, wall-like and stubborn. She mumbled something, then flung her shoes off to the side, where they clattered like dice. She put her weight on one leg, then the other, and her butt swaying like that made him yearn for jungle women and their long spears.

He joined her and thought she'd draw away, but she didn't.

"You don't have to stay with me," she said, "if I'm boring you."

"Not a bit."

"You seem smart," she said scanning the palm trees below. "Are you?"

He wasn't sure what "smart" meant. He explained, "I know Mr. Bemis from before. He's a friend who has helped me considerably. He's given me money for my trip to the Amazon. I want to go again even if I have to *beg* him" He chuckled, surprised at his joke.

Rosea didn't move.

Jeremy rubbed his hands, cracked his knuckles by mistake, and heard her toes cracking as she dug her bare foot into the floor. It was like he hadn't spoken.

"So," Jeremy started again, "your mother was from Brazil. I've been there myself."

"Oh? I haven't."

Jeremy could hear the party inside humming like mosquitoes. The congas seemed loud, and he wished he wasn't here. His thoughts drifted for a bit, then he said: "I saw women who looked a bit like you. It's amazing."

"Amazons," she said, not a bit surprised. "They could kick your ass."

Jeremy was startled at her frankness, her titillating vulgarity, and the fact that she even *knew* about the Amazons. "Well," he leaned into her, taking the opportunity to move in closer, "they almost did."

With that, Rosea threw her head back and laughed deep in her throat, her brown neck undulating like the river, her muscles quivering with her belly laugh. Her thighs must be like dangerous cliffs, he thought. When she stopped, she stared straight at him. This is when Jeremy saw himself shrunken in her eyes, his light-brown hair (then full) exploding from his head and dissolving into the whites of her eyes. This must have been the last thing Dr. Robert Maxwell and Dr. Franklin Bisby saw of themselves before they disappeared into the jungle, like old mariners who decided to follow the sirens and jump into the sea to their doom. She pressed her face forward for him to kiss her. His mouth met hers with such force he felt himself being ground between her teeth, sucked into the whirlpools of the Rio Solimões, the kind that can trap a small boat and leave it swirling for eternity. Their tongues and lips sloshed at first, then they kissed with the powerful silence that precedes a jungle massacre.

Chapter 9

A Amazônia, Rio Solimões, Brasil
O Ano 1966

Carvajal, a village situated on a tributary that began at the junction of the Solimões and the Japurá, was named after Friar Gaspar de Carvajal, who recorded Francisco Orellana's voyage down the Amazon in search of the famed gold city, El Dorado. According to Carvajal's journals, Orellana was set upon by a fierce tribe of warrior women, brown skinned, tall, robust, and fine, who not only fought alongside the men, but clubbed those who tried to desert the battle. Orellana captured one of these Amazons and questioned her in front of his crew. The prisoner, who wore the gold amulet of a wide-hipped woman, told of how no man could stay in the

village after dark, for he would be captured, ravaged, then released. Be
forewarned, the Amazon warrior said, that he who entered this jungle as
a boy returned home as a man.

The small riverboat *Beija-Flor* whirred along the shore lined with
houses on stilts stained with various water-level marks, their narrow
porches decorated with colored shorts and T-shirts drying on the rail-
ings. The rising waters of the *várzea* had deposited on the floodplain
birdnestlike tangles of dried grass and brittle branches. The sandy penin-
sulas, nonexistent during the rains, reemerged, fanning into beaches or
narrowing into footpaths that led straight into the river. A passing squall
had bounced the boat and made Jeremy's stomach feel all green and
gringo, but now the rain had stopped, and large mats of grass floated
calmly on the water. Yet he felt alive in the tropical torpor, looking out
the open side of the large cabin at the palm trees and loose clusters of
towering *munguba* trees, thinking of the Amazon women just waiting to
make him into a man.

He lay on his hammock inside the boat's single cabin and imagined an
Amazon, her gold bracelets around her ankles, sitting beside him on a
small stool. Her loincloth would hang between her large brown thighs as
she taught him the ways of love. It would be secret; he wouldn't write an
academic paper on the meeting, no matter how much he wanted tenure.
Her words would be buried in her shameless whispers.

Carl Dotson and Don Kemp, the two other associate professors of anthropology besides himself, lay on nearby hammocks inside the cabin
and slapped woody-sounding flies from their ears. Their emeritus-bound
supervisor, Dr. Robert Maxwell, sat upright in his hammock, his pressed
shirts still tucked into his EZ-Travel pants, and he furiously wrote in
his notebook, tabulating the treasures bought in small villages west of
Manaus, including Waiwai feathered diadems, long sticklike Jívaro spin-
dles used to spin home-grown cotton into thread, Kayapó burial mats,
a beautiful *cavaquinho* inlaid in mother-of-pearl that probably had belonged to a rubber baron and that now belonged to Jeremy, and ten
gourds attached to a rope made of palm fiber.

The other soul on the *Beija-Flor*, the little hummingbird of a boat, was
the ghost of Dr. Franklin Bisby and his obsession with the Juarouá tribe.

Jeremy had read all of Bisby's academic articles and books on the tribe, texts regarded by many as important as the Dead Sea Scrolls. Bisby wrote of the tribe's rectangular houses with thatched roofs that were built on high ground facing the river. He found the natives to be friendly, and no wonder; Juarouá was the Indian name for the manatee, a gentle creature with fleshy lips, and pink creamy skin, and, below the fins, two human-like breasts that leaked milk during calving. But despite the tribe's apparent mild temperament, Bisby was beginning to see influences of a harsher modern world, and this he couldn't fathom. For one, all the natives asked for money. If they had any spears with carved barbs on each side, the shaft painted in black geometric shapes on the natural wood, or shields made of manatee and tapir hide, or turtle-shell axes, or hand-painted cloth, or jars and pitchers glazed and decorated with black-painted coils like miniature labyrinths, or Santarém Phase clay bird whistles made by grandmothers, they all were up for sale. And the Juarouá dressed like caboclos, the men in faded cotton pants and shirts and the women in old, dumpy house dresses. They ate manioc griddlecakes cooked on a butane gas stove brought from Manaus. "But, my God," Bisby was recorded as saying, "don't you people mold your children's skulls anymore? What happened to the flat foreheads, such a sign of beauty?"

The real treasure was when Bisby brought with him Nazaré, a Juarouá native and a treasure of innocence among the neurotic scholars. On Bisby's lecture tour, Nazaré wore a wool suit, his big hands with their tense and clawed fingers hanging out of the sleeves like false appendages. His bare, wide feet were splayed like a fan, and when he raised his foot and showed the audience his thick, cracked soles, a few members scrambled to touch the old scar tissue. Nazaré, in broken Portuguese peppered with his native tongue, proclaimed disgust at cars and tall buildings, and winced at the taste of ice cream. He talked about his forests, about how the motor of chainsaws drowned out the cry of birds, about how the trees came crashing down, hurling monkeys into the river. And he told them of his vision: his people would be destroyed. He didn't know how, but there would be no one left to dig the graves. His testimonial had the audience weeping.

Jeremy imagined taking Bisby's Nazaré aside, begging the man: *take me with you.* He had a compulsion to disappear into the jungle. He didn't know why back then. But Bisby beat him to it. When Bisby took Nazaré back to the Amazon, the scholar never returned.

Jeremy was jealous of Bisby's stunt. What was Bisby trying to do, make himself into even more of a legend than the caciques of El Dorado who painted their bodies with gold dust? Did he want people to obsess about his genius? Did he want to be known like Lope de Aguirre, going mad on his river raft through the Amazon and getting tangled in the lianas that grew from the small splits in his skull? Was he waiting—smugly— for them on the *Beija-Flor* to discover him wearing just a small apron and a parrot-feather crown in sublime tribal integration, and offer him back his tenure position? Would the meeting start with something like a "Dr. Bisby, I presume?"

Jeremy watched as Dotson got up from his hammock and wandered over to the doorway to look out at the river. Jeremy didn't like the man; he was a brat prof in contemporary social anthropology, and God knows who had given him a grant for this trip. Dotson's cheeks were red and flushed like a child who has just gotten up from a nap. A half-submerged oil can bounced in the current. Dotson pouted, sliding out his wet lower lip. "Look at that trash. They're slobs!"

Jeremy snapped back. "Mr. Dotson. We are here to observe, not make judgments. Leave your prejudices at home, in your blasted classroom. They don't belong here."

Dotson waved Jeremy away. "Can't you be a frickin' human being for once? Some things are piss-poor no matter what culture we're talking about. The Juarouá may be slobs. Littering may be a part of their RELI- GION. Ever think of that?"

Damn brat. Jeremy got up from his hammock abruptly, went out to the deck and forward to the bow. The pilot, who called himself Jacaré, or Crocodile, steered the boat with his middle finger hooked on the wheel. He had no front top teeth, just a wide gap between two canines. His laughter sounded like bubbly water. The interpreter, Aristotle, leaning on a nearby rail, stroked his ropelike braid wrapped in red fabric and slurped in *portunhol*, the strange combination of Spanish and Portu- guese. When Jeremy came near, the men looked at him askance and slit-eyed; then Aristotle took his red braid, flopped it up and down several times, and the two Brazilians crumpled in glee.

Just then Jacaré whipped around, blew the riverboat whistle, and headed to shore. A few boys emerged from a grove of palm trees, ran to the shore, and waved. Aristotle swept into the cabin and announced: "Carvajal! Put up your hammocks! Get your things!"

Maxwell spoke oh so patiently. "Aristotle. Carvajal is our home base. We are staying on the boat until tomorrow morning."

Aristotle pinched the end of his braid. "Staying on the boat? Porquê?"

Jeremy felt sweat grabbing at the back of his shirt. Maxwell carefully explained: "We're going to stay on *this* boat and take a *smaller* boat to visit the Juarouá. The Indians, remember? Just six kilometers from here? Remember our deal?"

No, Aristotle shook his head rapidly. "The Juarouá no are here. They are gone."

The boat thumped against the pier.

Maxwell caught his breath, a bit shocked, and sighed deliberately, maintaining his professorly caution. "No. This is not true. Dr. Franklin Bisby was here just eight years ago. He met the Juarouá."

Aristotle threw up his hands. "No Juarouá, my friends! I tell you! They are dead!"

Maxwell took a handkerchief from his pocket and wiped his sweaty forehead. "How do you know this, eh?"

"I know! I know! How can I say?"

"Aristotle. The reason we came is to see the Juarouá Indians. That's why we paid you. From here we hire a small motorboat to take us to the Indian village. Remember? If they are all dead, why didn't you tell us before, eh?"

"I *tell* you this before," Aristotle insisted.

Just then Jacaré bounded into the cabin shouting, "Cadê suas malas? Estamos pronto?" Where in the hell are your suitcases? The boys on the dock are here to help you!

Jesus Christ. Maxwell blew out his tension. Aristotle and Jacaré rattled off a discussion, then Jacaré exclaimed, "A Juarouá estão mortos! Kaput!" Then in English: "Dead!" Dotson and Kemp flew about like chickens, squawking, "Wha-wha, what's going on, the caboclos are ripping us off **95** blind!"

Aristotle threw up his hands. "You think all Brazilians cheat! I know! I see all the time! I hear tourists in Manaus say, 'this Brazilian man is too nice — he want money?' Hein? I tell you. The Juarouá are dead. There is no more, entendes?"

Maxwell strolled to the doorway of the cabin and looked out at the river. "Well, if it's not money, how can we get you to take us to the village then? We have come a long, long way for this."

Aristotle let out a drawn-out huff. "OK, amigo. You want to go to the *village*, I take you. Amanha. OK. OK. Maybe I make mistake. Maybe you are lucky." With that, Jacaré and Aristotle stomped out to the deck, threw a rope around a wood post, and pulled the edge of the boat close to the dock.

Jeremy, setting himself apart from the others, wandered back to the stern. Now he thought: perhaps Dr. Bisby did not choose to disappear but was met with a jungle fate reserved for missionaries and fortune hunters. He thought of those dumb cartoons, the ones with men in a cooking cauldron, the natives in grass skirts. He tried to shake those thoughts away, but the voices of the mocking children on the shore echoed in his ear as they shouted and pointed to the souvenir canoe strapped to the top of the riverboat. "Bote na agua!" Put the boat in the water! Boats are made to go in the water, you idiots!

☾

The night passed with oily restlessness. The riverboat rocked with the current, slamming against the pier. The darkness was lit with pools made from a full moon. The two Brazilians went into the village for the night, but everyone else slept on hammocks with mosquito netting draped along the wide doorway of the cabin. Jeremy lay on his hammock, listening to his snoring colleagues and to the strange insects beyond. He thought he heard a human cry out in the wilderness, but it blended in with all the other strange cries.

The next day everyone was ready to go. Jeremy hoisted onto his shoulder his small duffle bag of gifts for the natives — transistor radios, knives, and T-shirts mostly—then he climbed onto the pier. The rest followed. Maxwell carried his backpack to a makeshift bench in the shady area near the water's edge, sat down, and double-checked his notes and cassette tape recorder. Maxwell seemed to feel no dread that what had happened to Bisby would happen to them. "It could be local superstition or something to scare us." Maxwell smiled sheepishly at them. "Don't worry," he said, "these kind of folks try and screw up anthropologists all the time. It's like having a bad informant. Just keep your head on straight."

The sun burned the early morning and heated their impatience at Aristotle and Jacaré's maddening lateness. In the river, a dolphin sliced through the thick water. A group of young boys came from a dirt side street. Two of them carried fishing poles, and one had a pail. They goofed around and didn't see the anthropologists at first, then one boy heard Dr. Maxwell humming as he wrote in his notebook and elbowed the others. The group of them came over and asked unabashedly where the men were from. Argentina? São Paulo? Maxwell grinned kindly and answered with his hard American accent. "Oostados Oonidos." The boys stared as if unbelieving, then glanced at one another. One boy tapped the ground with his fishing pole. Maxwell closed his notebook and looked quizzically at the young boys. Jeremy watched. Maxwell was so professorial even here in this blasted heat. "Conhece os Indios Juarouá?" Maxwell asked.

The boys grew excited as they talked about the disaster. "Estão mortos, estão mortos," they all pealed, shooting make-believe arrows in the sky, "Peeuu! Peeuuu!" The anthropologists looked at each other. A collective lie? The truth? Both? "Como eles morreram? How did they die?" A collective shrug, their young brown eyes sparkling with frisky danger, their tongues rapidly prattling the tale of woe.

In the middle of the boys' explanation, Aristotle and two young men strode past and onto the pier, and the kids scurried after the three men, shouting that the Juarouá were dead "if you must know." Aristotle waved them away. "Puxa! Scram, will you?!" The two young men climbed onto two small boats with outboard motors. One man wore a torn T-shirt and a pack of cigarettes rolled up in the sleeve, and the other, who had blue

eyes, wore an old, wide-brimmed straw hat with a cut-away crown revealing a fluff of black, curly hair.

"OK, OK," Aristotle called to the anthropologists, "get in the boats!
Go! Go!" The old motorboats leaked oil onto the water, and blue flakes
from peeling paint floated on top of the gooey slick.

Jeremy hesitated.

"Don't worry," Aristotle barked, "They are not broken!"

Jeremy climbed down the small ladder and got into the boat he would
ride with Maxwell. Dotson and Kemp took the other. Two kids on the
pier ran over, grabbed the duffle bag with the gifts for the natives and
handed it down to Jeremy. Then they squatted on the edge of the dock
and held out their hands for tips. Jeremy absent-mindedly reached into
his pocket and gave them each a couple of centavos, which, from the
looks of their young frowns, must have been very little money. Well, so
be it.

Aristotle glared at the anthropologists, then stepped into one of the
motorboats. "You people are crazy. I sacrifice my life for you."

Maxwell rolled his jaw. "We appreciate this, my friend. We too must
be risking our lives." Then the young men revved the motor, and the two
boats headed toward the bend in the river into an *igarapé*.

The water of the igarapé was black and still, and the greenery around
them muffled the sound of the outboard motors. Aristotle pointed to a
submerged crocodile, its eyes and snout making a rolling V in the water.
Sheets of dead leaves undulated in the small coves and clung to the mangrove roots. One of the boatman hummed a tune that, for a moment,
Jeremy thought sounded like "morto, morto."

Aristotle called out something to the boatmen, and they began to steer
their boats closer to one of the banks. Then Jeremy could see something
— a small beach of rust-colored mud. The boatmen shut off the motors
and let the boats drift. Each grabbed an oar and with long, hard strokes
moved the small boats across the thick water until the prow scraped on
the shore.

There the group disembarked and climbed up the muddy embank-
ment. The boatman with the torn shirt said something, removed his pack

of cigarettes from his rolled-up sleeve, and offered one to his friend in the other boat. They lit their cigarettes and rested their arms on their roughened knees.

Aristotle translated, "They wait here."

"Wait here?" Jeremy said as he lifted the duffle bag of gifts onto his shoulder, "What if they leave us here?" Jeremy could feel Maxwell's hand on his shoulder, trying to calm him down.

Aristotle looked at them and narrowed his eyes. "They wait here. Have trust for them." Then he led the way down a narrow path cutting into the bushes. The rest followed his red-wrapped ponytail that looked like a thermometer about to burst. Jeremy glanced back. The boatmen were staring at them and puffing on their cigarettes. The bark from the trees crackled, thick leaves brushed them on all sides, and small pronged thorns caught their clothes. Aristotle slapped something off his arm and swore under his breath.

They reached a clearing in the jungle, a patch of red dirt like a splash of blood. "OK, here," Aristotle stopped. "Here is the great Juarouá village."

It was true, what everyone said.

Jeremy set down his duffle bag of gifts. He could see where the dwellings had been — the collapsed piles of thatch, dried fronds flapping in the wind that blew from the river, flattened huts overgrown with vegetation. Strips of trapped dried grass fluttered from underneath the woody vines that spiraled around tree trunks. Maxwell squinted. He looked pale and apprehensive, with a sunscreen smear on his forehead. His fair blue eyes seemed to blur into cotton balls.

Kemp started taking pictures of the ruins. Jeremy was making his way over to a collapsed hut when Aristotle called, "What I tell you? Everyone is dead! You believe me now?"

Jeremy tossed aside old pieces of thatch. He didn't want Aristotle to see his fear or his ignorance. He didn't want to see Bisby's dead body. There was a rumor about cannibals, but Jeremy didn't quite know what the rumor was.

Suddenly the jungle fell silent. One doesn't notice the noise until it all stops, until the howling and squawking is stunned, as if slapped silly. Jeremy crept toward the clearing. Everyone was converging; the jungle

stillness was not his imagination. Aristotle's eyes glittered with fear, and
he swallowed hard, his slender brown neck rippling. "Meu gente," he announced, "I go. I no want to die. I have four children." As he turned to
go back, the bushes rattled violently, and two horses with women astride
them bolted into the clearing. Then came two more women on horseback and two more. The largest women Jeremy had ever seen. Their
chests were broad like men's, and their breasts, so heavy and full, hung
crowded together, and some of them had severed one breast, leaving only
a scarred lump. They had decorated their bodies with painted sworls of
black *genipapo* dye around their breasts, and with slashes and fringe on
their chin and cheeks. Oily balsam gleamed on their skin, smeared over
new and savage-looking wounds. Their thick legs clamped the horses
bellies, and the horses' rib cages puffed in and out of breath. The women's
black, frizzy hair blew out like a storm. Some had decorated their hair
with crowns of feathers, and some had wound shanks with twine.

One of them let out a shrill cry, and two more women on horseback
bounded out into the clearing. The men were surrounded by the women's
wide faces and large mouths with blocklike teeth. The women grasped
blood-tipped spears and held them down at their sides.

Jeremy could hardly believe it, this gruesome sad luck. What a fitting
end. He had finally made the greatest find of his life, only to die before he
could write a word about it. Dotson's cheeks now sagged on his childlike
moon face. Kemp's head bent forward with the heavy cameras weighing
around his neck. The women looked at each other and spoke in a strange
language. Dotson looked at Aristotle. "Translate, damn it." But Aristotle
shook his head and mumbled that he couldn't recognize the language.

One of the women said something and slipped off her horse. She was
not a giant, yet she was tall, about six feet. Her hair fell down her back,
and a strip of curly hair had slipped into her armpit and remained lodged
in sweat. Her eyes were black like flint arrows, her lips rolled and thick.
She wore an apron of woven fabric, and on her belly a black *genipapo* serpent spiraled around her navel and pointed its head toward her crotch.

The woman grinned, her large teeth so flashy and yellow it would almost have seemed comic to the men except for their fear. The woman
approached Maxwell, grabbed his upper arm, and pulled him forward.

Maxwell dropped his backpack and wavered, muttered the name of his wife, "Please say something to Alicia for me," something about his love for her.

Jeremy reached forward to pull Maxwell away, but one of the women hollered, and horse hooves scraped the ground. In unison, the women on top of the horses raised their spears slightly. The woman tugged Maxwell forward again, holding his arm, but not roughly. She undid her apron and ran her fingers through her black, curly bush. Maxwell stepped back, but the woman yanked him forward, harder, so that he almost smashed his face against her shoulder. The other men watched from behind, and for a moment Maxwell's white hair looked blond and boylike. The woman opened her legs, took her thick fingers and spread apart her vulva so that they could see her purple labia peering from the cleft of her fingers. Then she pushed up a bit more so it hung like tongue. She laughed, then with both hands, grabbed ahold of his belt. Maxwell, terrified, stood there as she struggled to rip the leather. She called out and held out her hand. One of the women threw her a knife, which she deftly caught. She brought the knife forward, and Maxwell gulped and closed his eyes. She quickly took the knife and ripped up his shirt, slashed his belt, then continued with the knife down both legs of his pants. Jeremy shuddered as he expected to see Maxwell's blood and balls splattering at their feet, but instead she had merely succeeded in undressing him. She flung the knife back at a woman who caught it atop her horse. She pushed Maxwell down on the ground and got on her knees and straddled on top of him. She reached between his legs and pulled and kneaded. Jeremy tried to close his eyes, but had to stare, seeing her brown hand undulating like a small animal. Jeremy shuddered as he imagined her fingers warm and leatherlike on his own skin, and her strong raw breath grazing his own face like a large bear. Fear made the artery on Jeremy's thigh quiver. The woman slipped her hand away, widened her straddle and sank her crouch down. Her hair fell in front and licked Maxwell's face. Maxwell stared straight ahead, arms out to the side with his fingers pointed softly upward because she was holding him down at the wrists. Jeremy kept telling himself not to look, but he did; he wanted to see the end. Finally Maxwell shuddered, his head gave a twitch. Jeremy knew. All the men knew.

The woman slowly released his arms and smiled. Maxwell shifted and slowly reached up and brushed her hair off her face. Her smile faded; she looked at him curiously and pulled away and stood up. Maxwell rolled over to his side and lay curled up in a fetal position. Some of the women turned their horses and headed back into the jungle.

The attacker stood there still looking at them, then backed away. She scooped up the duffle bag of gifts and Maxwell's backpack and tossed them up to one of her cohorts on horseback. Then she jumped onto her horse, getting her belly up to the horse's back. Her enormous buttocks seemed a reflection of the horse's haunches. The backs of her legs had thick muscles starting from her buttocks and twisting together ropelike at her knees. She swung these loglike legs around and got on top of the horse again, then called out to another woman and pointed to Jeremy.

Jeremy didn't know what to do. He swallowed and pretended to misunderstand. One of the woman carrying a spear rode her horse up to him and, with one motion, pointed her spear at his chest. Jeremy shook and flinched at the point pick. His captor had a leaner face and was a bit smaller that the other one, and she had one long breast the shape of a jackfruit. Half of her hair was bound with twine, the other half hung to one side. Jeremy had an absurd thought that it would make a good fashion in the United States. He didn't want to have such an absurd thought at a moment like this, but he did.

Just then the large woman who had attacked Maxwell returned, carrying a child in front of her. She brought her horse up to Jeremy, and the spear was withdrawn a bit. The large woman took the child by the wrist, lifted him off the horse, and lowered him to the ground—dropped him, actually, as it was a long way down. He landed on the dirt and began whimpering. Jeremy stared at the small deformed boy. His head was rounded like a helmet, but slightly flat on top, and seemed attached to his shoulders because his neck was so short and thick. Black hair grew down around his ears and mixed with the green florescent feathers that grew at the nape of his neck. His lips gathered in a pucker, and his cry warbled like a bird. It was hard to guess his age he was so small and shrunken. The little one turned around and with his bowed legs waddled side to side over to the horse. He gave little hops with his arms upraised and his sharp shoulder blades poked out. But the large woman took the blunt end of her spear and gave his belly a jab, nudging him away.

Maxwell stumbled up, naked, and the men drew away and started back down the trail. "Wait!" Jeremy called, but now he had two women threatening him with their spears. She spoke to Jeremy sharply, while the small boy was given another nudge forward with the handle.

Jeremy backed away, then turned slowly to go, hoping he wouldn't see the woman kill the boy. Instead, the kid followed him. Jeremy could hear feet hopping on the dust and small breaths coming out in hoots. He stopped and looked back. The women led their horses back into the jungle, and the small boy remained, standing in the middle of the clearing. Finally, Jeremy picked him up and carried him to the boats.

When Jeremy and the boy arrived at the motorboats, Maxwell was huddled into one, and Dotson and Kemp were on the shore, ready to get on the other boat. Dotson turned. "What are you doing with the kid? Are you crazy? You want them to come after us?"

Jeremy held the child and held him closer. "They gave him to me. They were going to kill him." The boatmen laughed. What a headache you have, amigo! And one of them patted Dotson on the butt with the oar. Dotson jumped and grew even more livid at Jeremy. "Who do you think you are? Dr. Bisby, bringing yet another one of his freaks for the world to see?"

"Hey!" Dr. Maxwell shouted. They turned to him, but he said nothing more, but stared at them, his face getting longer and watery as he shivered and held the pieces of his clothes at his crotch.

Aristotle looked at all of them seriously and motioned to the boy. "Leave him here. They try to trick us."

"Let's go quickly then." Jeremy pulled the strange kid tighter to him, pushed Dotson aside, and got into the boat with Maxwell. The two men got into the other boat.

Aristotle sat in the canoe in front of Jeremy. "Vamos embora! Let's go!" the interpreter shouted, and the boatmen rapidly paddled away from shore. The small boy in front whirtled mournfully. "The boy is big trouble," Aristotle said, "my English is not enough good to explain."

Jeremy's two colleagues on the other boat glared in jealousy. They

were coming away with nothing, not even a Santarém clay pot to piss in.
Jeremy had the part of the Amazon woman that had been inside her and had emerged from between her legs. It was like he was the father. This is what the Amazon warrior had told Carvajal: you enter the jungle a boy and come out a man.

When they got back to the riverboat, Jacaré took one look at the boy, shook his head, and waved his hands — Back, back, give it back.

Jeremy explained in haphazard Porto-English: "Uma mulher gave him to me."

Jacaré and Aristotle looked wide-eyed as they argued among themselves. Jacaré tugged at Aristotle's shirt and gesticulated crazily. Abruptly, Aristotle held up his hands and announced, "Deixa acontecer," and both the Brazilians scrambled out to the bow.

Dotson and Kemp were still glaring at Jeremy, their chests shiny with sweat, their look accusing him of doing anything to get tenure and suggesting he just go into the jungle himself and shack up with Dr. Bisby. But when the boy's hand clutched Jeremy's fingers like a parrot and wouldn't let go, the anthropologist felt a strange jolt inside him. "He's mine," Jeremy proclaimed, and he named the child Birdboy.

During the night, Jeremy nestled Birdboy in his arm as they slept in the same hammock. Jeremy tethered Birdboy's small ankle to his own so that he would know if Birdboy was being snatched away during the night. Through the mosquito netting draped along the wide doorway, Jeremy saw the ravaged Maxwell on the deck with a bucket of water, washing himself between his legs like a woman, drying himself with a towel and struggling on his pants. Then Maxwell leaned on the rail and looked across the river. He didn't seem to care about the raging mosquitoes, but reached out as if to touch and gather something tangible, someone of the flesh. Then he folded his hands back on the railing and gazed at the shore teeming with shadows of dark, round, massive shoulders as if he would follow them.

Amazon behavior is more pointed than their Tupinambá counterparts and is less predisposed to ritual. Upon receiving guests, the Tupinambá women seat themselves at the foot of their visitors and wail about the misfortunes that have befallen the family, misfortunes that are supposed to arouse great pity. After this crying bout, the visit proceeds as normal, and the guest is entertained. With the Amazons, the women determine at first glance if the stranger is favorable to them. Most are not and are killed immediately.

—*Carta de Carlos Manoel Teixeira da Cunha a João Vicente Cardim da Almeida, O Ano* 1641

Chapter 10

O Ano 1977

Joe arrived home from work, his shiny sequined jacket rumpled, the seams rubbing against the tender skin of his armpits. As he unpeeled his jacket, he stood in the bedroom doorway and watched Sherri taking a nap. A light blanket covered her legs, and one foot stuck out of the bottom edge. On either side of her, Jeffy and Keffy slept, their pudgy arms splayed out, greedy with the space on the bed. The baby bottles, which they drank from as a matter of habit, had fallen into the small spaces between them and their mother. Their T-shirts had wet spots just below the chin.

Joe slipped off his uncomfortable clothes. This fake Cubanness and the lies he told on his tours were suffocating him. What made it bearable was Rosea, this interesting woman at work. She was brash the way she would deliberately forget her cigarettes so she could bother him for one. She smoked like a man, shoving the cigarette into her strong teeth and puffing furiously. She sat with her legs a bit spread and bragged that she could crack coconuts with her thighs, which would come in handy if that spazzy secretary Desiree ever pushed her last button. Rosea could be funny, too, mocking the B movies she had acted in, the ones with out-of-control Amazonian anacondas and pygmies and piranha feeding frenzies — the ones where she played the wild jungle *goona* lady and wore leopard-skin miniskirts and attacked delicate Europeans in search of some lost temple, only to be killed by some crazy volcano with a thousand-year curse. Joe laughed with her — yes, yes, the American Latin America of tropical puzzlements. She did a fine imitation of Chucky, that slant of the eye and sleazy sneer: "Someday, baby, I'll do it with the machine gun," and she'd throw her head back savagely and howl, "Yeah, yeah, how about the machine gun, how about the handcuffs, the strip-down butt check, yeah, why not? Have a martini, hey!" Then she'd stop laughing suddenly and take a deep breath, shove her fingers between the buttons of her blouse, tug at the underwire of her bra, and say, "Jesus, I'd love to hurl off this motherfucker." In the middle of her dazzling performance, Joe always reminded himself that he was married, and when he would show her a picture of the twins, she'd say, "Aw," and get almost teary. "I never knew my real father, and you're such a good one, Joe, I bet you make a great husband." "Aw," she'd coo again and tap the photo with her large thumb, "This one is cute." "They're identical!" Joe would say. "Oh, oh, ha ha ha," Rosea would peal, "good job, you!"

Joe slipped on his bathrobe and opened the window to let the breeze blow away the sour baby smell. Their new little house was better; the grassy smell from their backyard floated through the window. A wood fence in the back and a short chain-link fence in the front would keep their toddlers from wandering away. It looked like a real American home, something apartment dwellers in Rio only dream about. How lucky he was to have this little *casinha*, he reminded himself.

Joe went over to the bed, reached out and touched the top of Sherri's head, her blonde hair tangled and knotted in the rubber band of her ponytail. He felt the emptiness of longing; he had hardly made love to her since he first got her pregnant almost two years ago. A couple of times here and there. How could a woman go so long without a man's love? Maybe it was this culture, who knows? Joe wished she were awake; he felt unsettled because of something Rosea had said to him.

It was as if Rosea came home with him, and he felt a bit afraid. Today she had talked about how she was imprisoned here and how a prison can be anywhere—even this concrete slab of a city, this L.A., this one big tombstone; and her wild glee turned to anguish as she lowered her eyes and hugged herself, her hair coming part undone, her lips turning soft. Rosea said, "People can go crazy here, and I am crazy for you, José. That's the truth."

Joe let strands of Sherri's hair slide through his fingers. He wanted to stay calm when someone touched his skin; he didn't want to flinch from his past life; he didn't want his skin to burn from beatings or kisses to send electric shocks to his balls. He didn't want to feel as if he had been forced to pace the cement floor all night. He still dreamed of Brazil and of Sonia's last words to him. It had been years, but he couldn't forget. He needed someone to be patient with him, to love him in his foolishness, because the past was strapped under his tongue, and he couldn't bring himself to speak of it.

His boys looked foreign, doughy and soft, with a line of blond hair just in the middle of their heads and gray eyes, determined not to be blue or brown, but instead—indifferent. In a while, Sherri would wake up to go to work, and then they would wake up too and bawl until he could get them into the kitchen and stuff food into their little gummy mouths. Sherri had taught him how to make rice and potatoes and ground beef and hotdogs. Men in Brazil never cooked, and that was something else he had to get over. He thought of the child he wanted with Sonia—way in the back of his mind, but still. Jeffy and Keffy were like ghosts of his Brazilian child, filmy pale spirits of his past hope.

Yet they were his. Joe sat on the edge of the bed, took Jeffy's hand and stroked the curled fingers. The twins' faces looked puckered and peace-

ful. The breeze from the newly opened window ruffled their hair like
small warrior feathers. Jeffy's hand clamped around Joe's two fingers, like
a small handshake, *um apertozinho de mão.*

Sherri roused from her nap, but when she saw him sitting on the bed,
she shut her eyes hard and pushed the blanket down to her waist. Her
shirt was rumpled up, the soft flesh of her stomach exposed, with a red
streak across her skin from the elastic waistline of her panties.

"Home already?" she said. "Shit, what time is it?"

"I am always home at this hour." He grabbed her toe and wiggled it.
"Four o'clock. Time to bring you the car."

"My god, I'm late." She leaped out of bed, and the movement of the
mattress jostled the two kids awake. She darted into the shower and
shouted out instructions to him like a dictator. Meanwhile, the twins
squirmed and turned their heads to face each other. They blinked lazily,
their cheeks bright red. They made sucking sounds and slowly reached
for each other, gently scratching the sheet where their mother's sleeping body had been. The sound of the shower started to rouse them. Joe
cooed tenderly, but braced for the big bawl. "Hello, babees. Acordem,
dorminocos." They heard his voice and scowled.

Sherri burst back into the bedroom with a towel around her body,
hair dripping, and ordered him to change their diapers. Hearing their
mother's "I'm in a rush" voice, the twins rolled over on their bellies and
started to scream as they crawled around on the bed. Now not only did
Joe have to change their diapers, but he had to fight them, calmly; otherwise, everyone would be screaming. Joe got two diapers from the drawer
and set them on the bed. Then he grabbed one by the feet and pulled
him down. Jeffy ended up being first. He bawled loudly as Joe wrestled
the pins out of the wet cloth diaper. Jeffy had such fat legs and kicked
with powerful jabs. Joe shouted, "Que chato você é! When will you use
the toilet, eh?" and Sherri snapped back, "Don't swear at the babies." Joe
just kept wrestling with this little bull. Keffy, red faced, sat up in bed,
and cried softly with his red lower lip sticking out. "I don't understand,"
Joe hollered, "how they can be so upset with the idea of getting comfortable?" He finished Jeffy, tumbled him aside, and pulled down Keffy.

Keffy was more cooperative, and Jeffy had stopped crying for a bit as he sat near his brother and poked his fingers in Keffy's ear. Sherri was slipping on her shoes. "Don't let Jeffy poke him."

"For god's sake," Joe said, holding a diaper pin in his mouth, "I can watch my own sons." Finally the chore was done, and both of them crawled to the edge of the bed, flinging out their hands for their mother.

"Catch them," Sherri said breathlessly.

Joe lifted Jeffy up onto his hip, and the baby wailed again and flung his upper torso back in a screaming backbend. Joe jostled him a bit, and he tried to croon, to Ricky Ricardo him, but the kid didn't have a Latin bone in his body; rather, he had that dry scream of overfed boys. "Why do you go to work?" Joe argued with Sherri as Jeffy struggled in his arms. "If I could work full-time instead of coming home early, I could make enough money for both of us. How much money do we need?" But Sherri wouldn't listen; she was always so modern and such an expert, shouting over Jeffy's wails instructions about food, bedtime, and TV programs like Joe was a damn baby-sitter. Joe clenched his teeth, driven crazy by Jeffy's screams until he finally pitched his son on the bed. Jeffy landed face down against the mattress. Sherri stared incredulously as she jabbed on her earrings, "Joe! He'll break his neck!"

Jeffy sat up with a puffy face and stared at his father with quiet respect. Joe shook his finger at them. "Vou te ensinar como ser um homem! I'll teach you to be a man."

Sherri groaned as she put on mascara. "None of that Latin shit."

He didn't like when she blamed everything he did on being "a Latin," as she called it. He wanted to belong to this house, not be some damn foreigner. He took Sherri's wrist as she held onto her mascara and lifted the stick from her hand. The brush looked like a tiny insect.

"I want you tonight," Joe said, "I don't care how tired you are."

Sherri rolled her eyes. "Please. You don't know what it's like to work for hours—"

"I don't?"

"Well, OK, you work, but—" She fell silent and looked down at her fingers. "I'll be all greasy."

"That will be fun."

Sherri smiled and plucked the mascara from Joe. "Yeah, big talker."

When she left the house, there was a big brawl as usual as the boys waddled to the front door and cried. Joe put on his Brazilian records, his sweet bossa nova, his dear Carlos Antonio Jobim, oh *cantador* and father of love! Joe picked up both sons, held them on his hips, and started dancing, gliding around the floor. He could feel the movement of his hips rubbing against his sons' fat diapers. They gradually stopped bawling and listened. . . .

He thought of Rio, when after he closed up his newspaper stand, he'd take a shower and a nap, then he and the people who worked in the shops would go to small restaurants for a beer and perhaps a plate of grilled meat, rice, and black beans. Outside, the military police wandered about, and the sounds of rapid footsteps and the cries of loved ones being dragged down the street pierced the night, but inside no one could hear because a bit of bossa nova or a new electronic Tropicália tune with subversive lyrics was playing. The restaurant would be a bit dark, and the people would slip in and out of shadows and look at each other with frightening knowingness. They would get up from their tables, sometimes not even finished with their meal, and would start dancing as if it were the most natural thing in the world. We the lucky ones, they'd think to themselves as they moved around together in a strange kind of courtship. Men with white shirts and women with tank tops light enough to show the little knots of nipple—all undulated, catching a bit of blue or red light from outside, the color from their clothes sliding and disappearing into their warm skin. Crucifixes, *figas*, and gold hearts hung on small chains around their necks and rested in the soft, sweaty dent of their chests. People would dance close so as not to be frightened; they rubbed against each other, rubbed against each other's tired bodies, relieved, glad to live another day. Men smelled musky in their armpits, and the women had a saltier scent as their skirts opened around their legs. And the aroma of fried meat was everywhere. Glasses of beer clinked, and the people, who had for years just burst into conversation, a talent that indeed had saved many from absolute misery, now had to learn how to be quiet. The samba started from inside the hips, fueled by the fire of fear in their hearts, and demanded a Brazilianness, a Brazil that was at the core of all their troubles. This dance, more important than the national anthem, was a dance too beautiful to destroy, as the samba dreamers in their hope rubbed against each other just enough, not for sex, but to feel each other alive in the belly of Brazil, where the flame of the samba and its gentler brother the bossa nova was fueled by a desperate passion to survive.

Joe looked at his boys. Their soft faces were pallid and shell-like, their mouths passive and bowl shaped. Jobim's voice was in his background, in another room, from another time. But the twins grasped the sides of their father's bathrobe and worked the thick terrycloth with their fingers.

The day Joe was not sure he wanted finally came. Usually he made a point of leaving work before Rosea so he wouldn't have to face the "Do you want to go out for a drink?" question. But today he stood at the doorway of her office watching her hold in her contempt as she made reservations for Hollywood Celebrity Tours. Her legs barely fit under the desk, and with her large body trapped in her small office, she kept slamming her elbows into things. Her costume was a 1930s-style dress that pulled tight on her shoulders and grabbed at her ass. She heard Joe approach and whipped her chair around quickly. She looked intently at him. "You always seem sad."

Joe gave a little chuckle. "The day is finished. Finally."

"So am I, *meu bem*."

He trembled when he heard these words, *meu bem*, 'my dear.' The sight of her naturally tan skin made him burn inside. Down the hall, they heard the Mickey Rooney driver humming, then swinging out the back door.

"José?" she said with a soft Brazilian J. "We can go somewhere."

Joe sputtered out automatically, "I'm married."

"I know. You told me this morning that today is your wife's day off!" Rosea laughed, swiveled back and forth on her chair, those vulgar coconut knees a bit apart. "A beer, José. A beer. I'm not out to seduce you."

Really, he said, really he couldn't. It was Sherri's day off, fine, but he still had to go home. Besides, he reminded himself, Rosea looked like trouble. She was so beautiful — well, not really, but she had something about her. She could have been his soul mate, perhaps —

She got up and grabbed her purse. "A beer, José. Let's take my car." The way she said his name, Jzo-se, she was so deliciously demanding, and what was so bad about a beer anyway?

Rosea drove a ways to a bar called Nuestro Lugar, with a sign depicting a bandito with two guns drawn. She got out, drawing her skirt way up past her knees. Her feet swelled in her shoes, her hair hung down trashy-sloppy. Joe got out and followed her in. Rosea towered over the men. The pool balls smacked, and the men at the pool table puffed hard on their cigarettes, stared at her, and went back to their game.

The ones at the bar, their eyes as watery as mirrors, raised their glasses, *salud*, and Joe nodded. He didn't want to be here. The bar so dark, the hunched-over men so unhappy — when Rosea said "let's go for a beer," he thought she meant a botequim, an outdoor drinking place, not a place like this. He wondered if Americans needed to be so sad to drink. "This," Rosea said, "is a typical American bar, José."

José. The way she said it again. Jzo-se. She sat at a small table off to the side and shouted "Two on tap!" to the bartender who was leaning on the bar and running his hands over his mustache. The bartender slowly grabbed two mugs with one hand. Glasses not even refrigerated, not even cold. Maybe Joe should find a good bar next time.

Rosea became Miss Business, opened her purse and shuffled through the "stuff," dumping out the contents — women do this all the time when they are nervous around men; they take their purses and spill out their lipstick, coins, birth-control pills (oh, excuse me, you weren't supposed to see that). Well, Rosea was looking for her cigarettes, and Joe pulled out his pack, hit the open end against his finger, and one cigarette popped out halfway. He offered it to her.

"Oh yes, like in the movies," her voice rumbled. Then she leaned over and puckered her lips as she drew the cig out of the pack with her teeth.

Joe chuckled, a bit embarrassed, lit a cigarette for himself, then took his cigarette and lit hers with his lighted tip. "This is like the movies, too, né?"

Rosea grinned and took a few languid puffs, holding the cigarette between her forefinger and thumb. "Did you like how I got out my cigarette? Did you like that, José?"

"You smoke like a man," Joe said.

"So do you," Rosea slinked her eyes.

When the bartender brought the two beers, Joe started to pay, but found out that Rosea had a bar tab here.

They took a few sips. The beer was cold, but not cold enough.

"Who do you bring over here?" Joe said.

"I usually come here alone."

"Aren't you afraid of—" Joe motioned to the men who had gone back to their business of being lonely.

"Being attacked?" Rosea made a deadpan face, then threw her head back and laughed. "They should be afraid of me."

Joe let the beer run down his throat and waited until she finished laughing. "I would never be afraid of you. I have really been afraid. In my life. You would be easy to handle. You would be a relief."

Someone played Mexican music on the jukebox, the same kind he had heard when he had first come to America. He felt the crushing saudade again, almost overwhelming him; he longed now for a botequim. To relieve his tension, he said, "Someday we can go to Brazil and drink beers on the beach."

Joe expected an "oh, that's nice," but, instead, Rosea leaned forward and unleashed a passionate torrent of stories, how her mother had come from Brazil already a star and the terrible treatment she had gotten here. Her mother fell in love with a little man in bikini trunks who came to fix her pool, and this man became her mother's business manager, then her husband. Mr. Bikini Man stuck around long enough to produce little Rosea Socorro Katz, then he left, taking a lot of her mother's money. "Bam, the thief was outta my mother's life in less than a year."

Rosea had abandoned her beer now, and she was grabbing the sides of the table, holding on tight and looking strong enough to throw it to the other side of the room. She said, "I am stuck with the name Rosea Socorro Katz, named for that thief, and God knows where he is. Then this lousy town finished her off. You know how she died? Pills. I found

her dead the next day, still wearing the costume she wore on the *Jimmy*
Durante Show. She died looking like a parrot."

A few strands of hair stuck to her cheek. Rosea pulled the hair off her neck, then sighed angrily. She smashed out her cigarette in the ashtray, glared out at the bar, and fumed. Her lower lip pulled out slightly, half of it wet, the other dry with lipstick.

Joe wasn't sure what to say, if he should respond. He took another sip of beer and thought of Sherri, how he should be going home. He was about to say something when Rosea faced him again and leaned a bit forward so that her shoulders hunched. She went into another story, of how her mother went back to Brazil and said it was stunning with all these birds and dolphins, and how she had been planning to go back to live, but, oh no, never did. Rosea wanted to go to Brazil, but had never been. "Oh, it must be a lot better there than here. This country is shit. Look at this, José. Most whites would never come in this bar because bam, they'd get cut up. With knives. Cuchillos. Big old switch blades." Rosea slammed her fist into her hand. Bam. Then she took a deep breath and winked. "Does that scare you, Joe, the part about knives?"

Joe smirked. "No, there are worse things."

"Does this happen in Brazil, Joe? I mean, have you ever been deathly afraid? I bet people there are so mellow. So mellow. Jeez, I can hardly wait to get out of here. Well, how about you, Joe? Why did you come here? Do you think your lounge lizard uniform is going to be the end of your hassles? Do you know what's going to come next? They're going to eat you alive. OK, José, let's go to Brazil and drink beer by the beach, why not?"

Joe became a bit tired of her babble. He set the glass in front of him and wrapped his hands around it as if it were a neck. "Rosea, if you must know, America is my home now. Believe it or not, I ran away from a lot worse." He took a deep breath, didn't want to say more, but Rosea leaned over, so attentive, so open to him. She reached over and grabbed one of his hands.

"What, Joe? Ran away from what?"

Joe kept his head down because he couldn't look at her. He told her of the dictatorship, about the politics, about weak President Goulart, who was trying to be a communist like his inspiration, Fidel Castro, but got thrown out by the military. He told of how the tanks from Minas Gerais rolled into Rio and how everything was covered by a dark, evil cloud. Joe stared at the table; he could see the cracks in the old wood. It looked like a thick door; he looked closer as if he heard someone knocking on the other side. He went on, still with his eyes on the table. "Oh, it's not all beaches, Rosea. We had to be very careful of what we said. You could get killed. One journalist was tied to the back of a car, his mouth forced to bite the tailpipe, and was dragged until his guts burned—"

Joe stopped, his insides burning, too, and he took a big gulp of beer. He lowered the glass, felt a bit sick, closed his eyes, and leaned his forehead on his fist. He sat that way for a long time. He could hear the pool players' shoes shuffling around the table, their hard leather soles creaking the floorboards. He heard a couple of men mumbling secretly and scratching their heads. It was quiet, as if Rosea had left him.

He opened his eyes cautiously. Rosea gazed at him; she hadn't moved and still held his hand. "José," she whispered, "José."

Joe straightened up and smiled vaguely. "I am drunk on one beer, and I must go home. Americans are a bit bored with politics, I'm afraid."

"You're not boring me," she said, her face softened, "you couldn't bore me in a million years."

Joe nodded and drank the rest of his beer.

"José," she said, "can you dance? I don't mean cha-cha; I mean soft-music dance." Joe nodded slowly; he loved to dance, but it would be too much for him now, really.

Rosea snatched her purse. "Don't move," she said and rumbled through her perfumed junk. She pulled out a couple of dimes. "Stay there," she ordered, going over to the jukebox and popping in a few coins. Then she turned around and walked over to him, her arms hanging loose and open to the side. She held her hand out.

Joe eased himself up, not as drunk as he thought, just extremely tired at the moment. She pulled him up to her, and he tried to hold back, but he couldn't. He slipped his arm around her waist, and she placed one of her legs between his so that their hips moved together. It felt like water, both of them so in rhythm. She was so tall, his crotch hit her thigh. She bent her head down so that she would not seem towering. He buried his face into her hair and kept going deeper until he touched an earring with his nose. He brushed her hair away and saw the bones of her jaw, firm yet soft, and he stroked her cheek with his lips. "I'm married, Rosea," he said, "you know this."

"So?" she whispered in his ear. "I'm not after your wife."

This made Joe chuckle a bit.

Rosea gave a wide grin and held her mouth close to his. He felt himself getting hard and pulled away from her. She grabbed him by the back of his belt. "No you don't," she said, "I know exactly where we can go."

☾

"You know the Hollywood Hills?" Rosea said as he slipped into the car.

"I don't know much about this city, Rosea." He smoothed his sweaty brow with his thumb.

"I know more than I care to." She drove without saying much, only vaguely grinning to herself once in a while. He opened the window more and let the cool air blow on his ashamed face. He didn't want to look at her, but he glanced her way and saw her knees apart under the steering wheel.

"You need a bigger car."

"Yes, well . . ." Rosea smacked her lips, "if I ever get married and have a husband and kids, I'll get one of those big station wagons."

Joe knew she was trying to get to him. He shrugged his shoulders like nothing. "Well, of course, my car isn't—a station wagon, I don't think."

Rosea laughed deep in her throat as she drove up a hill. To one side was a large, empty lot surrounded by a tall chain-link fence. The tall eucalyptus swayed their spindly branches from side to side. She stopped next to a large gate locked with a chain and padlock.

"We're here." Rosea jumped out of the car and stood near the gate, hiked her dress up to her thighs, then leaned on the edge of the fence and pulled the gate back away from her. Joe watched as she wiggled her pelvis through the space between the gate and the fence, and finally she slipped through to the other side. She stood there, reached up under her dress and straightened her slip. "You coming?" she said. He'd be doomed if he followed her. He watched his hands pushing the gate out from the fence and heard his belt buckle scrape against the gate as his soft belly squeezed through. "You're strong," she whispered. He ended up on the other side of the gate with her. She smiled triumphantly, grabbed his hand, and led him up the hill.

Their footsteps crunched through the dry weeds and released a flurry of burrs and white fluff. Beer cans and the hard nut eucalyptus seed pods littered the ground. Joe looked at Rosea's face, her skin like the clay of earthen pots, dark whorls of hair falling around her ears.

Her voice seemed matter-of-fact as if she were giving him a tour. "These hills belong to Galaxy Studios, where my mother used to work. This part here was used for outdoor location shots. Quicky TV things. Caves had been dug into the hills, built up with chicken wire to make it look like rocks. Then the studios just left the sets here, and they got decrepit, bits of plaster breaking apart, and chunks just dangling from the chicken wire. Black widows build nests all inside these things. That's Hollywood's view of nature. If they don't like what's up there, they build it. They build trees all the time. Half a tennis court built down there, just half-a-one. They'd build the actors if they could. Then they could trash more humans than they do now."

Joe released her hand. "Don't talk of the movies. I have to talk of the movies all day."

"Of course." She took his head in both hands, like a trophy, and brought his face close. He started to say something, but it came out in Portuguese, and he couldn't speak in any other way now. He thought of the dangers around him, but when he felt Rosea's wet lips on his, he wrapped his arms around her and pulled her in. This was the end. The end. In the distance, he thought he heard someone shooting a gun. His mouth opened, and his tongue scraped her teeth. Her hands slipped between the ruffles and folds of his Ricky Ricardo shirt, unbuttoned it, and unfastened his belt buckle and zipper. A cool breeze hit his chest. He ran his hands up and down her skirt, silky and smooth, and he could feel the muscles of her thighs shifting, trying to keep her balance on the hill. He imagined men coming down a long hall, then finally jangling the lock to his prison cell, and he grew more excited. His hand went under her skirt, and he fumbled for those nylons women must wear. He captured the waistline and started to pull them down, and she helped them down the rest of the way, flinging them off. "You are not too cold?" Joe asked. "Not in a million years," she whispered as she opened her mouth for a kiss, then held his tongue fast with her teeth.

He stuck his fingers in the imaginary sand, and it felt spongy, and her moist hairs sent electrical shocks down his back. He held onto her, and it felt like someone was pushing him down. He grabbed onto her rump. Through the slit of his half-open eyes, he saw Rosea hovering over him. She pinned his arms out to the side by his wrists and straddled on top of him so that he was inside. She moved slowly up and down, and her cunt sucked him like a ripe mango. She slipped her hands away from his wrists, leaned over, and dug her fingers into his curls, then smiled and looked straight at him. Joe took a handful of her hair and stuffed it into his mouth to keep from crying out. The scent of eucalyptus mixed with her musk, and grass crackled next to his bare skin. Rosea dug her fingers into his mouth, removed her hair, and flung it up over her head so it hung like a curtain. As if hiding behind it, she lowered her breast to his lips. He drank her like the sweet coconut milk pouring from a gash made by a machete. At first, she tasted metallic like the blade, then the sweetness leaked into her tough brown fibers full of splendor and sand.

These women mate with man or beast and bear the result.
After giving birth, they keep the females and abandon all else.
I have heard that some abandoned boys are raised by wild
creatures and can be seen lying on their bellies on top of tree
limbs, dangling their sinewy legs and purring like jaguars.
Most of these boys perish while young, as none have the
natural dexterity to kill as quickly as do other jaguars, nor
the wit to build weapons.

—*Carta de Carlos Manoel Teixeira da Cunha a João Vicente*
Cardim da Almeida, O Ano 1641

Chapter 11

O Ano 1977

Jeffy and Keffy grabbed handfuls of sand and watched as it spilled
through their fingers. "Put it in your pail," Sherri called as she stood
near the water's edge. She needed to get out more and do things with
the twins on her day off; she hadn't been to Santa Monica in ages. Down
the beach, some teenagers ran splashing into the water, their jeans soggy
and wet. Their feet must have been freezing. One girl threw herself in—
in the rough surf, too—and as a large wave crashed against her face and
swept over her head, she scrambled back to shore, laughing as her friends
slapped her on the back, shouting, "Are you nuts?!" There might have
been a bit of a suicide try here, but it was too fun to stop now. Sherri

could tell these kids had cut school because she had done the same thing. After her twin sister died, she and her friends used to hang out at the beach where the broken-up pilings from an old road guard had tumbled down. Following a storm, they would sit on the half-buried pilings at the water's edge and wait for a big wave to come and wash them away, wondering if it would.

The clouds were gray and muscled. Jeffy and Keffy watched intently as the foam swirled onto the sand. Sherri laughed. They looked so cute in their matching seahorse pants and blue sweatshirts. She had wanted to dress them matching, even though Joe thought it was silly. She wondered if all husbands were like Joe, if all marriages were like hers. She wondered if dissatisfaction and boredom from day-in, day-out schedules were normal. OK, she didn't have the looks of a teenager anymore, and she had a thick waist — not too thick though. But she had had twins, don't forget. Were there any pretty women where Joe worked? She hated to admit that when she crawled into bed at night, with him already asleep, she sniffed his hair, then slipped under the covers and drew in the smell of his body, searching for the odor of another woman. But instead his sweat and the scent of coconut oil gave her a small nudge of desire, and she would plant a kiss at the base of his neck. She could do this only if he was asleep. Awake, he wouldn't let her touch him, and though he talked of sex constantly, he hated the feel of her hand. In his sleep, he called out another woman's name — Sonia — but he mumbled in Portuguese, rubbing his face against the pillow and pleading with someone to let him live. Someday Joe would say, "I want to leave you." In English. Someday he would curse the new land he'd been shipwrecked on. Someday she would curse herself for not being the "heart twin."

Her sister, Susan, was the heart twin.

On the last night of her life, Susan confided to Sherri that she was in love. Sherri looked at her twin sister's face, the mirror of her own improved reflection; but whereas Sherri was the aggressive head twin more like Jeffy, Susan was the heart twin, like Keffy. They shared a large bed with each other. Susan slid under the covers, her voice whispering with conspiracy, thick like plots. She spoke of how love felt like your body melting, like hot wax. She had a little book of poems, too, and showed

Sherri where she scrawled notes on the pages, *this one is good* and *oh so true!* Sherri answered with a smirk and a "Huh. Guys don't deserve us. Get over it."

The next day just as school let out, Susan stood forlornly under a palm tree and told Sherri she had broken up with her boyfriend. Sherri remembered how the hush of palms sounded like the rustling sheets of their large bed. Cars zoomed back and forth on the street. Susan looked up and spotted the guy of her heartbreak on the other side of the thoroughfare, with one of his friends, another guy, and they were laughing and jabbing each other with their elbows. Susan took a deep breath and darted into traffic. Cars screeched as one car hit her, sending her reeling sideways, and another car, trying to swerve, hit her with its headlamp and plowed into the side of another car. Her sister ended up on her knees, her head down on the ground, like someone in deep prayer. People rushed out of their cars, including a man whom everyone recognized as Bernardo Feliz, the crooner and Latin lover featured in the movie *Breathless in Granada*. He had black, rippled hair like the folds of an accordion. Bernardo lifted Susan and held onto her, weeping, "I'm so sorry, little one, my heart is broken," and he repeated it in his lovely Spanish. When he mourned, it was a song. Sherri looked up and saw a seagull heading out to sea, carrying away her other half, the part that knew the songs of love.

Now, on the beach, Sherri looked back and saw Jeffy holding his pail and pointing at the water. She looked around for Keffy, but couldn't see him. "Where's your brother?" Jeffy gave a blank stare and looked around. Sherri scanned the beach. In one direction, the older kids who had been playing in the water were heading up to the sidewalk, jostling against each other in a loud bundle. In the other direction, the sand stretched like sick skin, and in the distance a man jogged with a dog bouncing beside him. She swooped over to Jeffy and grabbed his arm. "Where's your brother?!"

Jeffy pointed weakly.

Sherri looked. Not there. "Where is he? Did he walk over there? Did he go swimming? Did he go swimming?"

Jeffy shrunk away and dropped his pail. Sherri grabbed his arm harder.
"Where is he?"

Jeffy struggled to pull away.

Sherri let go, almost pushing him in the sand. "You stay there! Stay there!" She ran into the water, and the waves hit her knees and thighs, a bit of an undertow sweeping her feet. "Keffy!" she screamed, "Keffy!" The sea answered with a horrible frothy grin. She clutched her head, I can't believe it. Her terrible luck—her heart that had been torn in half now ripped into fourths. There would be hardly any of it left. Keffy was so quiet, he probably wouldn't even call for help. He probably just stood there, with a pained expression like his father's, as he got swept away.

Sherri panicked, snatched Jeffy, and ran up and down the beach, calling. She ran toward a small sandy dune, thinking she'd find Keffy crouched on the other side and making a hole in the sand, but no, the sand was smooth, not even marred with footsteps. She clung onto Jeffy and ran on the hard wet sand at the edge of the surf. Jeffy began slipping down her hip. She shoved him back up to her waist; he was so damn heavy. The waves in the distance chopped like scissors cutting the water, and the clouds curled into ashy fists. She could feel herself weeping, but her throat was raw as if she had been screaming. Jeffy looked silently beyond her shoulder. A jogger, a young man with a UCLA T-shirt, came toward her, and she ran over to him. "Please, have you seen my son?"

"What does he look like?" He seemed unfazed.

"Well he's blond, about—" then she snatched Jeffy's face, rumpling up his cheeks, and turned his head toward the man. "My son looks like him. Twins!" Jeffy's gray eyes grew large and smoky from the overcast.

The man shook his head. "I'll keep an eye out," he said. "You should call the police." And he continued on.

She turned and screamed at his snotty cold back. "The police! What in the hell would the police do? The police can't do shit! Fuck you!"

Again Sherri looked around desperately, then spotted two skateboarders on the sidewalk. She ran up to them, and they stopped with a flip of their boards. "Have you seen my son?"

"What does he look like?"

Why do people ask that? Do people see so many lost children that one needs a description of a certain one? She grabbed Jeffy's face again. "Like this." They shrugged sorry and scooted away.

She ran down to the shore again, up and down, until Jeffy and her grief became so heavy she dropped him and collapsed crying. She could feel Jeffy press his nose against her shoulder. God, did he see his brother washed away? Her hands dug down to the damp sand, and she could hear Jeffy crying, but it sounded as far away as her own on that busy street so long ago.

She lifted her eyes and saw among the waves the top of a dark head. "Oh my god!" she panicked, but just as she got up, a boy glided in with the waves and let the water scoot him into the sand. He got up and brushed off the sand on his belly; he had been body surfing. His black hair with bits of green spilled down the back of his thick neck, as if he had feathers. His lips were pursed like a clam; his body was thick, and his legs thin and bow-legged. Her heart fell in dismay when she realized the boy was someone else. Still, she managed to ask: "Have you seen a small boy? Blond?" The boy squinted at her with his black bean eyes, then he pointed. Sherri turned and saw an old man wearing a white caftan with blue stripes. The wind blew his caftan back, and he seemed to be floating. She ran toward him, and Keffy appeared in the middle of the puff of fabric, holding the old man's hand and toddling alongside. Sherri let out a shriek, ran and scooped up her son. She pressed him against her and cried into the folds of his soft neck, then shook him a little, "Where have you been? Why did you run away?"

Keffy whimpered. She carried him over and set him next to Jeffy. Oh, the comfort of it—twins! The salt and pepper shakers, the heart twin and the head twin, the light and dark, the love and the hate. She knelt before them and gave them each a kiss on both cheeks the way Joe did, both meticulously equal, both with a sweet pain, then snatched them up together and hugged them fiercely.

She looked around for the old man. He was walking toward the strange boy who had been swimming and held open a towel for him. The strange boy wrapped the towel around himself and hopped up and down.

The old man turned to her and smiled. He had bony eye sockets and

two prominent folds separating his cheeks from his mouth. "I was walking along," he said, "and your boy followed me. You were nearby, but
the next minute you were gone."

Sherri looked out at the sea. "I almost died. You better believe it."

The old man looked at the two boys. "As Isaiah said, a twin always has
the mirror of the other in his own reflection. Eventually they find each
other."

"It was you, sir, who found him." She held her sons on either side of
her. "Don't you dare go near the water," she said to them. "Don't even
move. Stay with me."

The old man sat down, and she sat down next to him. The twins stayed
close to her and smeared their hands over the sand. He mumbled. Sherri
turned to him. "Don't tell me you speak a foreign language, too."

He turned and smiled again. "We all speak a foreign language." The
strange boy flung off his towel and trotted around them, flapping his
arms like a bird. It was hard to guess his age. He was fragile like a small
child but led the twins to play as if he were a little older.

The old man chuckled. "He's called Birdboy. He can't speak. His vocal
cords are deformed, but he hears fine."

"Goes to school?"

The man shrugged. "His adoptive father is a college professor," he said
simply.

Jeffy and Keffy got up and started flapping their hands and mewling,
imitating the Birdboy. She wanted to snatch them back, but the man
touched her wrist and told her to let them go, they'd be fine. He wrapped
his arms around his knees and sat watching the roaring ocean. His thin
skin floated on the thick veins of his hands.

Joe doesn't know she almost lost their son, and now she's here, talking to a crazy old man. She'll tell him when he comes home; he won't
know how serious it all was. He'll only say that this was one tough day.

She started talking to the old man; she couldn't help herself because
she hardly had anyone to talk to. She told the old man about her boring
restaurant job and how her kids were everything to her and how she had
wanted kids since Day One and how anyone else would have gotten an
abortion, but oh no, not her. She told him about her sister, Susan, being

in love and how love killed her and how the whole street wept when they saw the accident. Sherri felt guilty that everyone wept but her, and how she seemed like just some high school student waiting for the traffic light to change. "But," Sherri insisted, "sometimes a person is so sad they can't even speak. I don't know if you know. . . ." She mused as she smoothed her hair back and stroked herself on her cheek. She mentioned a bit about Joe, that she was married, and he was nice, she guessed, but sometimes she was not so sure. . . .

Suddenly she felt exhausted, with almost losing Keffy and the confusion of an attentive grown-up here beside her. She lowered her head to her knees. She felt his hand go up and down her back. It was warm and steady, and though he trembled, his hand did not. She couldn't think of what to say. She raised her head, keeping her eyes closed. If she had been the heart twin, she would have burst into tears.

She heard the three children's voices behind her and felt safe. She opened her eyes to look at him, and he was shivering in the cold, his thin lips like a strip of bluish rubber.

"Are you cold, sir? Do you have a ride?"

"No. I took a bus here."

"I did, too. My husband took the car to work, and I took a bus here. If you come home with me, he can take you home when he brings back the car," Sherri said. "I can make you a hot lunch."

"Oh, please," the man waved his hand, "that's fine."

"Yeah, but you must be cold. That's not fun."

She got up and took his thin hand, helping him to his feet. They walked along, and the boys followed, frisking and squawking together like gulls.

She learned that the old man's name was Melvinor. Melvinor never quite stopped shivering, even though she gave him one of Joe's sweatshirts to wear. He nodded off as he finished lunch. She got up and started to clear the table. "Would you like a nap? I've got a pretty good bed." Melvinor smiled quietly to himself, but not leering like most men. They left the kids at the kitchen table, and she took the man to her bedroom and

watched as he slipped under the covers and straightened his long caftan
around his body. "Why do you wear that hippy thing?" she said.

His tired eyes peered up. "If I had dressed sensibly, I wouldn't be in
your bed now."

Sherri smiled and backed away. She didn't know what to think, his
sinking into the warm covers like that. If he were younger, she'd almost
be tempted to crawl in with him, but his old body, or the thought of his
old body, kept her backing away toward the door, waving her fingers,
whispering a gentle "sweet dreams."

She put all the boys into the twins' room, and they crashed almost
immediately. She covered each with a small child's blanket. Bits of sand
grit still clung to their hands. The house was quiet. She went back to the
kitchen and got herself a mug of tea, then curled up on the couch. Joe
would be home in an hour, and then she'd have to roust the old man,
and Joe would take him home. It was her day off, and there was no rush.
The old man seemed like a miracle, someone put there by someone else:
a movie director, God, someone. She never really liked L.A., but things
happened to her just in time to keep her life moving, to keep the movie
exciting, to keep the characters alive so they'd be ready for the next twist
of fate. She set her tea down on the coffee table, stretched out on the
couch, closed her eyes and listened to the rare sound of soft, contented
breathing—it was like music in her lonely house.

Sherri woke up with Joe nudging her aside. He sat on the edge of the
couch and passed his hand up and down her leg, almost pressing down,
as if sculpting her. He stared at her a bit strangely, his face scrunched
and dark. Then he passed a hand down one of her arms, took her hand,
examined it, passed his lips lightly over her palm, then turned her hand
over and kissed the knuckles. He leaned over and kissed her on the cheek,
then on the mouth. He smelled like grass.

Sherri pulled back to get a better look at him.

"Why aren't you in the bed?" he said.

"Because someone else is sleeping there."

"Who?"

"A man, but don't worry—"

He sat up, gave her almost a smirk, then leaned his elbows on his knees and smoothed his hair. He seemed to be laughing to himself.

Sherri reached over and rubbed his shoulder. "He's old, Joe. Come on. You can have a duel over me, OK?"

Joe's face closed as if thinking of something else. He looked at the floor and pushed a toy matchbox car with his foot. She could see his shoulders rolling, trying to shrug off some burden. "Joe," she said again, "this man saved Keffy's life."

Joe turned toward her, and his eyes narrowed.

"I was at the beach, and I lost Keffy. The old man—"

Then Sherri felt the pain all over again. She covered her eyes with her arm and began sobbing. She wailed with fatigue, with loneliness, with the longing for her sister, how someone could die for love at that young age. Keffy would suffer being so sensitive in such a world. She felt Joe's hands cupping her face, the way he did with his boys. He moved closer to her, so close his dark eyes melted together, and he kissed her on the mouth. "I'm sorry," he said, then kissed her again. "I'm sorry," he said again, then kissed and sorried and kissed and kissed and said, "Sorry, meu bem, sorry." Sherri took a deep breath and pushed him away. He could be so overwhelming.

Just then they heard footsteps coming into the living room. They sat up and saw Birdboy, yawning from his nap. His hair was all grizzled, and he scratched the florescent green flecks on the back of his neck.

Joe's eyes widened. "Who is that?"

"It's someone the old man"—she reached over and picked a burr from his shirt—"is taking care of." She rolled the burr between her fingers. "Where were you today?"

Joe saw the burr in her fingers. He got up abruptly, brushed himself off, then went into the babies' room. Sherri sat up. Grass and burrs stuck to the cushion where he had sat. She brushed them off carefully, fearfully. The burrs floated to the ground and hid in the carpet. She tried to picture a vanload of laughing tourists covered with grass, fresh from a picnic on the lawn of the L.A. County Museum, picking the stuff from their hair. Perhaps the lawn had a few weeds, a few flecks of carelessness. Lazy gardeners, but she couldn't imagine it; she just couldn't imagine starchy tourists being crazy like that. Maybe it's something with Joe and this Sonia, but only a country hick would do it in the weeds — maybe.

She collected the evidence in the palm of her hand. She knew it was time to wake up the old man, the man she had found in the sand, the man who had saved Keffy's life and, in a sense, was going to save her life, too.

Chapter 12

O Ano 1952

"Does our Carmen Socorro seem a little squeezed out? Has the "punch" gone out of our fruit punch? Maybe a vacation in the tropics is the order of the day."

Carmen read this in *Photoplay* and broke down in tears, realizing how tender her career had become. She had been at the top, her songs filling the movie houses with happiness, pouring out of scratchy records with such *carinhoso*, the kicky *choros*, the hip-whacking *batuques*, the popular sambas, the romantic boleros. The fans used to come to her with autograph books open like holy missals. She was photographed in the bathtub. Brazilian men proposed to her with flowers even though they were

married. Her husband, the swimming-pool repairman, became her manager and had a way of cooing out bookings and swell contracts from the
toughest cookies. He was Jewish, and at that time people wouldn't trust
the wooden-nickel types who were good with money, so he changed his
name from Moses Katz to Moises Gato. Moises was savvy about what the
public liked — some flame, some flirtation, and some cha-cha. He wore
his wavy hair like the Cuban singer Pico "Toto" Garcia and grew a little
mustache and sported a purple florescent dinner jacket with black velvet
lapels. He learned to puff Tiparillos like a hidalgo and told witty jokes
in bad Spanish that made Carmen laugh.

But this didn't make her laugh: he skimmed money off the top of her
movie contracts, accepting kickbacks and committing other monetary
hanky-panky. Then he fathered Rosea, which scarred Carmen's sexy virginal allure that the studio had created; in those days, famous hens had
to hide their chicks. Look what happened to the Swedish actress Inga
Johanssen when she had her baby! What did Carmen have now but a
wooden-nickle contract, a baby, and a crook for a husband?

But ah, Rosea was born to avenge him; he saw his own flesh and blood
— with a fierce cry and a full set of teeth at three months old — ready
to spoil the fun. The cologne that clung to his skin evaporated, and the
poisonous chlorine swimming-pool smell oozed through his pores. He
doffed his Latin identity, returned to being called Moses Katz, gathered
up his pool-cleaning equipment, and left for Florida to swindle little old
ladies from Manhattan.

With the baby and the contract scandal, the Brazilian millionaires went
back to their wives. The new movies were less sparkling, more cynical
about love. Her Brazilian gardeners mournfully looked on, too overwhelmed with her celebrity to approach her. Carmen's spirit needed re-
kindling, and she decided to go back to Brazil, not to Rio, where her
singing career had started, but to where she was born — the Amazon.
She wanted to curl up in the big maternal arms, press against the large
jackfruit-shaped breasts of women who smelled like balsam and genipapo dye, women who would feed her boiled cassava and fish. Her spirit
was sad and broken, and she wanted to go home.

On the deck of the ocean liner, Carmen waved farewell to her eight-year-old daughter. Rosea stood there, glaring, so tall for her age and so resolute, unsettled and bursting at the seams of childhood. Carmen thought, she seems more Amazonian than I, which made it hard for Rosea, who was supposed to hide herself in the concrete kingdom of Hollywood. Curly serpentine fell around Rosea as the ship pulled away from the harbor. She grabbed a handful and tore the bunch in two, as if snapping the fragile veins that held them together. Carmen whispered, "Te amo muitíssimo, minha filha," as the strip of water widened between herself and her daughter. Then she made a deep, almost impossible wish.

The ocean liner stopped at Belém, then Carmen took a riverboat to Manaus and a smaller riverboat to Carvajal, a village closest to where the Amazons were said to be. As the ship pulled into Carvajal, small boys climbed up coconut trees and waved as her boat came in. Did they know she was a movie star, or were they just being friendly? People waited on the pier for the riverboat, and as soon as a crewman threw a hitch over the edge to tie the boat to the dock, people clamored onboard, wanting to carry her luggage. Two bigger boys wrestled their way through the crowd and grabbed her trunk, nudging others who were trying to snatch the cargo away. They hauled the trunk off the boat and hurried into the village. She chased after them, calling in Portuguese. The two young men, slim, with a trace of rib cage showing, turned, "Fique tranqüila, senhora," and motioned for her to follow them. One boy had long blond hair like a lion and dark skin. Another had black, frizzy boof hair like Carlos, the drummer in her band. Carmen slowed down, adjusted her sunglasses, so mysterious and taciturn, and felt alone in her foreignness. She wondered why she had even brought her silver turban with the bluebird print, her green-and-yellow turban tied up with red plastic cherries, her red- and white-striped blouse with Cuban ruffles and matching ruffle split skirt, and the same-style Cuban garb in hot pink. She had been in Hollywood for so long she had forgotten that other Brazilians wore normal clothes.

The two boys hauled the trunk to a small house made of brick and plaster and placed it on the porch next to the pool table. Then they stood on either side of the trunk, looked earnestly at her, and clasped their hands in front so that one hand remained cupped like an offering bowl.

Carmen tipped them both—an unwittingly large tip given the pleasant
lift of their eyebrows. Then she looked around. What was this, a hotel?
Someone's house? A refrigerator and a sign with a beer bottle that said
"Brahma" probably made this the town botequim. From the doorway,
the two boys called into the dark living room. Carmen heard someone in
zoris flop-flopping out to the porch. A man emerged, scratching underneath a T-shirt that hung on his bony shoulders. He saw her and grinned
with a rubberlike pleasant smile, motioning for the two boys to put the
trunk next to the wall. "Quer um quarto?" the man asked.

"No room yet," Carmen answered in Portuguese. "First I need to hire
a guide with a small boat to take me up an igarapé" (for maybe her relatives would let her stay with them!).

With a wad of American dollars, she hired a man named Chico who
had a canoe. Carmen changed from her linen and silk traveling clothes
into a two-piece floral swimsuit, a terry-cloth cover-up, and sunglasses
with zebra-striped frames. She slathered her body with suntan lotion and
insect repellant, then stuffed a bottle of clean water and some napkins
in a straw bag, and headed down to the pier where Chico waited.

Chico stood up and stroked the water with a long oar. His amazingly
stiff hair looked combed out with wet concrete. He wore baggy shorts
and a wrinkled but clean short-sleeved shirt. Carmen stretched out her
legs and fondled her long braid, at last free from turbans. Though her
roots were in the Amazon, everything here appeared exotic: an explosion
of blue araras overhead; a tree covered with yellow parakeets; the current of the stream splitting, then converging around half-immersed trees;
gray *botos* with their dorsal fins rippling like silk scarves under the water.

Carmen sat facing Chico and gazed at the warm, rolling muscles of his
shoulders as he pushed the oar through the water. The group of charms
dangling from a string around his neck nestled in the black curls of his
chest. She could do with someone like him. "Pra onde você vai?" Chico
asked. Carmen said she was going to a village where the Amazons were
supposed to be, where perhaps she had family. The boatman stopped
paddling, sat down, and placed the oar beside him. "Ah não. De jeito
nenhum." He would not go farther.

Carmen became incensed. "What do you mean 'ah não'? I paid you a lot of money. More than you make a year. You don't have to visit them with me, just wait on the shore."

"Ah não, senhora," he announced. "Nem mesmo o homem mais machão arriscaría uma lança entre os olhos." Not even the manliest man would risk getting a spear between the eyes.

"Jesus," Carmen said, ready for a Hollywood tantrum, "they're my family, for god's sake. I'm part Amazon, don't you realize that! You're not afraid of *me* are you?"

But the boatman squinted, his eyes tight with refusal, and stroked the amulets on his neck, passing his thumb over the figa. The boat drifted to the side and slid into the duckweed.

"What the" — Carmen looked around. The boatman sat there with his arms crossed in a snit.

Furious, Carmen grabbed the oar and pushed herself into the middle of the igarapé again. The oar was long, so she held it awkwardly at midlength. The boatman shouted at her as he hung onto the sides of the wavering skiff. "Cuidado! Cuidado! Be careful!" The boat knocked against something. He tried reaching for the oar, but Carmen pulled the oar through the water, and again the boat rocked, then floated downstream.

"Olha ali!" he pointed to splashing ahead. And there they were.

The Amazons waded waist deep, facing away from the boat. The ends of their long hair dimpled the surface of the water. "Mulheres selvagens," the boatman hissed, "e eu não vou mais longe."

"Fine, don't go farther. Stay here then." Carmen slipped off her terry-cloth swim robe and stuffed it into her straw bag. Her resoluteness made Chico nervous.

"Espera aí," he said as he grabbed the oar, "ao menos, vamos esconder." He steered the boat to the shore under a hanging thicket to hide. "No swim," he warned.

She kept on her sunglasses, stretched her leg out, and put her toes (with their red nail polish) into the water.

He had a fit, calling her crazy, holding out his hand and counting the dangers of the river on his fingers. "One, a crocodile! Two, anacondas!

Three, piranhas! Four, *candiru*, a little bug that will make it so hard to pee-pee you will pray to the devil! Five, the devil herself!" and he motioned toward the women.

"Don't worry," Carmen waved him off, "I know this water." She held onto a low branch overhead, lifted herself up, swung over, and plunged into the water, swimming toward the half-submerged women.

She was still wearing the sunglasses with large navy-blue lenses and zebra-striped frames. She peered over the frames and saw the igarapé was not as dark as she thought, and she placed the glasses on top of her head. Her braid floated behind her like a strange tail. She breaststroked silently except for a little plop-splash. At first, the Amazons walked deeper into the river as their heavy breasts sank and their hair floated on top of the water like weeds. Then they heard, turned around slowly, and faced her.

As Carmen swam closer, the women started to shift, a couple of them eyed one another. Gradually, one swam to the shore and climbed up a slimy trail; then another scrambled up the reddish-brown mud, and another and another.

Carmen began swimming a faster breaststroke and cried, "Wait! Espera aí!" but their enormous bodies slipped into the underbrush. By the time Carmen reached their bathing spot, the branches had closed behind them. She swam to the bank and clamored onto the shore, the soft mud oozing between her toes. She tugged at the underwire of the floral top of her two piece, straightened the zebra-framed sunglasses on top of her head, and looked around. A small wet drop landed on her shoulder. Suddenly, her feet were covered with evil flicks of fiery pain. She looked down and saw tiny, miserable ants crawling up her feet and ankles. She bolted to the river and dived in. The pain shot up her legs, and she kicked the water, calling out her name. "Socorro! Help!" She called for the boatman, but he didn't answer. If piranhas were to attack, it would be an improvement over the ant burns.

Carmen looked back to the shore and saw a woman standing in waist-high brush; the sun filtered through the trees, splashing directly overhead and bathing half the woman's body in light, the other half remaining in shadow. Carmen treaded water and gazed at her. This was the time for the rendezvous, the contract, the meeting of warriors, the clasping of two worlds. She wondered if the Amazons thought her too Amer icanized. She slowly raised her hand out of the water and above her head. "Hi!"

The warrior's bronze shoulder rotated, and Carmen called out again. "It's me! I've come home! You recognize!" She clenched her fist to show her power. She shot back aways, then swam forward again. The woman slowly undulated her arm. Then Carmen saw her holding a spear and screamed, "Don't!" and ducked. Underwater, the mud and tentacles of roots and floating pieces of old animal hide swirled. Something thumped in the water, and Carmen surged up for air. The wooden shaft of a spear stuck out forty-five degrees from the surface of the water. Carmen grabbed and pulled at the shaft, but the spear stayed rigidly in place as if it had grown there. The woman disappeared. Carmen, trembling even in the warm water, let her hands slip from the spear. Sadly she made her way back to the canoe. Her feet burned anew.

When Carmen reached the skiff, she found her boatman slumped over in his seat, sitting in his own blood. The warriors had shot an arrow through him; the shaft grew out of his back, and the point had busted through his soft stomach. His shirt was nothing but a bloody red paste. Too stunned, as when a disaster leaves you acting in a bit of a fog, Carmen climbed into the canoe and waded in the man's blood. She sat facing the prow, grabbed the oar in the middle, and with long mournful strokes took her faithful boatman back to his village.

The pier was empty. She wanted to show someone the dead boatman, but she wanted it to be the right person. She made her way back to the botequim where she had stored her trunk and to her horror found men wearing her turbans as they played pool. One leaned over to pop the cue ball, and the cluster of cherries dangled in front of his eyes. "Take that off!" she screamed. The man laughed and pushed the cherries away from his face with a cue stick. Dazed, Carmen wandered outside the botequim and collapsed on the bench against the wall. Two small girls ambled past her, the Cuban-style costumes floating on their small bodies, the tops tied to their torsos with shoelaces and the flounced skirts dragging in the dust. Carmen let out a cry and patted her forehead as if she would faint. A man leading a donkey by a rope shouted his greeting to the pool players and tethered his beast to the foot of the bench Carmen was sitting on. The donkey, a basket strapped on either side of its belly, wore her loop earrings snapped onto the tips of its ears.

Carmen put her face into her hands and wailed. The ant bites burned, and she looked down to see thick red welts running from her feet to her knees. That wasn't the worst. She worked in her head how she would explain to Chico's family in her tenderest Portuguese. "He was a hero who died for my sins. Ele era um herói que morreu por meus pecados. My sin of too much pride. Orgulho demais. I'm such a miserable movie star!" She cried so loud that the turbaned men came over and stared. The man with the donkey cried, "Que é isso?" The small girls in the Cuban costumes made their way back to her, tripping on the ruffled skirts. The donkey shook its head, and one earring flew off. This was a jungle joke, a fantasy, a horrible dream, the Amazonianized Hollywood of a pathetic movie created by a director with the DTs!

Then she heard the voice of the botequim owner. "Cadê Chico?"

Carmen lifted her exhausted head. "Murdered. I brought him back to the pier."

He stepped back, not believing. "Foi assassinado? Como?"

Carmen shrugged.

The small Catholic crowd crossed themselves with the flutter of hands.

"Como? Quem o assassinou?"

"The Amazons of course. With an arrow."

Ah! All at once the old man started chewing her out: "How dangerous! The Amazons, those cold-blooded women! Why would anyone go there except a stupid American?" He paced and waved his hands at her. "You are irresponsible! You killed him, you know that! What will I tell his wife? With six kids! Six!" The botequim owner screamed, "Go! Take your things and go home! We don't want you here! You are not one of us!"

Carmen stood up shakily and huddled in her swimrobe. Of course, that's the problem. "Keep the damn trunk," she sighed, "I'll just get on some dry clothes."

Carmen sat on the pier with her straw bag and what was left of her clothes and waited for the next riverboat.

Chico's canoe had been cleaned and was now upside down and drying on the pier. She wondered if his family knew already. The six kids would be crying. A small boy came up to her and offered her a banana leaf of cooked cassava. She waved it away. She heard the boy say something to her, rustle the banana leaf, and come forward again. She couldn't look at him and turned her head. Just a way down from the pier, she saw the two little girls wearing her fantasias and playing along the shore of the river. The Cuban ruffled blouses and skirts rustled among the reeds, stirring the muddy brown water, and the girls sang softly to themselves a tune Carmen recognized.

Carmen never admitted to Rosea that the journey was a disaster. She convinced herself that she just decided to stay in Hollywood because it was more civilized anyway. She ended up planting magnificent young trees and vines and bushes and flowers in her garden, and from mustached sea merchants ordered tropical birds and monkeys to add them to the backyard as well so that it would be the Brazil that would love her in spite of her foolishness. She told Rosea that Brazil was still as beautiful as when God first created it.

VON ZONNEVELT: These women seem to be absent of love. They are inhuman and hard, and one would hardly believe they have souls.

DA CUNHA: On the contrary, these women can suffer heartbreak that would render the most fervent poet useless. I saw a woman who, against the orders of her tribe, fell in love with a sugar planter. This woman went mad, first killing her horse with her spear, then piercing her flesh with sticks; shunning the balsam that would have helped her wounds, she chose to bleed to death.

VON ZONNEVELT: But do they believe in the afterlife?

DA CUNHA: It seems apparent that they do. The dead are bound with hide and twine and are brought to the river where the current rushes forth. The women mourners place the body in the water, where it heads toward a waterfall, and it is hoped, toward the sea, where it is said that a great fish meets them and carries their soul away.

—*Diálogo entre Carlos Manoel Teixeira da Cunha e o recém-chegado pastor holandês Pater Von Zonnevelt* (Dialogue between Carlos Manoel Teixeira da Cunha and the recently arrived Dutch pastor Peter Von Zonnevelt), *O Ano* 1642

Chapter 13

O Ano 1977

Among the many quizzical treasures Carmen brought from Brazil was a *carranca*, a devilish statue carved from a small hollow log. A carranca's face is carved so that the knife slashes and gouges form coils of hair, the wide toothy red mouth, and upslanted evil eyes. Nowadays people would think Carmen ripped off the figure from Mann's Chinese Theatre. Carmen said that in some Brazilian rivers these weird dragons were strapped to prows of large boats to keep away bad spirits. She put one of these statues in their hallway facing the door, like a guard dog to woof away malevolence from the house. Then she took to her room and stayed there for a year, leaving Rosea, a human carranca, large and fierce, to wander through the jungle of an empty house filled with wails, solitude, and grieving for the unspoken that had happened in Brazil.

"What was your mother like?" people would ask Rosea later.

Rosea barked: "How in the hell did you know Carmen was supposed to have a daughter? That was supposed to be a big-ass movie-industry secret. My mother was supposed to be a virgin. How else was she going to attract Gene Kelly?!"

Rosea didn't tell them how she watched as her mother sat at the table for hours and traced coffee stains on the tablecloth. Sometimes, to Rosea, Carmen was no more than a hand clutching the door or bare feet with red toenails. Sometimes she had a strange stare, as if her boat had sunk and spilled precious cargo that now floated in the water, cradled among the legs of mangrove trees.

Sometimes people would shake their heads and tut-tut, "That must have been *some* trip to Brazil."

"I wouldn't know, I wasn't there, now was I?" Rosea sneered. "I wasn't *supposed* to know."

Sometimes Carmen emerged from her room excited, wearing a formal dress (like the kind they wear for the Academy Awards), to tell Rosea that soon they would be going back to Brazil, where they would be free to be a family, out in the open, and drink beer with relatives and listen to soccer on the radio. "Rosea, you could even swim out to sea as far as you please because dolphins would bring you back to shore." Carmen called them *botos*. She said botos knew the sea like the backs of their fins. Botos were our brothers that cared for us. Botos, at night, would turn into men to meet ladies, then by morning return to the sea.

And so the botos came to visit Carmen for a while. The appeared as men who came in droves to look up at her sitting on the veranda in her underwear, greeting the world with luscious half-songs. They hung jewelry and love letters on the branches of the rubber plant next to the front entrance. They were foolish men like Mickey Rooney and Hanson Dulper, who played squirts in the movies and were now child-men running after fading stars. When they saw Rosea baring her teeth like the American artifact she was, they drew back and exclaimed, "Who in the hell is this! Where did you get *her*?"

After a while, after Carmen's pills and shock treatments, the men gradually shrugged their dorsal fins and went back into the sea. Then Carmen would lay on her stomach lengthwise on the railing, like a jaguar resting on a branch, one foot on the veranda, the other hanging over the edge, and scream that she hated Hollywood and that the best thing that could happen would be for an earthquake to shatter the city into pieces so the ocean could wash it away. "Não passa de uma grande mentira! It's nothing but a big fat lie! It's nothing but a bunch of plastic bananas!"

One day Carmen burst back into life. She emerged from her madness and decided, "No more creaking around the house! It is time for a come-back!" She decided she would plant her garden, turning a Hollywood ho-hum backyard into somewhere she could live.

Carmen ordered her gardeners to cover the mountain with banana trees, palm trees, coconut trees, and *pau brasil* with its upright reddish-brown trunk and its woody dark-brown berries; rubber trees with rough, pale-green bark and yellowish-white flowers that bloom in the summer; trees that produced guava with its pink pulp and pebbly seeds; and small vines that would spread over the ground and climb up the brick wall. Carmen told her gardeners, "Release the monkeys I have ordered from Brazil, and the capuchins and the howlers and the araras: the red ones with turquoise wings, the blue ones with golden bellies, and the green ones with aqua tails." The men released the animals, and Carmen cried for joy that now her world was like when God first made Brazil.

The only men Carmen had after all the other men left were the Brazilian gardeners she'd entertain after they finished working. The men sat awkwardly on her fake–jaguar fur couch. They drank beer in silence — she was a movie star, and they were not. Rosea slipped behind the door, so she could only see their slight movements and hear their lonely sips of beer as her mother spoke to them: "Você sente saudades? Do you feel homesick? Why are you here in America? Are you here for love or money?" Then her mother would kiss them one by one. Rosea could see their sunburned faces nestled in her mother's shoulders, their warm, heavy-lidded eyes closed, their lashes shiny with tears.

Only years later, when Carmen died after appearing on the *Jimmy Durante Show*, did she return to Brazil, her turban turning into a whirlwind, and blowing across the seas. Rosea found her mother crashed on the floor and cradled in the puff of her yellow-and-green satin skirt and starched petticoat. The studio took the body away and didn't tell Rosea the funeral was in Rio because there was nothing left to bury but a dream.

Just after dusk Rosea drove alone up De la Gente Drive, then turned on San Fermin to her mother's old house, in spite of what Joe said about it being forbidden. She made herself stare beyond the iron gate. The veranda was still there, the one where her mother had gazed beyond the hills, where Rosea had stood looking up, raising both hands, and getting nothing but silence and an Amazonian spear through the heart. Rosea continued driving up the hill alongside the stone wall, a shallow token of protection, a laughing cinch to climb over. She drove past the houses, past the spying eyes of Neighborhood Watch groups and pudgy-faced security guards, past, past, until there was nothing but the natural scrub of hills on one side of the road and the garden on the other.

Rosea parked the car near the wall and turned off the engine. The night was grasping the city in its fist. The last pink cloud had long since folded into darkness. She quietly slipped out of the car and stepped onto the hood. The metal popped. She placed two hands carefully on the wall, hoisted herself up, then vaulted to the other side.

At first, her eyes were not used to the dark. She felt her way among the trees, grabbing a low-lying branch, then another. She snapped off branches furiously, tossing them to the side, impatient with the idiocy of the way it was, the hodgepodge of confusion, American plants and tropical ones, oak trees with palms, blue jays battling disoriented parakeets that kept flying into the madrone bushes, spearing their little yellow bodies on the twisted red branches. Hell, look at this! The dried-up bromeliads clung into the crooks of branches, their roots penetrating the trunks down to the tingle, planted by Brazilian gardeners who eventually disappeared into Carmen's room.

The imaginary odors came back to Rosea: leaves that smelled like her mother's perfume and coffee and palm oil and oranges, sandalwood, carnauba wax, coconut. The house down the hill was lit by floodlights, and

Rosea remembered the pearl-shaped pool that glowed at night from the lights underneath the water.

Rosea covered her head and sank down. She caught her breath. It was too much. She started to wheeze, then realized it was chuff, and it was at this point that the evil carranca she had been, the prow of her mother's ghostly ship, broke open, revealing emptiness and termites. Rosea let out a jagged wail that only an Amazon was capable of, a cry that shook the earth and disemboweled it. She rolled around, back and forth, grilling her body on the tortured broken branches, grabbing fistfuls of dirt and smearing it down her cheeks and through her hair.

Rosea suddenly heard the footsteps coming up the hill. She scrambled up and headed toward the wall, trying to escape, but zigzagged, which threw her off course. Her pursuer jangled something made of metal, maybe keys. Then came a snort. She knew then. Guard dogs. She blindly veered off to the side again, batting branches, smashing into bushes that snagged her shirt as she clamored free. Vaughan Peters, a high-paid man of action, star of adventure flicks, had turned himself into a huge Doberman guard dog! In the movies, he mowed down foreign goons, blew up yachts, and killed hysterical Third World dictators, but now he and his Doberman pals were running alongside each other and using their snouts to jab at her legs. Carrancas with real fangs! Jesus!

The dogs growled but didn't bark, which made it more terrifying. One bit her jeans. Rosea yanked away her leg and, trying to dart to the side, tripped over the other dog and twisted her ankle. She almost screamed, but kept going, limping on the side of her foot. A dog swung its head and clicked its teeth. Her ankle gave out, and suddenly she sailed forward and landed hard on her stomach. Her liver gave a jolt, almost knocking her out of breath. She doubled over, grabbed her ribs. A black four-legged shadow lingered, and the metal disk of his dog collar shone like a strange eye. Rosea crawled on her belly. Her ankle, her knee, her ribs were in pain. She vowed to kill the dogs, "I promise you motherfuckers I'll shoot you to hell; I don't care if your master does have the hardest balls in showbiz!" The black four-legged figure relented and moved to another doglike figure nearby as if to talk things over. Rosea threatened, "You don't believe me, then?" But the pain made her words feeble.

Finally their footsteps rattled on the dry leaves as they trotted off downhill, their bodies one giant shadow. They disappeared as quickly as they had attacked. Exhausted, Rosea sunk her head to the ground. "I'll hollow out your head and tie you to the prow of his damn yacht."

☾

Rosea drove over to East L.A. to look up Geezer Ortiz, who sold guns from his house. She used to carry a gun on her street forays, but never used it. A parolee should not use a gun. Shouldn't have one. Rosea knew this. She wasn't stupid. Shouldn't be in the garden in the first place. But she was going to buy a gun, even though it was the worst thing she could do. For all she knew, someone had heard her in the garden when she screamed and fell. Maybe the police would find a piece of her clothes or her flesh, snagged on thorns. Or maybe the dogs were speaking dogs, the kind in children's TV shows, real snitches, real *puxa sacos*, as Joe would say. But life couldn't just be a job, an apartment, a happy parole officer. The garden made her feel pure, clean. Like Joe, pure and clean and sweet. As pure as when God first made Brazil.

Some of her *compañeros* were married, but Geezer had a long way to go to get straightened out. Oh, it had been hot back then! Her love for Mexicans started when her mother told her of the pachucos and how elegant they looked in their linen suits woven with sparkly thread, their sleeky baggy pants, the thick silk ties and matching handkerchiefs. And the knives that appeared out of nowhere—a breast pocket, their girlfriends' beehive hairdos—knives surprising someone like a slippery, deadly eel. Carmen had told her about the action at the Sleepy Lagoon, where some cop killed a Mexican, causing one *grandissimo* fracas, and Rosea, in love with defiance, grew to seek the fire that went with it.

Many people considered this neighborhood a flick-of-the-knife, fuck-you-gringo sort of place, and so of course the kids today acted like it was scary, too. Instead of the smashing zoot suits, though, they dressed in black Ben Davis pants and buttoned-up flannel shirts, big blue jackets puffed like bruises, peaked hats like wooly elves. They looked like corpses left in a ditch somewhere. The pride and the snazz had disappeared.

Rosea was older now, her heaviness had softened, and she carried more tragedy around. She looked at these street kids and wondered what she had wanted here, way back when. What drove her from the Hollywood Hills to the barrio? She seemed out of place now, in her sweatshirt and jeans, her thick ponytail, no lipstick, and dangly earrings. She hoped Geezer Ortiz, her old boyfriend, was still in the gun business. Once Geezer had brought a gun to her house and had shot coconuts from the trees in her mother's yard; the coconuts had shattered and splashed cool, sweet milk, and she and Geezer had stood under the trees with their mouths open and tongues out, trying to taste the exotic rain as it splashed down.

Rosea remembered the two-story apartment, and she wondered if he still lived there. She drove to the apartment and pulled to the curb. Nothing had changed: not the faded green paint, the rusted rain pipe along the side of the building, the brown water oozing from cracks in the plaster. More graffiti on the wall in front, though. Rosea sat in the car, getting up the nerve to go in. She didn't want to just go up to the front door, have a stranger open it, and say, "What in the hell do you want with us? We are a clean family; we are tired of your element." But oh, Geezer had been swell in his burst of glory, still young, with a gorgeous beard shadow on his ruddy face, his skin white like a *güero*, and boot-black hair. Jesus, he had been cute and a *chingón* to the max.

She got the nerve to get out of the car, climb up the concrete steps, and wander down the corridor until she found the metal number 10 nailed over the door. Rosea knocked. She could hear a loud TV and a bunch of children chattering. The door opened, and a small boy with large eyes and a dirty Sesame Street T-shirt stood hanging onto the doorknob. Rosea asked, "Ortiz?" The boy ran away from the door. Rosea stood at the doorway. From the dark hall, she could see the blue glow of the TV in the living room and could hear cartoons with their thump-ti-dump of frantic characters running around and slamming into walls. The little boy who answered the door ran back to the two other kids watching TV, lolling on blankets and pillows scattered on the floor.

A young man came from the lighted kitchen, stood halfway down the hall, and called out, "Quién es?"

Rosea tried to get a better look. His features danced before her in the shadows, the side of his face lit by the pulsating light of the TV. She guessed it was Geezer's brother. "You Scooter?" she said.

"Yeah."

"You don't remember me, Rosea Socorro Katz. I used to go with Geezer, remember?"

There was a long pause from the skinny, dark figure. Old cooking oil sizzled in the kitchen. "Geezer's dead," he said.

"Shit."

"Shot. Long time ago."

"Too bad." Rosea was not surprised.

"What do you want?"

Rosea asked then if someone had taken over Geezer's business. Scooter turned abruptly and walked toward the kitchen, and Rosea hung back, not knowing whether she should enter or leave, but Scooter stood at the doorway of the kitchen and called, "You coming? Close the front door behind you."

Rosea stepped inside, made her way to the kitchen, and sat at the table. A large stack of dirty dishes climbed out of the sink, and a pile of wrinkled clothes lay bunched on a chair. An old woman stirred some chorizo in a pan but didn't look up. Scooter went into the pantry, brought out a shoe box, and put it on the table. "Two hundred dollars. Look first." Rosea pulled the box toward her and opened the lid just enough to peer inside. A gun lay there, a .22, with a handful of loose bullets rolling around in the box.

Rosea felt sweat on her upper lip. She wished all this could happen outside in the fresh air, but of course it couldn't. A small girl, about four, came in, took one look at her, then at the shoebox, and she knew. The girl, so fragile and tiny, wore a small T-shirt and floral panties. She said something to Scooter, who told her to shut up. Then the little one turned and left, unaffected by the harsh words, and her skinny feet pattered back over to the cartoon room. Rosea pulled out her wallet and counted out a bunch of twenties, saved up from Hollywood Celebrity Tours. Jesus. Innocent tourist dollars smelling like perfume and Certs and midwestern innocence. She slid the money over. Scooter counted it and nodded, pointing to the box. "Be careful," he said, "it bites."

"I know." Then Rosea remembered her and Geezer shooting coconuts in the backyard. She turned to the old woman at the stove. "I'm sorry about Geezer. I was a good friend of his."

The old woman didn't even look up. Rosea suddenly felt sick about the whole thing, made worse by the mixture of smells from fried chorizo and rotten fruit and stale kitty litter. This place was a filthy dump, and she was a nobody. Scooter frowned. "Life is tough here, Rosea. Always was."

Rosea nodded and slipped the box under her arm, then she turned and left. She used to think it was so cool going with Geezer and being a *chola* tough chick and a part of his fully Mexican family, instead of everything in her life being "not quite Brazilian." She used to ride behind him on his motorcycle and snuggle her face into his neck smelling of hair tonic, her long hair snapping freely in the wind. She used to think she needed nothing else, but, remembering Geezer's face floating in the apartment window and his sardonic wave to her as she headed toward home in Beverly Hills, she realized now how his family must have despised her.

I dreamed I saw our galleons in flames, like floating lanterns, and great pieces of burning wood fell into the water with a loud hiss, spewing golden sparks far off into the night. In the light of the fire, we saw war canoes leaving the crime and sliding into darkness and heard the laughter of the oars. I woke up from this terrible dream only to see a glow from between the trees.

—*Diário de Carlos Manoel Teixeira da Cunha* (Diary of Carlos Manoel Teixeira da Cunha), *O Ano* 1643

Chapter 14

O Ano 1977

The house where Joe and Sherri lived was on Yarber Street off Tartley Avenue, names with so many Rs that Joe could barely pronounce them. But it was an American house, and the sky was blue overhead like in Brazil. Their rented tract house was a little casinha of perfection in a row of five, each with a red roof and wooden gate, each with small embedded tiles making a Spanishy arch over the front door, each with a square front lawn surrounded by a thigh-high scalloped wire fence, some with climbing rosebushes. They suffered in the summer because they were far from the beach.

But suffering or no, this was their home. And someone should have told the old man.

Joe drank his coffee silently and peered across the table at Melvinor eating breakfast. Finally, he and his wife happened to have a day off together, and Sherri went and brought this old man over to the house. But, being a prisoner of guilt, Joe had to be careful. No explosions, no complaints — only silence and forced humility. Sherri probably suspected him and Rosea; women tend to know these things. Last night he had beckoned Sherri to dance with him, shuffling his feet and undulating his hips as he held her close, but her body had locked in displeasure, and when she saw her pink hand engulfed by his brown one, she said, "You want a dark woman, don't you?" and pulled away.

Melvinor took a slice of white bread, spread butter and jam on it, and folded the bread in half like a child. He sat between Jeffy and Keffy, who were perched on booster chairs that Sherri had brought home from the Eye and Rib. The twins were acting cozy with their new grandfather, and Keffy kept giving him little fistfuls of food. Joe took a loud slurp of coffee. It was easy being an old man; you're too exhausted to have desire. Melvinor began babbling about the Brazilian Birdboy and wondered out loud how people in Brazil could abandon kids just like that and let them starve.

Joe leaned his forearms on the table; he needed to hammer the truth into this American knucklehead: "There are men who would gladly take care of their kids. But it's all up to the woman. If a woman wants to dump the kid in the garbage or just throw it in the ocean or send it to the moon, there is not a thing a man can do. All this, yet a woman always wants love, but when you try and try, she kicks you in the balls. Eh, Melvinor? Don't tell me this hasn't happened to you."

Melvinor didn't seem fazed by his outburst. "Well," he continued cautiously, "Birdboy came from an Amazon native who didn't want him."

"Really?"

Melvinor shrugged. "A woman warrior. An Amazon. With a spear. Professor Millard — the gentleman I live with — doesn't tell much about his life. But it seems he had quite a journey."

Joe laughed and brought the coffee cup to his lips. "Amazons don't exist my friend. Only in our fantasies."

At that moment, Sherri sat down with another plate of toast. She tapped Melvinor on the arm. "Come on, another piece." Joe almost sensed a twinkle in Melvinor's eye and saw Sherri's uneasy grin. Keffy butted his head affectionately against Melvinor's shoulder, and, dammit, Joe wanted to grab Keffy and sit him down, hard.

Sherri put her hand on the old man's forearm and announced, "We're all going to the zoo." Joe grimaced. Sherri caught his expression and withdrew. "Well, Joe, you don't have to go, but Jeffy and Keffy want to."

"Of course I want to go. We hardly ever go anywhere as a family . . . ," and his voice faded. He thought of Rosea, what she was doing, probably something sick and depraved and interesting. Crazy woman. Sherri moved in a blur, and the twins looked straight at him, both chewing on triangles of toast. The world got back into focus. Joe's voice blared a bit too loudly. "OK! Let's go to the zoo, OK! Jeff and Keff!" Joe leaned over and tweaked their noses, "Let's see some wild animals! Wilder than your mother, eh?"

The zoo. Tape recordings of caged animals blared from speakers in the concessions stands, while in the distance a real lion roared. Footsteps cracked on gravel and sounded like pacing policemen, impatient and determined. Women pushed baby carriages, and men trotted behind like prisoners, carrying quilted totes and lunch boxes. Joe hated the zoo.

Jeffy and Keffy sat in their tandem stroller and stared up at the people. Inflatable dolphins and blue bears spun around, clothespinned to lines strung across two trees. Jeffy pointed, wanted one. "No," Sherri said, "you don't even know what they are." Joe looked around and tugged the strap of the diaper bag on his shoulder. It was a bit chilly to be at the zoo. And he didn't like this place; the zoo triggered a fear in him. The animal cages trembled, and memory crowded his thoughts—

Alberto Heinmann wails and tries to shake the iron bars of his prison cell, and the noise echoes down the hall. José tells the gaúcho *to be quiet. Alberto Heinmann, from Rio Grande do Sul, has a German name. He is not*

used to prison. He reaches out from the bars, half delirious, pleading, the
poor soul dehydrated from diarrhea. The guard swings his baton, smash-
ing the man's fingers, and he shrieks . . .

Joe grabbed at his head, then slowly let his hands fall as he concen-
trated—hard—on Sherri, who crouched in front of the stroller, pulled
out a tissue from her purse, and wiped Jeffy's nose. The baby held onto
her fingers, hollering and trying to pull her hand away. "Don't you want
to see the monkeys?" she cooed. Melvinor looked at him and smiled be-
nignly.

Joe glared. "Don't worry, old man. Bad animals are locked up. Don't
be afraid. Be glad it's them instead of us."

Sherri raised her eyes and caught Joe talking. Her glare made him
flinch. "What is wrong with you?" she said.

Joe moved away and shrugged. What did they know?

Melvinor pushed the stroller, and Sherri walked beside him. Joe
drifted behind. Sherri's bunda, full from her pregnancy two years ago,
churned like the cheeks of a large animal eating. Joe imagined his own
throat hot with animal anger, his teeth wanting to devour bits of her flesh.
The back of Melvinor's white hair blew into a cotton ball and made his
brains look airy and ignorant. His plaid sports jacket and loafers looked
like a caricature of an American tourist. Picture an old man and a young
lady with two kids. How nice. Joe was probably the only one in the crowd
spoiling the fun by thinking of prison.

Everywhere the information signs told of the animals going extinct,
especially in South America. The signs accused Brazilians of destroying their own country for greed and animal skins. The carefully printed
words in English gave him the middle finger: "This is for you, *babacos*,
and your love for money, your insipid carelessness, your love of pleasure, your chainsaw dick cutting down the rain forest, your oversexed
neuroses. Well, no wonder you have dictators there; if it weren't for zoos
in America, Brazil would be just one giant wasteland."

Then the monkey cages. Joe watched the monkeys' bewildered tropical faces behind bars, the unshaven shadows calling out in the name of
justice—

Alberto Heinmann, the gaúcho intellectual, brags that his subversive ar-

ticles and pamphlets and books got him in trouble. José rails at him, so naive, "Screwing a communist got me in trouble. This little affair with someone began as hardly anything, ended up as something. I have no feelings for the government, and I don't want to save the world! Cynical and resigned just like the rest! If God would just let me manage my newsstand and enjoy a cold beer, that would be enough. Punto. What good is it all now?! My newsstand has probably been bombed to pieces by the police, my prick is dead and useless!"

Alberto confides that he has dreams of the prison walls crumbling and everyone escaping.

"Bullshit!" José shouts right in his face. "Bullshit, you crazy fool!" But every night the gaúcho weeps and calls for his wife, while José blames Sonia for his mess.

The monkeys screeched and scrambled to the ground, then started swinging and swinging and swinging without stopping—

José, half-asleep, swats an imaginary rat crawling on his head. He opens his eyes, and feet dangle above him. José jumps out of bed. Alberto has hanged himself with his shirt and swings gently. The tension of the shirt, tied to the crossbars, has squeezed his eyes open, and drool spins from his mouth in a clear thread. José grabs the man's body and shakes him, "Socorro, socorro!" Other prisoners start banging the bars with anything they can find, swearing and screaming at the guards, "Dead man! Dead man!"

Joe backed away from the cages and bolted toward a large stretch of lawn; in the distance, he saw fences and small brown animals clawing to get out, screaming bloody hell. At the lawn, he collapsed and rolled onto his back. The lions roared far off. Laughter wandered by, chewed up by the sound of metal pulleys. He pressed his eyes, but the harder he pressed, the more he saw—

When they take Alberto down from the bars, they lay him on Joe's bunk. Alberto has a line of golden hair from his belly growing upward and spreading out to his chest and purple nipples. A piece of paper peeks from the waistline of his now urine-wet trousers. José lifts the paper. A love letter. He reads some, but not all; it is private. Poor man, trying to be smart in such a world. His dead cellmate's face is shaped like a heart.

Joe felt someone poking him, and he opened his eyes and saw Melvinor sitting on the grass, his face hovering. "Are you OK?"

"Go away," Joe said under his breath.

Melvinor drew back.

Jeffy called, "Daddy!" Joe looked up and saw the twins tumbling over each other and rolling.

Joe covered his eyes. "Stop it, for god's sake!"

"Joe," Sherri said, "We're at a zoo. What do you expect?"

Joe peered through his fingers and watched Keffy wriggling on the ground, his T-shirt crawling up his soft, vulnerable belly. Jeffy ran over and threw himself on top of his brother. Keffy kicked his legs and squealed, and Joe wanted to snatch them up, kiss them to death, adore them in their innocence. But all he could do was shut his eyes and suck in the tears to keep from crying out.

At daybreak, after a sleepless night, we went down to the beach to inspect our ships because we all had the same nightmare. When we arrived, the large crucifix that Padre Pedro Oliveira had erected in the sand was now torn from its base of large stones and hacked and charred. As if this blasphemy wasn't enough, we saw that our nightmare had come true: our ships were nothing more than burned masts, ragged sails, and broken hulls hidden underneath the water. I cried in despair and rushed over to the water's edge as if to touch this disaster with my own hand because I couldn't believe it! The surface of the water was covered with torn canvas, with water and wine casks revolving in the waves, with trunks, pieces of wood, and lumps of straw, and with the most hideous flotsam of all — Padre Pedro Oliveira himself.
— *Diário de Carlos Manoel Teixeira da Cunha, O Ano* 1643

Chapter 15

O Ano 1978

Joe opened the van door and stood to the side to collect tickets. He smiled the way he had to and gave his little speech: "Welcome to L.A. How do you like our Mann's Chinese Theatre with the hand tracks on the sidewalk?" Then one by one he collected the tickets. One guy commented about his jacket. "Nice and shiny. Do you serve martinis on the tour?" Joe took his ticket with, "My friend, there are many ways to improve the world. Unfortunately it's not possible." The next woman winked at him and asked him if he was a Latin Lover. Joe, humiliated by such a comment, said nothing but snatched her ticket and motioned for her to board. A few others handed over their tickets, and Joe closed the door.

He slipped into the driver's seat and raised his eyes to the rearview mirror: a vanload of fearful, innocent faces.

He had to do this tour with the truth in mind. Chucky had gotten some complaints about his lies. "There needs to be truth to your tales," Chucky said—"some at least." Joe couldn't believe this. Who knew the truth about movie stars? Wasn't a part of their lives a lie, and who complained? Who complained of cowboys and gangsters? If lies could come from Hollywood, why couldn't lies come from him? And frankly, he was a better liar because he had lied to save his life.

He had gone a week telling the truth, but something about this group angered him, he didn't know why. They seemed like such idiots. He pulled away from the curb and sped into traffic, forgetting to tell them about the Marlboro Man and about how all of L.A. was at one time a desert and every plant here was forced to grow. As he entered Beverly Hills—the sacred grove of eternal wealth, where streets had beautiful Spanish names like Rosalita, Reina del Mar, and Linda Verde Heights—he did a few houses the normal way, saying how much the mansion cost and what the swimming pool was like, and how many movies this or that person made. But this wasn't enough. He stopped at a large brick mansion of a movie star most people did not consider important, and his anger poured out of him, and he wanted to shake his passengers until their teeth rattled, until finally they saw the light, even if no more than that shed by a lightbulb: "The one who lives here, Jack Roberts, his real name was Roberto Cavanis. He acted in a few films. You may have seen him in *Outside Port Cecilia* and *Hidden Secrets*. His past life is not familiar to us, but I will tell you. This man long ago was a dictator who killed many people, and he cut off tongues so no one could talk. This is what they say, but I didn't see it myself. But finally he came to America to start his life all over again and got into the movies. But nobody can change completely. People say he keeps a dungeon with torture equipment. He has a pool in the middle of his living room because he has a skin disease where evil has eaten him. So he must struggle to have good skin so he can be a movie star."

Then Joe drove up the hill to another house, Spanish style: "This house is incredible. Belongs to Holm Miller, a famous producer in the old days.

His most famous film is *Attack in the Middle of the Street*. It is famous, né? I am from Cuba, and maybe I confuse a few words. Look. This house here, you realize, is made of adobe mixed with gold. He used to spend time in the Amazon with cannibals. Somewhere in the roof he put in human teeth that he got from his cannibal friends. People think it's bits of corn, but really it's not. It's teeth. How about that, my people?"

Then he drove to a house with a high gate and wall, the house hidden by a narrow tree-lined driveway: "Here is another producer, Jason Lair. They say he keeps a maid from Haiti who has put a curse on him. Sometimes I see her by the gate, crumbling herbs in the pocket of her apron and mumbling. He keeps her locked up because otherwise she'd escape to Florida. People don't change that much. When they move here from other countries, only their shoes are different."

The tourists looked at each other; one man had an angry face. Joe felt satisfied. "Well, my friends, evil is everywhere, even the people who live in fancy houses have problems. Just go through life, my friends. What else can we do?"

They laughed uneasily, but at least they got the message. Now Joe would smooth everything out, say, "That's show business," and "Não chora, there is nothing to cry about because America is a great country." Joe pulled out onto the roadway and did the rest of the tour as normal, but no matter. He saw in his rearview mirror that the angry man was making his way to the front of the van, his heavy camera swinging around his neck. Unfortunately, there was a spare seat in the front, and the man sat down, scooted forward, and held onto the back of Joe's seat. "Listen," the man said, and Joe knew what was coming. The man lectured about how he must tell the truth, that no one should be accused of being what they're not, and "that's not the way we do things in this country. Evil is not everywhere, and your damn fatalism will get you in trouble one way or the other." He hadn't spent his money to hear a pack of lies.

Joe could not resist arguing. "Well, you pay money for movies, don't you? Do you believe everything in the movies is real? Did Carmen Socorro wear her large hat to bed? Did she take a shower with it?"

The thick folds on either side of the man's mouth deepened, his stone-like cheeks flared. He said he would complain to the management, that he was sick of people cheating him, not being square, and, besides, he didn't believe Joe was Cuban or knew Desi Arnaz, or he would have seen Joe in *I Love Lucy* because his wife had been watching reruns for the past ten years. Again Joe replied, keeping down his angry exasperation, but curious to know what country he seemed to be from: "If I'm not Cuban, where do you think I'm from?"

The man snapped, "Mexican, you're all Mexican here, don't think I don't know," then he got up and headed back toward his seat. Joe looked at his rearview mirror and thought the man in his thick body looked so lonely, stepping over people, looking for the truth.

When the angry man got off at Mann's Chinese Theatre, he took out his little pad and pencil and scrawled out the number of the van. The rest of the group thanked Joe hurriedly and left, a bit afraid. Only one gave him a tip, a skinny college student who said he had enjoyed Joe's cynical attitude toward Hollywood. Joe watched as the people examined the sidewalk gouged with hand and footprints, the tender tracks of ghosts. Above their heads the shrieking dragons on the red entranceway to Mann's Theatre belched out fire. The city teemed with danger, but went on about its life so innocently that one could not even imagine the terror that existed.

❰

When Joe arrived at the Hollywood Celebrity Tours office, he already knew he was in trouble. The crazy Mickey Rooney stood by the back door and stuck his tongue out as Joe entered the building. "Chucky needs to see you, Cubano."

"Please. My name is Joe, not Cubano. Can you say my name? Eh?" Joe, his body aching, went into the staff room and punched his time card. Low voices mumbled down the hall as people talked on the phones, and his gangster supervisor barked the loudest of them all. Joe slipped his time card back onto the rack and wandered down the hall. He stopped briefly at Rosea's door, but she was busy, one hand grasping the phone to her ear, the other hand clawing the edge of the desk. Half her hair was stacked on top of her head and twirled and pinned at random. He loved this mess, this unruliness of hers. Her legs opened the way he liked, and she hooked her feet on either side of her chair, her thighs stretching her skirt.

Just then Chucky called him. Joe swung out of Rosea's doorway and into Chucky's office. Chucky was in his chair and looking up at the ceiling. "Please, my cha-cha friend," he pleaded, "be a good boy. We love having you. But don't pull this shit. They won't believe it if it's too unbelievable."

Joe sighed, sat down on the chair facing him. "The trouble, Mr. Chucky, is that some people want . . . boring facts. They should not go to movie stars' houses if they want boring facts."

Chucky looked at him directly, almost with something else in mind. "Well, cha-cha man, sometimes we have to take other people's wants into account." Joe eyed the machine gun hanging on the wall. Such fools he had to work with.

In the next room, Rosea clumped her chair loudly against her desk. She grumbled, slammed the appointment book shut, and rummaged through her purse. Chucky listened with his lips parted and his tongue rolled in his mouth. Then Rosea stomped down the hall and out the back door. Chucky leaned in and motioned to the next room, "Speaking of wants. You ever *talk* to her?"

"Who?"

"You know," Chucky bobbled his head, "talk to her. Do you and her—?"

"I don't know what you mean. I talk to anyone who talks to me. But I do not like to be *forced* to talk," Joe said simply.

"Oh, pretty boy," Chucky snorted as he picked up a pen and tapped the end on the desk, "fast talking is part of your charm, isn't it? Get in the movies before you kill that accent."

Joe left abruptly. The Mickey Rooney was standing in the doorway of the staff room and gave Joe a raspberry as he passed. Joe swung around. "That is so stupid when you do that. You know? That is so stupid!"

Mickey winked with a click of his tongue. "Some guys like it."

"Bicha." Joe rushed out the back door. Outside Rosea was smoking a cigarette and leaning against her car. "Are you coming, José?" she shouted. José. His name. The way they said it in Portuguese. It was Sherri's day off, and he didn't have to baby-sit. But he couldn't stay out late. He had to be careful. He had to pick some milk up at the store.

Rosea's black hair, dismantled from her hair-do, hung down her shoulders. He found himself wandering toward her, and the closer he came, the more her smile widened, and she tucked a couple of strands of hair behind her ear. She held out the pack of cigarettes to him and said, "Finally, I got some to share." He slipped out a cigarette from the pack and glanced to the side, afraid to look at her face as she leaned over and pressed the lighted tip of her cigarette to his.

He took a puff and leaned against her car, exhausted. "I had a terrible group today. Some man accused me of lying. Idiota."

"Don't worry, we're out of here." She opened the car door and got in, then let Joe in on the passenger side.

Joe didn't care where she took him. He was too tired to resist with "oh my wife, oh I'm married and have kids, oh, oh. . . ." He hadn't slept well in days. He dangled his cigarette out the window and listened to her shifting gears. She rambled about the perfect place to go, even a bit weird. He could use a fright, an electric shock. That's how he would know he was in love.

She tossed her cigarette away as she headed up De la Gente Avenue, then up San Fermin Drive. Joe realized this was the way to Carmen Socorro's house. "No, no, not here," he cried as he crushed his cigarette on the door. "For god's sake! We could lose our jobs!" She drove fast, bouncing on the ruts. "Rosea! I could be fired! I have a family!" She continued on San Fermin, flying past the Socorro home with its lush backyard, to where the trees had thinned out and yellowed, to where surrounding houses became scarce, and there was nothing but dried hills and a brick wall that still enclosed the estate. There, she swerved and stopped next to the wall. Joe shook his head resolutely. "I can't. I can't lose my job."

She flung open the door. "Come on, the coast is clear." Then she bolted out, scrambled onto the hood, and slung her purse strap over her shoulder. "Don't worry, I'll protect you." And with that she heaved herself over the wall.

Joe crouched down on the seat of the car so no one could see him through the windows. He clasped his knees and stared at his shoes. They would be caught, and he was still in his work clothes! They would know where he worked because no one else dressed this foolishly.

"Come here," he heard her call from the yard.

"Get out of there," he croaked, feeling ridiculous huddled in the front seat. Rosea kept shouting from the other side of the wall, "Come on, Joe, come on, I'm waiting," so loud that she might as well have been a police siren. Finally, Joe swung out of the car, took off his jacket, and threw it on the seat. He slammed the door, climbed onto the hood, and looked over the wall. Rosea stood below with her arms akimbo. "Unbelievable," she said, "you're going to join me."

Joe, threw his leg over the wall, and jumped to the other side, landing at her feet. He stumbled and looked around the garden. This? There were palm trees, yes, with dried fronds that had fallen and scattered like bones, and a couple of banana trees whose trunks had split open, a lot of bushes and weeds. It was as if these trees had been tortured and left to die.

"Look, Joe," she swept her arm. "Doesn't this remind you of Brazil?"

"No, this doesn't remind me of Brazil because if we were in Brazil right now, we'd be killed." Rosea grabbed his hand and led him through a group of trees. He pulled away. "I don't want to be here."

"Fine," Rosea said as she ambled backward. "But I do. And I have the keys to the car. Among other things." Rosea dropped the purse at her feet and took off her shoes. Then she opened the front buttons of her dress, shoved the dress down over her hips, bringing along her nylons and underwear, and slipping the whole thing off her feet. Her purple nipples, stuffed tight into her bra, showed through like splashes of blood. She popped open her bra and tossed it to the side. Then she spread her legs slightly and slowly smeared her hand through her bush.

The late-afternoon shadows from the trees spilled onto the ground, making the shapes of men. Joe thought he heard mocking laughter, and he backed away, almost putting out his hands to protect his face. The place frightened him, but the sight of Rosea standing there brazen like that drove him crazy with desire. The shadows made a large hand smoothing up and down her belly.

She went over to him. He touched her slightly on the arm, then on her naked hip. She leaned her head on his shoulder, embraced him, and smoothed her hands down his back. At first he flinched, imagining the touch to be from someplace else. She stopped—then began unbuttoning his shirt.

He shivered with cold or fear. He couldn't decide which.

Peeling away his shirt, then slipping off his T-shirt, Rosea looked sad, her throat swelling with the urge to cry, her thick brownness, her grand sorrow carrying him away.

He stroked the red marks where the bra had dug into her skin. The top of her chest was flushed with a rash. He blew on it softly. He began to feel dizzy and leaned on her to stand up.

The room with one light bulb. Day or night he can't remember. No windows, only the light in the policeman's eye. The policeman sits on the edge of a desk, says maybe he can be released today, who knows? A fly has smashed into the bulb, a sign there must be a door somewhere or a window.

It is silent as if everyone has gone to bed. Only the voice of the police booms: "Do you know we are near where they have the feira on Wednesday? Do you realize it is Wednesday and above you many people are buying food?"

What can José say? He has been in prison, hasn't bought vegetables in ages. And about Sonia? The policeman asks him the same questions about the meetings, about where her parents live. José refuses to say anything, says he just met the girl, for god's sake. He's nothing but a working man. "I'm humble. A good Catholic."

Rosea embraced him, found the long scar on his back, and ran her fingers up and down his slightly raised skin. "Don't—" he gulped and tried to speak—

The questions, the questions again and again. "The meetings? Where do her parents live?" José knows if he tells, the police will harm the family, too. But José remains faithful, like a machine. "No, I don't know where they live." The room is a box turning upside down, and both he and the policeman are rattling inside this box, like stones.

Suddenly from out of nowhere a door slams, and another policeman appears. Now two men are asking the same question, and José's tongue is numb from the same dull ticktocking; there is nothing he can do to change the questions. He has denied Sonia so much he almost doesn't know who she is anymore.

The policeman pacing around gets furious and hits José on the back with a belt. "How can a rapist like you defend the bitch the way you do?! You must be crazy! You must have two personalities, one a saint and the other the devil!" The policeman on the desk asks him the same questions again, then comes a another slash, and the question again. José falls face down on the floor. He can't even remember what he is saying; all he remembers is how loud the belt is when it hits his back, his roaring, which he's tried to hold back and now can't. It flashes on his mind: if they are near the feira, *can anyone hear his cries beneath their shoes?*

"Don't. Don't touch me!" He cringed and broke away from her, turning his back. Rosea went over to him, rubbed the back of his shoulders, then placed her fingers firmer on the scar and grilled his memory for more details. His back muscles went into spasms trying to block the prisoners inside him, banging on his ribs, screaming in indignation and terror —

Everything becomes quiet, and he hears running water as if maybe they are ready to wash him down. José turns to the side and sees one of the guards pissing, trying to aim for his bare skin, but instead the stream lands on the floor.

Joe wept wildly, uncontrollably. He didn't care if anyone heard his sobs. Rosea kissed his back, then slowly licked the long scar as if she were closing up the wound. Her tongue was light, dry, and steady. Then she pressed her lips against his skin and gnawed gently.

Joe lifted his head and saw the woman in white again, her skin glowing like mother-of-pearl. Slowly she raised her hands as if to stop someone coming toward her, revealing palms stained with *dendê* oil. It was the woman he had seen when he first laid eyes on the garden. She doesn't exist, Joe said to himself, she couldn't exist. But who cares. The idea of such a beautiful vision made his painful longing for Brazil something his heart couldn't bear.

Chapter 16

O Ano 1978

Joe and Sherri took the twins grocery shopping. The babies jerked and fussed and whined, and when one cried, of course the other had to cry, too. Sherri and Joe took two shopping carts, placed the twins on the kiddy seats, and rolled the carts down the aisles while talking of prices and what food to get, trying to keep the boys calm with promises of nonsense: "Wanna go to Disneyland, to Mr. Chili's to get a taco?" Both he and Sherri schemed together, thinking of bribes for the kids, and when that didn't work, Joe threatened to hold them upside down and swat them on the behind.

Sherri gasped, "Joe! That's like torture!"

Joe grew angry. "It is not torture! I would never, never torture my kids. Don't ever use the word *torture*! Hein?"

"Joe — Joe. I was kidding. Jesus. C'mon. We don't have *torture* in this country. You think I'm an idiot? You think I'm stupid?"

"Sherri, it's the word I don't like."

"Fine. There's a couple of words of yours I don't like either. Like *I'll only be a few minutes*, like *I'll be right back* and then you're gone half the day. I've had to ask the neighbors to feed the kids so I can go to work because of your goddamn — "

He let her yell at him, and he let her win the argument, too, because it was true. He and Rosea and trips to the garden: it was starting to become a dangerous habit. In the beginning, they went on his days off, then came more elaborate plans, lies of overtime, a long errand. He and Rosea would wander around the back of the estate where the garden had been left to die and reminisce about Brazil like old lovers, as if the memories had truly existed. His good memories were from before the Anos de Chumbo, when Sonia had loved him; Rosea's were from the Amazon, where she had never been. They'd crawl under a tree or a bush somewhere, isolated, hiding from those dogs that Rosea talked about, but that never appeared. They'd sink their bodies together and clasp each other tight, her thigh nestled between his legs. "I'm afraid," she would always whisper in his ear during their lovemaking, their bodies rocking on the ground sounding like birds pecking at the leaves.

"I am afraid, too," Joe would say, "but I have never felt so alive."

Joe's daydreams followed him home from shopping. Just as they pulled in front of the house, his heart froze as he saw Rosea standing at his front window, flashing a blank stare, then running — jumping the knee-high wire fence that surrounded their patch of lawn and darting toward the wooden gate at the side of the house. His fantasy turned into frantic reality as he scrambled out of the car and ran to the back gate. Rosea was already there, scratching the wood, jingling the latch. "Rosea!" Joe called. She whirled around, her face opened with fierce surprise. "What are you doing here?"

She took a deep breath and grabbed her hair, lifting the mass off her neck. Her large gold earring caught a rippled black shank in its loop.

Joe tried to keep his voice soft so she wouldn't explode. "Don't come to my house."

Rosea gave a throaty grunt.

"Rosea. I have a family."

"Well, I don't."

Sherri, bewildered, wandered around to the gate. She saw Rosea, and her mouth dropped. Joe turned to Sherri and tried to put his hands on his wife's shoulders—"She works with me. She needed to pick up some paperwork"—but Sherri jerked away from him.

Joe knew. Everyone knew, this lie about paperwork. And Rosea made it worse with her sudden broad smile, her red lipstick like a vulgar ribbon, and the stupid movie line: "I'm his secretary," she tossed her head, "really."

Sherri nodded severely, her brow ruffled.

"Sherri, meu bem, just some papers. That's all." His lie stuck to his throat.

Sherri made a simple smile. "If she came for paperwork, shouldn't you give her some?"

"Yes, of course," he muttered.

Sherri turned to go. Joe followed her out to the car.

"Help me, will you?" she snapped as she picked up and shoved Keffy at him, then she pushed a grocery bag against his chest, and he caught that, too. She struggled, pulling out Jeffy, who was having a fit, and set him hard on the ground. Joe put down Keffy, opened the chain-link gate to the front yard, and tried to lead the boys straight into the house. The twins stopped short when they saw Rosea. "Who's that?" Jeffy pealed.

"Get in!" Sherri ordered as she carried two loads of groceries.

Joe opened the trunk and grabbed one more bag, trying not to look at Rosea as he made his way into the house. He could hear her bracelets rattling like a bridled horse. Sherri stomped inside the house, dumped the grocery bags on the counter, then thrust the children into their booster chairs at the table. Joe quietly set the bags on the counter. He had never been afraid of Rosea before, but something about her boldness, here with his wife and kids, made him especially nervous. He looked into the living room and through the large window saw Rosea with her arms crossed, pacing back and forth in his front yard.

Sherri tossed some of the groceries in the refrigerator, then opened and slammed cabinet doors. She began to pull apart the boxes from a ten-pack of cereal, angrily rattling the cellophane.

Jeffy whined.

"Shut up," Sherri snapped.

Joe scurried to the refrigerator. "I'll get him some milk—"

"SHUT UP—"

Joe slammed the refrigerator door and bolted out of the house. Rosea stood boldly on the front steps. Joe, in one motion, snatched her by the arm and dragged her out of the yard and down the walkway to the sidewalk. "For the love of God—"

Rosea jerked her arm away. "Your wife is cute—"

"Rosea. Do not come to my house—"

"You were supposed to meet me! Where in the hell were you?!"

Joe ran his hands hard through his hair. His appointment with her had absolutely slipped his mind, but it would be worse to admit it. "I can't just drop everything. I couldn't get away. If you had a family, believe me, you would know that sometimes—!"

Rosea was fuming. Her tongue made a loud click like a gun. She hugged herself, paced, flung her hair back; she had learned this strut of contempt from the movies, or from the street. "Joe, I'm not an object. I'm not a goddamn Amazonian artifact. You love me!" she hollered, then she came in close and growled. "You love me."

Joe took her arm again and pulled her toward her car. He could see a group of young boys turning their heads as they rode by on bicycles, prepubescent boys already with the desire for her body. The kids were probably hoping he would push her into the car and fuck her.

"Rosea," he said again, fumbling, words coming out mixed with desire and stupidity. The reek of his sweat overwhelmed him, a shabby immigrant after all, a foolish family man. "Don't come to my house. Ever. Believe me. It will ruin everything."

"Hey," she said smoothly, "I just wanted to see where you live. That's

all. You can love your wife. Do you fuck her? Do you make her wear sun- **165**
glasses? Blindfolds?"

"Don't say that about Sherri, please. She is innocent. I love her."

"That's what they all say." Whipping around, she stomped over to her car and drove off.

Joe shuddered as her car tore around the corner, then went back in the house. The twins murmured in the kitchen, sitting alone at the table and gnawing on cookies. Joe drifted to the bedroom, where Sherri lay curled up on the bed, her back to him. He settled down on the edge of the bed and folded his hands. Sherri was rasping into her pillow.

"Meu bem," he whispered.

"Speak English."

He needed to tell her about what was on his mind, the reason why he couldn't stand her touch, and all the things that had happened to him. He would tell her things she never knew about, the time he was imprisoned, the dark time in his old life. Her hard face would soften with surprise, then she'd whisper, "Coitado, poor thing," and smooth her hand over his shoulder joints, which had been wrenched out, and kiss the scar on his back that she never mentioned except once to joke if he had been cut up in a hot Latin knife fight. And he wanted to assure her that he loved his sons and loved being a father — yes, as they say, "get the cards on the table." That way maybe he wouldn't crave Rosea. It would be hard, but he had to. That would be best.

Joe lit himself a cigarette to prepare himself. He looked at the smoke slinking upward. "There's something I need to tell you."

She didn't answer. He continued smoking, the lighted embers making little pops. He would tell her when he finished this cigarette. He could tell her now, but no, in a bit —

He finished his cigarette and crushed the butt on the ashtray. He reached over and with his knuckles traced her heels, flat and hard with a ring of dirt around her calluses, then he passed his hand over her hips and up her body. He leaned over and kissed her shoulder.

"Feed the kids or something," she muttered. "I've had it."

☾

Joe woke up at the usual time, feeling a bit sick. He sank under the covers, daring not to touch Sherri sleeping beside him. He dreaded going to work and seeing Rosea, who would threaten him and demand—what?

The white walls of the bedroom glared back at him with frankness. This was his home, his shell of carinho. He curled up like a baby. He wanted to hide here, not go out the whole day, just be here, home, no more temptation. This Rosea had shot off a machine gun her first day at work, and what did that mean? Maybe she was a gangster, someone violent who would demand money for her discretion, blackmail him, banish him to the desert of his shame, but no matter, he could take it. He'd been through a lot worse.

Little pajama feet shushed toward the room, and Jeffy appeared in the doorway, hanging on the doorjamb. Joe motioned him forward with his finger. "Daddy's sick." Jeffy stayed put, but looked surprised, so innocent. Joe climbed out of bed, slipped on his robe, then patted his son on the head on the way out of the room. Jeffy followed him into the kitchen. Joe picked up the phone on the counter. His head spun as if he'd been drinking *cachaça* all night.

He got his gangster boss on the phone. Chucky Weaver with his damn loud voice guffawed: "No problem, Hoe-zay, still got all your sick days, the honest Joe you are."

Joe glanced at Jeffy wandering out of the kitchen. "Thank you, sir."

"Yeah, well, you rest. If I hear you've robbed a bank, you're in trouble." His boss cackled at the other end of the line. Joe held the phone slightly away from his ear until Chucky had finished burbling.

"Yes." Joe started to feel dizzy. Maybe he really was sick.

"Hey!" Chucky yeked. "See you tomorrow."

"Yes." Joe lowered the phone, then hung up. Jeffy came back into the kitchen, this time with Keffy. Joe got out two bowls and two spoons and set them out. The twins climbed silently into their chairs. Joe got out the cereal and poured out colored, beadlike bops with marshmallows. He couldn't believe they ate this. Everything in America seemed like a toy, even the food. He got a carton of milk out of the refrigerator and poured it over their cereal. They both looked up, puzzled.

"What's the matter, you think I'm a monster? Huh?" He snarled. Keffy smiled, lowering his bottom lip and showing his tiny cubelike teeth.

Joe crouched between their chairs, held each of his sons by the chin, and kissed one, then the other. Joe kept his face close, and he could feel the boys tugging away. Their gray eyes blended together, making a watery pool. They mewed that they wanted to watch cartoons in the living room, so Joe let them go.

Joe made coffee and poured himself a cup. He'd have to get them dressed sometime of course, maybe after the cartoons. The boys were watching the *Jeffy and Keffy Hour*, a show that Joe always kidded was named after them. The cartoon characters on the TV, with their frenetic nerves, spoke fast and wonky as they chased each other around and bashed into walls and threw their enemies off cliffs.

He heard Sherri scrambling out of bed with a "shit!" and she came into the living room, struggling to get her robe on, only to see the twins in front of the TV. "Your father didn't change you? Didn't he go to work?"

"No," Joe called from the kitchen.

Sherri stood at the doorway. Her blond hair had a tangled nest in the back, and her face was still puffy. "Aren't you late for work?"

"Called in sick."

"You don't feel well?" she sounded annoyed as she went to the cupboard and rumbled around for a coffee cup and poured herself a cup of coffee. "Won't your secretary miss you?"

Joe bristled. This early and already like a whip. He drank a long sip. "Sherri."

Sherri ambled over to the kitchen table.

At first, Joe didn't say anything.

"What? The big confession?"

Joe gritted his teeth, the momentum for complete truth left him; it goes away so rapidly when lies become a way to save your life. "Sherri. This secretary has been stalking me. She comes here, she—is after me at work in fact—I am afraid of her."

Sherri looked at him askance. "Really? That's too bad. Maybe you shouldn't wear your skirts so short."

Joe smirked, pulled a pack of cigarettes from his pocket, and lit one. "You're smoking too much."

"This woman makes me nervous. You don't believe me."

"If she is stalking you, we must call the police."

"No, no," Joe said. "That isn't necessary."

"What do you mean 'no, no'?" Sherri gasped. "I can't believe it. No time to be paranoid now, Joe. We are going to call the police."

Joe couldn't tell if she was mocking him or not. Then she went over to the counter, picked up the phone, and began dialing.

Joe dashed over and snatched the receiver from her. "NO! It's OK! It is—OK!"

"Joe! The woman is stalking the house! That's a crime in this country. I know you hate the police, but—" She lunged for the phone. Joe yanked the receiver and sent the phone crashing to the floor. The plastic covering cracked and flew off, and small screws bounced on the floor. Joe hurled down the receiver, the whole thing. Sherri stood there stunned. Joe paced and kicked a piece of loose metal from the phone, and it skidded across the floor, disappearing into a corner. The kitchen creaked with his footsteps. The twins shushed across the linoleum toward their mother. The *Jeffy and Keffy Hour* blared through the frightened silence.

Sherri started to cry. The twins whimpered into the folds her robe. Joe sucked the blood swelling from a small but deep cut in the palm of his hand. He couldn't look at them; he was so ashamed of this thing he could not stop.

Captured!

—Diário de Carlos Manoel Teixeira da Cunha, O Ano 1643

Chapter 17

O Ano 1978

Ah, Melvinor, Sherri thought to herself, let me confess to you. I am jealous of Joe; he just comes to this country, and bam, a year later he gets a great job. A DAY JOB. Because he looks like Ricky Ricardo and reminds people of something they loved when they were kids. He reminds them of sitting in front of the TV in the summer, eating grilled-cheese sandwiches, with nothing else to do for the rest of the day, no job, no school, no nothing. But the frustration doesn't stop with memories of childhood. He meets new people every day and puts on the charm. Ends up with weeds on the seat of his pants from innocent company picnics. Women stalk his home, too.

Melvinor had been coming over for months until Sherri realized that he had never invited her over to his house. She had to ask, but felt like such a silly little woman. "Melvinor, I want to see what your house looks like. I want to be invited for coffee or something. Why don't you want me to visit you? Do you have a crazy wife in the attic? Is she like that wangy broad in *Sunset Boulevard*? Are you afraid something would happen?"

Melvinor rested his hand on her knee. Sand sprinkled off the sleeve of his caftan from one of their days at the beach. "Come on your next day off. Please, I'd love to have you."

"Thanks," she nodded, embarrassed. She was asking an old man for a date, kind of—she didn't want to seem begging for it. She didn't want it to seem like she was trying to make Joe jealous or anything, and she could say she wanted the car to do errands to see one of her waitress girl-friends or something. She didn't want to force Melvinor to love her. She was the head twin after all and couldn't expect much.

On Monday, she got the twins dressed up in matching denim overalls. She dressed them together, diaper-diaper, shirt-shirt, jumper-jumper. The boys liked to watch each other get dressed, and oh those pink fleshy plumpies with sturdy little legs! She should find some daffodils some-where and take their picture. The twins slipped out of the bedroom and ran into the living room while she got dressed. What? Pants or a dress? Her dresses looked out of fashion and had waistlines and full skirts. She almost wished she was an old lady. Then she could date Melvinor. They could be two cute, charming old folks eating senior-citizen specials and drinking watered-down bourbon. He was old enough to be her grand-father. He had the skin of an old man. Should that stand in her way? The oldness of his skin? That was the problem.

The dress with a waistline, then.

She pulled up to his driveway, turned off the motor, and looked up at the two-story house, the outside blond and well painted, the lawn seri-ously green and neat. She took a deep breath and honked her horn. She didn't want to pry the twins out of the car if Melvinor wasn't home or if she had the wrong address. The curtains upstairs flew apart, and some-one opened a sliding glass window. A man with thinning hair and glasses leaned out. "Yes?"

Sherri stepped out from the passenger side. "Is Melvinor home?"

"Of course he is." Then the man withdrew from the window and slammed it shut. Sherri kept her eye on the window, then opened the back door to get the twins. She'd never met Melvinor's roommate. Guess she would now. She snapped off their seatbelts, and they slid out of the car and ran up the steps to the front door. Jeffy began pounding on it, and Keffy copied him. The door opened, and Melvinor stood there in his familiar long, loose caftan, white and blue stripes. He leaned down and pinched their cheeks. They bounced up and down, wanting Melvinor to pick them up.

"No, guys, you're too heavy," Sherri called as she came up the walk. The wind blew out her flowered dress. She pressed down the bubble of fabric and felt a bit like Natalie Wood. Except she didn't have white gloves. She wished she looked like Natalie Wood. She wished Melvinor were James Dean in *Rebel Without a Cause*.

Melvinor looked at her with a kind of calm and held the door open as he guided her in, keeping his hand on her back for a few moments more. She stepped into the spare hallway, a clean space-age oblong with a shiny wood floor. At the end of the hall was a small stairway going up to the second level. Birdboy stood on the bottom stair, watching as she ushered in the twins. The strange fuzzy-necked boy was wearing only his underwear and T-shirt, and his knees, knotty and thicker than his legs, bent inward. His face looked dark in the shadows, except for his protruding mouth, which caught the light from the living room. "There's Birdboy, you remember him," Melvinor said.

Sherri nodded. Jeffy and Keffy tore out from behind their mother and ran toward Birdboy; the children recognized each other and began jumping and tweeting and twerping. Sherri lingered in the hall for a second, a bit worried about her boys, but Melvinor called, "They'll be OK. Jeremy is home, too." Then he extended his hand. She took it reluctantly, so strange to be holding hands like this, and patted her skirt, trying to feel like Natalie Wood, trying to feel young, trying to feel like a heart twin instead of a miserable head twin.

He led her into the living room, a bright, clean, and stylish room. Two big Mexican-style pots with aloe flanked either side of the front bay window. A grayish satin couch, bone-white walls, and a poster of a South American Indian in red body paint and words that said "The Amazon — Tupi or Not Tupi." No other pictures. One newspaper, compactly folded, lay on the glass-top coffee table. Sherri tried to connect Melvinor to the room, tried to comprehend his spareness, his simple ease with everything. "Who's the decorator?" she quipped.

Melvinor smiled vaguely, turned, and went into the kitchen without a word. Sherri put down her purse and followed him. The kitchen seemed clean and square jawed, with a nice blond wood table pushed next to a window with a view of the garden. It was solemn, but now made edgy by noise: the mugs clinking as Melvinor gathered them from the pantry, water roaring into the empty kettle, the gas flame hissing. Melvinor watched the water boil. She could hear the footsteps of her children playing upstairs and someone using a bathroom. The water boiling made a soothing white shussly noise, and soft steam puffed out the spout. It almost seemed Japanese, something penetrating and meaningful, empty yet full. Sherri thought she should say something, but felt too stupid to risk it.

Melvinor carried the kettle over to the table and put several boxes of tea bags in front of her. She selected mint, and Melvinor poured the water into her mug. Then he fixed tea for himself and left the room. It seemed so strange, Melvinor living with this man who had no family except for this bizarre son from the Amazon. That was all Melvinor seemed to know about his roommate. And the fact that he had an ex-wife. Sherri took a sip of her green-yellow tea and looked for a clever saying on the mug, but it was blank.

Melvinor came back into the kitchen with a notebook. "I want to read you something," he said.

"A poem?"

He opened the notebook, the kind with the hard black covers, and began reading from one of the pages:

Mona, like the whirlwind you took me away.
My dear Mona, away with the wind.

Heddie, my daughter, also with the wind,
Away, away, both of you with the wind.

His voice got high pitched with nervousness. He snapped his fingers as if to speed himself up:

Cancer took both of you, my sweets
and I am in a sandstorm, wandering the earth,
I find the words of Isaiah carved in the cave.
Oh the shining sun, Oh sandstorm
Oh my dear wife, my dear daughter.
As Isaiah said, vanities of one man can kill many lifetimes.

He stopped and seemed out of breath. Sherri squinted because she didn't know much about poetry; it seemed like a sad poem, though it didn't rhyme. She nodded. "Nice. Very nice. You seem educated, Melvinor. Not that I would know."

Melvinor thumbed the rest of the pages rapidly to show her. All blank. Like moth wings. "Look, I can't write anymore. I'm trying, but I can't."

Sherri ventured, "Are Mona and Heddie—?"

"Both died of cancer within a year of each other."

"I'm so sorry," Sherri whispered and took another sip of tea. She wondered what she would say if Joe died. She wondered what she would write.

Melvinor looked at her earnestly. She saw the tiny pink veins in the whites of his eyes. "I am so lucky." He spoke softly, "I had the most wonderful wife. Mona. When she died, there was no one else I could—" Melvinor looked down at his tea and rubbed his fingers on the handle. "Well, my daughter of course, but she was taken, too. Sometimes I get angry at God. Like Isaiah."

Sherri held her breath—

"It's not good for me to be like this after so many years. Perhaps my mind is slipping, but I will never forget how much I could love someone. Jeremy is different, of course. Love for him is bitterness. So bitter he doesn't want to talk about it. Won't even say his ex-wife's name because it's like swallowing nails. And I can't help him. Not one little bit."

Sherri felt something shake and loosen inside; she felt soft and foolish, then sad. She put her face in her hands. Melvinor had had the perfect marriage. Of course, how could she not guess? Mourning has made him basic, and a bit spiritual; his robe was pure and loose; he could fly up to heaven this instant and join Mona. How could Sherri talk to this man about her husband, who stomps around the house with his passionate pleadings? *"You don't understand! You don't understand!"* But, damn, Joe wouldn't tell her a thing, and now he was seeing another woman. A woman who *understood* him?

Melvinor reached over and held her hand. "Are you alright?"

"Fine." But she burst out crying. "Oh god," she said, "I can't believe this." She pinched the upper part of her nose to get herself to stop. Tears ran down her fingers. She wanted to kill Joe for making her act foolish in her stupid Natalie Wood dress, having tea with an old man who still loved his dead wife! "If you must know, my marriage is—" She choked on her tears. "Jesus, I'm sorry Melvinor."

Melvinor reached over and gave her a paper napkin. She took the napkin and cried in short dry jags. She could sense Melvinor's hand stretched out to her. Then she took a deep breath and blew her nose. "What a soap opera. Shit. Well," she sniffed long and hard, her sinuses bitter and burning. Then she stopped. "Well. Some outburst, huh?"

Melvinor smiled weakly, then took her hand. "Bring your tea to the living room." They both went into the living room, sat down on the couch, and placed their cups on the folded newspaper on the coffee table. Melvinor rested his skinny arm on the back of the couch behind her shoulders. She slowly laid her head against his shoulder, and he whispered barely audibly, "That's it." She looked out the front window. Across the street, a pepper tree's droopy branches swept the fence. His cheek swept the top of her head; she could feel his warmth. She almost wanted him to have a scratchy beard; she wanted him manly. With one hand, he threaded his fingers through hers, and with the other he fondled her hair. She could smell him, clean like soap with a tinge of orange spice from his tea, and the thickness of his breath. She let her head relax, her tight breath loosen. "Oh, Melvinor," Sherri said finally, "to be in love I can't even imagine it. Maybe I was born in the wrong generation."

Melvinor squeezed her hand and kissed the top of her head.

Sherri remembered her mother. After her father had left the family, her mother had brought home a lover, a man in a wheelchair. It was right after her sister Susan had been killed. Sherri had learned about sex from Susan and then, moments before the accident, had learned about love. And Sherri, being the head twin instead of the heart twin, had sat at the dinner table with no one to discuss this little matter of "how do they—?" She had looked at the withered legs of their guest and wondered—? She saw her mother, overly cheerful, forcing a laugh and good times as she carved the roast beef, and the man, waving his arms wildly, like a windmill, the only thing he could really move. She was a bit scared of him, crippled like that, and even with useless legs he seemed uncontrollable. After dinner, she heard her mother whispering to him, then heard her slowly pushing his chair into the bedroom, the wheels rubbing on the carpet, and the man laughing like a Charlie McCarthy dummy, and then silence. Until this day, the sound of a squeaky wheel gave her the creeps.

Is this the same thing? The wheelchair man and Melvinor? If he were younger, would what he was doing, kissing her this tenderly, seem so unusual? More tenderly than Joe?

She heard some running upstairs, and she was a bit concerned for Jeffy and Keffy, but Jeremy was there; he'd keep an eye on them. Melvinor stayed perfectly still, but not shifting uncomfortably. She knew they could stay like this for a long time, strangely comfortable, not really in love, but might be thinking about it.

The house cracked its lonely, aching joints, and for a long time things were still. Then Sherri heard behind her the sound of a man clearing his throat. She turned her head. Melvinor's roommate had been watching them intently. Melvinor looked back, too, and removed his arm from around her shoulder. "Jeremy," he said, "join us."

Jeremy shoved his hands deep into the pockets of an old sweater and sank into a chair across the coffee table from them. His appearance— loose sweater, flannel pants, large socks, and no shoes—reminded Sherri of babies when you dress them in clothes way too big. She even had a flash of thought, "he'll grow into them," but no, of course that was ridiculous. His eyebrows were arched a bit like Joe's, but much paler, and his skin looked ashy and drawn, made worse by his bony jaw and thin neck. Jeremy leaned his forearms on his knees, clasped his hands together, and stared incredulously at the two people in front of him, acting like lovers. Jeremy looked like he had just run out of a burning house, tossing on him whatever was available, leaving behind his belongings and his children, losing everything he had loved. The gray sweater made him look smokey and confused. He bunched up his body as he sank deeper into the chair. Sherri wanted to say, "I'm sorry you seem so sad," but she didn't want to make him cry. So she smiled and said, rather fake-perky, using her waitress voice, "I hope my kids didn't keep you from your work."

"He's driving me crazy," he said simply.

"Oh," Sherri got up, "I'm so sorry," pouring out her words profusely, looking for her purse, brushing herself off — the disoriented way mothers get, apologizing for being in the way, clumsy, a litany of *I'm sorries*, "I'll get them, they are — we must go — so much trouble — sorry to — "

Jeremy held up his hand. "It's not your kids, ma'am. It's mine."

Melvinor pulled her back down on the couch beside him.

Jeremy looked hard at the old man and spoke with his mouth tight, his soft chin almost trembling. "It's the Bird, Mel. What should I do? What should I do with the Bird? I'm at my wit's end. Where's the *book* to tell me how to *do* it?"

Melvinor sat back and crossed his arms and legs. "May God counsel you with your burden, my friend. I am just a simple old man. My wife and daughter died long ago, and all I remember is joy."

Jeremy's eyes darted between her and Melvinor. She clasped her hands together and smiled thinly at him, imagining she was a prim young lady wearing Mary Jane patent leathers. Jeremy rubbed his tongue on his upper teeth, keeping his lips closed. Then he took a deep breath. "Enough of this." He got up abruptly. "Mel, I'll tell you this," and he pointed toward the old man, "if anyone had told me I'd end up an ornithologist, I would have told them to flap their arms and fly to Machu Picchu."

With those blocky-sounding words, he left the room abruptly and went back up the stairs.

Sherri heard his footsteps going slowly, almost reluctantly; he seemed so lonely. "Doesn't he at least have a girlfriend?" Sherri asked after a pause. "Someone that smart with a good job, a teacher in a college? I can't even imagine a life like that. There must be cute girls in his classes."

Melvinor shook his head. "No. Just his ex-wife who caused him a lot of grief. That's it. Don't know much about her. She was in the movies, I think."

"Yeah," Sherri said, "movie folks. Crazies, that's for sure. Sometimes they come into the Eye and Rib and—"

Just then the ceiling above them thumped with whoops and cries. She heard the twins crying, too, tripping over something and calling her.

"My God, what happened?" Sherri jumped up and started up the stairs. Birdboy's screech penetrated the walls, a screech not quite boyish, something zoolike. Jeremy was yelling out of his wits.

When she entered the room, she saw her twins in a corner, dumfounded, not really hurt, both bug-eyed, with matching expressions and matching outfits.

Jeremy was struggling with Birdboy, pinning the boy under his arm. Birdboy kicked, flailed his arms, and made a small bleeding scratch on Jeremy's face. "Stop that!" Jeremy hollered as he slapped the twitching arms and legs, then pleaded, squeezing the boy against him, "Come on, please, little man!"

"Hey!" Sherri cried, "Let me talk to the boy. I know what it's like—"

But Jeremy roared, "Get away, please!" Birdboy seemed to calm down for a second. Then the boy leaped up, ran to the open window, and threw himself forward. Jeremy lunged over, grabbed his shirt, and then snatched him by the waist, trying to pull him back, but Birdboy clung onto the windowsill. Jeremy's face was sweating, and strands of his longish hair stuck to his forehead in a coil. He rasped in the boy's ear, "Please, please don't." Finally, Birdboy let go of the sill, and Jeremy fell back against his desk, then wrested Birdboy to the ground. Both of them took heavy breaths in unison, Birdboy's hand gently scratching the floor. Jeremy's shoulders fell as Birdboy relaxed underneath him. Jeremy cupped his hand on top of the boy's head to soothe him, then lay his head on Birdboy's back. "He says he wants to fly," Jeremy muttered. "How do you tell a child-development specialist that your kid wants to fly? Literally."

"You have a handful. I'm so sorry."

Jeremy carried Birdboy over to his desk chair and sat down with the kid on his lap. Birdboy curled up and covered his face with one of his hands. "It's something about falling in love with the wrong woman. In the Amazon somewhere. I went in as a boy and came out an old man."

Birdboy trilled softly.

"A Brazilian woman, then?" Sherri said.

"Yes."

"My husband is Brazilian. He can be difficult, too."

"It's more than difficult." Jeremy closed his eyes and rocked Birdboy. It was clear he wanted her to go.

Sherri went over to her twins. She squatted before them and gently stroked their little bellies with her knuckles. "Huh, fellas, OK now?" But they stretched their gaze past her and stared with fascination at Birdboy. She ran her hands over their hair, smoothing out their distress, listening for their little panicky short breaths. Instead, they both whirred in their light, human-baby voices.

"If I knew what was in Birdboy's heart," Jeremy piped in again as he combed his fingers through the boy's hair, "the way you do with your sons, I'm sure everything would have ended quite differently."

Sherri took Keffy's and Jeffy's hands, and they descended the stairs. They went back to the living room, where Melvinor was waiting. Sherri released her boys' hands. "They don't take after Joe, that's for sure. If they did, they'd have been in a state by now."

She and Melvinor stood facing each other, a bit shaken themselves. Melvinor smiled and put his hands on her shoulders.

"Well," she chuckled, a bit embarrassed, "I can see why you don't invite me over. You kinda do have a crazy wife."

Melvinor leaned over and gave her a small kiss on the mouth. "As Isaiah said, grief gives us other opportunities to show love." She looked

at his eyes; they were squinted, the way one gets when there is an at-
traction, but not enough courage to dare. She wondered what Mona had
looked like. Sherri imagined her with dark, short, curly hair. And his
daughter she imagined blond, probably a college student, full of promise. Both dying would be like having nothing. But Melvinor's grief made
him peaceful. She could stand for another kiss, but it might come out
too absurd; she might knock him over if she tried.

She felt the twins nestling against her legs, their cranky little heads
rubbing against her upper thigh. She reached down and fingered their
soft baby locks.

"I have to go," she murmured, "I think they're getting tired."

Melvinor nodded. Sherri wanted one more kiss, and she smiled, hoping to charm him. But he backed away, and she could hear the bones of
his feet crack. This house, now so completely silent, made her feel calm
but alone.

These astounding warriors are the very picture of filth and pestilence in household matters. The Amazon hut reeks of flesh and rotting vegetation. The meat, hung from bamboo hooks, is black with soot from the fire pit. The fetters, made from tapir leather, have dug into my swollen wrists. They will let me write only for so long; after that, they snatch the writing implements from my hand. We are not allowed to leave without an escort, and we are forced to accompany their hunting excursions in order to carry home their kill. They come to us with food constantly, as if we were cattle to be fattened. Baskets of fruit and grilled fish and *masato* are the more palatable items. — *Diário de Carlos Manoel Teixeira da Cunha, O Ano* 1643

Chapter 18

O Ano 1978

Antropofagia I
Cannibalism — The Hunger

Rosea carried her steely dog-killer .22 everywhere to protect herself. In her imagination, even in her dreams, dogs chased her wherever she went. She woke up as if still inside a dog's mouth. Her dingy bedroom smelled damp and warm from the freak early-morning rain shower; sunlight made a burning strip on the floor near the window, and the shadows of burglar bars snarled through the curtains. Rosea obsessed about dogs in the garden until it got to the point that she saw fleet-footed greyhounds chasing her car down the highway. At work, a mastiff crouched under her desk. The dark-blue alleys were Doberman nights, and weedy, dry, empty lots were German shepherd days. She thought of prison and dogs baying behind bars. She was asking for it, playing herself to the limit. Her world waited for disaster, its jaws poised.

Rosea knew she could chase Joe with doglike perseverance, with Amazon longing strong enough to bust three million coconuts. She imagined chasing him through Vaughan Peter's new movie *Capture at San Cristobal*, a blockbuster action flick where Vaughan single-handedly mows down an evil dictator from *somewhere* in Latin America with a large ball of fire that rolls through taco stands and burns up rain forests. She imagined rescuing Joe while firing her gun at a herd of FBI men and finally stealing a boat and taking him to a deserted island with nothing but palm trees and turtles and a freshwater spring. She had devoured her heart in the quest for love, and now there was a big hole. When she wept with desire, she didn't have a pretty dainty cry, a lace-hanky cry. She had an ugly cry, a hacky howl, the cry of anguish described in Amazon legends.

Joe followed her into the garden with the ghost of some warrior prodding his scars, licking his memory. Who knew what dogged *his* mind, only that she made him crave her. They kissed, their lips making small plocking sounds. His eyes sparkled as he craned his neck for her tongue to brush down his jugular, frightening him to death.

Antropofagia II
Cannibalism — The Steps

The ceremony is parceled in pieces. The warriors capture the prisoner and hold him for many months. He is fed and sleeps with women of his desire. When the day of celebration comes, he is taken to the river and washed, then led to the village square. The chief praises the prisoner for his bravery and skill in battle and proclaims that the honor of being eaten by his fellow man far surpasses being eaten by worms.

Rosea and Joe spread their clothes under a cluster of bushes hidden from view. Anyone who came up here would have to be looking for them.

Any dog that came up here would be shot. Joe lay flat on his back to hide his scar, but he had a smaller one, a white thread across his collarbone. He seemed melancholy, his manhood in soft, round puffs, too concerned with other things. He'd seen a vision a few times, he said, a woman in white, her hands stained with yellow palm oil. He didn't believe in visions because he was becoming practical here in America, but still . . .

Hands: Rosea ran her tongue between his fingers, then continued following the life line on his palm.

Joe stroked down her nose with his thumb.

She kissed his palm as if it were a flower, then—

Arms: Rosea traced her fingers up Joe's arm covered with dark, silky hair. She turned his arm so that his hand faced upward and traced the maroon veins floating underneath his soft, light-brown skin. He had a small scar in the crease of his elbow. "Where is this from?" she said.

Joe's face grew sad. "Soccer game."

She nipped his shoulder and sucked a small lipful of flesh. Joe raised his head slightly, caught her nipple, and pulled it into his mouth. Rosea stuck her hands in Joe's hair and wrapped a curl around each of her fingers.

Chest: Rosea ran her knuckles down his face, his neck, then placed her hands on his chest and licked a small patch of dark hair on his breastbone.

Stomach: She lowered her head onto his belly. He flinched, his stomach tightened, then yielded. Rosea traced an imaginary black genipapo coil starting from the curve of his ribs, making a dark spiral of trouble on his skin. The black genipapo dye drained into a whorl between his legs. She rubbed her mouth on the wiry hair, releasing the scent of a man. Rosea opened her mouth, and her tongue curled into a hook as if using it to pull in his entire body. Then she sunk into his flesh, and it disappeared just like that.

Loins, the Rest: Joe grabbed her shoulders, pulled her down beside him, and got on top of her. His hips slid between her legs. He took one of her knees and coaxed it up. She brought up her other knee and held him with her thighs. He closed his eyes and brought himself down, rocking until their clothes and leaves gathered in the small of her back.

Cannibalism — The Sacrifice

An honorable captive tries to fight back, argues with the chief that there are many people who love him and would fight on his behalf. In spite of his threats, his head gets smashed into bits with a club. The women of the village take the prisoner's body, lay it on its stomach, and begin to trace a knife down its spine —

A branch cracked. First, it seemed like nothing. Then footsteps shuffled the dried leaves on the ground. They scrambled up. Rosea grabbed her pants and began stuffing her large legs inside the tight denim. Then she threw on her shirt, leaving the buttons undone. Joe struggled to turn his pants right side out first, then managed to wrestle them on. A bush rattled, a few loose leaves spiraled in the air. Rosea grabbed her underwear and Joe's T-shirt and crammed them in her purse. She peered through the branches. A man was making his way through the trees, and the sun hit his belt buckle and sunglasses as he appeared and disappeared in flashes of light.

Rosea scooped up the shoes, and the two lovers thrashed out of their hideout as they tried to get to the wall. The approaching intruder coughed and pushed his way forward, flapping aside a low-hanging branch. Rosea and Joe hurried, flinching from their bare feet on the ground. "Go faster!" Rosea whispered harshly as they scrambled over a fallen log. "Keep going!"

"Hey!" a voice called.

"Shit," Joe cried, stumbling to a stop, "we're caught."

"Go," Rosea shoved him forward with her armful of shoes.

"Hey!" the voice persisted.

They turned around. Then she saw him. It was some kind of golf-links vision, here by himself. She knew this type. Anger in her grew and mounted into fury. It was a phantom from L.A., a big-time mogul's lackey or a small-time producer, looking studied snappy and bland like milk, hiding the lasciviousness. The man's pink scalp showed through his thin, sandy hair, and he wore khakis, a pink polo to match his scalp, and spiffo moccasins. He was holding a clipboard, but he spoke like a policeman.

"What are you two doing here?" he demanded.

"Well, what are you doing here?" Rosea fumed.

Joe nudged her. "We're going."

"Wait just a minute here," the man said, "this is private property, you shouldn't be here."

"We're leaving," Joe assured. Under his breath, "Come on, Rosea!"

"Well, who are you, Vaughan Peters?" Rosea bellowed.

"None of your business. I have a permit."

Rosea's back stiffened, and she dropped the shoes. Yeah, she knew these men. They worked with her mother. Galaxy Studio goons. And here they were again. The motherfuckers just kept multiplying like outer-space aliens. These men used to slip pep pills between her mother's clenched teeth as if she were a horse, and they poisoned her *mai tais* with hope. They were always laughing at some private joke and carried posterboard renderings of new ideas for torturous bingo-bongo hats. They loved tropical things gone mad. When her mother was on the outs, they scooted around like schoolboys with a lot of money and had jaguar convertibles and faggy boyfriends who worked in real estate. "If you hadn't had that kid," they'd say, "we could say you were still available, pure as Amazon snow." These brittle men drove lonely actresses to suicide, actresses who waited for the big break and for love. These men — their muscles slim and hard from weight machines, their flesh slippery and blue veined — these men, like zombies, never died because no one dared to kill them.

"I'm reporting you," the man barked, gesturing with his clipboard chock-full of great big money plans, wiggling his little butt as if he had a little tail bopping side to side, "and finish dressing, will you!"

Rosea unclasped her purse. He kept yapping about the shoes strewn on the ground in front of her, her exposed chest, and snorting like a Chihuahua. She slid her hand inside the purse, grabbed the .22 under the crumpled underwear, and pointed it at Mr. Golf Shirt. He blinked his beady canine eyes. "Hey there. Whoa. Whoa." She saw Joe's hand reaching over to snatch the gun. She pulled the trigger. Time suddenly sped forward like a Moviola gone mad, when the film just rips through the lens. A red spot flew onto the man's shirt as if his blood had been hurled at him. His eyes widened, his pouting mouth opened just a bit, then he fell straight back, landing with his arms out to the sides.

Rosea glanced back at Joe, who she expected would be collapsing or crying, but instead he was examining the body severely, with no expression. He motioned to her, just like that. "We're going now." Then he ran ahead of her to the car. Rosea stuffed the gun back in her purse, gathered up the shoes and limped after him. She turned to get one more look at the dead man. Papers from his clipboard fluttered on the ground like white birds trapped in a net. Rosea felt numb. The dead man just lay there in his pink shirt. He seemed like a toy, a golf doll, a Hollywood artifact just tossed under some bushes. Didn't even plead for his life. As if he didn't have one.

Rosea tossed the shoes over the wall, then climbed over using a toe-hold between the bricks. Joe was leaning over the car, his elbows on the hood and his face in his hands. His back was bare and goose-bumped, a large scar traveling from just below his shoulder to his waist, and other paler scars crisscrossing over his back, like confused purple roads. Rosea opened her purse and gave him his T-shirt. "Let's go," she said.

Joe slowly slipped on his T-shirt. He didn't look at her. "Give me the keys," he ordered, "I'm driving." Rosea placed the keys in his hand. He snatched them, went to the other side of the car and unlocked his door, got in, then reached over and unlocked hers. Rosea threw the shoes into the back seat and slipped into the passenger side. Joe started the car and tore off down the hill.

Rosea tried to decide what it felt like to kill someone. It was as if she had watched someone else do it. It felt like the times she would listen to the women at Frontera, discussing their murders. The women looked normal, almost nonchalant, and some had kids. They said that when they pulled the trigger, it felt unreal. As if all the things they were mad about in life just went "powie!" For a split second, they felt clean, almost virginal, but then they knew to flee like hell. They fled from the dogs that constantly chased them. Sometimes they'd see the dogs and sometimes not, but the fear was always there, and the howling in their ears was unbearable. Couldn't sleep without a dog eye gleaming right near their feet.

"Where do you want to escape to now, eh?" Joe muttered as they spilled onto the freeway.

"Drive east toward Riverside," Rosea said, buttoning her shirt finally, "let's get out of here."

Rosea knew she'd just have to *cala* her *boca*. Just shut her chops. No Amazon talk, no Sheena the Jungle Queen in goona flicks, no animal skins logic, no nothing. The shit's gotta get worse now, believe it.

Dom Marcus Pedro Ferraz de Lima knows the ways of the Petiguares, whose reputation for fierceness and cannibalism was well known, even among their French allies who bartered for brazilwood. Lima was captured with us, so we looked to him for counsel because we had never encountered such wild women. Some of our men had even mocked Friar Gaspar de Carvajal's account of Orellana's Amazons, claiming that these women were nothing but the fevered lust of a Catholic priest. Lima, our expert counsel, believes these women hold similar practices, at least in their fierceness, and he has instructed us to act according to the Petiguar customs if we ever hope to save our skins.

— *Diário de Carlos Manoel Teixeira da Cunha, O Ano* 1643

Chapter 19

O Ano 1978

The canal stretched as far as they could see, from cleft of the mountains at one end to the overpass at the other. They could not see the water in front of them because the concrete sides sloped upward, but in the distance the dark-green water looked like just another slab of colored cement. They stopped in a whorl of car tracks; they were not the only ones to come here. Joe turned off the ignition, reminding himself that Rosea had pulled the trigger, not he. He had known nothing about the gun.

"How did you know about this place, huh?" Joe said, but couldn't look at her.

"Don't ask." Rosea clutched her purse tighter, then jumped out of the car. "Come on," she said as she ran toward the incline.

Joe slipped out of the car and followed her. The air smelled like the rotting oranges from the grove behind them, the one they had driven through to get here, where workers had raked up piles of gray, powdery balls of decay. The ground hurt his bare feet because he hadn't had time to put his shoes back on. They stood at the edge of the water, and Rosea hoisted her purse onto her shoulder. She jabbed her chin forward, intently watching the olive green water puckering and rolling past them. Joe turned away, feeling a bit dizzy, afraid he'd fall into the water. The zipper from Rosea's purse growled. From the corner of his eye he saw her rubbing the gun with her shirt to remove her fingerprints, then dropping the gun into the water. She was so quick with it, just a splash.

A pickup rumbled out of the orchard and came toward them.

"Oh my god," Joe cried, "we're dead."

"Act calm," Rosea said. "If you fall to pieces, they can smell you from a mile." She grabbed his hand, and Joe tried to jerk it away, but she held on fast. "Hold on to me. Do a bit of acting, for god's sake."

The front grill of the pickup smiled through a cloud of dust. Joe lowered his eyes. The driver waved as he passed them and scooted off toward the distant subdivision.

Joe followed the truck with his eyes until even the trickle of exhaust had disappeared. "Tell me, Rosea, do you know what it is like to be in prison?"

Rosea made her finger into a hook, grabbed a strip of her hair, and pulled it across her neck. The dark shadows under her eyes made her look as though she had been beaten.

"Yes," she said finally, "I've been in prison."

"What did you go to prison for?"

"I burned down my husband's house."

"You're insane. I see it now."

"He drove me crazy. He suffocated me."

"He should have suffocated you."

"He loved me too much." Rosea flipped her hair back, her eyes slanting, defiant. "No, he didn't love me. He loved the fuckin' Amazon forest.

It's not even there anymore, and he still loves it. It got burned, too, and nobody gives a rat's ass about that."

"You Americans are so spoiled," Joe seethed. "You are loved, and you destroy everything. You deserve nothing."

"I'm on parole. I'm as good as dead now."

"You sure are."

"So are you, PAL!" Rosea exploded. "You are IN IT with me! You probably got your own rap sheet, don't you? I bet you were in prison, too, and you kissed someone's ass to come all the way over here to the land of the free and the home of the brave!"

Joe grabbed Rosea's arms and pulled her forward. Her face opened in surprise, and she mouthed "stop that," but Joe squeezed his hands tighter around her arms. "Listen to me! Listen to the truth!" he shouted.

"Fuck you!" Rosea turned her head away, but Joe slapped her, and she tried to bolt. He grabbed her arms again and jerked her forward, screaming, "Listen! Listen!"

He'd played that scene over and over again: the doors opening with the keys gotten from the bribed landlord, the two policemen grabbing him and Sonia, the apartment doors staying closed despite his screams, him riding blindfolded in the back of a van, the police mocking him that Sonia was not done, such a pretty *moça* like that. Joe, in a surge of anger, hit Rosea harder across the cheek.

Rosea screamed, "Don't hit me! Kill me, but don't hit me!"

Joe started thrashing at her, almost as if caught in a net. Rosea crouched, but kept screaming at him to snap out of it, but her screams were far away. He saw her face, wild within her hair flying through his hands. Finally he gasped, then stopped and pulled away.

Rosea sank to her knees and rocked back and forth, moaning. "Fuck you! Fuck you!"

Joe began shivering, and the low roar of the wind caught her occasional whimper.

Finally Rosea spoke, her voice steady. "I was in jail a long time, you know. I'm paying for my sins. Now I live in a dingy apartment. I get to watch my neighbors' kids play and have a normal life that I'll never have. I smell their barbecues. I'm already in hell, believe me."

Joe turned to go back to the car. "You don't know what hell is. You have no idea."

Joe came home late, and on this warm night he watched his boys in the front yard tossing around the soccer ball he had given them. The ball came up to their knees. He sat and watched their fat legs chasing it. He wished they looked like him, just a little, his curly hair maybe. He had the desperate urge to embrace them, both of them, one clasped in each arm. He wanted to demand that they love him; he wanted to feel their innocence and have it sink into his skin.

Jeffy, the aggressive one, tossed the ball, and it dropped on Keffy's head. Keffy looked stunned.

"Hey, hey," Joe called out, "não chora. Hit the ball with your head." Keffy needed to be taught how to act like a man. No, no. He wanted Keffy to cry so he could hold him in his arms and comfort him. But Keffy didn't cry, but instead looked at Joe a little vacuously, the wind flipping a few strands of blond hair. He rubbed his head, and they continued playing.

Joe remembered soccer on the beach when he was a boy. All the boys played it — scooting an old ball with their feet, batting it around from instep to instep, flicking it off the toe with a pow, squatting low and try-ing to hit it with the tops of their heads. He remembered brown knees, white knees, the sand with soft craters the shape of tumbling bodies. The goal posts remained as permanent beach equipment. Sometimes the boys chased after the ball as it rolled down toward the ocean and got caught up in the waves. He remembered lunging in the water, and the sounds of noisy trucks jangling, stray dogs barking, popping firecrackers up in the favelas. He remembered the sand fleas and their delicious itch and buzz, and how he played so hard that his stomach swelled with air gulped in excitement.

Joe went over and swooped up the ball. The twins looked at him.

"Come here," Joe called as he sat back down on the steps, "come here."

The boys looked at each other, then waddled over. Joe put his arms around them, squeezed them tight, wouldn't let go. Their little mouths opened like beaks. "Daddy loves you," Joe whispered and pulled them tighter. He kissed them hard on the cheeks, one, then the other, over and over again. He heard them squeal, but he was in a trance, getting his tears on their little T-shirts. Oh, little innocent Americans, little Angelenos, oh these angels from the City of Angels. *Beijos*, kisses, *ele beijou-os loucamente*, like crazy. *Podia continuar beijando-os assim pra sempre.* He could kiss them like this forever.

They both stared back at Joe, their two faces identical; they were his sons after all, one man — split in half.

He shivered and pushed his boys away. The metal gate and the short chain-link fence surrounding the yard glinted under the streetlights. The city! City of Angels! L.A. always pacing at night, rattling its bars, a stunned prisoner waiting for the next interrogation — !

— *Who did you vote for in '63?*

— *Don't remember.*

— *Goulart?*

— *Não sei. Não me lembro.*

— *What do you mean, you don't know, that you don't remember?*

— *Politicians are all the same.*

— *Do you know anyone in the Acão Popular?*

— *No.*

— *The Movimento Revolucionario?*

— *No.*

— *What do you know about Burke Elbrick?*

— *Who's he?*

— *Don't play stupid with me, babaco.*

— *I don't know him!*

— *How did you meet Sonia Mendes?*

— *Forgot.*

— *Why didn't you go to the university?*

— *I couldn't pass the vestibular.*

— *Too stupid to pass the big test, cara? Well, what do you think of the Fifth Institutional Act?*

— *No opinion.*

— *What do you think of Tropicalistas?*

— *No opinion.*

And it got worse from there. They say that the very act of torture makes you forget what you used to know. They say that when your torturers force you to type your life story, you should keep it short because they will ask for it over and over again, and if you forget one thing, they'll accuse you of making up your life. The purpose of torture is to tear down your previous life and rebuild it the way they want it. Joe was trying to rebuild his life here in America. He had rebuilt it and now was watching himself tear it down with truths that made no sense.

No, I did not kill her.

No, I did not kill him.

Joe wanted Sherri to go with him to a carnival at Griffith Park. "Come on, meu bem," he pleaded. "It's not just the Mexican stuff; they are supposed to have Brazilian music, too." Come on, meu bem, he continued in his head, get into an argument with me so I can fall to my knees and confess to my crime. Let me wrap my arms around your legs as if they were a whipping post and beg forgiveness. But Sherri said she'd rather everyone be out of her hair so she could clean house, and he could take the kids, too, while he was at it.

Joe pushed the double stroller through the gates and paid his fee. Sherri dressed the twins in matching clothes, and immediately people swooped down to admire the little ones — the old soft-faced *vovós*, pinching their cheeks with soft, padded fingers and cooing "que bonitinho!" and the young L.A. girls stopping their boyfriends to marvel at the two cute look-alikes.

Along with the red and green serpentine bow-tied with small Mexican flags, banners in Brazil's national colors, green and yellow, flapped in the wind as bossa nova blasted through the speakers. Joe closed his eyes for a second and imagined he was somewhere else. He could hear strains of his language among the Spanish and English, and people laughing and cracking open cans of cold beer; he could smell *feijoada* with its black beans and smoky meat. He opened his eyes, and the twins were leaning forward, reaching for something. Oh yes, of course, the twins wanted the balloons that a clown was giving away, the balloons with the name of a travel agency. The clown came over, exclaimed "Twins!" and delicately picked two yellow balloons for the identical boys with identical yellow hair. The clown held the balloons out by the strings, but Joe said, "No, give us a yellow and green," and the clown complied. Joe tied the strings of both balloons—the yellow and the green—to the front of the stroller. "There, meus filhos, is my red, white, and blue."

He pushed the stroller down the walkway, lined on either side with booths and small stages. Some booths played music from loudspeakers, others displayed primitive art, fake batiks, baseball caps, and inflatable beach balls made to look like giant soccer balls. Strips of meat fried on large grills. Metal bowls of lettuce rested in basins of ice water. Joe was hungry for the smells, but his belly felt too tight to eat.

Everything seemed far away. It flashed in his mind, *I am very different from these people here*, but he tucked his thoughts away again and focused on the sound of the conga drums and the twang of a *berimbau*. He turned and spoke Portuguese to a group of people, but they only looked at him because in fact they could not understand what he was saying above the loud music. The twins rocked gently in their seats; the stroller squeaked in rhythm. Joe saw the world blurring the way it happens during carnival.

He pushed the stroller over to an outdoor stage. A tinsel costume with silver wings, a giant butterfly, fluttered before him and disappeared into the glare of the sun. Music poured out of everyone's mouth in place of words. A man with a straw hat shuffled over and asked him for a cigarette in Portuguese; Joe pulled a pack out of his shirt pocket and watched the man as he took the cigarette, smiled, and lit it with a lighter. The man's brown and mottled face was crinkled like a basket, and his tired eyes were puffy and wrinkled from simple grief. Joe muttered "Senhor—" and then opened his mouth to talk, but out came a memory of Brazil, some words from a samba or maybe a ballad of sadness. The man spoke again, gestured with his hands, the cigarette in the cleft of his fingers. Joe must have been speaking Portuguese because the man kept answering him.

"De onde você é?" Joe finally asked.

"From Rio, just like you, my friend, I can tell by your accent," the man said. He said he made pizza for a living, and he was here in America to make money. Then the man grabbed his hand, spoke fervently, his tears so salty they hung in the corners of his eyes. A group of girls strolled by, and both men gave an ogle, normal in these cases, but the girls tossed their long dark hair in contempt; suddenly Joe saw them burst into green araras that flew once around the crowd and exploded into sequins. The man shook Joe's shoulder, "Meu jovem! Que aconteceu!" Joe's eyes followed the path of falling sequins, then turned to see the old man almost shouting in his ear. "Parece enrolado!"

Suddenly it was samba. A cheer went up. The drums, the *cuícas*, the tambourines, and—the sexy fantasia girls! That's what everyone came to see. The silver butterfly flew in front of the stage and turned into a woman in a fantasia with giant open wings. Women with green and yellow fantasias danced behind her. Their large colorful feathers curled at the tips, and a coil of sequin-covered wire held firm their small breasts. Draped strings of beaded necklaces rattled on their bellies and thighs, and the Americans sighed: oh yes, this is Brazil!

The man hadn't left, and, in fact, he drew his tired face next to Joe's and shouted, gesturing close to Joe's face. Then he paused with his mouth slightly open, waiting for Joe to answer. He smelled like tobacco and coffee, and a bit of beer. Joe felt the twins tapping his hand, but he brushed their little fingers away. They tapped him harder, but Joe couldn't take his eyes off the man.

Joe finally blurted out, "Eu assassinei alguém!" I killed someone. The man cried out and embraced him hard, leaning his head on his shoulders and began weeping bitterly, his gray hair stiff, as with fright, and badly cut with chunks shaved off behind his ears. He babbled out loud in Portuguese, "Yes, I have killed people, too, with my loneliness."

Joe hugged the man hard, as if to embrace Sherri and ask for forgiveness for destroying her spirit and causing her unquenchable unhappiness that he could not solve or sweet-talk away. There was no bridge between his two countries, only desert and jungle and water. Over the man's shoulder, Joe saw dancers carrying a large paper fish, its scales fluorescent green and yellow and swirling, people around it chanting and waving their arms.

Joe stood in the middle of the melee, clasping his Brazilian *compan-heiro*, hanging onto his Brazilian world. The Brazilian man lifted his face from Joe's shoulder, then without a word wandered away, zigzagging in his own smoke, not even noticing the beautiful girls with waist-long blond hair in his path. Joe called to him, "Amigo!" but the man disappeared in the crowd.

Joe heard children crying and found himself in the streets of Rio, being followed by small kids asking for money, reaching up with their little brown hands. Joe realized that the twins had climbed out of their stroller and were weaving through the crowd. He grabbed them and dumped them back into the stroller, from which they clambered as soon as he reached a quiet stretch of grass surrounded by eucalyptus. There he let them run free. Families sat on blankets eating meat on a stick or bowls of feijoada or falafel sandwiches and talking freely and loudly, the way he remembered. He wheeled his empty stroller over to a group speaking the language of his heart, but just stood there, afraid to be part of them. He lowered himself to the ground beside the stroller and watched silently as his boys ran and flapped their arms, yerping like birds.

Chapter 20

O Ano 1978

Ten Rules for Latin actors (or how to behave like one):

1. You must be named Pancho, Pepe, José or Rita, María, Rosita.
2. You must have a Mexican accent; even if you don't have one, get one.
3. You must always want sex.
4. You must never get sex.
5. You must dance or play guitar, or, failing that, you must know how to play cards and gamble.
6. You must always make shady business deals without a contract; if possible, seal all deals with a kiss.

7. You must live with the notion that the blond girl will be the star. Realize that your only function as a Latin actor is to return the blonde back to her Americano sweetheart.
8. You must have a hot temper.
9. You must be willing to play Argentine gauchos, Mexicans, Cubans, Brazilians, East L.A. riff-raff, and sometimes all of them at the same time.
10. You must realize that the good Latin parts will go to non-Latin *blanca* actors. Remember, you will be interesting enough for them to make a movie about you, but never good enough to play who you are.

Rosea's parole officer sat at his desk, him with his suit and striped tie, trying to look so hip with longish hair that curled behind his ears in two hooks. He was young, but not as young as he wanted to be. He was holding the *L.A. Times*. He flipped the paper over, showing her the headlines: DEAD MAN FOUND ON VAUGHAN ESTATE. "Did you know this?" he asked. "Amazing the guy would get shot just as you were on parole. Nobody even thought much about the Vaughan mansion, except it was a bit hard to get to, and all of a sudden you're out, and all hell breaks loose. Do you find that strange, Mrs. Millard?"

"Please call me Ms. Socorro Katz."

He didn't respond except to blink his dotlike eyes.

Rosea trembled inside but modestly smoothed her hand down her skirt. "Why would I blow it? I have such an excellent job."

Her officer handed her the newspaper, got up from his desk, and went through a file drawer. DEAD MAN FOUND ON VAUGHAN ESTATE. Rosea read the article while eyeing her parole officer at the file cabinet. The dead man lay there overnight until the production office got nervous and sent the LAPD onto the estate—with some dogs. That's a relief, the news about the body being there for a while. Rosea prayed no one had seen her escape.

"Did you know Mr. Driscoll, the victim?" the parole officer said as he found the file—*her* file no doubt.

"Never."

"Seems like he works in the movies. I think he was thinking of using the place for a film. Do you know anything about it?"

"I'm not in the movies. I hate the movies. Don't even ask me."

So the man who had gotten in her face was a Hollywood hoo-haa. The man who had seemed so distant, a zero, a nothing. A bad dream. He was probably trying to make sense of her mother by drifting through her property. Just some no-name drifting through. What did the man expect? What big secret was he looking for?

Her parole officer sat down and folded his hands over the file he had pulled out. "Have you ever visited the garden since your release?"

"Why should I?" Rosea snapped, "My mother doesn't live there. What good is it? Hollywood killed her off and left nothing but her platform shoes."

"Well. You work at a tour company. And one of the things on the tour is the houses in Beverly Hills, so it stands to reason I should ask."

"I have a desk job." Rosea tossed the newspaper back to him.

The man stared at her for a long time and twirled one of his wingish curls around a finger.

Rosea caught herself rubbing her forehead. She stopped and dropped her arm down. Why don't people just shut up about everything? She looked beyond him to the window, one of the old ones where the bottom half slid up. At five floors, Rosea wondered if anyone had ever leaped out and landed on the street in front of a lunchtime crowd. She'd take a leap if she had the courage. Or run away with Joe to Brazil. Wouldn't matter if they lived in a hut somewhere. They could go by plane or ship, wouldn't matter. If the plane crashed, no problem. If the ship sunk, she'd pull him down into the water and watch his dark eyes widen, his strong arms flail as he desperately tried to clamber out of the air bubbles. Then she'd clutch him as her hair floated and spiraled like an eel, and they'd tumble on the powder of the long undisturbed sand and rest their heads among the clams. Dead and forever innocent.

"You might want to be careful," the parole officer said finally. "You've got a rap sheet—no murders or anything, but . . . you know what I'm saying? I mean—I'm no federal judge. I'm just looking at you and thinking 'She's a big girl. A really biiiig girl with a lotta anger.'"

Rosea lunged at him. He flinched, and she pulled back. "Look. I've
been straight. What do you want, a martini? If I wanted to break parole,
I would have gone into the house and stolen the TV! You can't connect
what I did before! My marriage was totally different! I mean, everything
was different. Jeremy Millard was strange. He even slept with a monkey!
He was asking for it—" She stopped.

He looked at her admonishingly, narrowing his eyes. "I hope you're
through punishing people for all the bad things you think they've done
to you."

Rosea bolted up, whirled toward the door. "What in the hell do I have
to see you for if you're going to say shit like that?!"

The parole officer ignored her, opened the file, and started filling out
her parole report.

Rosea thumped her palms against her temples. "I can't believe this,"
she muttered, "everyone here is nuts." She paced in front of the beveled
glass door that blurred and buckled the bodies of people moving up and
down the hall.

Her parole officer was still writing. Writing a lot.

"Jesus," Rosea moaned, "you writing a book about me or something?
A man dies in my mom's yard, and you think I wouldn't be a little crazy?"

The parole officer finished writing, then spun his chair side to side,
eyeing her.

Rosea looked away. The other two desks in the room were empty. She
felt like the only one in the world on parole. Then she gazed out the window again, imagining herself plunging down to the sidewalk. Keeping
her eye on the other building across the street, she finally said, "If that
movie man was looking for some tropical thing up there, he'd be wasting
his time. The last toucan was roadkill a long time ago. Ended up just a
splat on the road with its beak sticking up like a dick."

As Rosea crept to her office, she touched the wall to steady herself. She
heard talking and laughing from the crowded reception area, but something was different. Chucky wasn't haw-hawing like a gangster, Tom Mix
had dropped his stupid cowboy accent, Mickey was acting like an adult,

and Bogey wasn't mouthing off. It almost seemed normal; they were acting like people from this movie decade of *Network* and *Deer Hunter* and
of Brit actors doing nude scenes, not like the usual funny bunnies from
the Silver Screen.

Desiree in her usual floral dress stuck her head out of the crowd,
spotted Rosea, and beckoned her. Rosea grunted and instead slid into
her office, lowered herself down in front of her appointment book, and
massaged her temples as if her head would split open. Desiree appeared
at the doorway and asked if they could talk. Rosea shuddered. Desiree
took it as a yes and sat down on the chair beside the desk, crossed her
skinny arms, and gave her perpetual cold shiver. She started rattling on
like a half-wit about how Chucky was the friend of someone's agent who
was representing someone doing a film based on Carmen Socorro's life,
but who needed advice.

Rosea squinted, "Who?" — feeling sick as hell — "Who needs advice?"

Desiree gave a little "oh," realized she was prattling way too fast, and
started more slowly, explaining that Chucky was a friend of Nancy West's
agent. "You know Nancy West, she played the girlfriend of Jason Hart
in the movie *Honey Hill*? She's young? Blond? I think she's dating Bran-
don Kahn, who starred in *Gunfire at Point Zero* with Vaughan Peters —
you know, the one shot in Guatemala? You know the Nancy West I'm
talking about?"

Rosea groaned and closed her eyes. She didn't know a Nancy West.
She hated movies, and she'd been chanting "I hate movies" to people
over and over again like a psychotic Buddhist monk. She heard Desiree's
voice in a haze: "They're making a film about your mother's life. You
know, Carmen Socorro? Chucky has offered you as an advisor to Nancy
West. She's the star."

Rosea heard the last line but couldn't believe it. *Someone* named Nancy
West is going to play Carmen Socorro, and she, Rosea Socorro Katz, has
to give advice? She shifted in her chair, her stomach in pain.

Desiree came back into focus. "Isn't it fantastic? After all those violent serious films, we deserve something to cheer us up. *Carioca Craze*.
That's the name of the movie. What's a 'carioca,' Rosea? I forgot. But no
one forgot your mother. She was always so happy. So much happier than

most. Ohh, ohh," Desiree gasped, looking at the wall, at the calendar, at anything instead of at Rosea, "how exciting for you. I would have done anything to be in the movies."

Rosea reeled over to her, flaring, "WOULD YOU HAVE GONE BUTT NAKED?!"

Desiree sat there red-eyed, her hair in the two aggressive, 1940s-style hair rolls. Her pointed chin quivered, and her boxy shoulder pads made her neck and arms look like sticks coming out of nowhere. "Oh, Rosea, that's beside the point. My career never got that far."

Rosea slammed back on her chair. "I gotta work."

Desiree got up and left. Rosea held the edges of the desk and breathed hard. She thought she'd faint right there. Desiree came back, tossed a screenplay on her desk, and hurried out. Rosea stared at the manuscript. *Carioca Craze.* She was repulsed but a bit curious. What would they say about her mother? She wondered how she herself would be portrayed and who would play her. Someone kind of pretty? Would the film have a scene where her mother brushed Rosea's hair and talked of the Amazons thundering through the jungle on their horses? Would the film include her mother's crushing saudade in which she wandered down the hall calling for her Brazilian gardeners? Who knew enough about Carmen to make a film?

Suddenly from the waiting room came an explosion of conversation about the murder. Rosea listened. Someone went on about the "one who was shot," some location manager, as if he were the star of the show. Bogey hollered, "Whoever shot that man should be shot himself!" and the cowboy added, "Maybe hung, pardner, maybe hung!" Rosea rubbed her tight and painful stomach pushing up against her lungs and stared at the script's faux-leather covering. Some guy died for this? All that's left of him is this screenplay, one of the millions of screenplays in Hollywood usually ending up as doormats or being handed back and forth like old whores?

Carioca Craze. She turned to the first page and passed her hands over the paper. It felt cold. The words blurred until she couldn't read. The letters were like ants that swarmed out of cracked and rotten coconuts. Rosea narrowed her eyes. The room started to spin; the words began to crawl up her fingers and inside her sleeve. The white pages liquefied and churned in her stomach. The room had a sharp, rotten smell. Rosea bolted, that white-chalk feeling rising up in her throat. She rushed to the bathroom and kicked the door open as if she were the police. Her stomach heaved, and she made a horrible gagging sound, producing only a spider thread of saliva. The bathroom walls were pink like human insides. Another wave hit her head, and, too big to sink to her knees over the toilet, she grabbed the edge of the sink and the toilet-paper dispenser and hung there, trying to bring up the poison guilt that had settled in her bones.

Rosea lurched out of the bathroom and collapsed back in her chair. Beads of cold sweat crept on her hairline. Desiree bounded in again —

"I have to go home, I don't feel well —" Rosea snapped. She shouldn't have said that. Desiree would suspect a nasty case of nerves. But instead Desiree pealed, "How sad, I'm so sorry." Rosea rolled up the screenplay like a club. She let Desiree advise her to go home and drink tea and watch *General Hospital*. And of course — Desiree winked — do some reading. Rosea slowly stuck the screenplay in her purse. Then she rose and carefully lifted her purse to her shoulder and staggered down the hall.

Rosea drove east to her old hang-out bar, Nuestro Lugar, to read the screenplay. She didn't want to be near Hollywood, where everyone who saw you with a screenplay craned their necks to check: Who are you? What are you reading? A spec or under contract or sold or what? Who's your agent? Are you very good?

A few boys strutted past her and hooted — "Hey, vieja!" A shopkeeper tossed out old mangos and tomatoes into a cardboard box while his assistant dumped a shipment of fresh oranges into an empty bin. Once in a while a fry cook would step out from a restaurant, lean against the wall, and light a cigarette. Old Impalas thumped by, the bass on their radios turned up, crystals twirling from the rearview mirrors and making small rainbows on the windshields.

The bar seemed bleaker than ever. The dull glint from the naked bulbs shining under red-glass lampshades reminded her of prison at night, where there was always the throb of a light. Joe was right. This is a sad place to be. She slipped away to her usual back table. The men looked up from their beer, and one group had the energy to play pool. The balls clashed together like knocking heads. A Mexican *norteño* song went on and on about *corazón y calamidad.* She ordered a beer and listened to the men's heels clicking as they went around the pool table. She heard a dime sliding into a pay phone. They say these guys are dangerous, knives in their pockets, guns hidden underneath their jackets. But here they looked innocent and lost, not knowing where else to go. They probably never killed anybody, probably couldn't even handle a knife or a gun; it would be too overwhelming to attack or kill someone and change their lives forever. They probably did nothing but drink in the morning and sit on their doorsteps in the afternoon, tottering to and fro while their wives went shopping and gossiped with friends about the old drunks they had married.

She sat with her beer and lit a cigarette. The smoke curled like a small fist, then spread out as a gray haze. She began turning the pages, creaking past the title *Carioca Craze*, past the character descriptions. Then she began reading . . .

Ten Lies from the screenplay that did not happen in Carmen Socorro's Real Life:

1. American Pete Shinsky discovers Carmen singing in a bodega in Rio.
2. He offers her money and a career in the United States, not like the cheapo Brazilians who offer her only a free beer.
3. She has a Mexican accent.
4. She always wants sex with her servants.
5. Her lovers play guitar, but are into gambling and making bad business deals that involve drugs.
6. Her Americano friend Pete Shinsky straightens her out, says she's

talented and can make it. He books her into various nightclubs. A lot of them. Including Broadway. Numbers involve big hats. Monkeys, bananas, and, on one, dancing zombies.

7. Thanks to Pete she is a hit. They get married.
8. She has a hot temper. Still.
9. Pete, her inspiration, is killed in a car wreck.
10. In her grief, she lights candles, somewhat mystically. She wanders topless around her garden (drums pound in the background). Then continues her career triumphantly. (Fade out.)

Rosea finished the manuscript and slapped it shut. The beer and cigarette thickened in her empty, upset stomach. The music played in the background, and at the pool table someone started a new game, smacking a set of balls. She heard a voice, "Otra cerveza?" She leaned over the table, crossed her arms, and lay her head down. No revelations on why her father, after his brief stint as her mother's cha-cha man, left for Miami to swindle chlorine-smelling ex–movie stars. No story of what happened in Brazil to cause her mother's heart to explode in flames. Nothing about a daughter making the plot too messy, watching everyone doing dirty things to each other. The only thing clear was that Mr. Pink Polo Man was where he wasn't supposed to be. Hollywood sticking its nose in everything, what's new? She wasn't sorry she had killed him. Not one little bit. She almost wished he would come back to life so she could kill him over and over again. Ah hell. She created in her mind ten Mr. Polo Men and lined them up against the wall, then took a machine gun and blew them away to bloody splashes. That's how the ending should go. End with a revolution. *Viva.*

Women were brought to us for our pleasure. Lima informed
us of the Petiguar custom, that we could request any woman,
for if a man is to die, they deny him nothing, not even a wife
of the chief. First, the old women were brought to us. They
had full stomachs that hung over their loincloths. Many had
cicatrices and scars from war and rashes from ringworm.
We refused them. Bring us the younger ones, we demanded.
—*Diário de Carlos Manoel Teixeira da Cunha, O Ano* 1643

Chapter 21

O Ano 1978

Joe and Rosea laid a blanket on the ground away from the water's edge
and removed their shoes. Rosea shoved her shorts farther up her thighs
as if she were ready to wade through mud. She said something under
her breath as she plunked down and made a big deal about rubbing the
sand out from between her toes. Joe eased down on the blanket — not
too close to her, but not too far either — and leaned back on his hands.
The ocean waves smeared a membrane of foam on the surface, and fleas
bipped around piles of washed-up seaweed. The dilapidated lifeguard
towers were spray painted with letters that looked like inky bird claws.
In the distance, someone set up a motion-picture camera on a tripod

and did nothing but film the ocean. It looked like some experimental Cinema Novo movie made by a crazy art student.

Rosea had wanted to bring him to the beach, and he had agreed to go, as much trouble as it was. They came to talk about what to do next about this guilt, growing so large Joe felt as if he had killed thousands. How do you think about something like this? Joe wanted to ask her, but when he saw Rosea clutching a tote bag tight between her knees, then rifling through its contents, he knew she was ready to erupt again. Then she yanked out what she said was a screenplay.

"Ah no," Joe grabbed the screenplay from her and shoved it back into her bag. "Nothing like this. I want to talk serious."

She snatched the manuscript out again and slapped it down on her lap. "It's serious, alright. You need to know what the end of the world might look like."

"I DON'T want to talk about the movies."

"Joe. They are making a movie about my mother!"

"I don't care. I want to talk."

"We are TALKING about LYING!" Rosea glared at him, her nostrils flaring. The wind ruffled the pages. She deliberately turned to the first page, and her eyes slowly dropped as she began reading.

He refused to listen; it wasn't important. He closed his eyes and willed the memory of Sonia; he did not wrestle with the memory; it did not come as a flashback, in a jolt of violence, but with sadness and pain. He let himself remember Sonia running toward the waves, her long hair down her back, hair so wiry, like wool mixed with air. He let himself remember how her bikini revealed the small of her back, a perfect place to put his thumb. *É prohibido prohibir.* It is forbidden to forbid. These words, the cry of the Tropicalistas, became the music of love. During this time, lovers split up, ran away, disappeared, and their cars burst into suspicious flames. It was a lot to go through for someone. But it was not forbidden to forbid. What the Tropicalistas meant was that *era prohibido amar.* It was forbidden to love. But nobody could follow the rules; the longing was always there. It hadn't gone away.

Rosea tossed the manuscript off to the side with a "whack!" Joe looked up.

"You insensitive motherfucker, you aren't even paying attention!" she said with fury. Suddenly she bolted into the ocean and ran into the water up to her thighs.

Joe sprang up. "For god's sake, Rosea! Don't be so strange! Come back!"

Rosea turned once to cast a look at Joe, her hair undulating in a long snake down her back, then she lunged forward, jetting into the water. She sank and rose like a large fish, her hair unraveling in the tide. Joe ran in after her, water up to his knees, then his thighs; he dived in just as she propelled herself forward through a loaf of water. "Come back! Come back!" he croaked as Rosea swam steadily away from the beach. He saw his hands dipping down into the water, first pale and glimmering, then disappearing as his body surged forward, over and over again. He screamed out Rosea's name, but his voice was muffled as the water lapped around his ears.

My God, was she crazy, trying to swim back to Brazil? Was he crazy to follow her? She wouldn't even make it to Panama. He found himself bobbing in the dark waves, watching her swim farther on. The ocean stretched around him, hopelessly remote, and the water underneath him swelled, then let go. He lunged toward Rosea and got hit with a mouthful of brine. He coughed, and his lungs burned. Thick ribbons of water flowed through his kicking legs. Rosea was out too far for anyone to catch her. He looked toward the rim of sand and thought of Jeffy and Keffy waving, of Sherri waiting for him with a bag of sandwiches, of his Brazilian family calling him home, telling him how it would be worth it to be in love again, if he could.

He knew he could not save Rosea. He had caught a current and was being taken back to shore; he wouldn't fight it. He imagined women with sunglasses and amazing hairstyles, standing around him and teasing: Why did you swim after someone so crazy, and why are you in so much trouble, José? How can you resist the look of our sunglasses when you used to love them?

His knees scraped on the sand, and he scrambled up onto shore, the water spilling from inside his shorts. Rosea had made it to shore farther down the beach, and she was stumbling and running toward him. She began crying as she got closer to him, and she rushed and clutched him hard, embracing him until their wet clothes popped between their chests. "I want to go home," she wailed.

Joe nestled his face into her hair. A small piece of seaweed had gotten caught in the tangle. "É nada," he whispered as he combed his fingers through her hair, "forget everything." A tiny spider made its way out from the depths of her black wet mass, scampered up, then dropped downward on a fine strand.

◖

Joe let the door swing open and stood at the threshold to the living room. His wet T-shirt clung to his chest, the legs of his soaked shorts flapped together, his dry arms bristled with goose bumps, and his spirit was so low it felt like a dream. Everything was happening in slow motion—the kids running, stopping with a lurch, a toy truck slowly falling and making a complicated clatter on the floor. Joe told himself to act normal and held his arms out, beckoning to his sons. Only Keffy came, waddling cautiously, looking over at Jeffy. Joe lifted Keffy, watching his son's face rise, then he placed Keffy on his hip. The boy set his warm fat legs against Joe's wet clothes and started to cry. Joe held him close, the crying sounding like from another time. Keffy's stomach tightened and puffed, his fat legs tried to wiggle away. Joe pulled Keffy closer, a bit more roughly, wanting to feel his son's aliveness, but Keffy struggled harder, then flung his body back and bawled, showing the mean little roof of his mouth.

Sherri ran from the kitchen to check out the commotion. "My goodness, what happened?"

Joe set the baby down, and the crying stopped immediately. He walked past his sons, cupping his hand hard on top of Jeffy's head. The twins cooed and shuffled together like pigeons. Joe continued to the kitchen, not saying a word. Sherri hovered, her mouth made a pop as he passed, and she finally said, "For god's sake, Joe, you're wet!"

Then Joe saw him. The old man, sitting at the table. Joe said nothing, but went over to the refrigerator and pulled out a beer. He imagined himself saying, "Watch how to drown your sorrows, old man. If you even have sorrows." But instead, his mind went blank, and he held the cold bottle in his hand, trying to think of what came next. Sherri swooped open a drawer and quickly pulled out a bottle opener. He opened the bottle and took a gulp.

Part of him wanted to say he felt glad he was alive. Part of him wanted to tell Sherri that he swam out to save Rosea, then decided not to and swam home. But he couldn't.

Sherri waited for an explanation.

"I fell in the water," he said simply.

Sherri moved closer. "What water? Where did you go?"

"The beach."

"The beach? We would have gone with you."

Joe didn't answer and took another drink.

The old man shifted in his chair but didn't take his eyes off him.

Joe felt a bite of bitterness. "Hey, velho, I bet you notice I'm wet, too."

Melvinor wavered a bit, then said, "You didn't fall into the water; you jumped in. And you jumped in because you wanted to drown."

Joe slammed the bottle down hard on the table, and beer erupted out of the top. "Cala a boca! You stupid old man!"

"Joe!" Sherri cried.

Joe wiped the foam from his chin and hurled the bottle into a corner; it hit the wall with a clatter, the rest of the foam spilling from the neck. "Stop thinking you know things about me! You know nothing!"

"Joe! Slow down!" Sherri cried.

Joe didn't care; he lunged at the old man and grabbed his shirt collar. The blue vein on the old white neck fluttered. "You are not part of this family!" Joe yelled and gave him a jerk. "You hear! You cannot be over here a hundred times a day!" He felt Sherri hovering, peeping, pecking at him with pleas and pleases. Joe brushed her away with his foot and grabbed Melvinor's shirt harder and tried to lift him, but the old man would not get up, stayed sitting, making himself damn heavy. Sherri pulled on Joe's arm, crying, shrieking. Joe ignored her and shouted into the old man's face, trying to drill the words through his skull. "I don't want you over here! This is my family! I am the man here!"

Joe let Melvinor go and hurled himself at his wife. "Either I'm the husband or he is! You can't have it both ways! Choose! If you choose him, next time I *will* drown!"

"Joe, of course you're the husband, but what is all this about drowning? Did you try to drown yourself, Joe?"

"There are some people in this world that need to be killed! Some people could use a gun shoved down their throat!" Joe didn't know if he was shouting at him or at her.

"Stop that! I'll have my friends over if I want! At least I'm not sleeping around like someone else I know!"

Joe snatched both her arms and shook her. "I am not sleeping around! I am not drowning!" He heard his voice catch, and he gave a small whimper. Sherri's small lips moved, and the lower lip pushed out a bit, defiantly. "You hear me?" he shook her again and saw her blue eyes snap shut.

Everything was crying around him. The kids threw their small bodies against them, bumping their foreheads on Joe and Sherri's knees, their wails so loose and wide. Melvinor got up and dug his fingers into Joe's shoulders, trying to pull him away from Sherri.

"Leave me alone!" Joe cried, still hanging onto his wife, "don't take her away from me! Don't take her away, God." Melvinor slipped away, and the twins fell on their seats and cried, yet the noise seemed far away. Joe took a deep breath and quietly smelled the grilled-meat odor on her shirt, then sniffed at her neck for a tingle of sauce, hanging on to her so she wouldn't run over to the old man. "Sherri," he said. "I'm sorry. I'm sorry, Sherri. I'm so sorry."

She held onto him and soft-voice kissed his neck with sweetness.

"Sinto muito," he whispered into her ear, "tenho medo." I am afraid of what comes next.

They brought for Dom Marcus Pedro Ferraz de Lima a large woman with one breast lopped off, the skin scarred with thick wrinkles. She had a healed slash across her neck and one slice across her abdomen. Her reddish-brown thighs were like two enormous logs of *pau brasil*. Lima laughed and waved his hand away, refusing her. Suddenly two women jerked him up, pulled him by the tethers on his wrists, tied a rope to his waist, and dragged him toward the river.

—*Diário de Carlos Manoel Teixeira da Cunha, O Ano* 1643

Chapter 22

O Ano 1978

Oh Nancy! Nancy West, slated to star in *Carioca Craze*, is the ingénue *type*, the romantic *type*, a box-office beacon *type*. She does romantic comedies mostly, playing young women gee-gogging over love. A decade earlier she'd have been fucking Elvis Presley on the sly inside a beach cabana. But this isn't movie history; this is now, and Nancy West is destined to play more challenging roles. After all these years, Hollywood is reviving Carmen Socorro into the joyful, vivacious performer we all knew. It was a bit like how Bela Lugosi came to near life as Dracula. Audiences loved the role no matter how long the legend had been dead.

Rosea was given a luncheon appointment at Ernie's Grill with Ms. West to advise the young star on the ways and means of Brazilian bombshell-ness; Rosea was a technical advisor; that was her job. She sat in a booth and waited. She didn't know what advice she could give and was—as they say in civilized society—"a bit puzzled." She looked around at the ocher and brown walls and gold paisley carpet, muted and manly as a depressed widower, and at the long, brown leather booths smelling like cigars. Along one wall were framed glossies, celebrity mug shots signed with a quick hand and a dry pen. Rosea hated ritzy restaurants like this, its clinkle-clankle of stemware, kissing and puffing, little business cards held between two fingers floating around the room like dead fish. She shifted in her seat and pulled down at the crotch of her tight leopard-skin stretch pants. Her white blousey shirt had elastic that pulled down off the shoulder for that disheveled coochi-coo look. A man looked up from his manuscript and stared at her. She teased him with an airborne smooch, then swept her dark mane off her shoulders and flicked her large, round, chariot-wheel earrings.

Nancy entered. Rosea recognized her right off, having forced herself to see *Honey Hill*. Nancy wore white linen pants so pressed and stiff and a colorful gossamer blouse so flattened against her chest she could have been trucked in on a handcart. She had blond hair with a perfect Lauren Bacall undercurl. Her body was small—oh, you Hollywood tinies, you, with your bony rib cages and tweaky heads! With your broad smiles and early eye wrinkles filled with moisturizer and pancake!

Nancy grinned and waved her small hand, and different people waved back. Jesus, how many people did this woman know? All who *could* wave did, then Nancy furrowed her brow and searched the room for anyone who *didn't* wave. Finally Rosea motioned to Nancy, who lifted her eye-brows, said something profound to the waiter, and made her way to Rosea's table.

Nancy stood in front of the booth and rolled her shoulders a little nervously, as if on a date with Rosea, with Rosea the Man, the notori-ous Latin Lover and Gangster Type. Rosea held out her hand for a shake, clattering the large gold bangles on her wrist. "Beautiful," Nancy said holding Rosea's hand and turning it to look at the rings of gold, "and such an honor."

Nancy slipped into the booth. "I *loved* your mother!" Her eyes shot upward in dreamy memory of fabulous song-and-dance numbers. She rattled on about all the Carmen Socorro films she had seen, how she was so glad The Musical was finally coming back, and how this one was going to make it, not like those other lemons like *Star* and *Doctor Doolittle*. "And oh, this movie is quite different; we need this film like medicine, we need a little perky-uppy after the Vietnam War. Biographies are hard to do and usually too serious to be fun. Like, you know — that film about Lincoln? But this movie will be both serious *and* fun. Won't it?"

Rosea stared for a bit, taken aback by Nancy's rapid-fire chattering, then glanced at the table with a "yes," her sudden shyness making her face feel fat.

Nancy leaned over to whisper, "You can relax with me. Your mother was a wonderful performer. Consider yourself lucky."

Rosea gave a quick smile. Yes. Lucky.

A waiter saved the day and handed them large leather-bound menus. Nancy held the menu in front of her, and Rosea admired her nails, so perfectly oval and red, tapping the leather cover. Finally, Nancy reached a decision, the large salad, which of course Rosea ordered, too, not to seem piggy, though she could have used some pot roast or something. The waiter took the menus away, and Nancy smiled sweetly and said, "We ordered the same thing, like sisters." Then she folded her hands and shivered in glee as she looked around the room. The men wore fedoras and wide-lapel suits, and the women wore saucy peplum jackets and pillbox hats with light nets softening their eyes. The people here were from a past that Carmen had raved about, when people dressed up in their search for love. The man playing the piano looked a little like Joe, both had dreamy eyes and copper-toned skin, though the pianist's was darker. The music Rosea recognized as having to do with chance meetings, with women who open their doors at midnight for the mysterious stranger who drinks good brandy.

Nancy went on for a while, her voice sounding like tinkling bells. Rosea didn't pay attention to her words, only that she reminded Rosea of her mother's friends who would gather at the pool, the same four women: Alice Taylor, Marni Lloyd, Trixie Evans, and Lola Manchester — looking trim in their two-piece bathing suits and wearing large straw hats to protect their skin from the sun and white zinc cream to protect their noses. These women would sit at the edge of the pool, laughing and stroking their bare midriffs (scandalous in those days) as they swished their feet in the water. Their red toenails and shaved legs glowed under the clear blue. Once in a while a woman would get too hot after chattering about her fading box-office beauty or of some love affair, take off her straw hat, slip into the water, and quietly paddle across the pool and back again, always keeping her well-styled hair-do above the water. Then the love chatter and midriff caressing would resume. Finally, Carmen, her long black hair free of her turban, would jump in, swim to the middle of the pool, and sink to the bottom so her black hair floated out in all directions like billowing ink. Then all the women would slide into the water and swim around, fluttering their red fingernails through her hair. Her mother would rise up for air in a big bellow of pleasure, and the movie starlets, "aging mermaids" as *Photoplay* called them, would finally, one by one, dive head first, filling the middle of the pool with loose gold spirals.

Rosea thought Nancy a little stupid, but knew someday she would be sad. Rosea almost felt sorry for her. But now the starlet was smiling, expecting to hear something good. Rosea, tugging the blouse at her shoulders, had to explain: "You remind me of someone I know."

(Did that sound like a come-on or what?)

Nancy was pleased and leaned her forearms on the table. "Who? Who do I remind you of?"

"Friends my mother had. Alice Taylor. Marni Lloyd."

Nancy beamed, "Oh, I loved them! I loved their work! Well, people talk about new movies today, but," she stretched her hands and patted the table, "the oldies are goodies, believe me."

The waiter came with glasses of chilled wine and a silver tray of bread, with matching silver bowls of butter pats on ice. Rosea hadn't seen food like this in so long she didn't dare touch the bread or she would massacre it. She watched Nancy's small fingers wrestle with the bread and tear off a piece. Then Rosea took the bread, closed her eyes and sniffed the tasty crust. This must be what a real house smells like.

Nancy clattered the knife into the cold butter. "Great, huh? I love the smell of fresh bread."

Somehow the aroma almost brought Rosea to tears, and she tried to take a polite chunk while concentrating on the roughness of the crust so she wouldn't burst out bawling. The bread and wine hit her tongue with such taste she felt as if she could eat and eat and never stop. Nancy ate heartily, talking about some producer while keeping a large piece of bread wedged inside her cheek. Nancy winked, "We're getting more."

Rosea took a gulp of wine. "I could eat here all day."

Nancy raised her finger, and a waiter came almost immediately at her beckon, as if her finger were a magic wand. Boom, more bread.

Nancy continued talking, and Rosea watched her intently, marveling at how she could talk so much. When she stirred on the leather seat, somehow Rosea could smell flowers.

"I like your perfume," Rosea said, now sounding awkward; it certainly would sound better coming from a man.

"Hibiscus," Nancy said, "a tropical flower, I was hoping you'd like it." "Uh-huh."

Nancy sucked in passionately. "Oh, I wish I were Latin."

Rosea bit down on a piece of crust. "Really?"

Nancy nodded. She went on about the fieriness, about how sexual they could be, energy just hiding underneath the surface, and though they looked warm and touchable, there was a bit of fierceness. Nancy said she liked things like that. She said whenever she ate an orange, she always thought of Pedro Garcia's mouth when he ate oranges in that Pancho Villa film. She oooed about how the juice must have gotten mixed up in his mustache, and ooh how she'd like to lick it off!

Nancy's forwardness was surprising, yet clumsy. Her body moved like a gringo learning the tango but impatient with the steps, wanting to get to the final sexy lunge. "Well," Rosea drank the wine and looked at the empty glass. "It isn't totally easy, you know. We don't have a million lovers a night, you know."

"Oh!" Nancy gasped. "Of course. Oh gosh, I'm stereotyping. But it's because I'm ignorant. That's why you're here. To teach me." Nancy's blue eyes searched Rosea's dark ones, her head wavering, the piano music swelling (if you can imagine).

"My mother didn't have a million lovers either. In spite of what that screenplay says."

Nancy shifted uncomfortably. Rosea decided she needed more wine. She raised her finger like Nancy, but her finger looked large and clumsy, and she didn't think any waiters would come, but one did, and she asked for more wine. The waiter brought them two more glasses along with the salads.

Nancy plowed into her salad as soon as the plate landed in front of her. "Starving," she said.

"Why did you order just a salad?"

"My weight. Oh," Nancy gasped again, "we have to, for the movies, but of course, you're — beautiful the way you are."

"I feel like Fernando Llamas." Rosea stuffed lettuce into her mouth.

Oh, ha, ha. Nancy twitched as if ruffling her feathers, then continued eating. Her fork in her right hand, a piece of bread in her left, she ate without stopping. Rosea poked a tomato with her fork and sank into sadness. She didn't want to talk about her mother. The screenplay was written, and nothing could be changed; everything she said would seem like worthless *Photoplay* chit-chat. Carmen demanded a life as rich as an arara's colors and as strange as the tale of the boto that turns himself into a man in order to screw all the girls in the village. That's just the way it was. Rosea lifted her eyes and saw Nancy gazing at her, placidly chewing away. Rosea decided to shake up this girl and gleamed a ferocious smile. Nancy smiled back hesitantly. With that, Rosea started her first lurid story, one well known among Amazons: "The one thing my mother loved — was women."

Nancy's eyes widened.

"You know what I mean, don't you?"

"Yeah. . . yeah."

"She never used men the way — say — you and I do."

Nancy slipped an olive between her teeth.

Rosea continued her story of how Carmen invited all these women for a special . . . game. "To begin, they'd wander through the middle of the exotic plants in her garden, some plants young and taking root, others already blooming, and there were always flowers attracting humming-birds and butterflies—American ones, of course, but where else could they go in this city? All these famous women would come. I mean famous like Marni Lloyd and Deanna Durbin and Trixie Evans, who always brought her special bean dip. Not Lola Manchester, because she was half-Mexican and somewhat of a Catholic. Sometimes Alice Faye came when she could get away from her husband—" Rosea winked.

Nancy gasped.

"So as part of this thing, this 'game,' my mother would invite these men to run through the garden while the women would chase after them, sometimes with spears or, if their wrists were too delicate, with steak knives! And these women would charge like Amazons ready to kill the bastards—"

By now, Rosea had wound herself up and began rising to her feet as she grabbed the table on either side. Then she caught herself and sat back down. "Well, the goal was to capture these men and tie them up. And you know . . .," Rosea caught her breath, "you know what happens once men are captured—"

By then Nancy had stopped chewing and just sat there, slack-jawed, her eyes swimming, her giddy face kissed smooth by the wine. She had a radish stuck to a fork, but her wrist went limp, for even the radish was too heavy.

Rosea took another gulp of wine, almost having to recall where she was and whom she was with. Two glasses shouldn't have really made a six-footer drunk, but what the hell if she were?

Rosea continued, now babbling whether or not Nancy was listening, though she was and how! "Well, the men liked this game, too, famous men, they were all there: Jack Grinnell, Manley Ficus, Perry Como. And surprise—Jimmy Stewart! No shit. Even him. Once the men were tied up, the women would kick them like logs, sometimes rolling them down the hill, just doing any sort of violence to them. Except killing them. Just to get them all crazy, you know. Then came—" Rosea mouthed the words *blow jobs.*

Nancy slowly crunched on the radish.

"But that got old. After a while my mother said, 'Chega agora. I'm too old to chase men.' Then she'd invite her starlet friends, who couldn't get cast anymore because they were considered too old. They'd meet in the garden, and they'd be wearing their orchid-print *kangas* wrapped around their hips, and their bare midriffs were kind of flabby like the way they get, you know? And their hair was blond and frizzy from so much movie-star hair goop. Imagine these women — just walking through that jungle, grabbing onto tree trunks, rubbing their" — Rosea mouthed *crotches* — "and they'd talk about love, maybe. Then my mother would get all her friends to sit in a circle. And she'd take out from her pocket a small bag of cocaine and a razor, and shake some cocaine onto a small mirror, then sort the cocaine with the razor to make four lines. This was way, way before anyone was doing coke regularly. The women took small straws, held it up to their nostrils, and sniffed the white powder up and over. And as you know, Nancy, when that happens, when people snort coke, they get happy. These women, clamping their noses, moaned in a delicious pain. Then ran their fingers through each other's hair and swayed with the music inside them; they sang . . . and swayed . . . and cried. They cried a lot about people who had screwed them over."

The amazed expression on Nancy's face brought Rosea back to reality. She had said too much. She had betrayed her mother, made her into some Hollywood pervert when all Carmen had wanted was to paddle a canoe down an igarapé and scream at the top of her lungs. Nancy took a deep breath and ate the rest of her salad in silence, mopping up the dressing with a piece of bread. Rosea wanted more wine, but knew she couldn't keep her mouth shut as it was.

Finally, Nancy looked up from her cleaned plate. "Wow. Incredible story. I can hardly wait to see that garden! We're going to film there!"

Rosea caught her breath, feeling the jab.

Nancy grew serious. "You heard about how our location manager was killed there? I mean, he was scouting out the place, and can you believe it? Shot. I mean — who would have — ?"

"Yeah. That's bad." Rosea snapped open her purse and drew out a pack of cigarettes. She noisily lit a cigarette for herself and pushed the pack and lighter toward Nancy.

Nancy refused the cigarette but continued dragging the tines of her fork over her plate. "Why would anyone do it? I mean, who would even be there? And Vaughan Peters, well, he must have dogs, electrical gates, who knows? Kinda like the Charles Manson thing almost."

Rosea felt her anger rising, a bit tempered by forced politeness. "I don't think it is—quite. Well, no one got cut up—as far as I know. Well, how should I know?" Her tongue was doing flips, feeling like a trigger finger. "Perhaps your location manager should have gotten permission to be there."

"He did. I'm sure of it." Nancy's face got a little blank.

Rosea drew out a long stream of smoke. "Of course he would."

"Well," Nancy shrugged, "you may know more about it than I do. I don't know much, except—this town is full of crazy people."

You know more about it than I do. What's that supposed to mean? What does she know? *This town is full of crazy people.* Rosea had to be careful, no more wine, be stealthy. Her head started pounding, and she tried to act nonchalant, rubbing her forehead. She couldn't get back Nancy's innocence if she tried.

Nancy impulsively grabbed Rosea's hand. Rosea saw the small fingers wander into the crannies of her large brown knuckles. "Hey," Nancy said, "I can see how it can be upsetting. God, your mother's house. How horrible."

Rosea couldn't look at her, but felt her brow tightening, her skin twisting. "Well, like you said, this town is full of crazy people."

"Some of the craziest work in the industry." Nancy gave Rosea's hand a squeeze, then let go. Rosea wanted to get out of here; the men at the place were starting to look dark and threatening like the film noir guys in *Touch of Evil.* But Nancy shot up her little pointer finger again, like the magic pinnacle of success, and ordered some coffee for two.

The steam of fresh, hot coffee hit their faces. Rosea's body felt clumsy, and guilt had nabbed her tongue. She continued puffing on her cigarette and couldn't think of anything funny to say. Nancy looked at Rosea and narrowed her eyes a bit as if seeing through the cracks of Rosea's lies. "Well," she said as she reached for the sugar, "we aren't detectives, are we? That's for another movie."

"Yep."

"You know," Nancy cracked a smile, "can I ask you something?"

"What?" Rosea took a big gulp of hot coffee and let it burn her mouth.

"How come you're not in the film? I mean, I was surprised when my agent told me you existed."

"Well," Rosea crushed her cigarette on her saucer. "Well, I didn't live here when I was a kid, see. I spent a lot of time in Brazil."

"Oh really? That's cool."

"Yeah. I spent time in the jungle. It took me a while to get a . . . a . . . what are those permission papers called? Not a green card . . ."

"A visa?"

"Yeah," Rosea lowered her eyes. "I couldn't get one of those. I had to fight the border patrol and alligators to come here."

Nancy broke into peals of laughter. "Wow, they should make a movie about you!"

Rosea smirked, her lips tight like a slingshot. They said nothing for a long time. Nancy drank her coffee and stared ahead. Someone waved at her, but she merely squinted. Rosea tried to see her mother in Nancy's crazy blue eyes and blond hair, tried to picture her as Carmen Socorro. She couldn't imagine it. This Nancy, this girl, probably had her family here, probably from Long Beach. Nancy's pale, simple face, a comfort to millions, was like a fragile egg that needed to be cracked open; Nancy needed to see the darkness stirring underneath the water in order to survive this film.

"You know," Rosea finally said, her insides now stirring with anger. "My mother was just a fool in a big costume. Just like you."

Nancy's face fell. "I am more complicated than I seem, you know. Acting is just a job."

"Is it, though?"

Nancy smiled uneasily and slipped out her wallet from her purse. "I'm afraid so."

Rosea saw she was about to leave in a pissed-off, cutesy way, just flutter out on her little butterfly wings.

"Nancy—"

Nancy looked up.

"Don't make the film. Nobody will ever get it right. Nobody."

"Well." Nancy got up and didn't even wait for the bill. "We'll certainly try." And with that she swished over to the cashier, paid the bill, and left.

Chapter 23

O Ano 1978

What a terrible day. On his last run at work, Joe had argued with a bald-headed man dressed in lime green Bermudas who accused him of lying. "What lies, you filho de puta?" he wanted to say. "What do you know about truth?"

At last in the living room at home, Joe kicked off his shoes, flung off his shirt, flipped through some mail on the coffee table, and snatched up a letter from his mother. He sat on the couch, reached over to the coffee table, and swept aside remnants from the twins' hard night: a bottle of liquid children's aspirin, a thermometer case, and several damp wash-rags. The house seemed quiet with relief; the sick twins who had kept everyone awake, struggling with their small goo-filled noses and rumbling lungs, were now taking naps.

Joe peeled tape from the seal of his mother's letter. Had it been opened by the police, or had his mother enclosed a photo maybe? Joe flipped through three pages of filmy onionskin, hoping there would be more, then passed his fingers over his mother's delicate handwriting, her crisp Portuguese endearments. He could almost hear the wonderful nasal sounds of *ãos* and *ães* whispering from the fragile paper. The creases from where the pages had been folded looked like the veins of leaves.

He heard Sherri in the kitchen clipping coupons and the small clatter when she set the scissors down. Joe read carefully his mother's words of love, "we've been thinking of you and we miss you and are you getting rich?" On the next page, his mother complained of inflation and how the price of everything was a robbery and how the TV had nothing but garbage compared to what was going on outside. Joe hoped she would say more about this "outside world," but she didn't and instead went on to talk about his youngest brother, Pedro, who had taken over the newspaper stand and now also sold *salgados*—little shrimp pies—and linguiça wrapped in dough. Pedro had married a nice girl from Rio who worked at a bank. They didn't have much money separately, but both of them together could afford a little apartment. Then his mother reprimanded—"Why don't you write? Are you still alive, *meu filho?* How expensive can postage be in the United States, anyway?"

On the final page, she talked of a family friend, Carlinhos, who had worked for President Goulart—"Carlinhos, our little Marxist friend and the godfather to Pedro." Joe remembered Carlinhos bringing a bag of *suspiros*, little sugary meringues, for a treat every Sunday. She said he had been over just the other day, and a week later he was gone, and she missed him so. Gone where? Joe frantically flipped the pages for more and peered inside the envelope. Dead? Disappeared? Such stupid, polite, delicate nonsense. Carlinhos dying in bed in the arms of his wife, or Carlinhos with an exhaust pipe stuffed down his throat or his balls zapped? At the end of the letter, his mother wrote, "Tenho saudades de você, and I know it's silly, but I miss you and wish you were here, *meu filho.*"

Beijos. Abraços com amor.

Vá com Deus,

          Sua Mamãe

Joe gazed at the letter. He missed Carlinhos, too. He missed his mother. He missed both the despair and the hope that life could get better with the snap of the fingers; he missed the newspapers and gossip rags, *Quatro Rodas* road maps, the horoscope, and *orixá* guides to love; he missed the lottery tickets and the *bichieros* who plied their illegal lottery. He even missed the bad things, the street children hanging around restaurants, hoping for leftovers; the shadows of *moleques* and crooks, knife threats and cocaine, the *subornos* to crooked cops, and the skulking fear that hovered over the sun-drenched sidewalks. He longed for the women who wore their frizzy hair in a ponytail on top of their heads, looking like palm trees split apart by lightning, their *morena* skin, cotton dresses caressing their slimness, white bikini panties and their dark bodies showing underneath. He even missed the veiled Madonnas in the churches.

Joe remembered the time when he had appeared at his mother's house after prison, as a hungry ghost of death scarred with whip marks, knowing that his nation had showed itself to him as indolent and hostile. He had hated Brazil then. And yet his mother, with her wordless love, her embrace, her silent knowing about his troubles, had taken him into the kitchen, heated some rice and beans, and fried some meat while he gazed at the sunlight shining on her houseplants on the windowsill.

Joe gazed at the letter and took a deep breath. Tired. His saudade almost split him in two.

It was amazing the silent mothering that Sherri did so well he almost couldn't endure it. Last night, comforting the two sick babies, he rocked Keffy while Sherri took Jeffy. Joe stole glances at his wife's heavy eyelids and marveled at her tender voice soothing Jeffy's outraged cries. This made Joe feel gentle toward Keffy, coughing and crying in his arms, and Joe stroked his son's soft, pale cheek with his thumb. Ah, Joe thought, if he could just rewind his life, go backward, start over, start from his mother's arms just like this. . . .

Sherri, wearing her large old slippers, shuffled into the living room. The fur on one of the slippers was stiff and sticky, matted together where

Sherri had washed it last night after Jeff had thrown up on her foot. She raised her eyebrows, the wrinkles on her forehead deep from worry, and said she had called in sick to work; she was just too exhausted. She saw the letter at his knee. "What's this?"

"Letter from my mother," Joe tossed the three pages on the coffee table.

Sherri glanced at it. "Good news? Bad news?"

"Not enough news."

"Hmm." Sherri sat down on the couch beside him, leaned her forearms on her knees, picked up the letter, and scanned the pages. "I should learn Portuguese. But your English is so good it would only confuse matters."

"Life is confusing enough as it is."

Sherri gave a tired laugh. They both settled back on the couch, and Sherri closed her eyes and sighed, "Do you miss her? Your mother?"

Joe reached over and took a small blond tendril of her hair and placed it behind her ear. "Yes. I do."

"Exhausted," Sherri muttered. "How did our mothers ever do it?" She yawned. Her soft breath, her chest moving up and down, filled Joe with longing. He reached over and stroked her hair again.

Hmm. Sherri was falling asleep.

"Lay on my lap," Joe said, "here." He moved to the end of the couch, then nudged her shoulder. "Come on, meu bem."

Sherri groaned sleepily, stretched out on the couch, and lay her head on his lap. She opened her eyes and looked up at his face. Her eyes were blue the way he first remembered them, but the puckers around them had gotten softer. Joe stroked her lips softly. She smiled and closed her eyes. "Hope you don't mind being a human pillow," she whispered, "You're almost too comfortable for me to move."

"No. You stay here."

Her face softened in her sleep, and her mouth dropped open a bit. The chapped skin on her cheeks looked like bits of powder. It was hard to get Sherri gentle and yielding like this. He fingered her hair, letting the blond strands slide through his darker fingers; he imagined his skin purple like the curtains on a confessional, the kind in Brazilian churches, where those waiting in line listened to the muffled sins of the guilty. Brazil was fading, just black holes of information in a letter. Yet he cherished the gentle bate-papo, chit-chat, the sweet carinhoso of news of the family that fluttered like birds over the dark sea of his pain.

❰

Joe went back to Wranglers' Eye and Rib to ask for his old job back. He wanted to live like the simple immigrant he was. He needed to be around Sherri, be a family man, and forget Rosea and the whole business in the garden. Rosea wanted him to come over after work because it was Sherri's day off, but Joe refused and instead decided to go to the Eye and Rib and talk to Manuel.

Ah, the familiar table tops of plastic wood, the Western lamps with red-glass covers! And those autographed pictures on the wall, too; in L.A. you couldn't eat in peace without some movie star staring down your shirt.

Joe slipped into the kitchen. The smell of grilled meat and barbecue sauce and mildew and dishwashing liquid brought his innocence back, the excited new-immigrant fright that had quivered inside him like a jewel. He scanned the kitchen staff for a familiar face, but everyone was new — and new to this country. The men at the grill — in sweaty T-shirts and aprons splashed with red sauce, their hair slicked back with water — muttered in Spanish as they speared the beef with long, cruel forks. One of the line cooks saw Joe and pointed down the hall toward the back. "Bathroom."

Joe shook his head, and the cooks looked askance, as if he might be *la migra*. "Eu trabalhava aqui. I used to work here." And the men standing before the sizzling meat nodded cautiously at him, motioning with their forks, and one said, "Me parece como un americano. You look Ameri-can."

"Não, não sou americano. Brasileiro." His voice was muffled by the sound of the fat splashing on the grill. The dishwasher, the man with his former job, sprayed full blasts of hot water over greasy plates, the steam rising above his head. The young man, wearing a cotton shirt with long sleeves cut short, had light-brown skin and serious eyebrows. When Joe had been a dishwasher, he already had dreams in the clouds, already thinking of the next plan, the better job, the better house. This boy looked indifferent, a bit rude. He would survive.

Finally, Manuel showed up from the staff room in back. A familiar face! "Manuel!" Joe called.

Manuel looked up and smiled, "Hey, amigo!" He went around to Joe, extended his hand, a thin hand that made his large ring stand out like a gold knob. They embraced and gave quick kisses, cheek and cheek. Then Manuel grabbed both Joe's shoulders, looked into his face. "Something," he said, "is not right."

"Come on, hombre," Joe pulled away, "I just came to say hello."

"Does Sherri know you're here?"

"No. Not yet."

Manuel eyed him closely, then motioned him to the staff room. They sat down at the familiar old white table with flecks of peeled paint chips. A portable radio on top played Mexican music and plates of food were half empty from busy workers nibbling here and there. "Have some food," Manuel said, "a whole table of people got tired of waiting and walked out just before the food came. Come on." Manuel got a small plate, dished out some beans and potatoes and a cutlet and offered the plate to Joe.

"Not so much. This is for the cooks."

"Taaa," Manuel got him a fork and knife. "Sit down. You are one of us."

Joe sat down, and Manuel pushed the plate in front of him. The steam rose from the beans and potatoes, and Joe suddenly felt a surge of emotion. He leaned his elbow on the table and pressed his face into his cupped hand and tried in vain to keep from crying. This was terrible, to cry in a kitchen in front of a man. He didn't know it would be like this; he thought he would have a little chat, then he'd buy a Coke and leave. The crying jolt took him completely by surprise. Maybe it was the warm food. The accordion playing on the radio didn't help either, or the words sung by a *charro*: "Mi corazón está triste pórque mi amor me abandonó por otro." Yes, my love left me, I left my love, everyone left, I will be lonely forever. "Estaré solo para siempre."

Joe rubbed his eyes, so embarrassed. "I'm sorry."

Manuel sat at the table across from him. "What is it?"

"I keep thinking of you. But I shouldn't come here."

"The Hollywood job is not good, huh?"

"The rich are all alike."

Manuel chuckled, "Ah, well, that's true." He took a spoon from his apron pocket. "Eat. It will make you feel better." Joe began eating the beans and cut a piece of meat.

Manuel joined him and dipped the spoon into the mashed potatoes, then the barbecue beans. "A lot of these guys here, you know," and Manuel leaned closer, "have no green card, and they come and go. About three months ago la migra raided the place, and everyone disappeared. For about two days I was doing everything myself, but sure enough we got new people in no time. And on and on it goes." He shoveled the spoonful of potatoes and beans in his mouth, nodded, made another concoction, and ate that too. He licked his spoon. "Sometimes I don't know why they come here. Of course, I know it's about money—but sometimes I feel like saying to them, 'Yes, it's rough over *there*. But *there* is where your soul is, you know. And here . . ." he shrugged. "So when people tell them 'speak English, speak English,' it's no matter, yes? Well, speaking English has been worthwhile for you and me, but—" Manuel shook his head and would say nothing more.

Joe continued eating. This food tasted so good, not like the bland food he had to cook for the twins. The spices danced on his tongue, and the grease comforted him like the smell of his mother's chicken cooling in garlicky, oily broth. He shook some hot sauce onto everything on his plate. He wanted to tell Manuel more about his job, the living hell, and the problems he had gotten himself into. Joe wanted to pour out how he suffocated under others' desires to be stars, to be images of images. He hated the sleek bodies of everyone in the business, the tough lizardness, the hard-lipped grins. But Manuel said nothing, stared ahead, and listened to the radio, chewing on a french fry. In fact, Joe had come here to get his job back, but he couldn't explain why.

The meal would end soon, and he would have to say something. He took a look at the staff room, the sacks of flour and beans on the shelves, the giant cans of jalapeños and fruit cocktail, jars of pickles and mustard, the radio whispering love, "amor, te queiro," that sounded like humiliated men with their pants down.

Joe knew his mistake, deep inside. But men don't talk of these things. Nobody goes backward, not even Manuel or the men at the grill. Joe realized: we from other countries know the moment we step out onto this new land that *só podemos seguir adiante*. We come here in the first place to move forward, and this country with its giant hand pushes us farther. We try to leave the past behind because we think we are safer in the present. Chucky has fallen for his pin-striped suit and machine gun on the wall, for his Jimmy Cagney movie world. Chucky is safe because Al Capone is dead, and Chucky does not have to worry. But the past furiously becomes our present. Chucky is not a gangster, but a nut. Brazil is part of Joe's present life, even here in America. No, Joe couldn't work at the Rib and Eye with an innocent heart. He no longer had excuses for his misunderstandings.

Joe got up and offered to wash out his plate, but Manuel said, "No-no-no, let the dishwasher boy do it."

The dishwasher boy. Joe smiled to himself, wondering if Manuel had ever called him the dishwasher boy. "Well, amigo," Manuel rose, and their hands came together in a handshake that sounded like a loud pop, "Hasta luego."

"Até logo," Joe said, a bit quieter. Then Joe and Manuel went through the kitchen, and Joe left his old boss speaking Spanish among his line cooks. Though nothing was said outright, Joe had a feeling that Manuel knew why he had come.

Senhor Carlos da Cunha will come to my rescue! As will the powerful Capitão Armando Silva Perreira and Abdalmo Catete de Souza! Padre Pedro Oliveira will pray for my soul! Constanzo Jaime Lima de Branca! Vicente Previ Gonsalves! João de Bragança! These men have fierce weapons! My mother, Graciela María, and my father, Mauricio Luciano, and my brothers, Oswaldo, Mauro, and Luis, and my sisters, Maria and Isabella! All the saints and São Sebastião! São Martin! Nossa Senhora de Fatima! All of you pray for me!

— *Gritos de Pedro Ferraz de Lima ás portas da morte* (Pedro Ferraz de Lima screaming at death's door), *O Ano* 1643

Chapter 24

O Ano 1978

Jeremy Millard pulled the new book from his briefcase and sank down in his office chair. He held the book closed with both hands, almost afraid to read it. The afternoon light came through the window of his home office, causing a too-bright glare. He thumbed the pages of this new little treatise written by anthrosquirt Dr. Carl Dotson. Dotson, the one on his Amazon expedition, who had looked after his hide more than at the culture surrounding him, was now an *expert* on Amazonian ephemera — *ephemera*, a word that sounds like wind blowing against silk, but means the junk people throw away. It sounds like *ethereal*, as in "an angel flew down to earth on *ethereal* wings." *Ethereal ephemera* — the study of sacred junk. Jeremy turned to the chapter entitled "Past Amazon Exploratory Gatherings" and began pushing through the scholarly text and the suffocating new theoretical lingo the kids were writing nowadays. Then his eye caught his name:

> The theory of Amazon warriors proposed by Dr. Jeremy Millard in 1966, though now considered a hoax, is still useful in that it provides us with a perfect illustration of how even twentieth-century anthropologists succumbed to the early European fear of the primitive embodiment of provocative female traits, which include nonlinear formulation of thought, emphasized in the importance of randomness, surprise, and intense sexual engulfment.

Jeremy couldn't believe it! The *theory* of the Amazons? The idiot Dotson had seen the warrior women himself! He had blubbered at the sight of Dr. Robert Maxwell's "deflowering" and had gone into hysterics when Jeremy tried to bring Birdboy into the canoe. Dotson HAD SEEN the Amazons, he HAD SEEN Birdboy! How could he deny it? How can one trade truth for tenure? Truth! Truth, for god's sake! What happened to Truth in all this newfangled theory? What is the purpose of scholarship if not for discovery? Well, of course, that's the thing—your research has to be believable and can't be too challenging, or people won't believe you. It's easier for anthro blue-bloods from Berkeley to specialize in Yanomami hammocks than to unravel the emotional meltdown gotten from chasing women who copulate with great birds and devour men in one gulp. Dotson could be writing about straw hats for all anyone cared, yet he couldn't seem to resist denouncing Jeremy's Amazons as no more genuine than the Piltdown Man!

Jeremy wanted to smash his fists against the walls. Oh, he could just see the punk Dotson at anthropology conferences, tossing his little head, puff-puffing his way to sublime admiration while slashing Margaret Mead, claiming her *Coming of Age in Samoa* to be a useless exercise in Western naïveté. Dotson probably bragged that he had bundled his balls with palm leaves and twine and had taken part in a Kayapó manhood ritual because that's the fashion for anthropologists now. The man infested the world with his footnotes, sprinkling minuscule tidbits of scholarly thought like fleas. Ah Lévi-Strauss, ah *Tristes Tropiques*, sad tropics, how sad you are, fading into oblivion!

Jeremy slammed the book shut. He had nothing but contempt for these sham colleagues: they ate at him with jokes about his assumed fatherhood; they laughed openly to his face. Their voices raw like their tweedy Ivy League jackets; their humor glib but dull. They were aggressive like warriors and already had their claws bared, ready to push him aside, open the tender throats of scholastic funding, and dig for the Fulbrights and Guggenheims to get themselves the fishing nets and shell necklaces and llama boots and live monkeys. The shiny dust cover of Dotson's new book reflected Jeremy's lean, haggard face; his perturbed expression bled through the portrait of a Tupi with a crown of yellow plumes.

Birdboy opened the door cautiously and sneaked into the room. Startled, Jeremy jumped. The kid had appeared out of nowhere and was staring at Jeremy's despair. The boy's eyes gleamed.

"Get out of here!" Jeremy cried and swiveled his chair from side to side, then roughly pushed away from the desk with his foot.

Birdboy, around fifteen but with the maturity and size of a five-year-old, had the scorn of an adolescent. He huddled against the bookcase.

Jeremy's anger surged. "Why did you sneak in here, huh?" Then Jeremy got up from his chair and approached him. "Quit huddling like that! Why are you acting like such a coward! Do you have any idea who your mother was? Do you?" Jeremy snatched the boy's arm and pulled him forward. "Look at me! Look at me!"

Birdboy kept his face low, and his fingers gently scratched the air, like he always did when he was tense. Jeremy grabbed the kid's chin and looked into his eyes. He saw the reflection of his own thin face, now pained, bleeding into the whites, the way it had when he saw himself in Rosea's eyes.

Jeremy felt a surge of emotion, and he wrapped his arms around Birdboy's head and held him tight to his chest so he could hear Bird's muffled churtling and whistling and the small pops from his neck. Birdboy struggled away and bolted out of the room.

Jeremy took a deep breath, trying to calm himself down. "I'm sorry,

Bird. Sorry." Jeremy stuck his hands into the front pockets of his sweater and paced around his office; god damn it, he missed the things lost in the fire, especially his dear old books, enough to cover the walls, and his fishing net from Santarém, and his beautiful cavaquinho that he never learned to play, and of course—the monkey. The memory of the fire made him so ashamed that he could never say Rosea's name. The shame came from knowing that he had crossed a forbidden bridge, that he had taken a foolish journey toward love and away from knowledge.

Dr. Maxwell, after his encounter with the warrior women, realized that his knowledge meant nothing and that he would live for love, even if it destroyed him. Academia turned into hell for him, and he traded it in for a jungle purgatory. Jeremy often longed to do the same, disappear into the Amazon, for there was nothing for him here. The new young anthropologists were now keeping a foothold in their homeland, offering him "The Psychology of Rubbernecking and How It Contributes to the Way We View Our Work" or "The Study of Joggers and Their Body Anxiety" or "The Deconstruction of Deconstruction Addicts" as actual thesis proposals! Jeremy went over to his desk and fingered a little onyx box given to him by a student who had just returned from Yucatán. The box was really from a gift shop Jeremy had seen in Pasadena. Nice kid. Yeah.

Jeremy wandered to his desk and sank down in his chair. He opened the back flap of Dotson's book again. Married with two kids. He tossed the book across the room. What disgust, what terrible loneliness. He took a deep breath. Maybe he'd sleep on his hammock tonight and rock himself into oblivion. He should talk to Bird. Maybe he was too rough. But not as rough as the Amazons would have treated the boy. The Amazons would have killed him. Oh, excuse me, Mr. Dotson, Amazons are "legend" (as you say), the wilderness wearing a female fright wig. Let me tell you, Mr. Dotson (no I won't give you the honor of calling you Dr. Dotson), if you were sensitive, a real scholar, those Amazon giant-esses would have changed your life. You would have felt the bitter rawness of sexual guilt and engulfment. It would have haunted you. You would have chosen your woman because of it, not the college-professor's-wife-with-two-kids, but a tall woman to destroy your life. This longing for big-assed women with massive legs, prominent pubis, flagrant and oversized labia (vulgarity and all the rest) would have made you a fellow slave to unreason.

Jeremy knocked on Melvinor's door. "Is Bird in there?"

"Come in," Melvinor said softly.

Jeremy opened the door and found Melvinor sitting on his bed with Birdboy lying beside him, his head on the old man's lap. Melvinor looked up, his eyes floating in pinkish rheum. The room was spare: a single bed, a side table with a lower shelf holding a stack of notebooks, and a small lamp. He kept the house key by the lamp. No pictures. Just white walls, like solitary confinement except for a small window looking onto the backyard. Melvinor spent hours in this room doing what, Jeremy didn't know.

Melvinor's attention dropped back to Birdboy, and he ran his feeble fingers through the boy's bristly hair. Birdboy rumbled, his mournful eyes opening and closing in a grief he had no words to explain. The old one continued the story he had been telling: "Then Isaiah came upon a field of broken rock, which had once been a great temple. Water from hidden springs dribbled from the rocks like a new life emerging from the old one. From this ruin, Isaiah had a vision that one day God would return and save his people so that they could return to their Promised Land and" — he looked at Birdboy — "fly." Birdboy understood the word *fly* and cooed.

Jeremy saw those two, saw it was no use. He backed away. "Never mind. I'll get Birdboy later."

"Wait," Melvinor said, "I want to talk to you."

"About what?" Jeremy was in no mood for Melvinor's reprimand about his being an inadequate parent.

Melvinor pulled the covers and sheets out from their fastidiously tight tuck under the mattress and covered the boy. Melvinor's face was sunburned; he had been outside a lot. Lately he seemed to be dressing more youthfully, in hippy cottons, light-colored drawstring pants, and baggy T-shirts.

Jeremy sat beside him. "OK. Shoot."

Melvinor's normally roving eyes looked steadfastly at him. There would be no mumblings of Isaiah. "Jeremy," Melvinor said, "I'm in love again. Finally, I found someone to love."

Jeremy smiled vaguely and felt like saying, "We all think we're in love. But we aren't." But that's not what he said. He leaned in with an air of understanding, a professor's false sense of amiability when a student comes in and complains about the grade. "Who? Who are you in love with?"

Melvinor was serious. "Her name is Sherri."

Jeremy threw his head back and laughed. "Sherri? The woman who came here with her two kids?"

Melvinor nodded slowly.

"Look—" Jeremy said, stinging with impatience, "she's married, has kids, and, believe me, she's not going to leave anyone for you."

"Yes, but she loves me anyway. A married woman can love someone else. Her husband loves someone else. That is why they always fight."

"Mel, couples always fight. And they're always jealous of each other. And sometimes they do that other thing—with someone else. That doesn't mean she's headed for a divorce. Her husband probably makes some kind of a living? Supports her? You think she's going to leave and starve with you? You ever think of that?"

Melvinor's eyes glittered, as if his brain were circling like the globe, not as dead as he seemed. The man was serious. Faces of people in love are spooky, almost possessed.

"Melvinor," Jeremy said with a bit of a shiver, feeling the faint chill of jealousy. "It's hard to break up a marriage. Even a bad one. Someone would have to—"

"Try and kill you."

Jeremy's shame turned into anger, and he jumped to his feet. "That's not the point! We all try and kill each other, don't we? It's that she denounced me! THAT'S how women operate! I don't even know where she is. Alive or dead? Who knows? It's like she disappeared! Poof! Thank God! Just wandered back into the jungle"—Jeremy took a deep breath— "where the bitch belongs. And you are one crazy man, Mel."

Melvinor spoke with passion. "Sherri never told me I was crazy. The crazy. The only one who ever told me I was crazy was you. And I'm not in love with you."

"Well," the window reflected Jeremy's face as a fleshy smear, "that's good. That's good, Mel. Otherwise, we'd be in real trouble."

Jeremy looked at Bird with his head on Melvinor's lap. Bird didn't understand what was being said, but he knew emotion and was scowling and clinging onto Melvinor's knee. Jeremy indicated to Birdboy. "Make sure he doesn't leap out the window and try to fly, will you?"

Melvinor stroked the feathers on the back of Birdboy's neck. "He doesn't want to fly when he's with me. He only wants to fly because you want to fly."

Jeremy turned abruptly and headed toward his office. Just as he was about to slam the door, Melvinor called out, "Jeremy!"

Jeremy turned around.

"Sherri invited us to dinner, all three of us."

Jeremy gave his such-an-inconvenience sigh. "I don't know. I've got a full teaching schedule."

"She wants to know what's a good time for you. She can adjust her work schedule. They are expecting all three of us."

Jeremy, surrounded by the darkness in his head, gave him the ill-fated date. Then, with nothing more, he left the bedroom, returned to his office, and closed the door behind him. He slid into his chair, pulled his glasses off, and dropped his head forward, trying to stretch out the tense muscles in his neck. Not only was he being battered by Dotson's contempt, but he was being choked with Melvinor's newfound love. Was Melvinor insane, was his mind puckered up from too many washings? He tried to imagine Melvinor in bed with someone, forgetting how, forgetting how to stroke a woman's hair, how to whisper of love, so easy and free.

Jeremy drove to Sherri's house with Melvinor and Birdboy in the back seat. They arrived at a beige stucco house that needed fixing up. Just as Jeremy shut off the motor, the front door of the house flew open, and Sherri stood there in her apron. One of the toddlers, wearing baggy shorts and a T-shirt, shot out from behind her. She scooped him up and called, "Hi!"

Everyone got out of the car, and Melvinor walked ahead, opening the chain-link gate. The other tot wiggled out of the doorway, ran up the walkway to the old man and grabbed his hand. Birdboy jumped out of the car and ran into the house as if he were a cousin.

"Well," Jeremy said, following the pack, "this must be the old haunt."

"Oh yes, quite." The brisk motion of her head swung her ponytail. "Sherri. We've met."

Jeremy took her hand, gave a small bow, which on second thought must have looked stupid. "Of course."

"Whoa, you're different once you get out of the house," she said under her breath, like a little girl.

"I hope so," he grinned. "Things were a little tense the time you came over." He looked at her face, the small lines on the sides of her eyes, the hard shiny cheeks, the small nose speckled like a strawberry. She wasn't beautiful or exotic, but matter-of-fact and friendly. She swung her kid around with ease to her other hip. The kid played with the blond curl covering her ear. "You remember these guys. This is Keffy, the mellow one," she said, bumping up the one on her hip. "That's Jeffy," she pointed to the one holding Melvinor's hand, "he's our fighter pilot. You've met them before, but you probably think of them as the same."

"I know twins are different," Jeremy nodded agreeably.

"Oh," her face got vague, as if a memory struck her, "so different. One is the head twin, the other is the heart—but—" she set down the little boy, "both are equally heavy."

They sat at a long picnic table in the backyard. Her husband was stacking plates with chicken, ribs, and sausages and setting them on the table. "Are we expecting a crowd?" Jeremy asked.

"No. My husband got carried away," she said as she sat the kids down. "Joe's the barbecue expert."

Joe smiled sheepishly and rubbed his brown arms. His curly hair looked tousled as if he had just woken up. Sherri bustled around, "Sit anywhere please, Jeremy. Joe, get him a beer," then she swooped up, filled three kiddie plates with drumsticks, potato salad, and corn cobbetts. Birdboy sat between the twins, who pinched at his arms and made little bird squeaks to imitate him, then laughed hysterically. Sherri set the plates down in front of them and with the same swiftness filled three cups of lemonade. Birdboy shifted his eyes playfully, gnawing at a chicken leg, biting strips of meat, making like a parrot. The twins giggled and picked food from his plate; Sherri slapped her hand on the table. "Stop that, you two!" Birdboy smiled a bit and gave a twirl, which threw the toddlers into more hysterics.

Sherri "made plates" for everyone and sat at the end of the table in a lawn chair, with Melvinor on the bench next to her. Joe came out of the house with a large bottle of beer and two smallish water glasses and plunked down on a lawn chair at the opposite end of the table from his wife. He shifted restlessly, then poured the beer into the glasses and slid one to Jeremy. "For you, my friend."

Jeremy nodded. He sipped the beer to be a sport, but didn't like it, but if this was a working-class family, so be it. Everyone began eating, silently. Joe's narrow-eyed gaze shot from his wife to his kids and then to Melvinor as if he suspected something. Then Joe wiped his mouth with a napkin, looked at Jeremy beside him, and motioned a bit impatiently. "Please eat more, Mr. Jeremy. You only live once."

Jeremy took a sip of the beer, which tasted so bitter. What to say to this man, who seemed a bit moody? "Got a nice L.A. tan there," he said to Joe.

Joe gave a smirk. "It's my skin color. I was born this way. My sons," he motioned with a rib bone he had been gnawing, "got the pale side of the family. Sometimes I wonder if their father wasn't Norwegian."

Sherri put her chicken leg down. She had sauce all over her lips and wiped her mouth hard. "No, dear, they're yours. It only takes one time, you know."

Joe flushed with humiliation, then he quickly smiled at Jeremy, "American sense of humor, eh?"

"Ah yes," Jeremy wanted to change the subject quickly — "Sherri told me you're from Brazil?"

Joe took a gulp of beer. "My English is pretty good, no?"

"Excellent," Jeremy leaned forward. "I've been to Brazil!"

Joe nodded and grinned. "Good for you." He settled back and sized up Jeremy. "Where did you go?"

"The Amazon. Have you been there?"

"No. I don't have the right shoes, as they say here. Did you like it? Did you see crocodiles?"

"Many."

"Good for you." Joe gave one of his narrow-eyed looks, and then he seemed to shut off.

Jeremy didn't want to look straight at Joe because the man looked temperamental. There was something not right about him, and he acted almost like Rosea. He had the roiling restlessness, the agitation of inner drums, the frustration of a failed raid, the sense of longing for a place to fit in, but now he had to live in the passionless, cold, logical world where the Carl Dotsons ruled.

Joe suddenly jolted up, and the reinvigorated man went through the whole business of stretching clear across the table for salad and making a big deal out of piling lettuce on the twins' plates, telling them to eat, that they never ate enough salad. Then he offered Jeremy more salad and corn. Jeremy shook his head. "Thanks, I've eaten plenty."

Joe leaned back on his chair, reached into his pocket, and drew out a pack of cigarettes. "Mr. Jeremy, mind if I smoke?"

"Not at all."

"Disgusting habit," Sherri called down the table, her mouth full of corn. "I wish he would stop."

Joe leered, "I've stopped a few things, meu bem, but you can't have me stop everything."

"Joe! Enough!"

"Taa," Joe shrugged his shoulders and continued smoking in silence, flicking the ashes on the lawn. He stayed subdued, puffing and staring for a long time at Birdboy, who plucked his corn kernel by kernel. Finally, he turned to Jeremy. "I have seen him. Your son, no?"

"Not officially. I mean, not biologically." Jeremy didn't like for people to find any resemblance, "I brought him from Brazil, a long time ago. He was an orphan. Sort of."

"Ahhh," Joe's voice swung like a curved line. Then he leaned into Bird-boy and said with vigor, "Rapaz! Fala Português?"

Birdboy turned his eyes toward Joe, but kept eating, his beady eyes blank.

"Seu pai me disse que você é brasilero? Né?" Joe rotated his cigarette between his thumb and forefinger.

"I'm afraid," Jeremy said, "he was raised here. I don't speak Portuguese very well myself."

"Ah." Joe shrugged his shoulders. "Of course. My sons refuse to speak Portuguese. Well, 'what's the point?' I always say."

"Culture," Sherri leaned forward, "it's about learning their culture."

"Culture!" Joe said almost too loud, "what do you care about my culture, huh?"

Sherri glowered.

Joe puffed his cigarette angrily and scratched the back of his ear. "Well, what is American culture, huh? What amazing bit of culture is here in L.A. There is — the movies? Hein?"

Sherri filled Melvinor's glass with more iced tea, deliberately touching the old man's wrist as she held the glass steady. Jeremy expected the jealous husband to react, but Joe leaned back, crossed his arms as if he were hugging himself, and watched his sons a bit sadly.

Suddenly Joe got up, "Excuse me." He smashed the half-burned cigarette butt on his plate and went into the kitchen. The screen door slammed a little too hard. There was fumbling near the kitchen window. Jeremy turned to Sherri. "He alright?"

"Just needs to get his medicine," she dipped a clean napkin in her iced tea and wiped the sauce from her sons' faces. "He gets indigestion a lot lately. His job."

"What does he do?"

"Drives a tour bus through Beverly Hills. Makes him sick sometimes though, for some reason. A lot of pressure, these tourists."

"He shouldn't smoke. Can give him ulcers."

Sherri raised her eyebrows, "Well, what's a few more ulcers?" Then she got up, picked up her sons, and shook the food off them. "You don't need to get up, Jeremy," she said, shaking one, then the other, "these little guys can't sit for very long."

The kids took off and headed for the sandbox, then Birdboy left and sat under a shriveled dwarf orange tree and plucked a couple of unripe fruits. Sherri leaned over and whispered something in Melvinor's ear, and they both laughed. She held her hand to her chest, "My God, I swear," then jumped up and began piling the plates onto her forearms and in her hands, managing to cart away almost the whole table into the kitchen.

Jeremy would have rather not come to this picnic. A savage aspect of love was floating around, some turmoil that he didn't know if he should ignore or be a part of. He could try and understand it from an anthropologist's point of view, if he felt up to it. Instead, he imagined Joe in bed with Sherri; he was probably loud, demanding, sweating from his chest hair. Probably exciting, too, a bit exotic, a little kinky the way Rosea was. Jeremy shifted in his seat. He couldn't stomach Melvinor sitting there, being in love as it were. He'd talk to the old man when he got home. "Look, the woman's got a lot to handle. You can't deal with this Joe fellow and what he's going through; this is out of your league."

There was a small discussion in the kitchen between Sherri and Joe, Sherri's voice rising, then Joe saying something, one thing, very loud. Then Joe swung his head out the kitchen door and clapped his hands. "We are making coffee. I hope, Mr. Jeremy, you like it strong."

"Yes!" Jeremy said and got up from his chair, almost on an impulse to flee.

Just then Joe came outside carrying a pot of coffee and a pot of hot water, and Sherri brought out the cups and cream and sugar on a little tray.

"Sit down, Mr. Jeremy," Joe hollered as he set the coffee down. "We eat too fast here in this house."

Jeremy sat back down and watched Joe pouring coffee and then water into two large cups, which he gave to Sherri and Melvinor. He passed the milk and sugar to them. Then he took the two demitasse cups and spoke as if he were making a speech. "This is for me and Mr. Jeremy. I hope you like cafezinha, Jeremy. It is strong, but this is how to drink coffee after dinner. I can't get Sherri to drink it this strong."

"It's mud," she barked, stirring her coffee.

"Yes, well," he said ruefully as he leaned over and grabbed the sugar, "we compromise. You know what cariocas call American coffee?"

Jeremy shook his head. He really didn't know much about the civilized portion of Brazil, come to think of it.

"Xixi de freira. Nun's piss!" Joe burst out laughing as he shoveled sugar into his coffee. Jeremy laughed, too, but his chuckles always struggled out. Sherri touched her hand to her forehead. "So embarrassing," she muttered.

"Sherri!" Joe said half humorously, almost shouting. "*What* embarrasses you?"

Everyone gave an awkward grin, but answered only with tight sips of hot burning liquid. Jeremy ventured to reopen the conversation: "So, Joe, Sherri tells me you drive a tour van."

Joe swung his head almost like a bull. The oil from his curls made his head shiny, a bit greasy. "Yes, I drive a tour bus to the Hollywood homes." He gave a short smile, then took another drink of his coffee.

"So. That must be exciting."

Joe took another intake of breath. Stopped. "Yes. It's as exciting as I want it to be. No big shakes, as people say."

"Well," Jeremy added, the bitter coffee taste collecting in the back of his tongue, "it's a decent living."

Joe nodded. Another silence.

Melvinor piped up, "Jeremy is a college professor."

Joe looked at him from the corner of his eye, almost in contempt. "You are, huh? Good. Be careful." He took another drink.

"Can I ask why?"

"I went with a girl who was in college, she almost got me killed." His face seemed to swirl with emotion, his eyes angry. Everyone looked at him, expecting him to continue. Sherri and Melvinor froze, holding their coffee cups to their lips. Joe finished his coffee as if he had said nothing, then looked at the frozen faces. "Well," he said, "there is plenty more," and got up abruptly.

Jeremy got up, too, and joined Joe. The two men strolled along the
fence. Jeremy almost wanted to talk to Joe about Rosea; he had this impulse to shake Joe. Tell me! Tell me about love! Why do things happen the
way they do? Why do we risk going with women who are ready to kill us?

Ah no. Instead, Jeremy hedged. "So tell me. Does Melvinor come here
often?"

Unfazed, Joe looked at the old man. "I work during the day; she works
at night. I don't know who comes here for her. He's been here a couple
of times, yes."

"Do you," Jeremy was stepping on dangerous ground here, "worry
that maybe—?"

Joe laughed and scratched the back of his head. "Listen, if an old man
like that is what she wants, how can I stop her, huh?"

"You are an understanding man."

Joe took a deep breath. "Yes, I am understanding, I think. Sometimes
I understand a lot. Sometimes I understand a little."

"I don't understand—" Jeremy said, almost too emotionally, "anything, sometimes—"

But Joe drifted away, as if Jeremy weren't even there. Joe went to the
sandbox and snatched each of his sons, gave them a rough kiss, at which
they squawked, and set them down. Then Joe sat on the edge of the sandbox, slipped off his zoris, stretched out his legs, and poked the twins
with his bare toes. The twins took their pails and began piling sand,
burying his feet up to his ankles and then the cuffs of his trousers. One
of them held the pail up and poured the sand, which came down swift
and smooth. Joe placed his hands down on the sand and let his kids
bury them, too. Far away a screen door slammed, and someone shouted.
Jeremy imagined another fight like this one, another tumble of marital
discord, continuing without end.

Dripping wet from his river bath, Lima was brought back
to the village. The women circled around him, taunting him,
hitting him with sticks, and slapping him with stinging nettles.
Lima bore it silently, looking up to heaven, blood dripping on
his beard like Di Giorni's painting *Christ in Agony*. Then
the large woman with one breast who had been refused came
into the crowd waving a *tacape*, a club with a cruel blade
embedded in the center. At the sight of this, Lima's
composure broke.

— *Diário de Carlos Manoel Teixeira da Cunha, O Ano* 1643

Chapter 25

O Ano 1978

Nancy West's agent called Rosea at home. "No can do."

"What?" Rosea asked, "what? Nancy doesn't like me? What in the fuck
did I do wrong? Was I wearing the wrong kind of shoes?"

The agent said, "Nancy felt uncomfortable somehow at the things you
said. She said she'd rather just watch Carmen's movies."

"WHAT THE FUCK?!" Rosea bellowed into the phone, trying to slay
who's-it at the other end of the line just with her voice. "What does your
stupid movie have to do about my mother? What about her agent that
dropped her like a poison apple after my father took off! What about

that fairy in swimming trunks who couldn't stand the sight of my face and took off into the woods like King Kong? What about her nervous breakdowns and shock treatments when Hollywood told her to stuff it up her ass?!"

The agent sounded thin and evasive and shudderingly polite. Rosea would get her stipend, but, "We don't need your services. Really. Nancy is getting the role under her belt. She's doing fine. She'll make it. *Carioca Craze* is not a historical documentary. It's not anthropological. We aren't talking of Henry Kissinger's manual of foreign affairs. It's just a movie. Simple as that."

"Well, I'll tell you something else simple. Nancy West is not like my mother, that blond son of a twit. Who in the hell do you think you are, hiring a broad like that? Were you hoping for an Oscar nomination or something?! You know what I say to you guys? B-F-D! Big fucking deal and you STINK!" Rosea slammed the phone down. Damn. She paced around the room. Betrayed! Betrayed by that damn rich bitch Nancy West, who must have said, "Oh, that Rosea chick is SO strange!" For once Rosea put on her charm, and what did that skinny blond sexless weasel do but shoot her down! Rosea kicked at her bed. Hard. She had a strong kick and a cheap bed, so the cot flipped over and landed mattress down. She opened the curtains, saw a bunch of kids playing soccer — they put the wimps as goalie. She flashed the kids her naked breasts and yanked down her underwear, revealing her pubis. The game continued, cheating thud-kickers making goal after goal. Rosea snapped the curtains shut. Faggots. Gentleman Prefer Blondes, eh? Stupid punks.

And what! The next day she was invited for questioning! What kind of an invitation is that?! Well, have a martini! What could they pin on her? Why wouldn't they leave her alone? A girl tries to keep a job — a girl tries to be friends with — a girl tries to save the world, and what does she get? She might as well lie! Might as well lie to the teeth until her choppers all fall out from hot air!

The cop who ushered her into the interrogation room reassured her that she wasn't under arrest and she could relax and have "tons o' fun." Then the cop left and stood outside the door. He took a peek through the small observation window and grinned. The investigator was already there, sitting at a stark, polished table. There were two chairs, one for him and one for her. The investigator's face was long like a fish, with flaky gray cheeks and spiky eyebrows. Rosea sat quietly in her chair and leaned back, trying to look relaxed and nonchalant with legs stretched out in front and hands clasped together on her belly.

Last time she had been invited in for questioning, she had soot up her nose and monkey fur under her fingernails. She was in handcuffs and had been stripped naked and made to sing "The Lady in the Tutti-Frutti Hat." Now the cops were polite and let her sit down, and she didn't have to sing any tunes. But—

"We are looking into the Vaughan estate murder."

Rosea grimaced. "Oh. Well, don't look at me."

The investigator stroked an eyebrow with his thumb. He had a rash underneath his lower lip, which made him look like his tongue was hanging out. Rosea was curious how the fuck he knew, but she didn't want to reveal anything. "Why would I do anything against Vaughan Peters? I don't even know the man."

"It's not him." Was all he said.

Rosea got uncomfortable and leaped out of her chair. She paced. "Look. I burned down my house. One house. One time. My marriage stank. Have you ever had a bad marriage? Does ANYONE in Hollywood ever have a bad marriage? Oh no! Not on your life!! Yeah."

"Sit down, Mrs. Millard."

"Jesus, could you call me Ms. Socorro Katz? Could you do that for me?"

The investigator conceded with a nod of his head. "Ms. Socorro Katz, your car meets the description of a car seen in the vicinity of the garden the afternoon the man was found dead."

Rosea froze, and a shudder shot up her legs, her spine, rattled her gut, and she squawked out a retch. Then she strolled loosely over to her chair and flopped back down. "I got some kind of flu, but I dragged my butt in here just to be with you."

month?"

Rosea's face was stern. "There is no way in hell I'd go to that garden."

"Would you be able to give us an alibi if we requested it?"

"Yeah, those kids outside my window who play soccer. They are always waiting to see my pussy."

"Ms. Katz, that kind of talk doesn't help."

"Look," Rosea slapped her hand on the table. "Look. You think just because I got time for one thing, I've got to do every crime in the book. Oh, I did arson today, oh well—how about kidnap?! Oh, I never tried murder, how about blowing someone away?! You think people work like that? You think we are like druggies that go from grass to heroin and then end up in China smuggling diamonds in our brassieres?"

The investigator sized her up and down. "I can't hold you here because I don't have enough evidence, Ms. Katz. But I do suspect you, and you can bet I'll see you again. Of course, if you confessed now and saved us a heap of time, your sentence would be a hell of a lot lighter than if we have to come looking for you with a flashlight—"

Again Rosea suddenly leaped out of her chair as if it were rigged with electric volts. She lurched around the room, her body feeling jangly, and bellowed: "No way will I confess a lie just to make you happy! No way, Ho-zay! I'm straight! What do you want me to do, kill myself? Can't I live in peace without someone barking up my butt?"

The investigator was quiet for a long time. Rosea got nervous. She realized she had blown it and collapsed back in her chair. She wanted to tell him, "I try so hard. I try until it kills me. Something is making me so crazy I can't even think anymore. But I don't know what it is." But she said nothing. She didn't know how to make her voice small.

He looked at her without expression, his hands folded on top of his notebook, his pen sticking up. Rosea froze, then slowly her hand came up, and she pressed her knuckles against her mouth and could feel her teeth sinking into her skin. Her sobs clutched the back of her throat. Tears ran down her cheeks and began filling the spaces between her fingers, like a salty rain washing over dry arroyos. With this, he let her go.

Rosea, fuming, got into her car, slammed the door, and took off. She'd drive anywhere, until her gas or her nerves wore out. She wanted to mow down some people, flatten them like tofu-burger patties. She wanted to leave a tragic L.A. in her wake and see in her rearview mirror the grief-stricken, furrowed brows of the crazy mob coming after her, waving tire irons and lighted torches. A traffic light stopped her near Hoody's Laugh Club, where a line of people sat on blankets, wallowing in graham cracker boxes and cans of Diet-Rite and cheap paperbacks and rolled up copies of *Variety*. All this because at four o'clock Mr. Hoody held open auditions for an hour and could take only so many people. He wouldn't do sign-ups either. Hoody was some fat ass who sat in a dark auditorium snorting contemptuously while comedians sweated to be taken seriously.

Rosea pulled over to the corner and took a look at these hopeful comedians with hot swollen faces and sunken eyes, exhausted from sitting on concrete all day, their faces already bitter from trying to find something funny in this town. She leaned out the window and shouted: "SUCKERS! YOU GOTTA DEGRADE YOURSELF FOR THAT ASSHOLE! YEAH, PRANCE AROUND FOR SOME JERK, WHY DON'T YOU?!"

The comedians peered briefly from their magazines and other useless business, then went back to their waiting. Idiotic entertainers. Alfred Hitchcock once said, "Actors are sheep." Damn right they are.

Rosea zoomed away. She spun down Vine, hating the *film industry* with all her soul, the *film industry* with its accidents of fate: being born to celebrities, becoming has-been stars, getting laid, dropping dead. The shop windows displayed mutilated bodies, tiny torsos in silk shirts, legs with green hose and dangerous-looking, pointy-toed shoes, rows of heads in snappy wool beanies and floppy-brimmed sunhats, pieces of bodies, chopped up and lying every which way.

Marry me, Joe, marry me. Marry me and leave the country. Two tickets to Brazil. Quick! The words became numb like a burned tongue, but the pain was there: marry me, Joe. The people on the sidewalk passed her like zombies, their eyes hidden under sunglasses, their lips coated with pretzel salt, their teeth yellow from coffee. They carried bags filled with tissue paper wrapped around little expensive gifts. Rosea flipped off a man carrying a sign that said "KICK ME AND SLIP ME A FIVER,"

and the man shook his decrepit fist at her. The restaurants poured out
their greasy onion smell of chili burgers and fried fish. She gagged and
covered her mouth with the back of her hand, taking a deep breath to
try to calm the nervous tangle in her gut.

She prayed to have Joe, begged God to make his wife have cancer or
something so he could be a beautiful sad widower and then marry her.
Please, let me have Joe, and I'll want nothing else. I don't care if it's fash-
ionable; I want to be his wife and bear as many children as he wants,
ten, twenty. . . . Her joints trembled with anger that exhausted her; she
wanted to sleep; she wanted to die from oversleeping. She prayed to God
and to the devil at the same time to increase her chances of marrying
Joe: I'll be a virgin, a nun; I'll light tons of white candles, enough to burn
down the whole church. I'd even burn up the whole city if I could find
my beautiful husband Joe in the ashes.

It was 1:00 A.M. in her festery apartment complex, a group of creeps
jacking-off down the corridor. She unsnapped her three locks and
opened the door. Joe stood there under a naked porch lightbulb. His hair
tousled, his eyes sharp with sleeplessness. It was bad enough, he said, to
come to the same apartment building where he had stayed when he first
came to America, full of hope, but to come here in despair was almost
more than he could bear. She stepped aside, pulled him in, and shut the
door. She placed his hands on her breasts and kissed him, sweeping her
tongue on the ridges of his teeth. She pulled him over to her narrow
single bed and opened her bathrobe.

He drew back.

"What? What now?"

Joe shook his head as if to say *stop*. Start over. Start from when we
were innocent coconuts bouncing on the waves.

"I can't —" he seemed to say, but shit, maybe she wasn't hearing him
right. He said something about how he was such a bad husband and
father, and OK, so he was a bad lover also, something that diddly-squat
men say when they want to dump you.

Rosea flung off her bathrobe and squeezed her breasts together and hissed, "Feed off of these! Aren't I your pig trough?"

Joe turned his head away as if human flesh were disgusting all of a sudden. "Please, Rosea. We have to end this."

She stroked her bush with one hand and then shoved that hand into his face. He slapped it away. "I wanted," he tried not to shout, "I wanted to tell you here and not at work!"

"Hell no! I want to get married!"

"Marry you? Are you crazy?"

"Please," Rosea scrambled for her robe, "please. Marry me and let's get the hell out. Let's move to Brazil. Let's do what my mother never had the nerve to do."

Joe pulled away and turned toward the door. "Forget it."

Rosea leaned against the front door, blocking it. "You think I'm a whore, don't you?"

"You are not a whore, and I'm not a whore either. I do not kill people!" He almost started choking up, "Understand? It is not my fault!"

"Ah! That's good. That's really good, Mr. Innocent. Well, let me tell you something. The police not only can talk to dogs, but they got a lotta snitches working for them."

Joe swallowed. "What do you mean?"

Rosea didn't say. Let him panic a bit. Finally: "We better as hell leave the country."

"This is my home. I am not going anywhere with you. Let me go."

"You better not be running away from me!" Rosea brayed, pressing her butt against the door, "You better get used to THE LIFE, Mr. Happily Married Man. You think all the shit happens around you, and you are not the least bit guilty? Could that be? Huh? Hell no! We're all guilty. You think you can come to this country and play the innocent immigrant forever! I don't know what it's like back in Bananaville, but here in the movies either we fall in love or we die! You wanna die in prison? You wanna die together in the gas chamber strapped to my pussy?"

"Forget it!" Joe grabbed her and pushed her aside. "Look at you! Look at how you live!" he shouted as he left.

Rosea ran down the corridor and out into the street after him. He hurried to his car. She broke into a run, her bare feet slapping the concrete, her robe flying open, boobs flopping, hair glopped to her neck. Joe scrambled in his pocket for his keys as he made his way to the door on the driver's side.

"HEY!" She screamed. "STOP!"

Joe unlocked the car, then shouted to her over the roof. "I will suffer for what I did to you or Sherri! But I will not marry you or run away! I do not take bribes. I would rather be tortured!"

Rosea's anger veered out of control, and she pounded the side window with her fist. Joe jumped in and started the car. Rosea saw a rock in the gutter. She swooped down, grabbed the rock, and smashed the side window. Joe swung out of the car, slammed the door; he grabbed her hair and slapped her, his hand striking her jawbone.

Rosea flung him away with a swipe of her arm and shouted, "*Families* are from the movies. *Voodoo* is from the movies. *Tropicana Banana* is from the movies. *You* cannot survive in the movies! Neither can I!"

Somebody from the second floor of the apartment hollered: "WHAT IS THIS, A HITCHCOCK MOVIE?! DOES ANYONE HERE HAVE A JOB IN THE MORNING?!"

She ignored the neighbor. So what? She was so filled with desire for Joe she shivered. Joe paced back and forth, squelching his shouts, his "I'm sorry! I'm sorry! What can I do?!" She fantasized cutting his shirt open with a big knife; just imagining the sound of tearing fabric made her wet. She wanted to rip up his belt with her teeth. Joe swiped the air with his hands as if he would hit her again, but she lunged at him and began kissing him furiously, biting his ear, nipping his lip, surrounded by his confused breath.

Joe pushed her back. "I mean it!"

Rosea took a deep breath, then burst into tears. "God damn it, Joe! You loved me!" Crying gripped her stomach like the time she first laid eyes on him. She crumpled onto the pavement. The sidewalk at night was still warm.

"Please," he kept saying to her, "please, do not cry." His pleading made her love the danger. She loved him, even loved to hate him, and she hated to love him. She hated his lovely stupidity, his wetback simplicity. Rosea hacked loudly, tears and snot wetting her knees, drool smearing the back of her hand. "Kill me," she wailed as she rolled around on the pavement. "Kill me! I want to die!"

The second-floor man hollered out the window again, "SHUT UP DOWN THERE OR I'LL KILL YOU MYSELF, YOU DAMN WHORE!"

Rosea moaned, "Ah go ahead. I can't stand this life!"

Joe stooped down, and she could see his eyes like two hollow dents. "You will live no matter how painful it is," he said, his voice emerging from the dark. "You will live like you can't believe."

Then he got into his car and drove away.

Rosea stayed huddled, kneeling on the cement, tugging at her hair, moaning. She remembered her mother's story of how Amazon women after battle would do each other's hair while boasting of the men they had killed. The other Amazons listening would scoff and joke in an act of not believing until the proud ones would have to rise and physically describe their victims in intimate detail, praising the manhood of some, deriding the manhood of others. The women's fingers were covered with rings that, along with breastplates and feather collars, they had stolen from the defeated tribe.

Rosea looked up. The glass from Joe's broken window glittered like the winks of a dark river.

Saturday after the freakout. Rosea drove to Joe's neighborhood, houses bland as boxes, beige or light blue, with the old-lady rose gardens and scowling dry lawns bristly as a buzz cut. She pulled to the curb. Sherri's car wasn't around. Good. She slipped out and quietly closed the car door. Then she carefully opened the front gate and went up to the window and peeked in between the curtains. A toy truck lay upside down on the couch. Joe was probably in the backyard. She jumped the fence and slipped around to the side of the house and peered through the wood slats of the back gate. She saw the two boys playing, but no Joe. The gate was unlocked, and she eased it open, the bottom noisily scraping the ground. The twins turned toward her, with their pale round faces and matching blue overalls.

Rosea slowly approached them, not saying anything, so seldom had she encountered children who did not burst into tears in her presence. They acted as if they recognized her and remained perfectly still. Rosea got up close to the little idols and knelt in front of them. They seemed so soft, as if you could use them for a pillow on which to cry tears of comfort. No wonder Joe wanted to keep some semblance of a normal life. The twins held their padded and flat hands out to their sides. One of them lifted a pointer finger. They looked so alike, one with raised finger, one not. Both had bowl-shaped mouths like babies in toilet-paper commercials. One looked at her in fascination; the other was more fearful, the little blue vein in his milky neck quivering, his breath a little raspy. Rosea brushed one of their tummies with the back of her hand. The twins stepped back and continued staring. The one with the delicate neck vein looked toward the house.

She searched their faces for a resemblance of Joe. Perhaps they had Joe's apprehension. Perhaps his mouth. Rosea got on all fours and smelled their necks, their baby smell. She lifted her hand and ran her fingers down one of the twins' back, then cupped his butt.

They both turned abruptly and waddled away, their little bodies jostling under their overalls. As if in a dream, she felt herself running after them and scooping them both up. They raised their hands in the air, struggling, but her large arms clamped them tight. They struggled and snerked, and their bodies tried to twist loose, but her Amazonian strength held them fast as she jostled them harder. "Stop!" But they struggled even more and kicked, and one powied her in the groin. Her mind went blank as if she couldn't think, but only remember the long gray halls of Frontera, the walls of bars and shouting women, the guards and their noisy concrete footsteps. The loudest prisoner was a cellmate serving time for kidnapping a child; this middle-aged woman cried every night in her sleep because she wanted someone to love. Rosea heard herself breathing hard, flying out through the prison doors just before they automatically locked behind her. The twins by now were crying, and she hoisted one kid on each hip. Jesus, were they heavy!

She saw Joe's face coming closer as the last automated door shut behind her. Suddenly she felt so light with Joe and his sons around her — her crashing through the prison gates, and him greeting her with open arms, all four of them colliding in her freedom, swallowing each other with kisses and hugs of joy!

Lima's body was cut into quarters, boiled, then roasted in big pieces and eaten with gusto. The old women put the entrails and intestines into large pots and cooked them over the fire. They sang and danced around them, stirring the horrible stew with long sticks and laughing like witches. After eating the human flesh and fighting for the tenderest morsels, they brought out jars of *masato*, and these miserable women drank until their drunkenness felled them as sure as the club that killed our dear Dom Marcus Pedro Ferraz de Lima.

—*Diário de Carlos Manoel Teixeira da Cunha, O Ano* 1643

Chapter 26

O Ano 1978

When Joe heard the twins crying, he opened the back door and dashed out just in time to see Rosea running, hauling one of his sons over her shoulder and dragging the other by the arm. Jeffy and Keffy were howling.

"Wait!" Joe screamed and ran after them. Rosea stopped suddenly as if stunned. The twins struggled and reached for him. Rosea clutched them with her incredible strength. Not even Joe could carry them both at once anymore. Joe snatched one boy, then the other, and they grabbed onto his legs and mewed. He squatted and held his sons tight and whispered a small prayer into their ears. He adored them so, including their orange-juice breath. *Graças a Deus* he saved them just in time.

Rosea stood there with her hands in her back pockets, swaying nonchalantly. Her rumpled brow made a small lump on her forehead.

Joe pulled his sons tighter against him. "Rosea! Are you crazy? What did you want with my sons?"

Rosea didn't answer, but rolled her jaw to show she meant business and wasn't sorry. Joe took a good look at her. She had large, mulelike shoulders and dark half-moons under her eyes like a bad omen. Joe stroked his sons' cheeks with his lips. He hated her now, and when he looked at her ragged hair hanging like a dangerous curtain, he imagined her waiting for him, hiding, holding a dagger. Joe knew he was in trouble. He decided to say nothing and took each of the twins by the wrist and ushered them quickly toward the house.

"Wait!" she called.

Joe held his sons even tighter and continued forward. "Wait for what?! You tried to kidnap my sons! Are you crazy?! Are you positively nuts?!"

Joe could hear her muffled scream, her pent-up rage squealing against her palm. Suddenly she flung her hand away and let out a bellow. "MARRY ME!"

Joe stopped and turned around. The twins knocked against his legs. "I told you no."

Rosea wrapped her arms around her waist and doubled over, staggering as if poisoned, "Marry me, god damn it. You know what I want."

"What is this? I should say OK, I give up, I'll marry you? This is impossible. I don't want to be with you anymore. I told you the other night."

He brought the twins inside and put them in the living room. The boys stared at him a little too steadily, as if they knew. He squatted to be eye level with them. "Papai is here. He will never let you go." The twins didn't quite believe him, and they peered over his shoulder to look at Rosea standing in the entranceway between the kitchen and the living room.

Joe rose and spoke to her across the room. The couch was like a wall between them, but not a very tall one. "I told you to go," Joe said. "I have told you, not my children. There is a point where I don't make deals. No

jeitinho, no nothing. If you want my children, you will have to kill me
first."

"Oh," Rosea scoffed. "Pretty dramatic, Latin lover you."

She crossed her arms and leaned on the doorjamb as if intending to
stay. "Oh yeah, I'm relaxed here," she muttered, but her eyes flicked
around nervously as if looking for an escape. The twins emerged from
either side of him and stared at Rosea again.

Rosea sneered, ambled toward the couch, and sat on the arm. She
winked at Jeffy. "I think they like me. Like father like son."

"I don't care. You go."

Suddenly a car door slammed. The twins squealed and ran toward the
front door. Joe swept over to Rosea. "Go! Go, damn it!"

"No." Rosea said firmly, hooking her leg on the arm of the couch.

The metal gate squeaked open, and footsteps thumped toward the
house. Sherri's keys rattled in the lock.

He gave Rosea a shove, and she stumbled up, then he pushed her again
toward the kitchen, but the front door flew open, and Sherri entered with
groceries and saw Rosea. Her face fell. "Oh," she whispered, and her arms
loosened around the grocery bag. "Oh."

Rosea grinned, her upper teeth lifting from her lower. "Hi. It's me
again." Sherri grimaced as if she knew. Rosea was almost part of this
family. Joe decided not to say anything. Excuses would make the lie so
complicated he wouldn't remember it enough to retell it properly. Rosea
took one step, and she wavered, as if she would faint. "I came here to
steal your kids," she said, "because I want your husband to love me."

Sherri gave a short sob deep in her throat. "He does love you."

Rosea tightened her jaw so it flared like a cobra. She stuck her hands
in her pockets again and paced, trying to push the words out, emitting
small grunts. "No," she said finally, her voice rattling with near tears,
"no, he doesn't."

Then she tore through the living room, almost knocking down Jeffy,
and flung herself out the door; she managed to get in her car and drove
off zigzagging, hitting the curb and pitching out again, as if the road had
disappeared.

Sherri took a deep breath and looked into her grocery bag. Joe scraped his hands through his hair. "I'm sorry. She came in here like a thief. I was trying to drive her away from here," he said.

Sherri looked frankly into his eyes, her small wrinkles so fragile. "You were *trying to drive her away*? How come you didn't? Didn't you try hard enough?"

Joe pressed down his anger. It seemed like an iron ball was stuck in this throat. "Well. What should I do, kill her? You want me to murder her?"

"I wish you had never learned English! That way I wouldn't have married you." Sherri walked slowly into the kitchen and put away the groceries, leaving the twins playing quietly in the living room.

Joe joined Sherri in the kitchen, trying to think of what to say.

Tears began to form in Sherri's eyes, and she bolted into the living room. Joe watched her from the kitchen. The light coming from the half-open curtain lit her profile with silver. She bent down, and her exhausted, baggy shirt hung open. Jeffy pulled at the neckline and tried to look down her blouse. She murmured as Keffy caressed her hair.

To Joe, Sherri was always mysterious. The silent mourning for her dead sister who had died for love. The head twin and the heart twin. She who could not love loved that old man, that walking corpse. She probably loved the silly professor, too, the professor who studied Brazil but knew nothing of its soul. When Joe had come to this country, his full name, *José Francisco Verguerio Silva*, had fallen from the plane and shattered to pieces on the ground, leaving him—Joe Silva. The names between his head and feet were gone.

Sherri, with her sharp voice, her contempt, her iciness, was the most honest of anyone he knew. She resisted him because she knew he would never fit here in America. She knew they were too foreign for each other, that Terra Nova was a frightening place of strange grunts, threats, and leveled spears. He knew she didn't love him and never had.

The boys placed their little hands on their mother's cheeks, covering her face with affection. She gave a small whimper. Then she took their hands, turned, and the three of them walked slowly toward the master bedroom, not the children's room. From the kitchen, Joe heard sounds of motherhood: cooing, the slick crispness of sheets being pulled out and

tucked over the boys, the words *nap* and *quiet*, and the creaking of the
mattress springs as she leaned over and kissed one, then the other.

Sherri went straight to the living room, sat on the couch, and didn't say anything. He wanted to tell her the truth, how it came about — sin and darkness, on the one hand, desperate hope and longing, on the other. He had come to the United States because he was tortured. He said the words slowly to himself. *Eu fui torturado.* He had an accent when he said the word *torture.* Sounded like a foreign political prisoner, like when they get interviewed on the television news. Sherri wouldn't understand the whole truth. It was too complicated. Truth is never easy, she always said. There are always at least two truths.

Joe got up and went as far as the kitchen doorway . She would not turn to look at him. He stared at the back of her head, her hair fraying from her ponytail like loose wires. She lifted her chin. Joe made his way to the armchair and sat down. She had one leg curled up on the couch. His mouth was dry.

"Sherri."

Her head moved slightly. How would he start? How would he plead? Guilty, of course. The argument would come; it would be like cutting each other open piece by piece. The room had grown dim. He leaned over and flicked on the lamp. She squinted and put her hand over her eyes, drawing away.

"Look," Joe said, trying to stay calm, "there does not have to be any more arguments. I know you want me out of here. I'll go."

Sherri swallowed hard and paused, looking down at her hands. Her face rumpled with grief. The small blue veins on the side of her temple seemed to hurt, reminding Joe of pictures of half-formed human beings. "I can't understand," she said quietly, "why you would fuck a woman — in front of your sons. I know you do — elsewhere. But they are innocent. Can't you just let them be children?"

She brought her heels up to the seat of the couch, then rested her head on at her knees. She coughed softly. Joe didn't even know if she was crying. He had no beautiful words to say to her, no comfort; his own stupidity he gave to her on a silver plate, as they say. To explain that he was trying to drive Rosea away would mean he would have to explain about last night, which meant he'd have to explain the affair, the murder, and so on and so on. The truth would be so complicated it wouldn't be right telling her now.

Sherri glared at him and kept her arms clasped around her legs. He almost wished she would explode in a rage, but she gripped her anger like a grenade. "What else do I have but my babies?" she said. "Where's MY big Hollywood career, Joe? Where are the movie stars for me? My babies are all I have." Then her voice sharpened: "Go back to your country. You people poison everything you touch. You married me so they wouldn't ship you back to your damn jungle. You are no life. You are nothing but death."

No. She had his life all wrong. He had to tell it. From Point One, talk, say everything, withhold nothing. The whole world wasn't a police station. No, he could tell her something. Not to save the marriage, but to let her know how much he had wanted to live. How hard he had fought death. He sat on the couch near her. She flinched. "Listen to me," he said. He would tell her, he would tell her. "Listen," he coaxed, "listen, meu bem. . . . Listen, there is something so important—" he reached over and turned Sherri's face toward him. She snapped her head away. He trembled, trying to continue. To gather the courage would mean he'd have to remember everything vividly and tell it—truthfully. "Listen a minute, I have to tell you—"

Sherri shoved him aside and scrambled out of the couch. "I don't have to listen to you! You have lost the right to TALK! I am sick of your lying, deceitful shit!"

Joe snapped. "I tried to love you, but you are no use! Perhaps, when danger is all you know, it is all you can love! It is better to be in danger than to . . ."

Sherri glowered, then her expression crumbled. She staggered to the wall, turned her back to him, and cried bitterly, her wail so hollow.

"Ahhh—merda." Joe got up from the couch and stood, watching her cry; it was no use trying to touch her. He lost the will to fight. Sherri leaned her forehead against the wall and was crying to no end. He wandered around and began picking up the toys on the floor and putting them in a little yellow plastic box. Amazing how the twins could sleep with all of this going on. He took the plastic toy box to their room, then went to the master bedroom and opened the door a little. Their mother's weeping made Keffy's eyelashes flutter, but he stayed asleep. They were sprawled out, sleeping on the marriage bed that he hadn't slept in for weeks. The boys had kicked over the covers, and their arms and legs were flung out as if they'd been shot just after they experienced the love of which they had always dreamed.

Requiem aeternam dona eis, Domine, et lux perpetua luceat eis. Te decet hymnus, Deus, in Sion, et tibi reddetur votum in Jerusalem. Exaudi orationem meam, ad te omnis caro veniet. Requiem aeternam dona eis, Domine, et lux perpetua luceat eis.

— *Missa de réquiem por a alma de Dom Marcus Pedro Ferraz de Lima* (Requiem Mass for the soul of Dom Marcus Pedro Ferraz de Lima), *O Ano* 1643

Chapter 27

O Ano 1978

Variety's headline "Cariocas Go Crazy" peered from the news rack. Rosea swiped up the magazine and began reading it as she continued walking down the street. She read of how the cast and crew were going to Rio to shoot a few scenes. For their dead location manager, they planned to throw floral offerings into the ocean at Ipanema, the beach of the famous song "Girl from Ipanema." For Carmen, they planned a pilgrimage to the Urca Casino, where she sang her famous tune "Rio, você ainda está no meu coração." Rio, you are still in my heart.

Rosea imagined Nancy in Rio—the Rio of tourist snapshots, like bad movies sets: Nancy standing at the foot of the Corcovado with her arms spread to the side, Nancy riding the little tram going up to the Sugar Loaf, Nancy with a bottle of cachaça, Nancy in her sunglasses holding a small dog while standing in the middle of the Copacabana's mosaic sidewalk of white and brown waves. Nancy West the bug, the ant, the fluff snot from your nose, the puffballs under your bed. Oh you, Miss Nancy, little candy lips, the new expert on my mother, Nancy, you little pert puta. Oh no. The Amazon culture is pure. Oh, not in the romantic way, the way movies thought of, but the way it was in the beginning—violent, with spears that aim clean for the heart. The Amazons were part of a well-ordered society, clear judgment, the emotions rich and strong, their struggle hard in a world where there were so many ways to die.

It was too much. Rosea grabbed the first page of *Variety*, ripped it in half, wadded the paper fiercely into a ball, and hurled it toward a parked car along with the rest of the pages. Hurrying footsteps approached her from behind. Thinking it was the police, she started to bolt, but someone shoved his fingers into her back. She whipped around and saw a short man yelling at her, "You gonna pay for that?"

"What?" Rosea squinted. She could barely see the man's round face and brown-freckled cheeks floating in and out of a haze.

The man looked at her in dismay. "Pay for the newspaper, lady."

Rosea rumbled around her purse and pulled out a couple of bills and stuffed them in his hands.

"If you want change, you got to come back to the store."

Damn! Rosea left abruptly, charging down the sidewalk and across the street through a red light while cars slammed on their brakes and screeched and drivers yelled, "Hey lady!" Rosea stopped, looked up at the sky, and shouted, "Nancy is not going to Rio!" The drivers yelled at her again, and one got out of his car, grabbed her arm, and marched her to the sidewalk. Rosea jerked her arm away, but the idea in her head was too strong to stop for a fight. NANCY MUST NOT GO TO RIO! Nancy would cause a disaster, get people killed. Boatmen will be shot with arrows, children will be trampled, death will come to the villages. Nancy will not follow Carmen's footsteps; she will not revive or resuscitate her mother; she will not do her Miss Pert Pussy dance on her mother's grave.

Rosea paced back and forth and slapped her palm on her forehead so loud she felt a mumble rising from her throat, but she couldn't even mouth the words for what she wanted to say. Why did they link South America with apes? Why do they think all jungles have quicksand? Why do jungle explorers wear hard hats when the thing most likely to fall on them is shit from some canopy dweller? Why are brains called *coconuts*? Why are crazy people called *bananas*? Why is it called a Brazil nut? Why is South America called a Good Neighbor, as if she were some wiggy housewife baking cookies? Or a Bad Neighbor, as if he were some teen-ager playing his music too loud? Why, oh why?

Rosea jammed her hands into her pockets, shoving her fingers down so hard her knuckles cracked, while the sadness rose in her throat and opened her face with the urge to cry. She didn't know what her mother wanted her to do. The show would go on; there would be a riot in Brazil; all hell would break loose; Brazil would hate Nancy West the gringa fool, but love Nancy West the movie star. Was that so different than the great painful love affair between Carmen Socorro and Brazil, where two beings loved each other deeply, but did not know the true life in each other's soul? *Se lembra de mim.* "Remember me, remember," her mother had pleaded with Brazil while strolling in her great American garden filled with toucans and araras, and the faint whiffs of lost Amazon pleasure. *Se lembra de mim.* Even if Hollywood eats me alive. Rosea snatched at her hair and took deep breaths, then ran her hands over her face. She heard someone say, "Are you OK?" She looked out through her fingers and saw no one speaking to her.

Rosea drove to the Hollywood Hills, where she had first taken Joe, their first clamor at love. The hillside, belonging to Galaxy Studios, was covered with ever-dry weeds that partially buried decrepit plaster-and-chicken-wire caves, tree stumps, and hastily built cabins of now splintered wood. Nothing would make this place green, not a rain machine or genuine rain. Rosea slipped through the loosely chained gate, and on the uneven ground her scrambling footsteps sounded like a posse coming to get her.

Looking down from the hill, she saw a roadway, four lanes, and the

large chain-link fence that separated the roadway from the property.
Barbed wire was strung along the top of the fence, and a row of eucalyptus had been planted along the periphery to soften the look of the
chain-link and barbed-wire combo. Weak, broken-off tree branches lay
strewn around like a sweet, tempting fire hazard.

Rosea sat down in the weeds. She lit a cigarette and took a few puffs.
She knew. The home, the place to settle down, to imagine your brain
not in a vat of lye, to have finally, finally some peace, some love, where
Portuguese sounds as natural as water slapping muddy river banks — she
knew all this was not to be. Well, here's one for you, Joe, and the way
you hold your cig, so sexy in your brown fingers, what a sight to behold.
Her memory of the white sand between his dark feet and the delicate,
dark curly hairs on the knuckles of his toes made her long for him even
though it was hopeless.

She took a long draw of her cigarette. The clouds, heavy and bunchy,
tore into shreds as they moved through the sky. She felt the wind pick
up. Surrounding her, dried grass, the fire tinder of the city, waited for the
next big movie. She leaned back on her elbows and thought of the three
men during the criminal phase of her life: Jeremy, Melvinor, and Joe. She
could hardly believe it. Her men so angry with her betrayal, so aghast
in their deep shit. She must be something, hurling full force at them like
an uprooted tree in a storm. She felt a few wet sprinkles on her skin,
but the air was warm and muggy. She didn't regret what she had done
to anyone. Men are weak. They wanted her to sing a few tunes. They demanded it. But she would not be anyone's Carmen Socorro. She would
not try to be what she was not. She would not become Miss Bananaville
for a bunch of horny studio execs. So if the world had no place for Rosea
Socorro Katz, then tough shit.

She held the lit butt to the dried grass and watched as the blades caught
with a few flicks of orange. She thought, Why not burn the place up? And
she held the hot ash steady next to a cluster of dried pods. The weeds
caught on fire a bit, then petered out. The drizzle made everything a bit
damp with a silvery shimmer.

Damn, Joe consumed her. She tried again and again to start a fire as
the fire for Joe burned fiercely between her legs. She imagined exploring

his body; she imagined him waking up with nightmares and her soothing him back to sleep in her arms. And even the murder — yes, the memory could disappear between them until it would be nothing more than an ugly argument in their past. And if the police *did* come finally to arrest them, they could commit double suicide: first, they'd entwine their legs and arms around each other, and she'd smell Joe's crazy coconut sweat; and just as the police shattered the door, both of them would kiss and place the guns under their chins.

This made Rosea shudder. She took her still-burning cigarette butt and tried once again to light the grass, but it only sizzled. Angry, she pressed the lit end against the palm of her hand. She watched her skin turn red around the cigarette end. She didn't flinch, couldn't even feel it burn. She pulled the cigarette away and examined where her flesh began to blister.

She got up and went down to the gate, squeezed herself through, and headed toward the busy roadway. She passed under a jacaranda tree, the pavement stained purple and brown from the fallen flowers. She walked along the roadway and saw an old ocher shoebox apartment complex that looked a bit like hers. One of the apartment doors had a placard with a large fortune-teller's hand that said: MISS OLIVIA'S PALM READINGS. Rosea thought of her fortune, fucked up like this, wanting Joe so much and not being able to have him, and reached in her pocket and pulled out a rumpled ten. She knocked on the door as she brushed the burrs off her jeans and hair. She caught her breath, feeling a bit nervous because, believe it or not, she had never gone to one of these places before, even though L.A. was crawling with them. So she'd give it a try. Because she was Desperate. D-e-s-p-e-r-a-t-e.

Miss Olivia opened the door. Rosea was expecting some gypsy queen with large earrings, a full orange skirt, and a wide sash, maybe hanging bong pipes or something. Instead, Olivia was thin, heavily made up, her eyes like beetles and her mouth a big, muddy lipstick pout. Her curly black hair was awry as if it had been staple-gunned in place.

"How much for a ten?"

"Palm and cards. Normally it's twenty, but I'm short of cash." Olivia motioned her in. The living room looked "furnished," as in "furnished apartment," with a cheap brown-vinyl couch and a linoleum kitchen table with fake gold flecks. Olivia rubbed her hands on her black stretch stirrup pants; she smelled faintly of B.O. in her polyester flower shirt tunic.

They sat at the kitchen table. Rosea looked over and saw a birdcage near the refrigerator. The bird had a bald spot on the side of its neck. "That's Omar," Olivia nodded, then she sat opposite Rosea and clasped her hands in front of her, her long red fingernails practically touching her wrists. Olivia tumbled out questions, asking Rosea all this stuff about her life.

Rosea looked askance. "You're the fortune-teller. If I knew about what was going on in my life, would I be here?"

Olivia grinned like the crazy aunt in a B movie, then she held out her hands and asked to see Rosea's palm. Rosea gave her a hand. Olivia looked dismayed, and her sharp-looking thumbnail pressed gently around the burn. "What is this, my dear?"

"Accident."

Olivia sat back and sighed. "It's covering your fate line. Let's see your other hand." Rosea's other hand was covered with filth. Olivia sighed. "I'll get the cards then." She had a strong accent, Russian or Arabic maybe, and she spoke as she shuffled through a drawer. "Do you know tarot?" she asked.

"If I knew tarot, would I be plopping in here?"

"OK," was all Olivia said to that. Then she talked about the landlord, this cheap Chinese guy who had raised the rent again and always threatened to deport her even though she had a green card. She pulled out cloth napkins and a pack of birthday candles as she rumbled through the drawer to find something. Then she got out the cards and a candle the shape of a star. She brought both to the table and lit the wick on the top point of the star candle. "Don't touch the flame now."

By now Rosea was pissed she had even come in here. The woman was obviously a phony who couldn't even play the fuckin' part. Not even mysterious. Just another immigrant thrown here by the wind. The burn on her palm started to hurt, and she blew on it when Olivia wasn't looking. Olivia fanned out the cards, pulled out three queens, and asked Rosea to pick one. Rosea picked the queen with the blue dress, the one that looked half-asleep. Olivia looked at her from the corner of her eye. "Didn't think you'd choose that one," she said.

"Want me to pick another?"

"Oh no." Olivia placed the blue queen in the middle, then cut the rest of the cards and kept them face down. She placed a couple of cards face up on either side of the queen, then a card above and a card below. Putting the rest of the deck beside her, she tapped her fingernails absentmindedly. She sat looking at the pattern for some time. Rosea stared at the candle, which wouldn't melt but gave off an orange glow; she realized that the star was merely a plastic mold that held a regular candle. Olivia turned away and coughed into her fist, rattling her smoker's phlegm.

Damn, she was taking long with those cards, trying to make up some big-ass story. Rosea said, "Give me ten dollars' worth at least. You don't need to tell my distant future. Just within the next few days. They're kind of important, you know."

Olivia nodded. She had traced the whole shape of her upper eyelid with a makeup pencil. As if to remember the shape of her eyes.

"Well," she said, giving a wave of her hand, "I didn't want to tell you, but you are in bad shape." And she pointed to one of the cards, gave it a tap. "Here it says, a lot of sadness."

"Didn't need to pay ten dollars to be told that."

"But—" Olivia gave a dark wink and skirted smile, "there will be some big changes in your life."

Rosea slid on her chair. "Oh please—"

"I mean—" Olivia caught her with her voice. "This card here means 'home.' Something about home. In other words, your home will change."

Rosea leaned forward. "Like how? How will it change?

Olivia shrugged. "Cards give no details; they only sense what is in the air."

Rosea thought: home—perhaps with Joe—perhaps somewhere away from the movies—a small bungalow in L.A. Or maybe home meant jail for her. She slumped in her chair.

Olivia grinned, her lipstick smear making her mouth look stretched. She reached over and picked a few burrs off of Rosea's hair. "You have

had a rough time here." Then she rolled the burrs between her fingers
and grew sad. "Yes, well."

Rosea watched her for a minute, but Olivia sat there, sadly studying
the burrs. Rosea quietly got up. Olivia popped up her head. "Would you
like some tea?"

Rosea shook her head no thanks. She headed out the door, but turned
once to see Olivia in front of her cards, the star still burning, her black
hair making her skin so white. "Thanks, uh," Rosea said, then left.

Maybe she should have stayed for tea; Olivia was about as sorry as she
was, but eventually the woman would get weird probably, tell some dismal tale, and bring out a pet owl or a cobra. Who knows. Then Rosea
would end up blurting out some real truth and completely change the
way of the cards.

Gradually, one by one, our men wandered deep in the woods as if drawn to their own deaths. There were no more ships, and if a ship arrived, there would be no man returning home. Hardship and tragedy have turned our souls savage, and instead of feeling revulsion, we see the world as wondrous and beautiful as our most intimate desires. It is for these women that our wretched loins tremble, no matter how bleached our bones may become after their cruelty. Despair has given way to a hunger that we have not wit to name.

— *A última página do diário de Carlos Manoel Teixeira da Cunha* (The last page of Carlos Manoel Teixeira da Cunha's diary), *O Ano* 1643

Chapter 28

O Ano 1978

Jeremy came down the stairs, sat on the couch, and turned on the lamp. Birdboy remained curled tight in the corner of the living room, next to the large potted rubber plant. His brownish body, stunted and obstinate like a walnut, shuddered as his throat rumbled a low and guttural twerp. It was midnight. Jeremy wondered what to do. Birdboy hadn't eaten or slept in two days. His avian eyes, in the shadow of the large shiny leaves, glowed purple. Yes, kiddo, Jeremy said to himself, I've put you through a lot.

The outside world had caught up with the boy. Jeremy hadn't suspected Birdboy would comprehend in his forested mind, but he did.

There were news reports of the murder in Carmen Socorro's garden, and they were doing a film of her life that was getting a lot of press. These things brought into mind Rosea, and her ghost came crashing through their doors again. Her large size and dazzling fearful presence seemed to engulf them, her loud bellow swallowing everything within reach of her pain. Jeremy could imagine Rosea killing the man in the garden, defending some dream she had of her mother's life with the fury that must have made that bullet bolt from its barrel.

Rosea had hated living with him, something that was hard for him to admit because he had tried to make her so happy. He remembered watching from the kitchen window as she worked in the backyard, standing in a large square of plowed up dirt. She had made up her mind to plant a garden. She had bought some young trees and laid them on their sides all in a pile, their tender trunks knocking together, their roots still bound in burlap; she spread around bags of fertilizer and large trays of starter plants. In a flurry, she proceeded to dig holes for her plants, but no, that one wasn't any good, and she dug another, paced, didn't like that hole either, then in anger she hurled the shovel at the bags of peat, busting the plastic open. She smashed the boxes of starter plants against the fence and stomped on the young trees until their vulnerable trunks snapped.

Then came what would become Birdboy's horror for months to come: Rosea stood in the middle of her ruin, her angry throat puffed, her arms rigor-mortised with rage. Birdboy, still a kid, waddled out to the yard at just this fateful time. Slit-eyed and brain-fried, Rosea glared at the boy, then her mouth, shaped like a box in an evil smile, uttered, *"Fly, fly."* Birdboy cocked his head for a moment, and Rosea uttered those spiteful words again: *"Fly, fly."* Birdboy's face shimmered as if something touched him inside, and he started jumping up and down and flapping his arms. From that time on, she'd hiss in his ear anytime, *"Fly, fly,"* and he'd start jumping again. Sometimes she'd even wake him at night, *"fly, fly"*, and Birdboy would roll out of bed and head for the window; if it hadn't been locked, he'd have jumped out.

Jeremy tried to get an answer from Rosea: "Why do you tell him to fly? It possesses him!"

Rosea answered: "It is his free will. I don't possess anyone. I am not the devil."

"Well," Jeremy shuddered, "don't act like the devil then," even though she did.

Birdboy tucked himself farther into the corner. He and Jeremy looked at each other hard, but didn't move. What was there to say? It was as if she had destroyed their house, leaving only slabs of thatch walls in a big rotting pile. Jeremy turned off the lamp and lay on the couch facing Birdboy. He could see the boy's two eyes gleaming in the dark again. The streetlights from outside illuminated the drapes, making the folds look like pillars of an old abandoned temple. In his head, Jeremy saw the jungle; he saw a group of women cutting through a field of ferns, laughing on the way back to their camp. He heard the sound of a knife scraping against hide. The breath from plants exhaling in the cool night air made a cottony mist that swirled around the trees. The footstep of a human, of an anteater or a jaguar or a stork, is all the same: steady and purposeful. It is here, Maxwell would say—perhaps from his grave, if his soul were alive, lying amidst his tribal gifts of knives and jars of *masato*, his bones the color of coal—that they give you a decent burial. Here they let you die when it is time.

Perhaps this is when the rationality that Jeremy fought so hard to keep . . . snapped. Perhaps it was a jolt from the river that tipped over the boat. Perhaps here is where all of his fine academic ideas sank and floated into the mouths of crocodiles. Jeremy could hear the sound of the crocs' teeth, tearing the fabric, the same sound as when the woman tore Dr. Maxwell's clothes with a knife. Jeremy never forgot Dr. Maxwell's moan when the Amazon conquered him, a moan of pleasure, not fear. "It is something to see, the Juarouá," Dr. Maxwell said in the last lecture to his class, which Jeremy attended. Then the professor stopped, knowing it was a lie. He looked at his students staring at him, some of them already cold and cynical, and he knew they were the ones who would succeed. "There is no real scholarship or new findings or any of it," Maxwell continued in his last lecture. "Everything is old, and we've known it since birth, or even before we were born. If you are in this class, but want to understand the paradox of the human heart, then you should leave at once and never return."

Jeremy should have left right after Maxwell's lecture. He'd waited until now to leave, and now he would. He knew that in Brazil the dawn crawled up onto the edge of the earth, whipped her orange and pink flaming hair around the black shoulders of the night, and laughed a bit contemptuously, then breathed slowly as her fingers caressed . . .

Jeremy insisted they get seats by the window. They'd fly to São Paulo. From there, they'd fly to Manaus and take a ferry up the Great River. It was almost three days of travel on this circuitous budget flight. The plane was crowded with American missionaries in their pleasant benign softness and Japanese Paulista businessmen in stiff, clean shirts. Spiritual needs and money. Brazil would be wholesome after all, Jeremy thought ironically. He remembered his Portuguese—vaguely—but ended up speaking English to the attendants. Birdboy clutched the sides of his seat, gawk-eyed and afraid, his neck feathers bristling. He stared at the cup of sparkling *guaraná* that the flight attendant set on his tray, then peered inside the cup as if checking for exotic insects.

"Drink it," Jeremy said. "It's not beer. Not piss either. Tastes like ginger ale." Jeremy picked up the cup and held it to Birdboy, who shrank away. Jeremy put it down. Patience. How was the kid to remember anything about his homeland? Jeremy lowered his seat back and Birdboy's, too, but Birdboy continued to sit erect, staring out the window at the clouds below them.

"Well," Jeremy laid his head down and looked to the side, "we're flying, that's for sure. See that, Bird? You're not the only one who can fly."

Birdboy turned and looked at him quizzically.

"Just kidding."

But Birdboy remained steady-eyed.

"Birds fly," Jeremy continued. "Airplanes fly with a lot of motor, a lot of jet propulsion. First time on a plane is exciting, I know. You were on a plane before, but you don't remember. This is like your first time."

Birdboy looked outside the window again and pressed his face flat to the glass. His eyes glazed over like a fragile layer of frost. He stayed like that for hours, sometimes tracing the window with his finger. He wouldn't touch the food in front of him, nothing. Jeremy ate a portion of his son's meal as well as his own, handed the two trays back to the attendant pushing the wheeled metal cart, and apologized for his son. The woman smiled, and in English with that beautiful unmistakably Brazilian lilt she said, "He likes the sky."

Birdboy had to like the Amazon because Jeremy didn't know if they would ever return to America. He did not tell anyone at the college he was leaving so that his disappearance would be a mystery, a legend like the gold men of El Dorado and the Amazon warriors. He'd be like Francisco Orellana, whose raft got trapped sailing down the Amazon and who left behind his commander Gonzalo Pizarro to rot in the Andes. The anticipation of meeting a group of warrior women exhilarated him. He could die in ecstasy. If he died, he'd join the triumphant list of those who had disappeared before him. If other anthropologists got wind of Jeremy's demise, perhaps they would speculate that he was searching for something deeper than most who take this journey. They could speculate that he became king of a native tribe or a high priest, eccentric and wizened. Or perhaps they could speculate that he, Jeremy, found a miracle plant but was too bitter toward the diseased modern world to bring back its cure. They'd say Jeremy was looking for himself, for God, and, in a way, they'd be right. If God was anywhere, he'd be in the Amazon, back in Eden, trying to re-create the world from scratch.

Birdboy did not loosen his gaze from the window until darkness fell. Jeremy dozed during the dubbed American movie, but Birdboy sat quietly, not falling asleep, but staring straight ahead. At the first glance of the pink sky, Birdboy stared out again, not even eating his breakfast. When the plane started lowering from the clouds, São Paulo still in the distance with its gray buildings and brown smog, Birdboy began slapping the glass window, as if he wanted to break it. Jeremy held his arm. "Don't, Bird, get your seatbelt on."

Birdboy continued, more insistent, slapping and slapping, and a flight attendant came over and said in Portuguese and again in English that the boy must fasten his seatbelt.

Jeremy jerked Birdboy back from the window more roughly. "I said enough!" Birdboy halted abruptly and plopped in his chair. The attendant looked wide-eyed now that she saw the kid's face, no doubt surprised that he was older and stranger than she thought. Birdboy slithered to a sulk, and Jeremy dug around for his seatbelt and snapped him in.

After the plane landed, people slowly inched out of the cabin and hauled their carry-on baggage in front of them or over their shoulders. Jeremy kept Birdboy in front and guided him through the aisle of the plane and down the canvas-covered ramp leading to the terminal. A gust of hot air blew through the small openings in the covering. Outside, the men unloading the plane wore short-sleeved shirts and sunglasses.

Jeremy looked at the man in front of him, his tangled hair a snarl on the back of his head from sleeping on the plane. Suddenly the people at the front of the ramp lurched back. The man with messy hair stepped on Jeremy's foot, then scrambled around and shouted, his thick brows coming together in one dark line. A hippy, his blond hair frizzed with annoying bits of yarn, whacked the crowds on either side of him with his elbows. Something in the corridor was blocking the crowd coming down the ramp. The crowd at the front stirred, and someone smelled of oranges. In the middle of the ramp, a pasty-faced American missionary called, "Move forward!" in English, "move forward" — as if only the voice of the great Yankee could part these waves of panic. A Brazilian woman shouted contemptuously, and her husband, stuck aways from her, rattled off a reply. The crowd from behind surged forward, and the new jostle brought up the smell of ripe travel sweat and the odor of fried eggs mixed with airplane fuel.

Jeremy reached down for Birdboy just as two backpacks closed in front of him like enormous breasts. "Hang on, kid," Jeremy said. "Bird, we're almost there." He managed to look down, but Birdboy was not in front of him. Then he felt a thump to his kidneys, and he tried to look behind as someone with a spongy inner mouth yelled into his face. He imagined Bird underfoot, maybe under someone's heel. Jeremy started thrashing in panic, but the crowd held him firm. Then he realized the problem. The hall in the terminal was packed with groups of photographers flashing cameras and shouting questions, in Portuguese and in English. He heard snips of "carioca madness" and "Welcome!" and "Bem-vindo!" Someone shouted that the human traffic snarl was from a Hollywood movie crew that had just landed. The crowd groaned.

"Bird!" Jeremy shouted. He heard his ping of distress above the chaos. A woman from the movie entourage turned her head. Jeremy's eye caught her straw hat piled high with bananas and cherries, her hair strangely blond and foreign. Her face flashed in front of him. Where had he seen her? Some movie? She looked at him from afar as if she recognized him, then patted her brow with a handkerchief.

Jeremy called again, "Bird!" A camera turned his way, and a golden bulb exploded. A man put his suitcase on his head like someone from a refugee camp. The insufferable ones in the back kept bucking forward and shouting at the movie stars, and one threatened to cram all of the instigators of this carioca madness into a pit with dynamite. Others shouted how they were sick of Hollywood and their stupid banana flicks; and those in front barked at the heels of the entourage. Jeremy smacked his lips, trying to wipe away the metal taste. Sweat formed on his temples. Jetlagged babies on their parents' shoulders wailed over the crowds.

The movie entourage bolted forward. The cameramen pushed themselves through, using their cameras as shields. With that, the crowd from the ramp flooded into the corridor. Passengers tripped, others fell on top. Ayee! Ayee! The fallen screamed and clutched onto their carry-ons like pitiful tourist flotsam.

Jeremy ran through the milling crowd. "Bird? Bird?" People hurried into the waiting rooms and disappeared. The fallen began to pick themselves up. Left in the torrent was Birdboy's little backpack, dark blue and flattened like a splash of oil.

Jeremy frantically searched up and down the hall, the waiting room, the bathroom. He swooped up to a security guard and rambled in English, but the guard shook his head, not understanding, and took Jeremy to the front of a long line of passengers at a ticket counter. Jeremy spoke English to the harried woman issuing boarding passes, and she squinted, trying to translate in her head his panicky babble about his son. She swung over to a loudspeaker and made a general call about a *menino perdido*, lost boy, which brought another security guard, probably one who could speak English. The first guard excused himself and left. Jeremy took Birdboy's passport from his pocket and showed Birdboy's photo to the second guard. The guard stared at the photo. Birdboy had worn a turtle neck that day, which, along with his flattish head, made him look like a brown mushroom. The guard started to hand back the passport, shook his head, "Não tem problema." What was no problem? Jeremy held out his hand, but the guard pulled away the passport as if he needed another look. This time he held the photo close to his deep-set eyes. Jeremy thought, what was *não tem problema*? The way his son looked? Or was Birdboy somehow being taken care of with a bowl of hot soup? What was no problem? What?

The guard nodded and handed back the passport for good. Jeremy retraced his steps patiently, with the guard following him. Jeremy was almost in tears thinking of his irresponsibility in taking the kid on such a trip and how he, Professor Millard, had crushed his son under his own flabby books, his cursed tenure, his reeking boredom, his unrequited desire. The guard looked at him sympathetically and patted him on the back. "No problem, friend. We find him. We find him."

A man rushed down the ramp from their plane. He seemed like an official. He spoke to Jeremy's guard. The guard motioned to follow the man. The man pointed to an airline attendant rushing down the hall toward them. She moved her arms stiffly, as if agitated. When she reached them, Jeremy knew by her sad eyes and the drifting way she said she could speak English that something was wrong. She was so beautiful in the Brazilian way—her makeup, her green eyes, her natural copper-colored skin, her blondish hair piled loosely on her head. Her lips trembled as if she had the most terrible news. The little boy, it seemed, had made his way onto the top of the plane and jumped.

Jeremy stood stunned. He couldn't believe it. He slowly pulled out Birdboy's passport picture and showed it to her. She nodded yes. Then she motioned for him to follow her, and she led him, the guard, and the official into an elevator. The official and the guard made the sign of the cross, then clasped their hands and bowed their heads as if already at the funeral. The guard patted Jeremy on the back again. The woman pressed the buttons of the elevator and turned toward him as the elevator descended. "I am so sorry, sir. Your heart must be broken."

At that moment, Jeremy wept like he never had before; then the official and the guard wept, and the woman wept. God, why did I ever bring Birdboy away from here to such a cold, frightful place as L.A.? No wonder the boy never spoke. He probably had nothing to say.

The airline attendant led them out to the tarmac toward a group of baggage handlers. The conveyor belt had stopped, and there was a string of suitcases up to the plane. The attendant said something, and the official tapped the two baggage handlers to the side. When the small crowd opened, Jeremy saw Birdboy lying face down, his arms out to the side, like a crucifix.

Jeremy realized that Birdboy had attempted to fly, but had failed. In that moment, he realized that Birdboy really was his son.

Senhor da Cunha: You have not written, so I take the liberty of sending a letter on the next caravel. This is indeed an amazing land you speak of, and these heathen women have done much to enchant, if not overtake, your reason. Follow the way of the Lord, do not stray from your path. Terra Nova brings out the darkness of the human spirit and the longing for carnality. Our priests and their spirituality are rare in these heathen lands, and one must take care and nourish the soul. Keep longing for your homeland. Explorers are best if they are warriors, not poets. You began your journey as a warrior; take care that you do not turn into a poet.

—*A última carta de João Vicente Cardim da Almeida a Carlos Manoel Teixeira da Cunha* (The last letter from João Vicente Cardim da Almeida to Carlos Manoel Teixeira da Cunha), *O Ano* 1645

Chapter 29

O Ano 1978

After years of becoming "old hat," Carmen Socorro tried to make a comeback and got a gig on the *Jimmy Durante Show*. On the last show of her life, she did this thing with Jimmy Durante where he joked about her new and most spectacular hat bursting with Amazonian bounty. The forest of fruit and parrots started to press on her head, and she forgot the punch line. Luckily, Jimmy, so Mr. Showbusiness, picked up her cue, and no one noticed. Roots pressed against her head and tapped her skull. Carmen opened her mouth again, but missed another line. Again Durante saved her. Small veins on her temples started bouncing and pounding against her skin. Her heart pumped up water to keep the fruit and leaves alive, but to no avail. That night, when Carmen came home, she dropped dead before she had time to change. A coconut tumbled from her hat and rolled into the ocean. The current lapped up the coconut and carried it across the seas. It got picked up by Amazon waters and was finally flushed into the Japurá River, where a fine-breasted warrior woman laughed, then snatched up the coconut with her teeth.

Rosea's mind spiraled as she clutched the sides of her desk. The names and times penciled into the appointment book were nothing but a blur; she couldn't figure out what the hell all these people wanted. This new state of frenzy had to do with the trade papers this morning announcing that Nancy had returned triumphantly from Brazil. A big success. Made friends with the natives. Hell, Nancy is damn lucky to be alive, damn lucky. Rosea's lungs felt leaden; she could hardly breathe. She curled and uncurled her fists. Bet Nancy stayed at the Copacabana Palace in a big room with a view of the smooth, white, sandy beach — a beach so wide that it was said if you had something painful in your heart and started walking toward the water from the sidewalk, you would forget your misery by the time you reached the wet, packed sand. Rosea pictured herself pushing Nancy out of an airplane thousands of feet up and watching her tiny body swirl down and eventually explode in some corn-field. *Adios, muchacha*, good-bye, piña colada, bye-bye Miss American Pie . . .

Rosea opened the top drawer of her desk, took out her catalog of the Homes of the Stars, turned to the back of the catalog, and ran her finger down the index, scanning names. She found a page number, flipped through the book, and there it was. The house of Nancy West. It was on the "low-budget" side of Beverly Hills (low budget for Beverly Hills, that is) because Nancy was still an up-and-coming star. The photo of Nancy's two-story Tudor fairy-tale house smiled from the shiny pages. Rosea rubbed her hands on the picture, smearing it with all her bitter-ness and envy, and she thought of fire and of Nancy rising in a screaming column of smoke.

Night. The tires on the pavement sounded like flapping lips because the ground was wet from someone's ferocious lawn sprinklers. People in this neighborhood couldn't seem to settle down. If the residents were out, their security guards or butlers were in. Guard dogs trotted back and forth behind fences surrounding the houses. Floodlights everywhere, Neighborhood Watch signs with little eyes. Threats of terminal prison sentences. To live in this neighborhood, you better look the part, not like a Sleezoid-Ex-Con-Chingón-Filho-de-Puta-Motherfucker! Rosea stopped in front of Nancy's house. The lighter fluid was in the glove compartment.

Rosea rapped her fingernails on the steering wheel. She examined the house again. It was white with brown trim that made big diamond shapes on the walls, and there was a gently sloped pouty roof. Small floodlights lined the walkway. The unprotected front door gawked at the street like an innocent face.

A BMW drove by. What a laugh. Here she was with a chola vehicle in Beverly Hills, a sloppy-looking Chevy, riding low on the tail end. Shit, she might as well quit right here, turn herself into the police. Show them the can of lighter fluid. Talk of big plans to burn Nancy's house. Have a chit-chat. Have a martini. Hell, why not?

Rosea scrutinized the house again. There seemed to be a light on, way in the back. Nancy was probably in her bedroom unloading treasures from Brazil, gold nuggets, silver figas, an emerald necklace, a tiny bikini, all part of her little plunder. Vaughan Peters was probably with her, in his manly packed pants and pointy-toe boots, tying her to the bed with rawhide.

Just as Rosea pumped enough courage to get out of the car and set fire to the "estate," a policeman pulled up. Rosea's first instinct was to run. But no. Be cool. She grabbed a map from the glove compartment and rattled it open. The officer shined a flashlight on her face.

"Yeah," he said, "what are you doing here?"

Rosea knew better than to look a policeman in the eye. She had her map spread out, cleverly dropping her gaze at the streets, the swirls of lines that looked like cracks on a concrete wall. She stared at the design of the city before her. Go figure.

"You need to move on," he said.

Rosea cracked a smile. "I'm a bit lost. I seem to have gotten stuck—"

"Where do you want to go?"

"Home."

"Where is home?"

Rosea paused a bit. She honestly couldn't remember. Then she said, "Show me to the 405, then I can make it."

The policeman made a big deal of directions. Take a U-ie here, then turn there, and bla-bla diddly-squat. He gave a snort, flaring his nostrils and sniffing her breath for alcohol. Thank god the lighter fluid was hidden in the glove compartment, talk about stiff drinks.

She drove off, but didn't go home. She parked along the ocean, her eyes snapped open like the roll-up shades in her apartment. The waves ruffled toward the shore like curtains on a nice princess bed. The kind of bed Nancy must sleep in. Finally, the sky began to lighten.

At 5:30 A.M., Rosea, dry-eyed and wired, drove back to Nancy's house. Who knows. Maybe she'd look less conspicuous in the daytime. A bit less menacing. She could disguise herself as a gardener or something. She should have brought a hoe or shovel to make herself look industrious and productive. Suddenly, the garage door opened, and Nancy's small red Porsche slid onto the driveway. Rosea caught her breath. She could burn the house now, but—would Nancy know who did it? And know why it was done? The m-o-t-i-v-a-t-i-o-n? The garage door closed. No. No. Rosea had to tell Nancy something, she had to think of something, one last reminder about the last scene, maybe. Perhaps the Academy Awards, "please thank my—"

The Porsche pulled out of the driveway and onto the road. The arson could wait. Rosea started her Chevy and followed. She remained at a distance, but the Porsche eluded her. The red car continued zipping down the hills, and Rosea chugged after it. Amazing how Nancy didn't even catch on she was being followed by an ugly old heap. The Porsche tootled

down some short-cut side streets, and Rosea felt this link between herself and Nancy, Nancy toting her along, a kind of match of fates, Nancy
driving them both to their destiny.

The Porsche finally headed toward the ocean. The road was getting
thick with commuters. A couple of cars pulled in front of her, but Rosea
kept her eyes glued on Nancy's red car. Nancy rolled down the window
and leaned her elbow out. Good move, now Rosea could follow Nancy's
little white sleeve as well.

Up ahead Nancy flicked on her turn signal and pulled into a beach
parking lot. Rosea drove to the far end of the same lot, near a cluster of
fan palms and a closed-up Snak-Shack. Nancy parked her car, locked it,
and jogged toward the beach. She was wearing powder-blue shorts and
a white terry-cloth top. Rosea waited for a bit, then she, too, slipped
out of the car. She wandered slowly toward the sand and watched Nancy
prancing along the shore. She flung off her shoes and ran on the sand.
Nancy's white terry-cloth top wiggled way ahead, jerking like a caught
fish. Rosea began to run after her, but keeping back. Then she picked
up speed, running on wet sand. She thought she would tell Nancy one
more thing about Carmen, her mother, but she wasn't sure what.

Nancy trotted in the distance, and Rosea broke into a faster run. Her
legs felt large and powerful, chewing up the sand, her feet wide and
brown and splayed. Her black locks trailed wildly behind her, screaming
a war cry. Rosea finally got close enough to see Nancy's arrogant little
flingy ponytail and her fuzzy terry-cloth top. Nancy must have heard her
because she turned around, saw Rosea, and gasped. She stopped, probably hoping Rosea would just barrel on by. But oh no. Rosea stopped
right in front of her, faced her, and blocked her way. Nancy's expression
widened with fright while Rosea threw an expressionless glare, a nervy
move she had acquired during her street bitch days. Nancy gulped, put
her arms akimbo, and tried to be friendly, her voice shaking. "Hey now.
What's with you, huh?"

Rosea stood before Nancy and said nothing, but watched her small
breasts heaving the small teddy bear decal up and down. "What? What?"
Nancy flung her arms out. "I have nothing for you. Please."

Suddenly Rosea grabbed onto one of Nancy's arms, then the other one. Nancy tried to writhe away, trying her self-defense step-on-the-instep move, but Rosea felt no pain. Rosea jerked her forward, like Clark Gable would. Nancy's blue eyes were wide and pleading, her lips pale because she didn't have on any makeup. She was crying softly, like a kitten.

"For god's sake, Rosea! What do you want?!"

Rosea swallowed hard. "I need to tell you something else about my mother."

"What? What then? Let me go, I'll listen!"

Rosea moved toward the water, her huge strength getting out of control as she hauled Nancy along. Nancy tried to fling herself back, her throat squeezing out cries, her legs missing a beat, stumbling, then tripping in the water.

"Stop it! I'm not going in the water!"

Rosea continued into the water, the waves splashing her knees, her thighs, her hips. "There's people!" Nancy screamed, and Rosea saw a few people far away, walking, oblivious to Nancy's distress. Oh, Nancy might be large and important on a big screen, but here she was just a zero in a lotta trouble. Pleading to be let go, Nancy reared back wildly, her ponytail tossing, her arms twisting in Rosea's grip, her blue eyes filling with tears. Rosea dragged Nancy neck deep into the water until she was just a screaming head with plucked eyebrows and a mouthful of straight teeth.

Rosea felt a rush of anger and lowered both herself and Nancy down under the water. She watched Nancy struggling and trying to kick, but held onto her with ease. Bubbles poured out of Nancy's mouth, her face surged forward. Rosea popped up, gulping air, which also brought Nancy up with a watery scream. Then, as Rosea went for a better grip, Nancy slipped away and shot backward in the water. Rosea, tall as she was, stood up on the sandy bottom. An oncoming wave splashed saltwater on her face, and she snorted out the burning brine. Nancy treaded, spitting out water, making a cluster of foam near her chin. She looked so small with her wet hair plastered down on her head. "Don't touch me," she coughed, struggling to keep the tide from pushing her toward Rosea. "Don't touch me. Killing me won't bring your mother back."

In the middle of Nancy's sputtering words was the truth: Carmen was a shell of happiness, a fancy tree with shallow flimsy roots and a kissy smile. As if she didn't really exist but in song. Joe had talked about the riots on the day of her mother's funeral, a funeral Rosea never saw. He tried to explain it: "Carmen Socorro reminded us of how desperate we Brazilians are to break free, yet how heartbreaking it is to be free. Being Brazilian is feeling both full of hope and full of despair. You can imagine," Joe told her, "the confusion of it all. A Brazilian always looks home because that is what never changes. At least it shouldn't. To a Brazilian, saudade is so strong it can kill you like drinking bad *pinga*, or it can keep you unbelievably alive like beautiful music."

"I'm sorry about your mother," Nancy called as she treaded water. "It's a price we all pay. We all know it. All of us do." She glided away with soft backstrokes. Small, white-capped waves broke against her; then she slowly turned and swam toward shore until her feet touched sand, and she scrambled up to the beach.

Rosea looked up. The clouds were breaking apart; it would be a beautiful day. Yet this city engulfed her in loneliness, looked at her incredulously as if to say, "You had all the chances, Rosea. Except the chance to be in love. But so what? You could have made up for that with a little patience." Then she saw Nancy running toward a group of people, shouting in distress and pointing at her.

Rosea felt prison walls come crashing around her, crushing her limbs and trapping her eternally. She'd have to live with so much regret; she'd spend the rest of her life imagining different endings to this bad, bad movie. Her hands would be trapped; she'd never touch warm skin again. It would be too much never to see Joe; it would be too much to long for him. Suddenly she felt the sea pull at her again, like it had so many times before, even in the middle of Melvinor's dusty broccoli fields when the fish had swam to her, ruffling their razored fins.

Rosea turned toward the horizon, and her arms shot forth like arrows. She cut through the strong current. The sun was coming up, and the waves began to sparkle like strands of Yemanjá's hair drifting toward all the shores of the world. Ribbons of kelp caught her leg, and the pulse of the waves straightened the seaweed out again, making it well behaved and rational. Rosea continued on, following the sparkle, not thinking of L.A. or Hollywood or Jeremy or Melvinor, or even Joe, but she surged ahead as the waves rattled against her ears like the fortune-teller's cards. The open sea faced her, cold, flat, and straight-eyed. Rosea was swimming home.

Home is where the truth is. Think of home, and you will not die.
— *A continuacão da última carta de João Vicente Cardim da Almeida a Carlos Manoel Teixeira da Cunha*
(The continuation of the last letter), *O Ano* 1645

Chapter 30

O Ano 1978

When Joe looked into the doorway of Rosea's office and saw the empty desk, he knew, before anyone told him, that she was gone for good. Chucky broke the news to him, that joggers had met up with Nancy West, who told them how Rosea tried to kill her and then escaped by swimming out to sea. Chucky patted Joe on the shoulder. "That's life, pal. That's what this crazy town does to people."

Joe waited until Chucky went back to his office. Then he went over to Rosea's desk and sat in her chair. He leaned back and closed his eyes, remembering her first days here. She was doomed from the start with that tight, misshapen dress and this furniture that trapped her like a cage. He thought she would be happier now, happier in the Brazil of her mind. Joe pictured her death as she might have wanted it:

A few Indians were standing on the shores of the igarapé, spearing fish. They were hungry, and they sought the large fleshy ones, perhaps a manatee or a boto or a *pirarucu*. A strong young man speared a dolphin, a fine boto, and held it up for the rest to cheer.

Then they saw a strange fish coming toward them in the current. It didn't move as normal. They held their spears, too curious to hurl them. The strong young man dived in the water, determined to wrestle the fish into submission, but as he swam toward it, the fish did not swim away. He reached out and grabbed some hair and knew then it was a body, a large one. The fishermen on shore fell silent, as when they find one of their own killed. The swimming man gathered a handful of the hair and toted the body to shore, where the others helped hoist the curious load onto the narrow beach. They lay the body out and saw it was that of a naked woman, a large woman. Wet hair covered her face, and her features had been eaten by sea creatures, her legs lashed with man-o'-war burns. The young Indian let out a cry that he knew this woman and that she had disappeared long ago, and he had thought she was dead. But here she was. Then the fishermen put the dead woman in a canoe and got in themselves, perhaps with pails of the fish they had caught, making their way back home.

Joe gave a sad chuckle. A perfect ending to a troubled life.

Today, on the route of his Hollywood tour, Joe did something he had never done. He gave his tourists the truth about the movie stars, how they struggled, and how their smiles saved them — for a few years. Then he said to them, "My friends, I will show you a house not on the tour. It was the first thing I saw when I came from" — he was supposed to say "Cuba," but said "Brazil." He stopped at Vaughan Peter's house and was so moved by his tumbling emotions that he almost couldn't continue. His tourists got very excited because Vaughan Peters was a huge box-office success, and his house was the site of a semifamous murder. But Joe pushed on and spoke of Vaughan Peters — how he had started out as a stunt man and became an action hero. Then Joe told of Carmen Socorro, a previous owner, and how she came here from Brazil, enticed by American success, and ended up being one of the richest women in Hollywood. But her fame came at a price. She had to endure her torturous hats, and when she tried going back to Brazil, her people rejected her. He told them how she ended up broken, dead before her time, and how her body was shipped back to Brazil, and of the near riot at her funeral. He continued, a bit angrily, telling them how Carmen may be loved by drag queens and was used to advertise bananas, but she should instead be a symbol of immigrant heartbreak. This country, Joe said, is both beautiful and cruel, innocent and guilty, the head twin and the heart twin.

The people in the van didn't move. Patches of white flushed over their sunburned faces. Their cameras sat like deadweight in their cupped hands, and no one chattered or laughed through his speech. Joe took a deep breath and looked at the mansion and the palm trees that he knew extended up into the hills, and he held in his memory the flowers that struggled to survive, the painful saudade, *o cheiro dum amor perigoso* — the scent of a dangerous love still lingering on the leaves — and the vision of a woman in white to remind him how unlikely life could be.

Joe's neighborhood appeared almost as in a dream. The houses, spread apart and singular like sugar cubes, seemed empty. His house didn't seem like his house. Without Rosea, things even seemed calm. It was almost murderous, like the quietness of being stalked.

Melvinor sat in the kitchen and watched the kids running around. Sherri was fixing something to eat. Joe stood at the kitchen door, and no one noticed him at first. The calmness of death muted their words. Melvinor murmured to Sherri about something of his childhood. Joe envied how Melvinor could speak gently without needing to make a big point. Keffy ran past Joe, and Joe scooped him up. Keffy let out a squeal, and Sherri turned and said, "Oh, you're home. They're about to eat."

"I will eat him." Joe kissed his son's young belly, then let him down. Joe went over to Jeffy, who was a bit harder to nab and had to be cornered, but when Joe bent down, Jeffy climbed into his father's arms. Keffy came over. The twins looked at their father with a startle, as usual, and Joe studied their sameness, their matching eyes, matching heads; they seemed like cotton balls, round, melting in. Jeffy swung at Keffy, which sent Keffy whining. Joe took them to the table and put them into their booster chairs. Melvinor didn't even bother him anymore; he could be their dear old *vovô* for all he cared. Sherri brought for each of the kids a plate of scrambled eggs and buttered toast and half a banana. Joe sat at the table facing his sons. He stared at their mouths chewing, imagining how many muscles, how much life, it took to feed yourself, to be happy. He tried to imagine Rosea this small, perhaps too big to be cute. Probably already with dark hair, dark eyes, and an impatient fist.

Sherri and Melvinor talked around him, didn't really say much. Sherri placed a beer in front of Joe and a bottle opener. He opened the bottle and remembered when Rosea had thrown herself in the ocean. Though at first he had tried to save her, he had made the decision to swim back, come what may. He knew his world was waiting for him to return. He knew his people — from the beautiful women with sunglasses to small beggar boys in baggy shorts — were on shore, standing under the coconut palms and waving and calling out, "Vamos! Come on now!"

He sat back and drank his beer. Melvinor fit in so comfortably here. Melvinor talked through the chatter of the kids and didn't examine their faces for motivation or for meaning. One of the twins handed Melvinor a piece of egg, and he ate it, just the way a father would. Joe took his beer to the patio and gazed at his flat green lawn and the twins' sandbox at the far end of the yard. This is what people dream of when they dream of America. He remembered Rosea here on her knees, half-cowering, half-treacherous, eyeing his sons, her long hair flowing down her back, wanting desperately that which she could not have.

That night Joe played a soft bossa nova for his sons. He lifted one at a time and danced, pictured himself with Sherri, who was always so embarrassed to move in this Brazilian way. The soft, rolling ticka-tac, the cuíca cried like hiccups, the guitars made your eyes into half-shut shells, the drums caressed your back and hips, and the words kissed apart your mouth. He danced with Keffy. Keffy didn't move as if he were trying to

understand, and his little cheek felt like soap. When Joe was done, he
kissed Keffy, who wriggled away.

Then he faced Jeffy. "You're next!"

Jeffy bolted, and Joe caught him. Jeffy did not like to be held dancing, romantic-like, so Joe held him upside down by his heels, shuffling ke-te-ki-tek-ki-tek as Jeffy squealed with delight.

Then, with the music of Noel Rosa playing, the saddest of songs—for Brazilians like to see how sad they can possibly get with a broken heart—Joe sat on the couch and placed the twins in front of him. He stroked their hair, then slid a finger down their little noses and stroked their mouths in unison, both hands going at the same time; Keffy's was softer, Jeffy's a bit firmer and more resolute. Joe smiled broadly. The twins began stroking his face; Jeffy pressed in his nose, then they fumbled to compete sticking their little fingers in his mouth. They continued tracing their fingers down his arms, making little car sounds. Then they traced his legs. Joe began speaking Portuguese, not knowing if they would understand. The twins touched his toes, then traced up his legs again. Joe cupped each of their heads, golden and gentle, into his hands. He told them, in Portuguese, that they would have to dream of the samba now, because he wouldn't see them for a long time.

The twins looked at him quizzically, then both crawled onto his lap as if they understood.

Long ago, great warrior women waded navel deep into the river and stood with their legs apart. They dug their large toes into the sand, placed their hands on their hips, and watched for war canoes and riverboats, and chatted as the fruit from their wombs positioned themselves just so. Flies, attracted to their ear wax, buzzed around their heads. Then one by one, coconuts, covered in green husks, emerged from between their legs, first shooting down into the water from the uterine contraction, then floating up to the surface and bobbing in amniotic foam, washing past the silvery fins of fish. Some coconuts begat other coconuts in the life-giving waters. Some coconuts washed up on the faraway shores of Manaus or Iquitos as empty dried-out hulls far away from the mothers who bore them. Other coconuts landed on the splendid beaches of Salvador and Rio and went on to prosper as best they knew how.

— *Uma lenda das amazonas, autor desconhecido* (An Amazon warrior legend, author unknown)

Epilogue

Rio de Janeiro 1997

It wasn't hard to spot them in the customs line at the Galeão Airport, even though the last photo Joe had received was years earlier and now they were adults! Besides, how much can pictures tell you? The twins were taller than he imagined, and they had soft builds. Both of them wore glasses; one had thick brown rims, and the other wore wire rims. He could guess that the one in big glasses was Jeffy, and probably Keffy wore the gentler wire rims. They looked wide-eyed in the middle of the nonchalant Brazilians tugging their oversized luggage through customs. Joe paced a bit, and his wife, Mariana, grasped his hand and held it tight. She couldn't stop talking, wondering if she had cooked the right things, and maybe their house wasn't so clean. "Mariana, how nervous you can get!"

As soon as the twins were released from customs, Joe shouted to them. They turned, looked almost surprised; they still had that incredulous stare. Joe saw them approach, and they seemed so American, walking with large steps, and they had small noses like Sherri. Their hair had darkened a little. They grinned like young Americans in TV commercials and held out their hands for a shake. Mariana started to cry and speak in Portuguese, "Ah, Zêzê! Seus filhos!" Joe wrapped his arms around one and buried his face in his son's shoulder. The shoulder stiffened, resisted a bit. "You must be Jeffy." "Yes," Jeffy said in his ear, and he was the one with the big frames! "They call me Jeff now," his son said so confidently.

Mariana embraced the other—Keffy. She was so short, and her dark curls must have tickled his chin.

Joe wiped his eyes, and they traded twins. He grabbed Keffy, who gave in more, a large squeeze, and his wire-rim glasses made him look like a professor.

Joe drove down the freeway, while Mariana, who spoke no English, chattered incessantly, apologizing for their small apartment and saying how they had a bed free because their son was spending some time with relatives in Belo Horizonte. Joe looked in the rearview mirror and watched his sons' innocent faces, peering at the favelas and the brown smog creeping around the cinderblock walls and old plywood roofs. The freeway here was lined with sadness, yes it was true. This part of Rio was probably as much a shock for them as the sparkly clean L.A. was for him. Joe cut back and forth in traffic, which he had got used to doing again, and said, "Don't worry, our house is a lot better."

The two young men giggled in relief, and they looked at each other and smiled. Mariana pointed to Keffy. "Professor?"

Keffy shook his head. "Nothing that smart. I'm a pencil pusher."

Mariana tapped Joe. "Que è um 'pencil pusher'?"

"Ele trabalha num escritório." Joe was a bit dismayed, hoping Keffy would be something more than an office worker, something different than the pale men of the L.A. streets. Jeffy said he was a restaurant manager.

"Really," Joe, said. "You know I worked — "

"I know." Jeffy pushed up his heavy frames.

"Do you manage your mother's restaurant?"

"No. A lot nicer one. People don't eat meat like they used to."

"Really," Joe said, "why?"

"Not healthy."

He remembered the feijoada Mariana had made. "You still eat some?"

"Whatever."

Joe's slang was rusty, and he figured "whatever" meant yes. He remembered first seeing Sherri at the restaurant when it all began, then, when things began to fall apart, trying to get his job back, thinking he could turn back the clock.

"So, Jeff. Do you hire immigrants?" Joe asked after a pause.

"Yes."

At home, the jet-lagged twins slept, one in his son's bed and one on a mattress on the floor. Joe peeked into the room. They slept in their underwear and had covered themselves with a sheet, but had kicked off the blanket. Rio was hot for them. Jeffy slept on his side, tightly curled, while Keffy slept with his arms out and open. Their stomachs were soft, and their large feet hung over the edge of the mattresses. Joe remembered the last time he had seen them asleep, the night before he had left Sherri, sleeping the same way on a late spring day, but in training pants and small T-shirts.

Joe went into his room, flopped down on his bed, and cried, keeping his face pressed against the pillow so no one would hear. He had thought that because he hadn't seen the boys in so long, and because there was very little connection to the land he had once tried to make his home, his two boys would seem like friends, like very welcome guests. But Joe felt in his heart a connection to his sons, somehow. He couldn't explain it; he was so Brazilian now, yet too overwhelmed for words — English or Portuguese. Mariana came into the room, and Joe pressed his face deeper in the pillow, then turned his head slowly away from her, to seem asleep. But Mariana knew. She took off his shoes and slipped off his pants. Then she took off her clothes and crawled into bed, pulling the sheet up so he wouldn't get a chill. She gave him a kiss on the shoulder and one on the back of his neck, then curled her body next to his.

The twins woke up talking about the beach, and of course Joe took them to Ipanema. The twins sucked in the salt air, their strides kicking up the sand; their bathing suits were baggy shorts, like those worn by Americans. They gawked at the girls with their tiny *fios de dental*, their swimsuits hiding in the cracks of their asses — their bundas as brown and toasty as baked rolls, their breasts small but unapologetic, and their incredible mulatta hair, thick and wavy and stacked lazily on top of their heads.

The twins sat on towels and stripped off their shirts. Their skin was so white and pale, their youthful muscles floated shyly underneath. They would someday be a little fat. "Take your shirt off, Joe," Jeffy said.

It startled Joe to be called by his name. He expected to be called "Dad" at least, but that was too much to ask. "I must warn you," Joe said, "I am an old man now."

Keffy shrugged. "We'll get there."

Joe took off his shirt and passed his hands over his chest. He had many gray hairs now. The two boys looked out at the sea. It was calm, rolling in softly. A row of young women dived in, their dazzling bundas like large brown hearts disappearing into the waves, then their heads emerging from the white foam. A sinewy vendor walked by carrying a large, full plastic sack and shaking a small rattle.

"Oi!" Joe called. The vendor stopped. Joe took out some money and gave it to the vendor, who handed back two packets of biscoitos de polvilho. Joe opened a package. "You must try this." He pulled out a puffed-up cracker shaped like a ring and gave one to each of his sons. "When I came to the States, the thought of biscoitos almost made me die of homesickness."

The twins laughed together and nibbled on the biscoito in almost the same way; it was amazing.

Joe was silent for a bit. "How is your mother?"

They both nodded.

Joe waited for more of an answer. "What does that mean? I know she's alive."

"Still working," Jeffy said, "she still lives in the same house."

"I know her address. She writes once in a while. Little notes, you know. Nothing fancy." Joe paused for a bit. "She never told me—about the old man. Who used to—visit a lot."

Keffy squinted, "Who?"

"Melvinor."

"Oh," Jeffy said, "He died a long time ago."

Joe felt a bit glad Melvinor was dead. "Well, he must have moved in after I left."

The twins shook their head.

"No?"

"No, he never did." Jeffy said. "We were really young when he died."

"Why didn't your mother remarry?"

The twins looked a bit sad, shook their heads "don't know." Then a small soccer game on the shoreline caught their attention.

Joe dug his toes in the sand. He tried to imagine Sherri older, probably rather cuddly, sweet probably. But she should have married again, when she was younger. She hadn't enjoyed it with him, but perhaps she might have with someone else. She deserved a wild fling at least, not sitting around with an old grandfather. She had been too afraid maybe. Perhaps he should have been more afraid; his fearlessness had almost destroyed everything they had. He wondered if Sherri missed him, if she had any regrets. When she wrote, she talked only of the twins, never of herself. He never knew whether to bring up their past. Maybe he didn't have the courage. Or the heart.

The same bunch of girls who had dived in now emerged from the waves, giggling and jostling each other. He thought of Rosea somewhere out in the ocean, forever trying to make it home. The girls caught his sons' eyes again. Good to see some things are the same in any country.

The twins' backs were getting a little burned from the sun. They'd burn quickly. "Did you bring sunscreen?"

The twins looked at each other. "We forgot."

"Forgot?" Joe said. "You know how hot this sun can be."

They shrugged, "Well."

"Cover your shoulders then."

The two boys obeyed and put on their shirts, but kept the front part loose and open. "Go in the water," Joe said.

"Can't swim," one of them said.

"No kidding?" Joe shook his head. They sat there, calm, covered up, watching, watching. They did not look like ones to spring to action. Joe wanted them to ask why he had left them, why he had had such a dangerous affair with someone like Rosea, why he had chosen to come back home even though he had to start his life all over again. But they didn't. Joe didn't want to press, but he wanted to talk about his crazy, long ago passion. Perhaps it is the Brazilian way, perhaps it is his fate, who knows.

A soccer ball landed right at their feet. A young, dark-skinned, hyper boy clapped his hands, "Passe a bola!" Keffy shoved the ball forward with his short white toes, and the ball rolled gently toward the boy. The boy snatched it and continued playing. The twins continued watching, as their pale knees started to turn pink with the gentle burn, hidden by the cooling breezes.

Acknowledgments

Several books in particular inspired me for this work, among them *Brazilian Bombshell* by Martha Gil-Montero; *Dialogues of the Great Things of Brazil* by Ambròsio Fernandes Brandão; *Brazilian Cinema* by Randal Johnson and Robert Stams; *The Anatomy of Captivity* by John Laffin; *A Grain of Mustard Seed: The Awakening of the Brazilian Revolution* by Marcio Moreira Alves; and *Tristes Tropiques* by Claude Lévi-Strauss. The music of Chico Buarque and Caetano Veloso added the soul.

An excerpt of the novel, titled "Rosea Socorro Katz, Coconut" first appeared in *The Raven Chronicles* in 1992.

I owe thanks to the following individuals for helping me with ideas, drafts, and support: my cousin Maria Cristina and her husband, Carlos Alberto Fellet, who told me about the coup as we were driving along

300 beautiful Botofogo Bay in Rio; Yasmine Mogul and Vance Bourjaily for helping to make it happen finally; James Brown, Gwendolyn Bikis, Megi Nacimiento, Luciana Castro, copy editor Annie Barva, and editor Patti Hartmann. Special thanks to my husband, Lewis Campbell, who kept the flame alive when I thought it had died.

Glossary

abraços e beijos (Portuguese)	hugs and kisses (a common expression used to say "good-bye")
babacos (Portuguese)	jerks; idiots
bandeirantes (Portuguese)	soldiers of fortune in Brazilian colonial history
bicha (Portuguese)	"faggot"
bichiero (Portuguese)	a bookie for the illegal but popular gambling lottery *jogo de bichos*

botequim (Portuguese)	bar
brocha (Portuguese)	sexually impotent
caboclos (Portuguese)	persons of mixed white and Indian descent; usually refers to those who live in the back country
cachaça (Portuguese)	popular Brazilian rum
cadê? (Portuguese)	popular expression for "where is?"
cala a boca (Portuguese)	"shut your mouth"
caló (Spanish)	street slang in U.S. barrios
carioca (Portuguese)	citizen of Rio de Janiero
carne seca (Portuguese, Spanish)	sun-dried beef
carranca (Portuguese)	dragon figurehead on a boat, used mainly in the northeastern part of Brazil
chingón (Spanish)	U.S. barrio slang for a tough but cool guy
deixa acontecer (Portuguese)	"let it happen"
desculpe (Portuguese)	I'm sorry (as in apologizing)
É prohibido prohibir (Portuguese)	"It is forbidden to forbid"; also the title of a famous Tropicalista song by Caetano Veloso
farofa (Portuguese)	condiment made with manioc flour and eaten with rice and beans

favelas (Portuguese)	slums
filho (Portuguese)	son
filho de puta (Portuguese)	son of a bitch
filhotes (Portuguese)	cubs, as in bear cubs
forró (Portuguese)	spirited dance of Northeast Brazil
genipapo (Portuguese)	a fruit that produces a black dye
güero/a (Spanish)	light-skinned Hispanic
igarapé (Portuguese)	a small tributary in the Amazon that feeds into a larger river
jeitinho (Portuguese)	a little "favor"
orixá (Portuguese)	pantheon of Afro-Brazilian deities
pau (Portuguese)	stick; also the derogative for penis
puxa saco (Portuguese)	"brown-noser" (sycophant)
"Que bonitinho!" (Portuguese)	"How cute!"
"Que chato você é" (Portuguese)	"What a pain you are!"
"Que loucura" (Portuguese)	"What madness"
saudade (Portuguese)	intense longing or homesickness
tacape (Portuguese)	a club with an embedded blade used as a weapon by some Indian tribes
várzea (Portuguese)	floodplain of the Amazon basin

velho (Portuguese)   old man

vestibular (Portuguese)   college entrance exam

vovó, vovô (Portuguese)   grandma; grandpa

About the Author

Kathleen de Azevedo was born in Rio de Janeiro, Brazil, but has lived much of her life in the United States. Consequently, her subject matter often explores the conflict between the Brazilian/Latino culture and the American myth of progress and self-determination. Her work has appeared in many publications, including the *Los Angeles Times, Michigan Quarterly Review, Boston Review, Hayden's Ferry Review, Greensboro Review*, and *Américas*. She also was a frequent contributor to *Brazzil* magazine. In 1992, her poetry was featured in the *Best American Poetry* series. She received her MFA in creative writing from the University of Washington and currently teaches English at Skyline College in California. She received a grant from Stanford University's Center of Latin American Studies to research the *literatura de cordel*, folklore poetry of northeastern Brazil, and many of her current projects deal with that area. *Samba Dreamers* is her first published novel. She currently lives in San Francisco.